A French Ex

CW00341745

Many special thanks to Capt. Fr
to fly, and the lovely people and friends who assisted in the
research.

The Monteverdi 375S is still one of the most desirable super cars of the 1980-.90's and only 80 were produced.
Special thanks to Paul Berger, owner of Automobile MONTEVERDI AG for his kind permission to use the photographs of the Monteverdi as featured in the Book.

The photographs of the Monteverdi are not used in the Kindle Version.

Introduction

A French industrial chemist Pierre Saar made a discovery, the discovered substance that gave extruded and moulded plastic's incredible strength, this additive revolutionised the plastic industry. He called it Loyplas, Loyplas was unique, very quickly plastic manufacturers around the world realised the potential of this product and demand outstripped supply, Pierre's company, the Vista Plastic Company, launched a huge expansion program. The original factory was based in the outskirts of Paris. Pierre decided to situate the new factory in Montreal and opened a new office in the centre of Paris then sales offices in New York and Hong Kong.

An insignificant accident claimed the life of Pierre, leaving the company in turmoil, only after his death, did the company discover that Pierre had kept the knowledge to reproduce Loyplas a closely guarded secret. Exhaustive searches of his office and other places refused to give any information on how to reproduce Loyplas. Many sought the formula and ever eager competitors stepped up their research departments to reproduce the substance, the plastic industry required a stable supply and Vista Plastic was running out of stock. All who sought the formula were ignorant of a dangerous fact, Loyplas incorporated a deadly secret; during the manufacturing process it would kill the operator without warning.

With Pierre's death the company was thrown into turmoil, problems encountered from the plastic industry, and then the infighting between dependants trying to grab Pierre's estate, forced Pierre's father to make a decision. He declared that his properties and personal items were going to be disposed of at public auction.

By pure chance, I attended that auction, and I had the successful bid for his Monteverdi 375S Coupe sports car; also, I acquired his entire wardrobe of expensive clothes and some of his computer equipment.

Then; discovering a share certificate, hidden in the car, written on the reverse side was a long list of figures, equations and symbols; I thought a formula, I had no idea of what it described or how valuable it had become. Further investigations lead me to into an adventure thwarted by intrigue, covert agents, industrial espionage, sabotage, murder and then his delightful mistress's.

Then someone tried, to kill me...

How did I become a target?

Characters as they appear in the book

Ross Todd.	The Hero & main character
Elaine.	Initial companion to Ross
Pierre Saar.	Deceased main character
John.	The village bar keeper
Simone.	Johns Partner
Jules.	Policeman extraordinaire
Louis Pascal.	Jules superior officer
Patrice.	Auctioneer
Jacqueline.	The house keeper of Pierre Saar
Harold Whittle.	English factory owner
Darrell.	Employee of Whittle Plastic's
Janine.	The secretary of Pierre Saar
Derek.	Accountant to Ross
Max.	General Manager Vista Plastic's
Luis.	Canadian Chemist
Ulley Lange.	Canadian Factory manager
Wayne.	Canadian computer expert
Dawn.	Canadian good time office girl
Claudette.	Receptionist Vista Plastic
Pongo.	Ross's Dog
Thomas Boisseneau.	Government Minister
Otto von Gertle.	Austrian Chemist
Albert Jacks.	Paris factory Manager
Maxine.	Mr Jacks secretary
Jon	Paris Lawyer
James Grimshaw.	Accountant and fraudster
Anne	Whittles secretary
Mr Smith	Shareholders Whittle plastic
Mr Joiner.	Whittles father-in-law
Sydney.	English Computer engineer
Capt. Frank	Pilot to Whittle
Gladys.	Ross Todd's Receptionist.

Karen.	Ross Todd's Secretary
Philip.	English Auctioneer
Harry.	Business Adviser and sales
D.S. Harris.	English detective
Terry.	Business Buyer
Mr Twist.	The polite heavy thug
Hermione	Capt. Franks lady friend
Jack and Edith.	Friends of Janine
Frances.	The villa Maid
Officer Pascal.	French detective
Officer René.	French senior detective
Bruyère.	Female helicopter pilot.

I have made a list of the characters in the book as they appear, also as a reference to who is who.

I printed the list and put it in the actual book as a book mark, it did aid some readers that found the different characters complicated.

Chapter 1

On the spur of the moment, I suggested a holiday to Elaine, my companion for several years, life for both of us had been uneventful in the latter years, hoping that the holiday might be the ticket to help the ailing relationship.
Where too? Elaine asked.
How about a driving adventure into France, we could stay in small hotels and guesthouses, take life as it comes and explore the region south west of Paris.
She agreed, packing over the next couple of days as we prepared for the trip.
I always enjoy the ferryboat journey, however this trip needed something different, the new rail shuttle through the Channel Tunnel would be an experience.
We started our short holiday leaving early on the Thursday, we were heading towards the channel tunnel terminal, where cars and vans were loaded onto specially designed rail carriages, I was impressed as the loading was quick and well organised.
We parked up in a steel cage, then waited until you are instructed to drive off, reclining the driver's seat I soon fell asleep to the distant rhythmic clatter of the carriage wheels as we hurtled through the dimly lit tunnel.
I was shaken from my slumber, the bright sunshine shone on my face as the train hurtled from the tunnel, no sooner we were loaded than we were on the new road link on route for Paris on the northern motorway.
A muffled chime from deep within the dashboard together with a flashing warning light in the petrol gauge informed me of low fuel, a motorway service station just ahead gave chance to replenish the go juice.
Paying for the petrol, the exquisite aroma of freshly ground

coffee hooked Elaine and myself towards the adjacent café, a cup of freshly ground and a gooey Belgian bun satisfied out needs, then it was time to press on.

Elaine now sustained, soon fell asleep leaving me to drive on myself, nothing new there I thought.

Road signs on the overhead gantry gave me the option to either drive straight through the centre of Paris or to bypass it using the Peripherique. Le Peripherique is the motorway ring road around Paris.

My personal transport was a Japanese Honda Legend, a big fast luxurious car with plenty of extras, it is a delight to drive; and the powerful v6 engine outstrips slow drivers and problem traffic with ease.

We drove on in a south westerly direction for many hours stopping to take a comfort beak and another coffee Elaine roused herself as the setting sun was becoming uncomfortable in my eyes, it was time to find a place that offered bed and breakfast.

Slowing for a road junction, a clump of signs on the opposite side of the road; announced the village of Laroche; another sign nailed to a tree indicated that first class B&B was available at John's Bar. A larger faded yellow sign with a word, when translated from our easy French book read 'Public Auction' An arrow clamped by a large wing nut pointed in the direction of Laroche.

Elaine decided that it sounded enchanting, lets investigate, we headed towards Laroche.

Road side trees had overgrown the road providing a welcome canopy blocking out the setting sun; shortly we entered the village square of Laroche and drove into the sunshine again. The village square had four roads accessing it, Le Bar was located on the North side of the square; a quaint old styled establishment was typical of an 1800's village coaching inn. It was painted white with green window frames, a Routiers red and blue sign swung lazily in the evening breeze; also, a B&B sign was placed in the upstairs window.

Parking my car, I ventured into the bar; the patron addressed me with a hearty 'Bonjour!' a great set of teeth were displayed as he beamed a great smile in my direction. I summoned my best version of the lingo and requested the availability of a room for the evening.

'In addition to your request for a room, would you like a pint of Boddingtons or a large Dandelion & Burdock Monsieur?' Boddingtons is a famous northern English beer; Dandelion & Burdock is equally popular soft drink.

Well, what a surprise, here was I, deep in the French countryside, discovering a northern gent just like myself.

'Yes',

'To which'?

'Rooms or Drink'

'Both' He confided in me that we would be welcome to stay, his rooms were getting scarce today, I conveyed the message to Elaine; she suggested a quick room inspection. She declared the room was clean and tidy, and very acceptable, the charges were acceptable with our budget, it was a good deal; if we stayed for a couple of days, John added that he would include all meals. Elaine accepted the proposal and we moved in.

Later in the bar, enjoying a small beer, John asked If I had I have any knowledge about the Triumph Bonneville motorcycle, I confirmed that I had owned a couple of Triumph's in my early years.

'Great! Maybe you could help me, I have one in the Garage, but I have had problems in getting it going, I declared I could take a look, not promising anything mind, as I knew they were a problem, and I was on holiday.' John pointed out of the back window of the bar, 'It's out there in the yard, have a look.' The Bonneville was Triumph Motorcycles best loved model in its day, although the electrics and the paintwork left a lot to be desired. Triumph relied on their history for sales, not realising that the new threat, The Japanese motorcycle industry, would kill the British motorcycle industry within years. Triumphs were OK, if serviced by official dealers, but when serviced by their owners, the skimping and saving pennies, meant the motorcycles became prone to breakdowns, and horrendous oil leaks.

As I stood observing the sorry looking machine, it was evident John's Bonneville was a typical example. This cycle had been unattended for many years, it was covered in rust, the aluminium engine was pimpled with little white clumps of corrosion, most of the moving parts looked and probably were seized solid. This was a job that would be grimy and long term, noticing a tin of oil on the shelf I read the label, it was light penetrating oil, I gave a liberal covering of the oil to as many areas I thought would that could cause problems.

'Let that soak in for a while then we will review the condition of the beast in a couple of days.' Placing the oil can back on the shelf, I noticed a small brass key hanging from a nail in the edge of the shelf. Before we left, I could not resist the temptation to turn the engine over using the kick start lever, initially the engine refused to budge, remembering I had found this fault before, I rectified the problem by selecting a gear, then giving the rear wheel a good tug backwards, I heard a distinct clunk from inside the engine, the backwards movement released the jammed kickstart ratchet, and the engine turned over. I reapplied pressure to the kickstart lever, this time the engine easily turned over making a chuffing sound.

It was a good sign; 'John if we could try some petrol, possible connect a charged battery it might even fire up.' Suddenly John's interest renewed: it was more important to have this engine running than attending the bar, a battery and some electrical jump leads appeared from the boot of John's car. Some petrol was poured into the fuel tank, the ignition key was missing; I tried to turn the ignition key slot with a small screwdriver but it would not budge. Retrieving the small rusty key from the shelf, it fitted and turned, the ignition light in the speedometer had a red glow turning the petrol tap levers open; I proceeded to prime the carburettors. It had power, petrol and in all it was ready to start.

I stood astride the motorcycle, balancing myself onto the kickstart lever, then applying my weight the engine spun over briskly, on the third kick a muffled explosion could be heard, and a curl of white smoke expelled from one of the carburettor's, it was a positive sign that life was still in this beast. The fourth kick proved better, the engine fired, then continued to turnover firing on one cylinder, slowly the engine revs increased, then suddenly both cylinders fired, its long sleep had ended. Quickly the engine warmed and the revolutions settled into a rhythmic beat as it idled, there were no mechanical noises or obvious oil leaks, the smile on John's face was a treat.

The door to the bar opened and a couple of locals came rushing to see what the noise was about, John was delighted and displaying his new noise machine to his drinking public, he stood by the side of his motorcycle proudly accepting the admiration.

Just then the motorcycle engine petered out, and produced a resounding backfire from the exhaust. A stunned silence, then someone, voiced a quick remark, which brought a round of hearty laughter, the floor show finished and much to the amusement of the onlookers, they sloped off back to the Bar.

John was ecstatic, 'Bloody marvellous and bollocks to them,' the Triumph worked, and it would work again, after making sure everything was safe and sound with the motorcycle we returned to the bar.

What is your best poison John waving his hand across the rows of bottles displayed on the Bar wall.

'A good brandy'

John looked at me, by the way what is your name?

Ross, Ross Todd, I replied; in all the excitement I had not introduced myself, John's easy-going attitude to life, we had forgot the formalities.

Sampling the pre-dinner aperitif 'What's this Auction caper? I saw the sign at the end of the lane. Ah John replied touching his nose as if he was flicking a fly from it, 'The viewing is tomorrow many people are coming; a lot of whom are staying as guests. I am glad to say the accommodation is full, we must have been very lucky to get a room. While we were talking another five prospective clients entered and requested lodgings John gave them directions to another Hotel close by, it was a shame he could not accommodate them all.

A local had included himself in our discussions on this auction, they conferred and chatted about the history of the local French scientist. It was headline news at the time when he made the fabulous discovery;

The local rummaging around in the pile of old papers in the Bar produced a paper proclaiming.

Magnifique Discovery By Local Chemist Caused Revelation in the Plastic Industry.

NEW PLASTIC PRODUCTS FIND
LOCAL SCIENTIST MAKES FABULOUS DISCOVERY.

Then the local still rummaging showed me the paper,

PIERRE SAAR LOCAL SCIENTIST & PLASTIC MOGUL FOUND DEAD

He continued to explain via John, 'The chap concerned was a local industrial chemist who had accidentally popped his clogs. The chap's personal effects were up for sale. In fact, a whole château; and the contents, are going under the hammer.'

Within the next few minutes of conversation, John told me how he came to be living in France; fed up with teaching in England he decided to move to France. As luck had it, he walked into a lucrative position teaching English in a school in Clermont; the opportunity professed a better future together with meeting Simone, a delightful French lady, it changed the course of his personal life. After a few years of teaching, the bar at Laroche came on the market. John thought the Bar seemed a good challenge and took the chance.

I have attended many auctions, both buying and selling. When you sell at auction, everyone wants the highest price and vice versa when people buy, they want the lowest price, after all, everyone loves a bargain. To make sure of good prices, place a reserve amount on the goods to be auctioned. This can go wrong so an underhand way is to bid up your own items. If Auction Fever happens then somebody will outbid you; at this game you have to create the bidding excitement for others to be interested, then, pull out when your price is reached. It can go higher if two people bid for the item.

Elaine and Simone seemed to have something in common and became pals immediately. John dropped into his

Yorkshire accent, explaining that there were other people staying at the bar who were interested in the auction; conversing about matters in our local accents gave us an aspect of secrecy. It was John's intention to go to the auction sale and acquire as many bottles of the wine for the funds he had available.

John thought it would be a good idea if we teamed up to sort this lot out. We set to the plan and perused a purloined, pre preview copy of the contents of the sale, only to stop for the odd glass of wine and a meal prepared by Simone. The meal consisted of roast beef and vegetables cooked in red wine. The meal lasted hours, not forgetting the pastry and cheese.

The good wines mixed with other delights become a blur towards the end of the evening.

I awoke to sounds coming from the open bedroom window, the village was coming to life. I quickly glanced outside and spied a small boy on a bicycle being chased by a group of children.

I could see across the square; a man was loading baskets of fresh bread into the back of a grey van. Other residents, mainly little old ladies dressed in black were all heading for the bakery.

I showered and tried to wake Elaine by shaking some drops of water on her. She told me to go away, then turned over and went back to sleep. I went down to breakfast.

The breakfast table was crammed with cheeses, croissants, hams, pastries, fresh breads, a choice of spreads, chocolate, jams, marmalades, coffee, tea and fresh fruit juices. The guests were arriving and starting on their breakfast. The room filled with people munching, discussions abound, prospective auction buyers discussing the morning's actions and possibilities.

There was an officer of the Gendarmerie in the bar talking to

John as I entered the room. I wished him a good morning and he returned the compliment. John, he beckoned me to join them, introducing me as an Englishman on holiday. The young Gendarme introduced himself as Jules. a good-looking chap, slim, dark haired and looked extremely fit, he spoke in a version of English that was rough but understandable. Jules was interested in the v6 Legend car parked in front of the Bar. He had not seen one before and as most French males are car enthusiasts he wondered if he could take a look at the car. I obliged, and why not? A friendly policeman is an asset.

He was well impressed when I lifted the bonnet to reveal the V6 engine shoehorned into the engine compartment, any spare space had been crammed with ancillaries. I offered a test run later; Jules eagerly accepted.

Another gendarme joined us, casual greetings were given and received. Jules introduced me to Captain Louis Pascal; he was his superior officer. They had urgent business, said their goodbyes and sauntered towards the market place.

John stuck his head out of the bar door, 'Auction viewing in one hour, the girls are going to the market.' Elaine and Simone had decided to browse the market while we went to the auction.

John offered to take me in his Triumph Dolomite Sprint, a very quick motor car in its day, rapidly becoming a classic. We travelled through the village, crossing a bridge over a river up the hill, and an impressive château confronted us, John pointed towards the chateau 'That's the place' a sign displaying 'Vente aux Enchère' was placed on the outer wall.

John parked the Triumph in the grounds, then we checked in at the auction office.

I acquired two copies of the auction catalogue. We were ready to go. Next task, to scan the list of items on sale, looking for the obvious bargains, scan again, then look for blank numbers, this is where additional lots can be added by the auctioneer. We Also searched for mistakes and misleading item descriptions.

As we walked towards the house perusing the catalogue, I was full of enthusiasm, and chatting to John about a past auction related experience. I told John how I once missed out on an item, at a Ministry of Defence auction, a 'Laser'. This item was listed under computer equipment so both my colleague and I assumed it to be 'a computer Laser printer'. It sold for £200, then we discovered it was actually an industrial light laser, similar to the one used in a spy movie when the villain was attempting to kill the hero. Laughing at my misfortune I missed looking at the first page of the auction catalogue. John was pointing the way to the crockery, we decided to start here. John was delighted with the amount of crockery and wines. 'There is enough wine in these cellars to keep the bar open for 30 years, the bidding on that alone will be furious,' John claimed.

The smell of fresh coffee drifted past our noses, we followed the aroma to a stall by the side of the office, a lady had a table laid; she was offering coffee, small cakes and biscuits. Requesting two coffees and a couple of cakes. John was nose deep into the catalogue and was oblivious to her presence. I watched her as she prepared our order, she was a shapely woman, possibly mid-thirties and very attractive, she placed coffee and cakes in front of me, she smiled looked at me but her thoughts were far away.

I offered her payment, she refused.

'May I thank you for this refreshment,' I replied, she seemed not to understand. John piped in translating what I had said, she thanked me again and John for the translation,

'Vous Anglais?'

'Oui mademoiselle,' I replied smiling, she gave me a cheeky

look and smiled. John said quietly the correct term was, Madam, 'I know but mademoiselle gave her a compliment, which she accepted.

The coffee was wonderful, the aroma complemented the taste perfectly, it was the correct drink at the correct time.

I returned the empty cup saying 'It was wonderful coffee, thank you very much,' giving her a wink. She smiled, accepting my appreciation.

We commenced to view objects in the sale, comparing item lot number with the description in the catalogue. In items of interest to me, John had a partial interest, but sometimes we were both stumped on some items. Then, with the occasional verbal excitement from other auction viewers, hurried notes were scribbled into their catalogues, even we had to try to work out what it was they were interested in, the occasional viewer looking over our shoulders. 'Nosy sods,' John remarked.

I told John one of my interests was in the watches and computers. He relayed his findings on a couple of items I may find interesting

Item 23: Montres Breguet 18k. Reading the description, John translated, '18k Moon phase Perpetual Triple Calendar automatic wristwatch, listed in the catalogue as Not working order.'

Item 24: Montres Corum 18k gold (Admirals cup model).

Item 25: Montres Cartier tank, stainless steel strap.

These were nice but expensive watches, we continued the viewing, inside the main house, we ended upstairs in the master bedroom, a clothes rail placed at the end of the bed had an array of jackets and suits. A nice blue jacket caught my eye. I tried the jacket, a good fit, then I tried the jacket from a dark suit, this fit well, the material was superb and after trying on the trousers they were an excellent fit. This

Chap must have been the same build as myself, I wondered what he might have looked like. The labels in the Suit and jackets, some names were known to me but some were not still the cloth felt good; manufactures of quality clothing, use quality cloth and these were good, well worth a bid. In addition, was a well-stocked accessory wardrobe consisting of many shirts, casual and sportswear in abundance. All items were clean and nicely pressed.

'Pardon'. a quiet voice from behind, focused my attention to lady who had served me with the coffee. She was standing close to me; and made slight adjustments the jacket that I was trying. Expertly she slowly smoothed the material with her hands over my shoulders, down my back, and over my buttocks.

She spoke to me then realising that her English was not adequate called out to John, he obliged 'I think that you are the same size as Monsieur Pierre. I hope that these clothes do not end up in the market, it would be a great pity and a waste Monsieur.' she sighed.

I removed the jacket; she took it from me placing it back on the clothes rail. I continued trying more of the clothes, then as I removed the trousers I pulled on my own trousers. I became aware she was watching, I glanced in her direction, she was smiling and responded 'Pardon. monsieur,' and walked slowly from the room looking at me over her shoulder.

'She likes you,' John said with a wide grin. Giving the statement a brief thought, I felt excitement and a stirring in my groin as I thought about her.

I continued the viewing of my catalogue, marking a small x for items I was interested in, and a double xx for items with heavy interest.

We scoured through the house, kitchen, cellar, the contents of the garage, some tools and a small hydraulic jack but nothing remarkable. John intermittently checked the time from his watch and suggested a hasty retreat back to the bar; we will be in deep trouble, if we are not back for the midday session. 'OK, let's go.'

Elaine and Simone had enjoyed the time in the market and had bought some fruit and other delicious titbits to eat later.

Simone had prepared a sandwich lunch for us; Elaine scanned through the pages and was reading out the items I had marked. She had a fancy for a couple of items for home. Simone also required some things but only if the price was correct.

'What is a Monteverdi,' asked Elaine. I replied

'It is an incredible motor car. If my memory is correct, the Monteverdi was a 2+2 coupe made in Basel Switzerland by a Peter Monteverdi.' The story, as I remember, he had a Ferrari Dealership but could not find the perfect car, so he made one.

The result was the Monteverdi 375 series; it was just about correct the first time and orders came in abundance from rich clients for similar vehicles. Monteverdi's are rare, later models are expensive and some versions are almost impossible to find.

Where did that name come from, I enquired,

'What was it like?'

'What was what like?'

The Monteverdi at the auction, did you not see it?'

'What!' I was on my feet and taking hold of the catalogue, her finger pointed to the entry

Page 1
1. Monteverdi 375S,

2. Renault Alpine,
3. Volkswagen Golf GTI convertible.
There were three cars listed, yet there were no cars present, apart from cars parked in the car park. We looked in the garage and it was empty, I was disgusted with myself for missing, what could have been my dream car.

English auctions would usually keep such choice items until the end, or midterm of the auction, in case the interest waned and no one wants to stay for the end.

Even John commented there were no cars in his catalogue, then discovered his catalogue had two pages stuck together, it was the same with mine, Elaine did not comment that the pages were stuck together when she prised it open.

I remembered idle chatter with John just after getting the new catalogues, I chastised myself for missing a serious item again, 'I am going back to the auction to have a look at the car and have a second look around.' Elaine and Simone decided to join me, they also wanted to have a look as well. Parking the Legend in the same place as before, the girls disappeared into the house.

Requesting information from a Monsieur Patrice, who was the head auctioneer, I asked him about the cars that were going to be in the auction.

He asked which car was I interested in,

'Item one, the Monteverdi',

'Ah, a problem, an unfortunate accident had happened with the Monteverdi 'Patrice explained. The vehicle had been damaged while being transported from Paris but they were hoping that it would be here today or first thing tomorrow, but well in time for the sale.

The other cars will be here shortly, as we spoke a car transporter carrying some of the cars swung through the gate, 'Here we are,' Patrice waved his hand in the general direction of the transporter.

I had a niggling feeling which triggered a question, 'Is there any problem in me buying items from this auction?' I am just checking, as I am not fully knowledgeable of French auction regulations. The rules and regulations were explained to me it turned out that there was virtually no difference to the auctions, but there could be a problem.

Patrice asked, did I live in France?

'No,' Then to comply, I would have to register and supply a guarantee from my bank to cover all bids.

'Pardon, Monsieur.' it was the same lady from that morning. She placed a cup of coffee on the desk, and a small plate of biscuits, two round and one straight positioned in such a suggestive way I laughed heartily out loud when I saw them, she seems to appreciate that I saw the joke and stifled herself from laughing. I continued filling out the required details, the auction house faxed the paperwork to England, my bank responded almost immediately giving surety of enough funds to cover anything I wished to buy; a friendly bank manager is a rare commodity. I watched this flirtatious lady while I stood drinking my coffee. She busied herself serving other customers occasionally glancing in my direction as our eyes met, she smiled. While my thoughts were drifting from the auction to other seductive thoughts, then they were shattered by Elaine saying,

'Where's mine then?'

'What?'

'The Coffee,'

'What Coffee?'

'The one in your hand.'

'The delightful lady in the black dress over on the coffee table gave me this cup.'

Simone looked at the lady then leaning towards Elaine

whispered, 'That is Madame Jacqueline. She is Monsieur Pierre's housekeeper.' Elaine corrected her English to 'was', and after explaining the change, they both laughed. Strange how thoughts invade your mind, 'Jacqueline,' thinking, 'I have never been to bed with a Jacqueline.'

The girls scavenged the house for bargains, with knowledge of what they wanted lodged firmly in their mind. there was no reason to stay, and I was quickly removed from the temptation of smiling large breasted women.

'Ross has an admirer at the Château,' Simone told John when we got back, I sat down grinning and sighing, 'at last, I have an admirer!' We all had a good laugh.

The bar was full, all rooms taken, people arriving for the sale. John said, 'we should have an auction every week.'

Jules arrived casually dressed, he was ready to go for the test drive. As good as time as ever we drove heading out of the village towards the main road, Jules indicated to a small road on the right. He said, 'that road connects to the main highway.' it is, as we say, a short cut. The narrow road joined onto the main road; we were heading towards Paris.

Accelerating to 70 mph, I flicked the special sports mode switch on the gear lever. immediately the engine revs increased as the automatic gearbox down, shifted one gear, the engine now ready for action, a quick stab of the accelerator launched the car in the 130-mph region in seconds. The automatic box easily coping with the power then it reduced the engine revolutions to a purr as it gained the cruising level, one of the Legend's added extras: electronic gear shifting. 'Mon Dieu.' Jules cries 'This car is incredible.' arriving at the next junction, I turned the car ready to return to the village.

During the return run, climbing uphill there was a flash of headlights from a silver car as he tried to pass. Pressing the magic button, we left the car as if he was standing still. Looking at him in my review mirror, he was shaking his fist or something at me, but he was disappearing in our dust. 'Jules, I think I have upset someone in that silver car.'

He remarked, 'No problem, he is behind, not in front, no matter.' He took a quick look back at the disappearing vehicle then returning his attention to the more serious matter in hand: the test drive.

An observation I noticed, when you are driving at high speeds, the bends in the road become very short and tight your senses adjust automatically to suit the increased pace your attention to the approaching road surface becomes very detailed. Jules gave a cautionary warning of the turn for the village. We slowed about a half kilometre from the turning, slipping quietly from the main arterial to the village. the following silver car now had caught us, followed us keeping at a distance into the village.

Parking in the market square the silver car slowly cruised past. The driver's face was hidden by the sun visor his companion a dark-haired woman was looking down at something on her lap, her hair falling over the profile of her face which made it difficult to see her.

We spent the rest of the evening consuming food, drinking wine, chatting late into the night. I was tired and made a move to retire; Finally, the warm bed clothes, were inducing my daily trip into the land of the sandman, a quiet voice from the darkness, 'An admirer,' then a finger prodded into my ribcage; the stabbing shock was electric, somebody was wanting to play, the sandman when would just have to wait.

Looking out of the window the early morning Sun was climbing above the tree covered hills in the East, its warming

rays quickly dissipating the morning mist.
I quietly left the bedroom and went downstairs for my breakfast. 'Bonjour John and Simone,' I tried my best French greeting as I entered the breakfast room. I was greeted with many returns greeting from most of the people in the room, speaking quietly to Simone I explained Elaine is enjoying her sleep she will be down later.
'A good day for the sale with bargains to be had,' enthusiastically commented John.
The breakfast table was well laid with all type of temping foods. I ate my fill and was ready to go to the auction; John was getting bogged down by a delivery. I was getting restless that the items I was interested were at the start of the auction and I wanted to view another couple of things. I just do not like being late for any auction. The time was 10.45, the auction started at 11:00. John finished and we sped off in the Legend, as we turned the corner, a traffic queue was backed up because of an accident. The time 10:55 I was getting uneasy. The sound of a whistle, I looked up to see a Gendarme he was standing at the head of the traffic queue, beckoning to us to advance. John yelled, 'it is Jules, get down the outside before anybody else.' I overtook the cars under instruction from Jules. At the entrance to the auction, Jules had kept the entrance clear for us and he saluted as we passed, turning into the car park.
I saw the Monteverdi gleaming still on the car trailer. It was a finished in a metallic burgundy as we approached, I heard the auctioneer accepting bids. John shouted, 'Which car are you selling?'
'Le Monteverdi Monsieur.' swiftly I told to John to bid in French,
'Whatever the bid is, double it.'
John heeding my request, cried out the bid.

A French Experience.

Chapter 2

As the bid landed, the gathered crowd were silenced by the nature of the bid and ceased what they were doing. Slowly murmurs increased as the punters discussed 'The whatever bid', all heads turned to see the new bidder. The auctioneer was holding the gavel high, brought it down accepting my bid. The under bidder looking back missed the last call.

The car was mine, now the question, how much did I pay for it. The whatever the bid double it, was a gamble I once took at an auction in England, the result was that I purchased a box full of rare motorcycle parts with an antique value of thousands, I paid £16, and lo and behold it had worked again. The secretary approached me, requesting my bidder's number. Luckily, I had pre-registered and showed her the number. 'Will that be the only purchase today, Monsieur?' 'No,' I replied, 'and could you tell me how much I bid for the car?'

The clerk inquired, 'Monsieur does not know how much he has paid for the car?'

'No, how much?'

'53,600 francs Monsieur.'

Wow! Divide by 9 and £6000 is what it cost. 'A bargain.' I was well pleased and I began inspecting my purchase, there was damage to the driver side wing, door skin, and front bumper. The damage had clearly been caused by a collision with a stronger object than the car. Still, no other damage, all the glass was in place, no headlights broken. Opening the door, the seats were finished in cream leather, a wooden detailed dashboard, finished off finally by a magnificent wood rimmed aluminium steering wheel.

I released the bonnet catch, lifted the bonnet to reveal the huge Chrysler V8 power unit. It was clean, no oil smears and a slight covering of road dust gave indications of an untouched engine. A quick glance around the engine compartment reassured me that everything looked in place. Closing the bonnet, I locked the car to protect it from souvenir hunters and niggling damage that upset under bidders might do.

I caught up with John, he was bidding on items that he wanted.

'Any bargains?'

'Odd bits and bobs, I am getting my stuff for pennies.' John enquired, 'how's the car?'

'Incredibly good, I am well pleased, it was only Six thousand.' He exclaimed. 'FRANCS!'

'Pounds,' I answered.

'Bloody hell,'

Patrice announced the next Lot: Lot number 24, the Breguet watch. I made the opening bid of a thousand, the price rocketed past 6,000 francs faster than I have seen. Finally, it was purchased by a small man with a frail outlook, 'a jeweller,' I thought.

Lot number 25, the Corum watch. Bidding started at 500 francs tailing off at 3000 francs. Same purchaser, 'everyone to his own,' I thought, wondering what was the value of the Breguet watch. Lot number 26, the Cartier watch, went to the same bidder. He looked unruffled, typical dealer, as if it was the normal thing to do on a sunny morning.

I was happy with the purchase so far. Elaine and Simone had made their way here and were getting items from the sale, then Simone called my attention to the fact that the content of the wardrobes was being sold. Elaine took over. She had seen what was on offer and was paying very little for the clothes, after about 30 items had been purchased by Elaine, the Auction was being slowed down by the clothes sale.

Auctioneer Patrice, realising only one buyer was buying, decided to offer the rest of the clothes in one go. Elaine made the only bid, quickly Patrice scanned the audience then slammed down the hammer. The bid was accepted.

I now owned thousands of pounds worth of clothes, which had cost less than two hundred.

I was feeling smug with my purchases and was having a good day; the auction was still going on.

The content of the cellars was now under the hammer. John managed to buy two lots of 5000 bottles and was well pleased, A small lot of choice rare bottles came on offer, they were snapped up fast, fortunes were paid by serious looking men, as they scanned the catalogue, they always grumbled to themselves, as if they are not happy with the price.

'John, why is wine so expensive and sought after?'

'Because it's the way of life; wine in the cellar is worth more to a Frenchman than anything else.'

The last lots were coming under the hammer. Monsieur Patrice announced a couple of extra lots to be sold before the sale of the château and lands. Extra item 1, computer and a printer. I opened with a bid of 1000 francs, it was mine at 1500. Extra item 2, portable computer including the carrying case. I again opened the bidding with a bid of 1000 francs, clinching the deal at 3500. Extra item 3, portable computer (not working, a broken case).

Launching a bid of 500 francs, to my surprise the next bid a verbal bid of 10,000 francs. Wow! At that sort of jump you do not even bid unless you have prior knowledge of what the item was or what it contained. I did not contest the bid, nor did anybody else. The bidder smirked to himself at his success of winning. I was sure I had seen him before, but where?

Elaine said, 'enough.' Happy and content with our goods, the

Château was the next lot to be sold, it would be good to hear and wallow in the atmosphere of ultra-high bids. Patrice asked for 2 million Francs, reducing to 500,000 francs until a bid was launched, then suddenly there was a shout from an official looking man forcing his way through the crowd, flourishing a piece of paper in the air. Monsieur Patrice the head auctioneer stopped the auction whilst he conversed with the official, quickly reading the paper. It was a district court order stopping the auction. Patrice declared that because of a problem with title to the château, the sale of this asset could not proceed, until this urgent matter was resolved. Patrice apologised for the problem and said that if respective buyers would leave their names with the auction clerk, he would contact them when the château became available for sale. Patrice continued to say that the auction had finished, all lots offered had been sold and the removal of goods could commence after each respective account had been settled.

With my bank guaranteeing my funds, I used a personal cheque to settle my account, the next task was to collect and remove the lots allocated to me. I made enquiries with the clerk to confirm transfer of title and arrangements for the car, export to the UK certain papers would be necessary.

As I approached the Monteverdi, the winning bidder with the huge bid on the broken portable computer, was standing with his foot on the trailer. He inquired if I wished to sell the car.

'Not at present thank you.'

He blurted out, 'I will give you two thousand pounds profit,'

'No thanks, I wish to keep it thank you for your offer.'

The man thrust a business card into my hand, 'Please call me if you ever want to sell it,' he turned to go, then as an afterthought, he turned back saying, 'I really would like to own that car, I will be prepared to give you Ten thousand pounds, above what you paid for it, can we call it a deal?

This guy stood holding his hand out hoping that I would decide to take him up on his magnificent offer, he seemed to be forcing a smile for my benefit, I was receiving bad vibes from him of detest, he was condescending to relieve me of this motor vehicle.

I wished no further discussion between us; he stood holding out his hand. I certainly did reconsider his offer, then a voice in my head screamed 'No! Don't, do it! There is something wrong, all this attention and sudden rush to obtain a motorcar; I decided to decline the offer.

Walking away trying not to look dejected he climbed into a silver car, it was that same silver car that followed us from the main road the other day. Also sitting in the car was the same dark-haired female; he must have been furious about something and it seemed she was bearing the brunt of his anger. he was a slight man with a shifty look dressed well but what a Berk, I suppose it takes all sorts.

I was mulling over his incredible offer, of £10,000 over and above what I had paid, either there must be something unique about this car, or some other factor involved, I decided to investigate before I made my final decision. I noticed Monsieur Patrice was making his way towards me, I congratulated him on an excellent auction, and offered my condolences relating to the problem with the official and his court order.

'It happens, are you pleased with your purchases?'

'I was well pleased.' I pointed with reference to the damage on the Monteverdi.

'That is the exact matter I wish to discuss.' The auction company accepts the responsibility for the repair back to its previous splendour, Also the car trailer is the property of the auction company. They would take the car to the repair workshop in Paris, making a priority to have it repaired within a week.

I thanked Patrice graciously.

'That was a better end to the auction for me, even at the end there is still a bonus.' I asked if it would be possible to inspect the vehicle before it goes for repair.

'Certainly, it is your prerogative as you are the new owner. I believe the auctioneer's driver is staying at the bar in the village, as the car would still be on the trailer and securely parked in the yard. We would take the car from there in the morning. Would that give you enough time to have a good inspection?' enquired Patrice.

'Yes, that would be perfect,'

'Madame Jacqueline will have all the clothes packed so you can take them with you.' Jacqueline: affectionate thoughts permutated my mind.

She had finished packing all the accessories, items and clothes into suitcases. As we packed everything into the Legend, Jacqueline enquired 'was I staying in the village?'

'At the Bar,'

'I have something for you,' she held out a bunch of small keys, 'These are for the suitcases.' She stroked my hand as they parted, 'I have a small Hotel if you wish to stay with me.'

'Thank you, I would look forward to staying at your hotel if I come back to the village.'

'I think you will,' She kissed me on both cheeks said 'Au revoir,' she turned, and walked away. I am sure she was purposely swinging her hips for my benefit. I admired the movement; it gave me great pleasure.

Loading the car with more goods, we started the first of many trips from the Château to the bar.

Simone made available a larger room for us to stay in and to accommodate the new wardrobe. We planned to stay a little longer than first intended; we liked this village. We browsed through the clothes, some of the styles were a bit flamboyant and currently not to my liking.

Some clothes brought spontaneous laughter and strange comments, making the evening pass quickly; Elaine continued to work through the immense stock, searching pockets for missed items and trinkets.

The computer bits I had won, also needed checking, I switched on the laptop computer, the majority of the documents were written in French, but I was surprised to find some were written in English. I was intrigued by the rows of numbers contained on the computerised spreadsheets; I wished that I could easily understand them, maybe, one day in the future.

I browsed through the English documents; this chap had been very important and ingenious.

I read about the company bond and share issue, but I could not understand the full implication at this time. I read letters to a 'Max', at the Paris office; then letters, to the Montreal factory, there were letters to a Canadian bank, also including a bank with an exotic name. It was the Hong Kong & Shanghai Bank.

There were letters that needed a password to gain access; I remarked to Elaine, 'This guy has secrets; some of these documents require a password.'

Finding no further items on the laptop I setup the desktop computer, I found more letters, each requesting a password. I opened a database listing the companies and the quantities for purchases of something called 'Loyplas.' In quantities of 1000 kilos at a time, most of the prices were in US dollars, showing a conversion into Canadian Dollars then into French and Swiss Francs. The figures on the database indicated low values, I had not realised my mistake of the decimal point location. I mentioned to Elaine that I was going down to the bar for a coffee.

'John, the documents and other stuff on the computer are all in French.'

'Aha, I have for you the very thing' he replied, then disappeared into the office at the back of the bar. Returning with a couple of computer disks,

'Load the program onto the computer; it will translate French to English, after a fashion, but makes the documents readable.'

After a couple of coffees my brain was stimulated by the intense caffeine boost. I returned to our room ok, and then followed the instructions and loaded the translation program onto the laptop computer. As if by magic, the letters started to reveal their secrets to me. After 30 minutes of reading, all the documents became boring and dreary, it was the documents which required a password that attracted my main attention.

Elaine was concerned about the amount of time I was spending on the computer. So engrossed I was oblivious to the time, meal times would have been missed, but deciding to give my eyes a rest, a meal is always a delight and worthwhile.

We chatted about our purchases from the auction, John was delighted, five cases of rare wines had been included in the wine he had bought, even Simone had made discoveries in her purchases, and everybody was happy.

After the meal, we drifted apart each having some tasks to do and I found myself with time to spare. I returned to that niggling password problem. I tried various combinations, I knew if passwords contain numbers, also upper- and lower-case characters, then they became difficult and even impossible to crack. In the short time I had spent I had gleaned enough from the computer files to have a mind's eye picture of him and his business.

One document, related to a plastic problem, something about a sample share certificate, this plastic would be used to make the share certificates for the forthcoming company floatation. He referred in his letter to having a holographic certificate number embossed on the certificate and it entwined in the design.

He was impressed with the sheet of plastic its smoothness similar to silk yet flexible. He wrote about the plastic giving a metallic sound as he flicked the edge or twisted it.

Then something I read I could not understand a brief history of Pierre's discovery and he listed it as follows.

'The event happened during a normal evening's work. I had not realised incorrect labelling of some new ingredients and I was disturbed when making the new batch, he went on to say he was adding polymers and other chemicals with the introduction of an alien strain of a titanium substance. All the ingredients were mixed totally out of sequence, but it worked.

I was the only laboratory chemist working that night all records of the premix were kept secret. I decided to name the product Loyplas.'

'Attention' remember to Xtract the gas. Judging by what I had just read this substance called Loyplas was a plastic additive that revolutionised the plastic extrusion industries; only one gram of the additive per tonne of plastic produced was required to give the plastic strength. Transparent plastic achieved shatterproof properties. Some of the wording I could not make sense of, I was not good at chemistry, at school and these documents contained information unknown to me.

He was concerned and referred to forgers trying to copy, and steal the formula, offering bribes to the Paris workforce for information.

Reading over a letter from his Bank, the manager suggested he should lodge a copy in their vault for safekeeping. There was so much pressure from all directions, finally gave Pierre the notion that he was the best person to protect the location of the secret. It was apparent that he distrusted bank managers, lawyers, even the police. In fact, he did not have a good word for some Government officials he considered not trustworthy. Wow I could not believe what I was reading; this was a man after my own heart.

It would appear that this Pierre Saar owned the Vista Plastic Company, a factory in Paris and one in Canada.

The Loyplas was shipped, from the Paris office and always referred to a Janine, I imagined this Janine, as a senior lady in the office, a lady who knew what to do wherever Pierre was. A reference to Max, showed him to be Pierre's managing director, there was another reference to a Jacqueline, concerned a small hotel where she would live. This must have been the Madam Jacqueline whom I had met today the housekeeper of Pierre, women of this ideal are a precious commodity and so must be nurtured with love and kindness. Obviously, Pierre had similar thoughts along those lines, she should have an additional source of income, I bet he secretly supplied funds for the small hotel.

Elaine brought it to my attention that another four hours of my time had disappeared into that computer.

I detected a serious hint of annoyance in her voice, which led me to suggest that we have a couple of days travelling to explore the countryside, 'first, let's enjoy the rest of the evening.' During the evening meal, the auction company driver finally arrived, I observed as he manoeuvred the car trailer and Monteverdi into the backyard, it looked magnificent, the yard only had limited light making it hard to see any of the finer detail, making sure it was secure we returned to the bar

The locals gathering in the bar that evening was rowdy and full of spirits, and of course a plentiful amount of the locally produced wine. We polished off our meal with a couple of excellent brandies I made a move to retire for the evening.

Chapter 3

The front door clicked shut behind me the rising sun just clearing the hills in the east, bathed the square in sunshine.

I had an urge to walk, an intoxicating smell of fresh bread hung in the air. Following my nose, I found myself at a bakery tucked away in a small side street. I perused the array of breads and pastries, I choose a couple of pain au chocolate, returned and sat down in the square near the War memorial. The warm sunshine was relaxing. I became engrossed in the taste of the pastry and oblivious to the world. 'Bonjour, do you always breakfast alone?' 'Sometimes.'

Looking towards the voice, I found myself looking into the eyes of Madame Jacqueline. She had seen me sitting in the square and decided to say good morning, she leaned toward me and carefully removed a flake of the pastry sticking to the corner of my mouth.

'Was it nice? le pain au chocolate?'

'Oui'.

'Oh, you could always share with me,'

'Sorry, but I have none left',

'That is a shame' she sighed fluttered her eyelashes and exaggerated the swing of her hips as she returned to her car.

Sometimes, I thought it would be nice to be single again, invitations like that do not come your way every day.

The flashing sunlight reflecting from the roof of the Monteverdi that was parked in the backyard of the Bar brought my attention back to more realistic matters.

The reflection was unstable, the car was being moved, I knew the car would not be going to Paris for at least couple of hours.

At that moment John opened the front door to the Bar and stepped outside, he stood and stretched his arms as if appealing to a higher authority, 'Anybody in the backyard?' I cried out

'No!'

Anticipating his reply, I was already on my feet and running towards the bar, I called back to John 'The Monteverdi is moving.'

Reaching the backyard, the gate, was open, cautiously I slid between the narrow opening into the yard; the Monteverdi's passenger door was open.

Bloody hell. Who has been in?

Did I lock the car?

I was sure I had locked the car.

The car was still moving on its suspension, then I realised someone, was inside the car.

Taking hold of the open passenger door, I asked what did he want in my car?

The figure froze, John appeared from the back door, "is everything Ok"

'We have a visitor'. With this slight distraction, the intruder attempted to escape from the driver's door. Making a grab at his jacket, I secured a good hold then I dragged him backwards from the car throwing him into the brick wall of the building, closing the car door shut I turned my full attention towards him.

Again, asking him his intentions, he remained silent, keeping his face hidden from me. John spouted forth the same question in French, still the figure offered no reply.

He seemed to be searching for something in his inner pocket, suddenly he held a large screwdriver and lunged at me. I Quickly stepped sideways; he missed me. He was very close to me I punched my fist toward his head as hard as I could, he collapsed to the ground, as he stood up, I punched him again, he sprang back at me, suddenly a dark clad figure pushed me aside and pounced upon my assailant. I was taken aback by this new figure it was Jules. His Police training in self-defence displayed itself as he instantly secured the offending hand which was holding the weapon. The assailant cursing profusely, was restrained and forced into a clearer area of the yard.

Taking the opportunity to look at this man, I recognised him as the chap from the auction, the same man who made me the unbelievable offer. But why and what were his motives, that had caused him to take such drastic action in breaking into my car.

Jules was questioning him accompanied with John eagerly listening to his answers. John then offered Jules instant English translation if the reply was not understood. Jules still unconvinced with his explanation, detained and escorted him to the police office for further questioning.

Simone appeared offering me a cup of coffee, 'Drink this, it will calm you.' if he had damaged my dream car, I considered only a public flogging would be an acceptable punishment. Calming myself I sipped the hot coffee and reconsidered the situation thoroughly. Why did he give me the immediate offer of thousands in cash so soon after the auction, and now this incident.

This motor vehicle had a secret, but what, something was in this car, I was going to find out before it left my possession. As John secured the backyard gates, 'you landed a couple of good ones. Any idea who, he is?'

'It was that flashy chap from the auction; remember the one who kept pestering me to sell him the car

'Something is in this car, and I am going to find it.' Elaine appeared and hurried to my side. She wanted to know what had happened, she had been woken by the commotion, and seeing Jules frogmarching the man across the square, wondered what was wrong. I explained the best I could satisfy her curiosity for the moment.

Opening the car doors, I stood and took a long hard look then started by removing the carpets. Next the contents of the glove box, any removable items from the boot of the car, then carefully I checked the interior for damage. I found there was damage to the passenger door lock which confirmed my worry, that I had locked it yesterday evening.

One corner of the rear seat had been lifted up away from its frame. John was voicing suggestions, that hidden diamonds and gold bullion could be hidden in the car. Gathering all the papers Elaine looked at each one but they revealed nothing, John also helped by translating any paperwork there was in French.

We returned them back into the glove compartment, putting the over carpets back into place. Still there was nothing out of place, I knelt on the front passenger seat, as I glanced over the back of the car that back seat squab, taking hold I pulled at it, it would not move.

Feeling around the edge I discovered a small lever, I pressed the lever the seat released and revealed a collection of coins, a single gold stud earring with a suspended jewelled pendant. Collecting the items, I placed them in my shirt pocket, I was about to replace the seat when I saw the reflection of bright metal in the bottom of a narrow crevasse in the rear floor pan. Inserting my fingers into the crevasse I tried to move the object, it was wedged tight, but with gentle teasing it came loose. The object turned out to be a blue faced Cartier gents watch very attractive although the closing clasp was broken; putting it in my shirt pocket with the rest of the finds, I returned and made fast the seat squab.

Turning around in the front seat, I heard a sound, it was similar to a sheet of tin flexing. Slipping into the driver's seat,

I continued the search on that side of the car. It was noticeable that this seat was softer than the passenger seat.

The central armrest lifted and revealed several classical music cassette tapes.

While searching the trunk section of the car, I checked the toolkit, every tool was correct and in place. The spare wheel had a new tyre fitted; together with a couple of car accessories, a travel rug completed the contents.

Opening the bonnet, I took my time looking around the engine compartment, all ancillaries and essential fluids were at the correct levels.

I started the motor, it growled into life, the engine revs increasing as the cold starter device kicked in, the revs settled to a slow idle, the engine was so smooth you could hear every cylinder fire in turn, Pressing the accelerator a couple of times the response was superb a nice engine and in excellent condition.

Sitting momentarily in the passenger seat, I again heard that sound of metal flexing. The seats were finished in light tan leather with moulded foam bases supported by steel springs, nothing should flex, taking a squint under the seat there was nothing obvious to be seen. As I brought my head back my eyes saw a silver blue flash of light, moving my head down again, I caught a glint from a shiny edge under the seat.

Lifting the seat cushion to see what it was, I retrieved the silver sheet. inspecting the item; it was made of plastic not metal as I first thought; the surface was an opalescence silver with an intricate embossed pattern which reflected a huge array colour, consisting of gold silver and bronze, and what seemed like a picture with some writing on one side.

Elaine returned from having a coffee, 'What is that?'

'I found it in the passenger seat.' Taking the article from me she inspected and read what was printed on it, 'Do, you know what this is?'

'No'

'It is a Bearer Bond Certificate,' She was about to say something more, when Jules appeared, Elaine slid the bond into the folds of her dress, Jules had come enquiring whether anything had been stolen or if the car been damaged.

I showed the damage to the door lock, this was the only damage I had found. If anything was missing, I would not know, unless that character, had something in his pocket belonging to the car.

Jules stated he was being charged with, malicious damage, together with attempted theft from an automobile.

'What about my action when I hit him?'

'No problem, he fell over resisting arrest. Also, you were only defending yourself'.

I was just about to tell him about the Bond certificate, when Elaine said, it was time for breakfast and this silly matter could be attended to later.

The driver was ready to take the Monteverdi to the body shop. I pointed to the damage to the passenger door, if that repair could be done at the same time; I said 'I would pay for that repair as a separate matter.'

The driver looked at the damage; he would pass on my request. The repair should be completed in about a week or sooner.

While having breakfast, I asked Elaine why she stopped me from telling Jules about the Bond.

She replied in a very quiet voice, 'If that Bond is correct, it's worth a fortune.'

'Fortune', I whispered

'Millions. Let's discuss this in private',

'What for',

Walls have ears, I have the Bond in my handbag, and it looks genuine. It's for 501 shares, there is more to read, but when Jules arrived, I thought it best to hide it.

I think you should say nothing about it, until we get home or find out more about it.

Somebody has already tried to steal the car, but I think it is this, that they were after', Elaine was showing a side I'd not seen before.

Could this bond be stolen?

Was it real?

Who would we call?

Who do we contact?

Who do we trust?

Returning to the privacy of our bedroom we examined the document. It felt like a thin metal sheet with a holographic picture of gleaming silver reflecting beautiful colours of aquamarine, silver, reds, blues. In fact, the full spectrum was being reflected from this item, it was lovely.

The Bond read,

****

The Vista Plastic Company.

Paris. France. Certificate Number 001

I promise to pay the Bearer the value of 501 shares.

Issued & Guaranteed

The United Federal Bank New York.

****

Written on the back in indelible black ink were six lines of calculations. Part of it looked like $(CxHz+O2+PF)$ polymer + $(T2H2 + heat) = \square$ plus loads of symbols, and lines of equations.

I was intrigued by the little skull and crossbones, this calculation must mean something, but as I was ignorant of this type of calculation and symbols, it had no meaning for me. Elaine suggested contacting our bank manager, or my accountant, but just what would we do about this Bond?

We decided to hide it, then see what the immediate future and the holiday brought, after all we were on holiday and instead of relaxing, we were both as busy as if we were at home.

Jules knocked on the bedroom door, Elaine let him in, we had matters to discuss.

Concerning the damage to the car, the man involved was of reputable character and origin, why should he have committed a trivial crime like this, and for what gain.

He is the Managing Director of Whittle Plastic, in England. He just kept repeating that he was a car collector; he wanted to buy the car. He even offered to leave surety of £1,000 to cover any damage he had caused.

Whittle had been charged and the surety deposited. If I called to the police office, they would give me the money, upon signing a receipt.

Jules and I walked to the office, a small amount of paperwork was completed, the surety paid, 'Fancy, smacking a guy in the face, and getting paid for it',

On the way back, I made the connection. A high value Bond Certificate from a Plastic company Whittle owned, Whittle Plastics, there is more to this, than he was willing to let on.

I decided against telling Jules about the Bond, as I fancied investigating the matter in my own way.

I made a telephone call to discuss the Bond with my accountant Derek, he would investigate on my behalf, if there any problems, I was sure he would advise me of the correct procedure. I explained the situation to Derek, including the exciting incidents that had taken place since the auction, he was intrigued.

Immediately he warned me on certain legal and currency matters, I could fall foul if I did not tread carefully.

He requested details from the Bond, I gave him the information he required, apart from the calculation written on the back. He assured me that he would make discrete enquiries and get back to me.

Chapter 4

Sitting quietly outside the bar enjoying a cool beer, I was browsing my options. Why not visit Paris while we were here, I could take a quick look at the business office of Vista Plastics, partially enter Pierre Sarr's world, and hopefully find out exactly what was going on. I made the suggestion of going to Paris for a couple of days. Elaine fancied a browse round Paris and Simone said she had access to a small flat, which we were welcome to use. I suggested to Simone that if she fancied two days in Paris, Elaine would have a companion to peruse what women peruse at their leisure. John agreed, he could cope in the bar for a few days, now all the auction action had finished he had many bottles of wine to sort and stack in the cellar.

I had no business clothes with me; selecting a conservative suit and compatible shirts from the clothing recently acquired, I was ready to go. Not knowing what to expect, I included the Bond certificate and the portable computer, then we left for Paris. Simone's apartment was in the south west side of Paris, located on a top floor; the apartment had two small bedrooms, a kitchen and sitting room. The view of Paris across the roof tops was good, 'It gets better in the evening', Simone added.

Checking the Paris Street guide, I discovered that the office of Vista Plastic's was within walking distance.

The girls were settling in and making tea, I went to explore and found myself standing in front of the office within fifteen minutes.

My heart was pounding, a feeling of apprehensive twisted my guts, do I go in, or call it quits and walk away, that little mind voice was yelling go, go and find out! Entering the foyer, the concierge requested my business. I indicated the company and was directed to the first floor. Slowly I climbed the stairs, I saw people milling around a glass fronted set of offices, I walked past not thinking that this was the place I should be, there was only one other office on that floor. Sauntering back to the office, the front door was wide open, still a copious amount of people both inside and outside, safety in numbers, I joined the crowd to observe. A lady in reception was taking details and making notes of people arriving, the receptionist spotted me as a new face, then addressed me the nature of my business. I was about to reply, when a hand landed on my shoulder, stopping me replying to her question. A familiar voice addressed me, 'Ross what are you doing here?' I turned to see who was speaking It was an old friend called Darrell. I worked with him in a plastic reeled film factory many years ago. He asked how Elaine was. I enquired what he was doing now and who he worked for. He had left the local factory years ago; he was in a senior management position with a Plastic Company based in Manchester. With the death of Pierre Saar, both he and his Boss came to ensure the continuation of the urgently needed supply of Loyplas.

'I work for Whittle Plastics'. Darrell tapped the shoulder of another who had his back to me, the man turned, and Darrell introduced him. The hairs on the back of my neck stood, it was him, the man who I had outbid at the auction, the bastard, who had broken into the Monteverdi. Although he wore sunglasses in a vain attempt to hide the crimson nose and a darkening bruising around his eye. I gained instant satisfaction, that all my punches had landed. Whittle grunted something at me, then just walked away. Darrell, noticing the ignorant rebuke asked what I had done to deserve that treatment. 'Your man has a red nose and a black eye; they are the result of him crossing me'.

'Oh my!' Darrell exclaimed, trying to curtail a smile. I told him about the car and the problems that he had caused. Darrell asked did I know that Vista Plastic had just floated on the stock market.

I did not know that, I chatted with Darrell for a few minutes and he told me more information I needed. The huge jigsaw was starting to take shape; my brain was starting to collate the information and calculate an outcome.

With Pierre Sarr's demise, there was a strong rumour that the company could not make the Loyplas; the company could crash and take the plastic industry into recession until this product became available again.

Darrell asked who I worked for and what was I doing here? I brought him up to date on the auction, plus some other events, declining to mention the Bond, until I could establish its importance. I was starting to become aware of the problems that this company seemed to portray, the value of the Bond was dropping faster than water down the drain.

A lady came out from one of the offices and addressed the group of people, requesting the attention of a Mr. Ross Todd. I said to Darrell, 'Nobody knows that I am here, just a moment, we will talk later.' As I left, I noticed a reflection in the wall mirror as Darrell's Boss grabbed his arm and dragged him to one side.

I held up my hand in acknowledgment, she walked up to me 'Mr Ross Todd' she asked in a pleasant voice, 'How can I help you?' I replied. 'An international telephone call for you, we do not normally take telephone calls for unknown persons but today is not a normal day, please come this way.' She ushered me into her office and pointed to a telephone, the receiver was laid by its side on the desk. The lady excused herself and departed leaving a delicate fragrance in the air.

'Hello Ross Todd speaking'; the call was from Derek, my

accountant. He apologised if he had embarrassed me by calling me at this office, but it was imperative that he reached me. He was speaking with an excited tone; one I had never heard before.

'That Bond is possibly worth millions.' He then went on to say, 'A very strong rumour is that the company could be suspended from trading because of the loss of a secret formula.'

'Is that for Loyplas?'

'Yes,'

'I met an old friend in this office, he told me the same story'.

I told Derek that the Bond had a calculation and numbers written on the back in of it. Nevertheless, I could not make sense of it. Enquiring how he found my location, he replied that he had called the bar, and a John had told him of our intentions. He had decided to call the Vista Plastic office just in case. I repeated the information passed to me and Derek confirmed it. He told me to take care, to remember that the Bond had a great value, but only if the formula was found. Thanking him for the information, I told him I would keep him updated with any developments. He said he would do likewise.

As I turned to leave the lady who told me about the telephone call was standing in the office door, her hand across her mouth, a look of disbelief on her face.

'Are you feeling, OK?' She replied with a delightful French accent and apologised, she had overheard what I was saying on the telephone and wished confirmation. She asked did I have the Bond connected with the company? I said that I did. She asked, 'was there anything written on the Bond?'

'There was.'

She declared that it was imperative that I met with Max, he is the company manager.

Would I agree to meet with Max now?

Now in the spider's web the excitement was phenomenal, I could feel my voice trembling in my reply, 'I will.' I was shown into another office; it had the appearance of a boardroom.

The room was well furnished with a large table and eight seats around it. Sitting on the nearest seat, I waited while the lady slipped away to explain the situation to this person Max. Within seconds a man returned with her and joined me, taking a seat next to me. He made immediate eye contact, whoever this man was, he was not fooling around.

He introduced himself as Max general manager of The Vista Plastic Company. The lady was introduced as Madam Janine, company secretary and director, she sat opposite me, many questions were asked. I answered all questions until my voice started to falter, 'may I have a glass of water, please?'

Max was still pounding away with the questions. He asked questions to confirm that I had no other interest in any other plastic companies anywhere in the world. I gave confirmation that I had previous knowledge of the plastic industry but only for a two-year period, and this was over twenty years ago.

Madam Janine served me with a refreshing glass of water. They discussed some matter in French. Turning to me, they wished to make me an offer upon the basis that I held this bond certificate and it had the lost formula written on the back. Before any offer was to be presented, they would need some proof. I opened my briefcase, removed a large manila envelope and slowly I started to extract the certificate from the envelope stopping halfway. If I had shown any more the calculation could be observed and I could lose my claim. Max approved of my caution. He confirmed he had seen enough; as he had seen the certificate before, when it was Pierre's and so the calculation would be correct.

They made the offer.

The company would have to be restructured into a three-way partnership, Max to assume the status of the M.D. Madame Janine would still be controlling the company accounts with myself as the other partner as I held the bond including the secret. The shares on it dictated that I held 51% of the company. They were prepared to work with me, as a silent partner. If I wanted to be a working director, they would both require that I had a period of instruction to be re-educated into their plastic industry, only then would it be possible to take a post as a working director. I would receive a salary equal to the others and have provisional, non-executive director status installed immediately.

Max proceeded to explain that although I had the calculations and the formula, they could be sold to any plastic company in the world for a vast amount of money. Max was worried that the company workforce be made redundant; he gave me the impression that he was a caring Manager, always looking out for the workers' jobs, and not forgetting he would also benefit that his own job was secure.

Requesting an hour to consult a couple of people and to gather my thoughts, I was left alone in the board room Madam Janine set the telephone so I could make calls. Derek was the first to be contacted, as usual, chasing Derek around different offices until he was located wasted time. Updating him on the outcome, he confirmed that it was a superb offer. Try to occupy a similar role as the former owner, keeping the formula secret until such times as it was appropriate to disclose the secret would give you seniority in your actions, be on your guard, call if you need me.

The haunting words from Derek made my back shiver. The events in the last couple of days would stand as trivial if the regime of industrial espionage, agents of unknown companies, who were prepared to steal, maybe even kill for this formula, permutated my thoughts. If the formula came back to the safety of the original company it would save the company, I would be safe; there was the bonus of directorship, and the value of the bond would make me financially independent.

The challenge of a new career was also of great interest. A final but vital piece of information was required; the man who could supply this detail was 30 feet away.

I left the office looking for Max or Madame Janine and found them preparing a statement for the gathered representatives. I requested that I would like to speak with Darrell before I gave them my decision.

The receptionist showed Darrell into the office with Whittle following. Madame Janine gave me a concerned look, looking at Whittle in the office.

Not wishing to hide anything from the matter in question, I asked, 'Darrell, if I had the power to pull this company out of its problems, what would your views be?'

Before Darrell could reply Whittle blurted out, 'If I had that formula, he would pay me a large amount of money if I sold it to him.' I held my hand up to stop Darrell replying.

Turning to Whittle 'Is your name Darrell?' He replied 'Bugger that, do you want the money'

'I wished to talk with Darrell, not! with you, will you please leave this meeting now!' His face went crimson matching his nose, spluttering, he erupted a stream of abuse.

'Get, out!' I replied.

Max a larger man in frame than Whittle, showed Whittle, still protesting ferociously, back towards reception.

Darrell whispered to me, 'He will not forget that.'

'Nor will I, I have had enough of arse holes like him in my life; his actions and attitude to me in the last day was, not to my liking, I will not put up with anymore.'

Max returned to the meeting grinning; Janine was also restraining herself from smiling. I asked Darrell to reply to my question, 'If this company was pulled back from the impending closure, it would save a lot of jobs throughout the plastic industry.

The answer to the question was agreeable, an answer that would save jobs and achieve a long-lasting future in an ever-growing industry was exactly what I wanted to hear.

Darrell voiced his concern about the affray, would that cause any trading difficulties for Whittle Plastic in any dealings in the future? Referring the question to Madame Janine, 'Is there a problem with this company?'

'No, they pay their bills.'

I thanked Darrell for his input, he returned to reception 'I bet Whittle is giving him a serious talking to at the moment,' Janine opened her door by a couple of centimetres observed the two for a while, 'Deep discussion,' Janine commented, 'you do not have a liking for Mr. Whittle.'

'No, I consider him a liar, cheat and a thief. I would not trust him, but please do not let my personal view cloud the issue, let us return to our present problem. Max re-joined us in the office and I explained my decision, together with the rule that I would be prepared to join the company. Max seemed to have the attitude: take what they want and dispense with me at a later date. Madam Janine had other ideas, she agreed with me, she liked my handling of Whittle. The sincerity of her voice, putting across a point of view, made Max relent, they finally both agreed.

Max explained what they intended to do and left to make arrangements, Janine poured two coffees, bringing them she sat beside me and placed the coffee on the desk. She confided in me, 'It is always better to be cautious than to be foolish, she felt that I was sincere and would be a good addition to the company.' There was something in her voice gave me an indication this lady was honest and straightforward. Possibly a person I could rely on in a crisis. I had a good feeling about this woman, I could not say exactly what it was, just something in her calmness and command of the situation. Max returned giving some papers to Madam Janine and asked for a copy of the formula; requesting a clean piece of paper, unobserved I wrote down the first line of the six-line formula onto the sheet of paper. Passing the paper to Madam Janine, she glanced at it, passed it to Max, who checked over the details then confirmed that it was the formula and what had been written down originally, although some of the symbols were incorrectly drawn, this could be down to my interpretation of the written formula. The Bond certificate was returned to the safety of the envelope then to my valise. I requested that if this was such a serious secret, it had to remain secret, but I would make sure that the secret would be made available if needs became critical.

Max went to the reception to give a brief announcement that negotiations were now taking place, there would be a statement released later today. Representatives could stay if they wished and coffee would be available. He reconfirmed that no announcement would be made until 3:00 pm. The company solicitor was summoned to attend the meeting. He drew up the agreement translated by Madam Janine. He assured me about the way I acquired the bearer bond certificate, secreted inside the car, purchased at a public auction was ok. If the item was not stolen, then it became the property of the buyer. Max reconfirmed that the first section of the formula was correct. I had the formula.

At 3:00 pm, Max read a statement to the waiting business colleagues, in addition there were members of the press and a television crew. Max claimed that the company was now safe. I was reluctantly introduced as a new director of the company. Max declared that we had plenty of stock to fulfil orders for the next two months.

Hopefully the industrial wholesalers and manufacturers were satisfied. The attending press reporters were eager to know more; questions flew in all directions, some were answered, some declined, happy or not with the answers given. A press photographer was taking some pictures.

Fresh coffee, the aroma wafted past my nose, 'What I would not do for a cup of coffee.' Madame Janine had already anticipated my thoughts inviting me into her office sitting me down and presenting me with freshly made coffee, together with a small snack.

Madame Janine asked where I got my suit. With caution I mentioned the auction; the housekeeper from the château had suggested that I acquired the clothes. Madame Janine replied, 'A very wise move.' Sliding over to me, she kissed me on the lips saying softly, 'Thank you for your kindness and understanding, in this business you have much to learn; I will help teach you if you will let me. Please call me Janine.'

'I hope I will not disappoint you.' As I reflected, she had soft lips, and an intoxicating perfume.

'The challenge of the future will be exciting. Already I have seen that you are not frightened easily.' Janine answered

'Frightened?'

Of course, 'Mr. Whittle was displaying the signs of somebody crossing you; it was impressive.'

Something inside me urged me to say 'I like your perfume, what is it?' Janine taken off guard blushed slightly and gave a name I had not heard of, she held a hand across her chest, I am sorry if I have embarrassed you, in asking about your perfume, 'No, I am greatly flattered by the comment' she replied. Janine suggested an evening of celebration. Remembering that I had two shopaholics with me in Paris, Janine suggested, 'Please bring them with you this evening.' A restaurant was suggested then reservations made. Max insisted on the company chauffeur dropping me at the apartment. With his expert knowledge of the Paris suburbs, I was at the apartment within minutes. He would return at 8.15 to take us to the restaurant.

Entering the apartment, I was accosted by two excited females Elaine and Simone wanting to know what happened why was I in the evening newspaper? 'Please, a moment, what is going on?' Simone had seen the story in the evening newspaper and translated the story to Elaine. Elaine chose to deny any knowledge of the Bond. I gave a quick explanation for Simone's benefit, about what I found in the car, the detective work, the chance meeting with Darrell at the office, the disclosure that the bond Vista Plastics were looking for, was in my safe possession. Oh, by the way, I forgot to mention, we were going to be taken in a chauffeur driven limousine to a restaurant this evening for a celebration dinner. If you wish to come, you should get moving or I will go on my own.'

When you offer two ladies an evening in Paris at a choice restaurant, imagine the scene: a bijou apartment, one shower, three persons all rushing to get ready. The hustle, naked bodies, the unisex shower which created an air of sensuality, the clothes show, hair spray filling the air, make up, then the transformation of two ladies was complete. Simone answered the knock on the door. It was the chauffeur respectfully announcing that he had arrived and would wait for us downstairs. Within minutes we were on route to an unknown destination. Simone requested the destination from the chauffeur, he replied, 'Gee Patron.'

Simone whispered that it was the best place in town, if you could get a reservation.

The chauffeur opened the door for us as we arrived then we were met by the maître d'hôtel, who ushered us quickly into a private area, where a small party of people were chatting. I introduced Elaine and Simone to Max, and Janine, Max conducted the introductions, to the people gathered, most were people connected with Vista Plastics. Max passed me telegrams from the Montreal factory manager, the Japan and New York Office managers, all offering thanks and congratulations. Finally, Janine greeted me by kissing cheek to cheek. 'I could get used to all this affection.' Her perfume was different, madam 'May I compliment you on your perfume yet again,' Janine thanked me graciously, 'I wondered if you would notice' she whispered.

The maître announced that dinner was ready, indicating the direction we had to proceed. Another gastronomic experience: escargots lightly garnished with garlic butter, fresh smoked salmon, and a selection of chicken and other choice meats, vegetables crisp and so fresh. My choice to follow was crêpe suzette. The wine and champagne flowed as if there were no end, followed by coffees and some excellent brandies, the evening I thought was a complete success. Quietly reflecting on my decision earlier, I assured myself that my actions were correct.

'Are you lost in your mind, Ross?' Janine asked.

'I am sorry, today has been so busy, I am content that everybody is happy with the decision I made.'

'Will you come to the office tomorrow?' We require you to attend some of our meetings, we all have lots to discuss and plan for the future.'

'A quelle heure'

'Parlez vous français?' Janine enquired

'Je ne parle pas français.' I will try hard to make my French improve as well as my knowledge of the business.

'It will improve; I will make it my personal challenge.' Janine replied.

The evening dinner progressed into the late hours; guests were bidding their goodbyes. As the party was coming to a close our car was waiting to whisk us to a comforting bed and a well-earned sleep before the early morning meetings. The girls decided to shop again in the morning, they would come to the office later.

Chapter 5

It was early as I showered then dressed for a day at the office, the ladies slept, totally unaware I had left. The morning walk was exhilarating giving me time to think. The Bond was now safe and secure, but maintaining its value would become a priority.

The old saying, 'A fool and his money are soon parted,' would haunt me from now on, until I achieved stronger control of the situation.

Arriving at the office the building was quiet, the Vista Plastic reception was in darkness, but a light surrounding Janine's office door gave an indication that the office was occupied. I pushed the front door, it opened, a chime sounded.

Max opened Janine's office door 'Bonjour, please come through, we are in here.' In the office people sat in discussion, each was introduced to me. Janine, her secretary, the company solicitor and his secretary, the Paris factory manager and his secretary, Max and myself completed the quorum.

This the first meeting of the new company, an agenda was prepared. The primary requirements - proposals for the future, the purchase of the company from Pierre's family, all these matters had to be attended to. The proposal was written up and the offer to purchase the company was put in place for the family to consider. The solicitor stated that if the proposals were agreed, it might take up to three or four weeks for the business to pass title, but as the company was solvent, he could not foresee a problem. He instructed his clerk to prepare the letters of proposal in the other office, we would sign then they could be forwarded to Pierre's family. If all went well, from Monday, the company with all its problems and glories would now be the responsibility of three new directors, hopefully giving extra security and fortune for the future. Little did I know that people in the meeting were already scheming and planning the company's downfall!

The meeting closed, the others departed, Max, Janine and I toasted the future again, wishing each other good fortune. I mentioned that any disagreement or problems should be discussed and settled as they arose; we were to keep no secrets, apart from the Formula. The entrance chime on the main door brought our attention to two people, loaded down with bags of shopping, looking weary and glad of a cup of coffee. Two coffees consumed and noses powdered, replenished the girls, who had decided to return to the village. We exchanged addresses and telephone numbers at Laroche. Max mentioned the need for future meetings as he had prepared and passed to me a proposed work itinerary to follow.

Janine spoke in English, 'Thank you, I hope to have you later.' Elaine whispered behind me, 'I did not like the sound of that.' 'It was probably a bad translation.' I gave Janine the customary kiss on each cheek as we left, shook hands with Max whilst saying, 'I will look forward to seeing you again.'

The chauffeur delivered us to the apartment, quickly we loaded our bags into the Legend, gave the apartment a quick tidy then we were ready to depart. Driving out of Paris Simone helped with the directions once we were on the road to Laroche both fell fast asleep it was a quiet drive back.

It was early evening when we arrived at Laroche, John was spellbound with the stories we told. He had read about it in the paper but could not quite understand what had happened, when I had enlightened him on the discovery of the Bond, he said sternly, 'Do not forget to inform Jules, concerning the Bond.'

That was a memorable evening of eating, drinking and telling of many tales. Jules appeared; I told him about the Bond certificate and other matters and also told him that now there was the possibility of a connection between Whittle and Pierre Saar. He promised to discuss this further in the morning.

A wine cooler had ceased to operate. John asked if I could check it out, replacing a fuse the cooler rumbled into life.

'Yu is clever with your mains!' 'Mains?' looking up it was Madame Jacqueline she was leaning over the bar watching me, after watching the television report on the discovery of the Bond she wished to congratulate me.

Testing the wine dispenser, I pulled two glasses of wine giving one to her I tried the other it was good. It was difficult to understand her accent. She decided to go home and wished me 'au revoir,' saying to me again that I would always be welcome to stay at her hotel. Thanking her for the offer, she said 'she had an electrical problem, could I visit her in the morning to have a look at it?

'Of course, I would be delighted to be of help.'

'A problem hmmm, and you'll have a look at it,' John looked at me then winked, also, 'Mains' she meant your hands not the electric mains. I rocked my hands from side to side as if holding a pair of water melons, could a pleasant shock whatever my mains were holding.

Sniggering John just shook his head.

Chapter 6

The bedroom was cold and the bed had attractive properties, from the window I could see the morning mist clinging around the tree tops like cotton wool on a Christmas tree. Elaine was fast asleep, probably going for the record morning lie in. I showered selecting warm casual clothes dressed and enjoyed a coffee with John. I fancied a morning walk, John reminded me, 'Do not forget your screwdriver insulating tape and bike.'
'Screwdriver, tape and bike?'
'Madame Jacqueline? Problem?'
'That is correct I remember now what this is about a bicycle I was going to walk.'
She has an excellent place to park one, John just about collapsed with laughter, 'I thought the joke was in poor taste.'
Picking a couple of tools I might need from the boot of my car, I called in the bakery first for a pain au chocolate, something to eat on the way. The meeting with Mme Jacqueline in mind, I made my way towards her hotel on the outskirts of the village. Stopping at the bridge over the stream, the parapet made an easy seat while eating my pastry, the stream gurgled as it ran its course gradually dispersing into a small lake. Pairs of water fowl scurried about on the surface of the lake, disappearing under the water then bobbing back up. They would disappear into the reeds at the edge of the lake reappearing seconds later, a likelihood that they were feeding their young.
The early morning sun had broken through the cloud, warming my back, I continued up the lane. The small hotel now on my right, I swiftly knocked on the door, I waited, turning around I looked back over the lane. The house had a

good view of anybody on the lane, still waiting for a reply I wondered what was the problem. Glancing at my watch, I was horrified. It was Seven o'clock on a Sunday morning; I was too early. There was no reply, great, she had not heard me. I would return at a more respectable time, suddenly a voice from above me spoke quietly, 'Bonjour have you come for the breakfast?' Looking up to greet the voice, it was Mme Jacqueline. She was on her balcony, dressed in a cream dressing gown. 'Please, come round the back of the house, I will open the door for you.' I apologised for being early and offered to return at a later time. She replied, 'You are here, I am awake, come, I will let you in at the back door.' She was waiting by the open door. I was still offering my apologies, she replied by placing her fingers on my mouth saying, 'You English always apologise for every little thing.'
'OK, I will not apologise again.'
'Perfect.'
Sitting me down at a small table she asked me why was I up so early? 'I have come to fix your electrical problem' She opened a cupboard and removed an old silver coffee maker which she passed to me, 'it is broken,' the coffee maker must have been made in 1920's or 30's with primitive electrical wiring. The fault was a broken wire in the plug, I quickly rewired the plug, it was working again. Mme Jacqueline washed it clean filled it with coffee and water, plugged it in, almost instantly the coffee machine started, spurting hot coffee, 'Ooh! You are an engineer' Jacqueline sighed. While the coffee machine did its work, I watched her preparing breakfast, manoeuvring round the kitchen picking things from here things from there, each time she passed the table something new was laid on it. Standing a moment, she looked at the table laid with fresh warm croissants, a single pain of chocolate, butter, jams and plates. She leant forward

to retrieve two cups from a shelf above my head, her bathrobe parted presenting me with a very close view of two ample breasts centimetres from my nose, although she unflustered by the exposure, I could feel the heat from the breasts on my face, she placed the cups on the table, closed her robe, retrieved the coffee machine poured two cups coffee. 'Sucre?' 'Petit sucre'
Voila! Placing the sugar bowl in front of me, we sat enjoying breakfast, drinking our coffees; she was discussing the news of yesterday in her version of French almost forgetting I was not fully conversant. I wondered how much of my discussion she understood, as she kept looking at me as if she did not understand. I slowed my speech, and gave simple answers where I could. She poured me another coffee, 'enjoy.'
Finishing breakfast, I made moves to go back to the village I would try my French 'Je allez le Ville'
She raised an eyebrow 'merci pour err, fix le coffee put.' She leaned forward, kissing me then she raised her hands hugging me around the neck. I was not prepared for the sudden embrace, she was smaller than I was my hands closed around her waist; to stop myself falling forward, the bathrobe had opened again, my hands touched on her nakedness, she held me close, continuing with the embrace.
She whispered, 'I have no secrets from you,' then she grabbed my belt buckle and pulled me out of the kitchen up the stairs towards her bedchamber.
A moment's pause for breath I glanced at her, she was smiling, and whispering to me in French. She had removed her robe revealing a curvaceous body most women would desire; as she lay together my hand fell into the natural hollow of her waist. Embracing each other, without stopping, inquisitive hands explored each other, time seemed to stand still, she manoeuvred herself on top of me then

continued with her lovemaking.

The view of her large breasts, gently swinging in a small circular motion in front of me, made me more aroused. We climaxed together and both fell together in a lingering embrace.

Within days of being total strangers, we could never be strangers any more. it was a wonderful way to spend a Sunday morning, as we were slowly relaxing, I took note of where I was. The bedroom was obviously hers; a wardrobe slightly ajar was brimming with clothes. A door to one side of the room, another on the opposite wall the windows was half covered by a lace curtain.

The head board was carved wood, with a flowing design it was nice to the touch a word 'HERSCHE' was carved in one corner, possibly the maker's name, beside the name was a number 01990 what significance it had I was unaware of.

A hand caressing over my chest, down over my stomach to the inner thigh, then moving over to the other thigh returned my attention to the female by my side. The exotic combination of soft finger tips and the slight pain of a scraping finger nail gave me an uncontrollable affect. She smiled, 'U R erect again.'

When someone has shared innermost secrets, a bond is formed; how you proceed is up to you. As I walked back, I reflected on the last hour I felt as if I had been taken, I felt as if she had engineered the situation to her benefit.

Back in the bar, I ordered a coffee, John inquiring did I sort the problem?

'It would not have fallen over.'

John exclaimed 'Not fallen over?' giving me a strange look as he pondered my reply 'What would not have fallen over?'

'The Bike'. John exploded into laughter Simone came to see what all the frivolity was about.

A telephone ringing disrupted the uncontrollable laughter, John answering, listened for an instant, and then passed the phone to me, 'For you.'

It was Max, he was enquiring if I was available to attend a meeting in Paris this Monday morning. 'A problem has arisen; stocks of the product have sold faster than anticipated. The plastic producers were panic buying and it seemed that one buyer is trying to corner the market, they had placed a huge order'.

'Was it Whittle Plastics?

'No, a German company Schyne Plastix had placed the order. We can supply the order, but it would make our stock dangerously low, Max declared that a fresh consignment of the formula should be started immediately to create enough stock to cover the coming next year's sales.'

To enable the product to be manufactured I would have to be in attendance with the formula.

'Where and when would I have to be?'

Max replied, 'The Canadian factory on Tuesday. We would be flying out on the first flight from Charles De Gaulle airport, returning back on the following Thursday.'

'Max, if we accept this order and successfully produce the product and keep the knowledge quiet that we have re made the product, we could let the buyers keep on with the panic buying. It would create the required funds to pay for the company. I would be interested on your opinion?'

'I will consider the probability factor and talk with you on Monday.'

'Ok, see you then.'

I told Elaine that Max had requested a trip to Montréal on the Tuesday, coming back Thursday.

Elaine decided that she would prefer to travel back to England. She could call and visit her brother on the way and possibly see a couple of old school chums. The Monteverdi would be ready just after we returned from the Canadian trip this would make me mobile.

We spent our last day in Laroche travelling around the surrounding countryside, driving through the smaller villages each was different some seemed abandoned with lots of derelict houses on the outskirts nevertheless they were quaint and quiet, finding a nice secluded spot by a small wood, we sat in the field to enjoy a small picnic prepared by Simone. It was good, a slight breeze cooled the heat of the sun. The cold grape juice plus the mini savouries and pastries this was exactly why we had come. I caught a movement from the corner of my eye a deer just partially hidden in the shadows another one braving the meadow come into the sunshine followed by a stag. As he walked into view the sunlight shone off his red coat, the enormous antlers made him stand at least 16 feet high. There were plenty of points on the antlers, which made him an old boy, but he still commanded grace and composure.

I touched Elaine's foot to make sure she had seen the stag. The creature surveyed the area, smelling the air then in a flash he disappeared from whence he came. Elaine had taken her shoes off, the stag probably smelt the feet then beat a hasty retreat, making known this observation I was thanked by a swift kick in the ribs. Stretching out in the meadow dwelling over the last couple of days events I fell asleep in the warm sun, dreaming of things to come. Elaine brought me from my slumber by tickling my ear with a blade of grass she was disappointed about cutting the holiday short. We made love in the seclusion of the meadow promising ourselves another holiday once all this crazy business had settled.

We returned to Laroche, and packed the Legend for Elaine to

travel home. John had prepared a small meal, a celebration on the house; he reminded me that I had not tuned his Triumph Bonneville yet.

Listen mate 'I have not gone home yet, Elaine's returning to England; I am staying in Paris for a couple of days then off to Canada. A distinct possibility I might be back to see you at the end of the week.'

'Great, have another brandy.'

Chapter 7

We left Laroche early in the morning heading for Paris. Elaine drove; the previous evening's consumption of brandy had an effect on my eyes, or was it the red wine, that was the cause. I slept for a while during the journey to Paris. Elaine adapted very well to driving on French roads, although she drove very well in any country. Negotiating the Legend through the Paris traffic following my expert directions which I retrieved from the Paris A to Z map; Elaine was enjoying the Legend's powerful agility; she parked in front of the office. I beckoned the concierge, to assist me with my luggage. I showed Elaine the route she should follow out of Paris, she leaned forward kissing me swiftly a little wave and she disappeared off into the Paris traffic.

Entering the office, Janine looked happy to see me, greeting me with a kiss on each cheek, this I have noted is normal for greeting male female, she was dressed in a short-sleeved cream blouse, buttoned at the front, a black slim pencil type skirt, black nylons and high heeled shoes: conservative business attire, she dressed well.

'You look appealing today,'

'Merci Monsuire Ross'

'Your perfume is enchanting.'

She smiled, thank you, she offered me a coffee,

'That would be nice'. Returning with the coffee, she leant forward to place the cup on the desk by me. It was hard not to notice the revealing view of breasts, alas they were restricted by a bra.

'Thank you.'

'No, reply in French, please.'

'Merci, Janine.'

Janine, I believe, would be as good as her word. She would

persevere with her personal instruction; my knowledge of the plastic business and the French language would increase. My willingness to learn from such an excellent teacher would ensure my attention at all times, together with the way Janine spoke English with an exciting French accent would ensure the tutorials a pleasure.

The business meeting was brief and to the point. We the three directors had a large amount of money to find, to pay for the business so it was imperative that we started production of the formula. Both Max and Janine agreed with my suggestion of accepting the order and produce the formula in secret. Janine thought it an excellent idea to capitalise on the situation; other companies were also trying to do the same. Max was still hesitant, giving an impression that he was not fully agreeable with me onboard. Something in his mannerism toward me. I decided to dismiss it, as Max did not know me and he would proceed with caution.

I requested somewhere to store my cases, also to enable me to repack a small case to take with me, a vacant office was made for my disposal. Once many years ago I travelled to the eastern seaboard of America, during the summer the humidity levels are high. Assuming that Ontario would be the same, I packed some lightweight shirts, shorts, socks and another pair of trousers. It all fitted snugly into a small hand case that also contained the laptop computer. Travelling light enables passing through customs easier. As a precaution, I had with me a backup copy of all the data files from Pierre's desktop computer, now safely stored with John. Returning to Janine's office, she asked,

"Are you ready to go to Canada?'

'Oui, Janine.'

'Bon.'

The chauffeur was called to take us to the airport. He

reported that we should go soon as there was a problem with the traffic. The Peripherique was closed because of an accident, we would have to go through the city centre on route If we were to make the flight at 14:00 hours we had managed to get booked on Concorde to New York, a meeting scheduled with the U.S. Sales manager, then travelling on by air taxi to Ontario.

Janine asked me to take some documents for the New York and Montreal office. Max appeared standing by the office door, 'Ready to go?'

'Yes', I forgot, 'Oui', picking up my case, I said, 'Au revoir, I will see you on my return'.

She replied, 'I will have you when I get back.' I looked at her with a mischievous smile, she blushed realising what she had said. She repeated 'I will see you, when you get back.', 'Please accept my apologies for the mistake, it is my translation, of the English.' 'There are two meanings to both phrases, both are welcome.' I leant forward kissing her cheek she offered the other cheek, 'No.' I whispered,

'None,' she replied turning her head towards me quickly I kissed her on the lips. She quickly realised the deception and smiled.

Max and I departed for the airport, destination Montreal, Canada. During the short drive Max, intrigued by my rapid rise to power within the company, quizzed me on the auction. How did I find the certificate? he became excited when I told him about the Whittle bashing incident, at least it would appear we had one thing in common.

Finally, I arrived at the Montreal factory I was feeling a bit tired, laborious meeting with managers and senior personnel, we had an extensive conducted tour of the Factory then we proceeded to the Laboratory No 2. The main Laboratory was undergoing a conversion from plans drawn up by Pierre; he had intended transferring the product manufacture to the new factory once the plant was producing then the Paris factory would undergo the same modifications, wondering to myself why did we come to Montreal if the laboratory was not complete, why not stay in France and duplicate in the Paris lab, why pay for the Concorde ticket when a normal flight would do. I felt that some questions would be brought up with the expenditure when problems with finance are paramount, these questions will be brought up at the next meeting

I watched mystified at our first attempt to make the formula we failed, probably it was me trying to be secretive with the formula, deciding to take Max into my confidence revealing to him the remaining part of the formula we tried again. Step by step Max followed the formula was very critical as he progressed through, the method to the mixing, was incorrect or ingredients missing.

We both decided to take our senior chemist Luis into our confidence, he would assist, once Luis had helped Pierre make Loyplas, but Pierre asked him to leave before it was completed and the final ingredients added. Luis tried the way he remembered worked up to the part he had not experienced everyway was tried including reversing the method, but alas we failed, Max and Luis seemed to have heated opinions during the process, I was oblivious to the conversation as they talked in French, I wondered if Max was out of his depth, just a gut reaction watching the two of them together.

Max spoke in confidence with me 'If we cannot crack this, we will have to declare that we are unable to continue manufacture and close the business.'

I was astounded by Max's defeatist attitude, 'What is wrong with you? I have what you wanted, you cannot make Loyplas and you are ready to throw in the towel

'What is, throw in the towel?'

Explaining the saying, also advising him that he was only one of three people and if he wanted to admit defeat, he could leave now, Max immediately recognising my annoyance towards him quickly revaluated his situation, and made a decision to keep going until we made Loyplas. Max called Janine in Paris explained the current situation. We all had a lot to gain but alas more to lose, the game was now played for extremely high stakes.

Mulling over the happenings of the last couple of days and how it was detective work that had solved some of the problems, a flash of inspiration came to me. Could; the answer lies in the private files on Pierre's portable computer.

Max was still taking to Janine; interrupting their conversation I explained the problem concerning the portable computer and the passwords. Did they know of any passwords or favourite words that Pierre had used, anything that could help? Setting up the computer as we talked, one of the files that I could not access I proceeded to open. Max observed the computer screen including the password location, 'This password could be one letter or fifteen letters long, it does not give an indication of the size of the password.' Trying all the letters of the alphabet in succession, the name 'Pierre Saar'. Did anyone know Pierre's mother's name, or her maiden name, his father's name, his dog's name, his car's name; all were tried.

We tried lots of combinations of words but still the computer sat there remaining uncooperative, together with the program security which would let us enter three different passwords then force us to restart the word processor program.

'Was he married?'

'He was not.'
'Did he have a lady friend?'
'He did.'
'What was her name?' Max did not know.
Janine, telephoning from Paris, asked to speak to me, 'Pierre
did have a lady friend.' She once overheard Pierre talking to
her, 'Could that be the house keeper at Laroche?' That could
be a good name to try, entering Jacqueline the computer file
remained closed, Then, cautiously, Janine let slip that Pierre
had stayed at her apartment; they had enjoyed each other's
company at dinner, but did not elaborate on that line of
information. We would talk later, wishing her goodnight,
understanding It was early in the morning European time.
Max had an inspiration, an idea for the formula, he
disappeared in the direction of the lab. Walking into the main
office, 'Is there any specialist computer personnel in the
company? Or did anybody know of a specialist computer
company in the area? I asked. Lots of shaking heads, nobody
had any idea, then 'Could I help?' turning to see a young
chap, coming towards me, he explained he had his own
computer at home, programming, and problem solving on
computers was his hobby.
Showing him the laptop, he grasped the situation, he would
have a go. Vanishing into the outer office he returned with a
small wallet, the wallet contained four computer floppy disk.
Selecting one 'Would it be OK to load this utility program
onto the laptop?' he asked first, 'This particular program is
worth having a copy, this program gives you the ability to
look into the computer data files and some programs. then
you can view what is in the file. You get an idea of what the
file contained even if you could not read it in its normal way.
By the way what is your name, I had forgotten to introduce
myself, or even have the courtesy of finding out his name,

my name is Ross Todd you are? I was labelled Wayne by my folks. Watching over Wayne's shoulder, the speed that he worked was impressive. He checked every letter and displayed them on the screen. Some were in English, he paused so I could read them, some were in French and Wayne translated them for me. Some of the letters I had already read, using John's translation program, but when a bilingual chap translates a better meaning is understood, I made notes on the contents of the letters but no passwords, keywords or additional information was found.

A couple of hours later Max returned. He had progressed to a full stop. Max said 'Who's this on the computer?' 'It is Wayne, he works in the main office, computers are his hobby. He is an expert.' Max started to laugh, 'Wayne, he is only a boy how can he be a computer expert? 'He is a computer expert, believe me! I am a company director!' Max saw the joke; we both enjoyed a good laugh, leaving Wayne cold on the joke. Wayne did not like that as he thought we were making a joke out of his age. We both apologised for our humour; we were inconsiderate. 'Please forget about it, continue with your valuable work, the discovery of the passwords.'

Wayne had managed to crack the passwords on all but three letters. The encryption code was good on these letters: not one password but two, both encrypting the file in a different format. This made it virtually impossible to decipher, but Wayne said that the first password was seven letters long and the second four characters long. He could write a program that would enter every combination of seven letter codes that there was, but that would take time. Did we have a couple of days to spare while this program was written and then set working? We had no option. Max was emphatic that we did not want the files to leave the office, Wayne could work here, and the company would get any piece of computer equipment he required. Wayne claimed he could work on the portable setting the program working within the hour. We gave him permission, giving instructions to the office secretary to get Wayne anything he wanted immediately.

Max said, 'We should eat and discuss matters.' Ulley Lange, the factory manager, invited us to eat at the German club in down town Dundas he would be pleased to take us, quickly we accepted. On the menu were varied Pizzas I helped to consume the largest pizza I have ever seen, followed by an excellent German beer. The German club was decorated as a German guesthouse. 'The woodcarvings came from Germany,' Ulley said. 'In most guesthouses in the French German border region the carvings came from one company every piece from that company had its name carved on it somewhere, the name of the woodcarver was Hersche. Then Ulley pointed to the name carved on the table. I said that in England a famous carver of furniture he also marked his work with a little mouse, every piece had one. That name Hersche was ringing an alarm bell in my mind. It was the same name on the bottom of Mme Jacqueline's headboard and the name was 7 letters long. Possibly, it could be the first password.

Thinking I had the first password, we headed back to the factory as we had finished eating. Wayne had the computer program working but he estimated that it would take 36 hours to complete its task.

'Try this name: HERSCHE.' The computer kept its secret. Wayne said, try it in lower case.' Hersche was entered, but still the computer remained silent. Wayne tried mixing the letters in upper and lower case

We tried with variations of the name using upper and lower case. As we entered the name spelt backwards, EHCSREH,

the computer emitted a beep, the screen cleared, 'Please enter your 8-digit code.' I cursed; Pierre wants to keep this secret a secret. Wayne said, 'I have already written the computer program for entering the numbers, it is quicker than the letters.' 'Set it going.' One single keyboard press and the program sprang into action. Max, pulling me away, said, 'How did you know that that was the password?' Up to a point, I thought, some secrets must be shared. I explained the situation, how I had discovered this name on Mme Jacqueline's headboard. Max said chuckling, 'lucky devil.' My memory flashed back to events in the bedroom of Jacqueline. Could it be possibly be that Pierre had had two lovers? A sailor has a girlfriend in every port, why could a company executive not have acquaintances dotted around the world? It could be a distinct possibility. 'Do you have Janine's telephone number at home? I would like to discuss something with her.' Having the presence of mind to be discrete, I called from an empty office, but not realising what time it was in Paris, I woke her from her sleep. What I was to ask could implicate her as the other lover. 'Janine, I am very sorry for calling at such an early hour, this is very important, do you have a carved wooden headboard on your bed?' She replied 'Oui.' 'Is the headboard made by Hersche?' She did not know, quietly asking me why did I want to know at 3.00 in the morning what make of headboard was on her bed. 'Could you have a look and see if anything is written on the headboard?' She said, 'I will have a look.'
'The name is carved on the headboard and a number has been written on the bottom, it is '18696981'
Thanking her I hoped she would be able to return to sleep, I would let her know about any further advances.
Returning to the office I asked, 'Any progress Wayne?'
'No, so I modified the search program.'

'Enter this number, see if it works.'
He entered 18696901, the computer bleeped, 'Incorrect, please re-enter code.' Surmising that we could not enter this code in variations, we entered the code again. The computer bleeped, 'Please re-enter' a new line appeared, saying '3rd try, last chance.' 'Wayne what does that mean. He replied that sometimes a program will only allow the pass code or password to be entered three times, then it would shut down.

The computer would have to be completely restarted; the word processor program started only then could the routine of entering passwords start again. This was to deter unscrupulous people accessing files quickly, which was exactly what we were doing but we had the time. Wayne said that he would have to depart soon as he was late for a hot night on the town. 'Female?' 'Sure, real female.'

'OK, show me what to do.'
Quickly Wayne showed me the process to enter the passwords and code, also how to modify the search pattern. Amazingly he had discovered a quick fix solution to restart the computer if the password failed; this reduced the restart by minutes. We set the program working. Wayne hot footed out to meet his pending rendezvous.

'Max, I hope he has better luck than we do,' We sat discussing the future, if after all this work, the three letters had no connection with the formula, the global plastic industry although still advancing could remain static until, either we rediscover it or a competitor discovers a similar additive.

The latter would be catastrophic for our company; the competition was closing on our heels, our competitors were kept at bay because Pierre's marketing idea, which was to sell it cheaper, than the competitors could research and develop the product?

Max seemed in a strange mood. I asked, 'Is there a problem with the business that you have not told me about? or any problem due to arise that Janine and I are not aware of'? Max was hesitantly was about to say something, when a telephone rang, he answered it.

He spoke to someone in English very carefully knowing I was listening, I could hear the other person a shrill voice leaked from the telephone receiver, which Max had not placed fully onto his ear.

'Who was it?

When does he return?

Is he just a European competitor?

What does he want?'

'When was he going to get the??'.

He broke off slamming the telephone down onto its cradle; He strode out of the office, claiming he was going to take a Pee.

I set my mind into rapid search and recollection of all the events that had happened in the past couple of weeks. Remembering how I had discovered found the numbers and the position that I had been laid in whilst in the bed of Madame Jacqueline. The number on the bed head was, what the fuck was it? '01990,' I tried but I could not remember the exact number.

Making a telephone call to Jacqueline, I asked her to do the same as Janine to get the numbers, from the bed head, she could not understand, I passed the telephone to Max, have a quick word, my French is not good enough to make her understand.

Max had talked with her before, chatting for a while, he jotted down the number we wanted, passing me the telephone back 'she wants a word'.

'Oui mademoiselle,' a little giggle came from the other end, 'Will I be coming to the village soon'?
'Oui je suis'.
'Please come and see I.' she replied, blowing a kiss over the phone, 'OK. Bye. Bye.'
The paper had written upon it '16900' from Jacqueline and 186969801 from Janine.
A girl from the outer office appeared with a pot of fresh coffee, placing it into our coffee machine, she glanced at me shaking a cup, I nodded, 'How do you like your coffee',
Jokingly I replied, 'Like my women, Hot, Black, and Strong and a touch of sugar'. She poured me a cup placing it on my desk.
Hello who are you? Have you worked for the company long?'
'Hi, my name is Dawn, I am a recent employee', she went on to enquire why an Englishman was working in a French-Canadian Company,'
With a slight boasting nature, I informed her quietly of my position. The minute I had told her I felt terrible regarding the manner in which I had told her.
'Sorry Sir I had not realised', she apologised.
'Please do not apologise, you were not to know,' this subdued my pompous attitude and statement, I reassured her she had not offended me.
Dawn sat on the edge of the desk talking, knowing she was displaying a fine pair of legs. Although distracting me, this gave me time to enjoy the coffee, and a respite from the password problem. It was to prove a worthy pause.
'Is everything OK in the factory?' she enquired, many of us especially the older ones are wondering what is going to happen, now Pierre has died.
'I assured her,' and asked her to pass on the message, 'that I will try and keep the company working, we have some

teething problems, but we are slowly succeeding.' Max burst through the office door, the swinging door caused a draught, the pieces of paper with the codes on fluttered to the floor, Dawn quickly stooped down to pick them up, displaying more of her legs.

As she gave me the papers, she spoke quickly, 'See you and good luck,' she turned to Max 'Coffee?' Max declined.

He watched as she left the office, 'Nice legs pity about the face'. A harsh comment..., I had the opinion, she was really nice.

Max commented 'I leave you for a second and you have another woman when I come back,'

'Well, it is not my good looks, I have no money, it must be my animal magnetism,' Max rolled his eyes, 'Yes he said another ten minutes she would have laid you, on the office desk.'

'Ten minutes, is that what it takes, Wow! I thought it was restricted to two'

Max exploded laughing, 'Your bloody English humour.'

I returned to working the computer, glancing at the paper Dawn had retrieved, the code was correct, there were two ways of reading it, I had read it the one way which was incorrect, simply turning the numbers around gave you two more passwords.

If Pierre wrote it whilst laid on his back, what was he getting up to? I stopped the deciphering program, then I entered 18696981, there was no response, I entered the second number 16900, no response re-entering 00691 the computer bleeped, the screen cleared to reveal the First of Three documents.

'Magic, I have it, I am in!'

Max rushed to my side, viewing the first document, lucky it was the document giving the formula details.

'Now I see, how and where we went wrong, it is so simple',

Max cried.

Pondering Max's reply if this was so simple, strange, that only Pierre knew how to make it,'

'Now there are two of us, that has the knowledge,' Max replied.

Immediately I sent a copy to the printer, it ejected a single sheet of paper, removing it; I looked for the first time at the secret formula.

Symbols and bracketed figures arranged in twenty or so rows, was this the chemical structure of the formula in its entirety, one thing I noticed in the characters, a character that looked similar to a small skull and cross bones, wondering what possessed Pierre to have placed a symbol like that into the formula; yet Max did not remark on the symbol, I did not give it a second thought.

Max had the bit, between his teeth, hankering to see the final outcome. Passing the printed formula to Max, 'Guard that with your life,' I said, 'now that you have the last clue, I will return to Paris, and will sleep on the flight.' Max readily agreed, he seemed eager to see me leave, or was I reading an incorrect vibe in the excitement of the moment.

Dawn glided into the office, placing some papers into the in tray on the adjacent desk.

I asked 'Would you do your Boss a favour?'

'Sure, what would you like me to do'?

'Find out the time of the next flight to Paris, and if there are any business class seats available,'

'Ok give me a couple of minutes,' returning to her desk, she made a telephone call then returned quickly saying, there was space. The flight leaves in two and half hours,'

'Great, book that seat for me.

Scanning quickly through the other two files, one portrayed an ongoing problem with Whittle Plastics going into depth that the owner was a serious problem. Pierre was on his case, a detailed list of the problems and with supporting names were in the letter.

The next document would not accept the number compatible to the other two. I had to enter the number given by Janine. The letter was addressed to Janine and marked Privée. Judging by the commencement of the letter, she and Pierre had obviously known each other for a long time. I did not read on, the contents of the letter remained a mystery, it was also in French.

I was almost ready to go, Max was talking with Luis on the telephone explaining where they had gone wrong. Just then, Dawn came back into the office, offering to drive me to the airport she had finished her work for the day, and as her place was way past the airport. She could drop me on the way.

Max thought that was a good idea, he did not want Dawn to overhear arrangements being made with the chemist. He indicated to me he would make the call in the next office. I tried to print Janine's letter then the other letter from Pierre. Before I packed up my laptop, I noticed the printer was flashing a red light, 'What does a red flashing light on the printer mean?'

'It is a paper jam' Dawn replied, she removed the wedged paper, then topped up the paper feed drawer, with a new ream of paper.

The printer reprinted the run, printing four sheets. I looked at the first and second sheet they both looked the same apart from Method printed on the top of the page. I must have told the printer to print two copies, thinking I would leave the copy for Max, then decided to take it with me, Max has his copy.

The other two documents were not for Max's attention I

folded them and placed them inside my jacket pocket. As I left the office I waved bye to Max, he left his telephone call and came to say goodbye he passed a small book for me to read.

The book title read Chemical Symbols Identified and explained. (With full analysis of all known chemicals). Heavy reading for an evening flight, still I was learning, it was imperative that I understand all matters. Dawn headed for the airport.

She drove skilfully missing all the other traffic on the road in her old battered Buick skylark.

We arrived at the airport with three quarter of an hour to spare, she looked at me and said 'What will you do while you wait,'

'I do not know, what had you in mind' I replied, she did not answer. Driving to a dimly lit area of the car park, she leaned over, opened the glove compartment and pulled out a small carton. 'You will need to use one of these' she held out a selection of condoms.

'I have not used one of these for years,'

'Safe sex is better than little brats eating you out of house and home,' I agreed with that and looked at the selection.

'What do you prefer banana flavour or ribbed? Dawn quickly replied 'Ribbed'.

I see why bench seats and automatic cars are so popular in America and Canada, plenty of room to manoeuvre. As Max had observed she was not the most attractive I have encountered but being of a different generation, she knew what she wanted, plus knew how to get it.

She ensured I was at the airport entrance in time to check in for the flight. She said 'You will sleep well on the trip to Paris, I hope to see you when you come back, and it's not true'.

'Not true?'

'You don't mind milk with your coffee' dumfounded, I stammered 'Thanks for your help, and the lift.' With a squeal of tyres, she disappeared into the night, on the rear bumper was a faded sticker, it read 'Smart People Do It in a Buick'. Oh well I thought I have just been elevated to the ranks of the Smart People.

I had to give her last remark some thought, then smiled to myself, as I remembered what I had replied, when she enquired how I took my Coffee.

Chapter 8

The flight normally departed at 21:00 however a slight delay had caused the flight to leave at midnight, arriving at Paris at 10:00.

Dawn had already pre-arranged a ticket for me which was being held at the reception desk. A pretty receptionist based on the check in desk, asked if I was Dawns friend,

'Yes,' I replied,

'A special upgrade for you into first Class,'

I asked 'are you and Dawn good friends?'

'Oh yes, we share an apartment together.'

I graciously thanked her for the upgraded ticket, requesting her to pass on my thanks to Dawn. During the opulent meal served, somewhere over the Atlantic, I contemplated on Dawns emancipated actions.

The choice of condoms, who would ever think of banana flavoured or come to think about it any flavoured condom, would it be curry flavoured in Asia or coconut flavour in the tropics the market variation could be endless.

Who manufactured them? Did we produce them in a subsidiary factory? After all it is a constant rising market, smirking at my joke, I reclined the seat closed my eyes and fell into a deep sleep.

I slept almost the entire journey until, a distant voice kept calling my name repeatedly; gradually I realised it was not a dream, it was the flight hostess wakening me to say an urgent message, had been received from Paris, someone would meet me in the VIP Lounge, where I was it was imperative that I meet with them.

After landing and clearing customs, I was ushered into the VIP lounge, where I was met by Janine. She ran toward me throwing her arms around me as if I was a long-lost lover, she held me tight, I could feel and hear her crying.

'What has happened?' I asked calmly. We walked to a quiet part of the lounge, found ourselves a seat, and she told me what had happened. Janine had received a telephone call from Montreal, the chief Chemist Luis and Max had become seriously ill whilst working in the laboratory, there had been a fire in the lab, and whatever they were working on had been destroyed.

Janine went on to say she had tried to talk to Max in the hospital, but the charge nurse informed her that he was in a coma. The security officer had informed Ulley the manager he which flight I was on. She was going to send the chauffeur but decided at the last minute to come herself.

'Shall I drive into Paris?' I asked.

'No, I will drive, I feel better now.'

We approached an immaculate Black GTI car, I deposited my case onto the rear seat. Janine skilfully negotiated her way back onto the main route into Paris, once we were on the motorway she floored the accelerator, and took her position in the outer lane and passed everything that she came across.

As we drove into Paris, Janine had re-composed herself to the lady in charge, I thought I had seen or discovered a chink in her armour.

We conversed, updating each other with the latest news from the office. The Englishman Darrell, had tried to make contact this morning; he had left a message to call him at the earliest opportunity.

She travelled at such high speed I reclined my seat. She was a skilled driver, drove around cars and changed direction at will; she had superb ability using the clutch and changing gear, which caused her skirt to slide up her thighs, revealing more than she wished. Trying to cover her legs and negotiate

Paris, she swerved slightly. 'I think it is more important to keep us both alive than to have an accident over a nice pair of legs,' Janine glanced at me for a moment with an impish grin then returned her full concentration to driving, leaving me to concentrate on finer matters. Arriving in a narrow street in the south side, Janine saw a parking place also being eyed by another driver, she accelerated hard and deposited her car, into the vacant space. I complimented her on her driving and parking skills. She thanked me saying I have a spare room and if you wish you can stay with me until you find somewhere.

I accepted her proposal, and we climbed the stairs to her apartment.

I was impressed with her apartment; it was comfortable and compact, the flat emitted a quiet, relaxed atmosphere. She showed me the spare room adjacent to the bathroom, I suggested that I take a shower. After the most welcome shower in an antiquated brass shower and bath tub, I changed into some casual clothes, I did not intend going into the office for the rest of the day. Returning to the living room I was greeted by the glorious smell of coffee, a cup was on the side table together with a warm croissant, Janine had also changed, we sat continuing the discussion over the trip and the developments at the Montreal factory. I felt inclined to tell her of my suspicions with Max's defeatist attitude toward the product, she looked a little concerned with me giving damning reports on a man now laid in hospital, unable to defend himself. As we chatted, the hours simply flew by.

Hunger pangs were gripping my stomach so I suggested we made a move and get something to eat.

Walking to a small café, not a stone's throw from her flat, we took a table at the back of the room, choosing something light from the menu and a glass of red wine. Janine's mobile telephone rang, partially understanding the conversation, it must have been the Paris office, she was receiving information, making decisions giving orders she was still in command. Janine sighed. 'Luis the chemist had died while making the formula, Max fortunately had been at the other end of the laboratory talking on the telephone, the mixture started to emit a greenish gas, Luis had shouted a warning about the gas then collapsed. Max rushed to help but he also inhaled some of the gas, not realising this he also collapsed. Both were rushed to the hospital for treatment. Luis was dead on arrival at hospital; there would be further details available tomorrow.

Telling Janine about the other two letters, I removed the printouts of the letters from my pocket. She started to cry as she read the script. She asked if I had read the letter. 'Just the first line where it was addressed to you and marked private, it was intended for you I could understand that much, but you know I was not that proficient in the translation to understand the full contents.

She declared that it was a personal intimate letter from Pierre to her, begging me to make sure it stayed that way. I said the only copy that I know of is on the laptop and I would delete it when we got back to the apartment. Showing the second document I asked her to tell me what was on it, as again I was mystified as to the contents. Janine read the letter, slowly going through it again, she asked, 'Have you shown this to anybody else?'

'No, why?' Janine proceeded to say that this letter contained Pierre's suspicions and concerns about a security leak from some members of staff. A reference to someone only referred to as 'M' was listed as a possibility. We could check the employees with Christian names and surnames starting with M. This we could do secretly, this matter was important, we would keep this information a special secret between the two of us.

The lights dimmed; the master of ceremony walked onto the stage. He gave a welcome to the café Senegal; this evening's entertainment would start with a famous international singer. Once this singer commenced his performance, although he was good, any further discussion was proving impossible. I looked at Janine, shrugging my shoulders. She replied with a similar gesture, saying, 'I think we should go.' I agreed. Entering Janine's apartment, a small green flashing light on the answer phone indicated a message was waiting. Janine pressed the button to receive the message, a Canadian accented voice proceeded to give details, translating the message Janine said it was the hospital requesting her to call. Returning the call she listened, presumably to the doctor at the hospital, she sat down slowly with a hand going to her mouth, thanking whoever she was talking to. She said in a frail frightened voice, 'Max is critical, not expected to survive. If there is an improvement or change, they will inform us immediately.' That call visibly shook Janine offering her my hand, I sat beside her, she snuggled into me, asking, 'What is happening?' She could not understand why all these problems had started or what would happen to the business.

Janine waved her hand towards a bottle of brandy, 'would you like a brandy'.

'Mâis oui, where are the glasses?' 'Dans la cabinet.'

I retrieved two glasses, pouring generous measures of brandy then sat next to her again on the couch. What had seemed to be a happy time was now turning into a chain of disasters, with no apparent way-out? Janine had fallen asleep on my shoulder, if I moved, she would be disturbed the couch was comfortable, the room was warm slowly, sleep overtook me as well.

Chapter 9

A stabbing pain in my arm woke me, the pins and needles in my wrist were painful, I could not feel my fingers, slowly looking around the apartment, my brain switched on full recollection of the previous evening came flooding back. I was still laid on the couch covered with a blanket, I was sleeping in my shorts but could not remember undressing, quickly glancing at my wristwatch it was 8:00 in the morning, calling out 'Bonjour' I waited for a reply, none came. Quickly looking around the rooms in the apartment I found Janine's bedroom; there against one wall I saw the distinct carved wooden headboard, different from Jacqueline's in design still it blended into the décor nicely, Janine's bed showed signs of being slept in but Janine was nowhere to be seen. I indulged in a welcome shower and a shave, then dressed room for a day in the office, I returned to the living.

There was no sign of Janine, had another bird flown the nest? What was happening in this new venture?

Remembering Janine had said to call Darrell in England, I rummaged in my case for his business card, I called him.

'Darrell... How goes it?'

'Ross thanks for calling.'

Darrell went on to say that Whittle had become incensed, he had regularly been on the telephone to someone in France, cursing them, shouting statements such as, 'Where is it, I have paid you for it?' Whenever I enquired, I was told to mind my own section of the business, this matter had nothing to do with you; once Whittle called this man by a name. It was Maximilian.

'MAX'. Could there be a connection? I explained to him events which had taken place in Canada with Max, and the accidental death of the chief chemist.

'A green gas emitted when mixing the formula Hang on.' he cried, he dropped the telephone on the desk, the line did not disconnect enabling me to listen to the event unfolding, Darrell shouted a warning to someone, then a klaxon siren started. He returned sounding breathless, gasping out, 'Thanks mate.'

He knew one of his chemists had been given a strange formula to make, details had arrived by fax from overseas that morning. Whittle had given this to him to produce. As I explained to Darrell about the Green Gas, he had already put two and two together and the sum was FIVE. He could see the chemist working, as a precaution he dropped everything to stop him working, he managed to clear the laboratory just as the gas started to appear, it was ignited by the gas Bunsen burner, causing a small explosion and a fire, the chemist was evacuating the lab and placed the room in quarantine.

'Darrell, please send me a copy of the fax in its entirety so I can compare details at this end. Send it to this fax number, it is safe, I could be having a problem with security.'

A noise from the front door made me break the telephone conversation with Darrell. I had just replaced the receiver when Janine arrived back. Coming straight towards me she greeted and then kissed me. 'I have something in this' waving a folder at me, whilst explaining, Max had a secret place in his office, she had noticed Max a few times placing papers into it, so I decided to retrieve everything.

Dropping to her knees she emptied the contents of the folder spreading them out on the floor. I sat on the couch looking at the paperwork. We examined the documents, apart from a strangely worded letter from the German Plastic company, nothing incriminating was found.

Janine looked at the German letter, then at me she said 'This is the company which bought all the stock of Loyplas.'

I spoke to Darrell from your telephone this morning, and told him about the green gas. A formula was faxed to Whittle early this morning from overseas, Whittle gave the formula to his chemist to produce, the green gas Luis and Max had experienced in Montreal was also produced in Whittles Laboratory, and this time no one was hurt.

'We have a spy somewhere in this business.'

'A spy?'

'Yes, a spy.'

'Darrell told me the name of a man he overheard Whittle talking to. It was Maximilian.'

'MAX!' Janine could not believe it.

'Is there anyone else called Maximilian working for the company?

Thinking back, I found the last part of the clue, on Pierre's old laptop in Canada, and then Whittle had the bloody formula within 12 hours, it could only be Max. He must have faxed the document from Montreal just after I left. It is no wonder Pierre was worried, not being able to trust anybody.

I looked at Janine "I do not know anybody in this company apart from you, I have to rely on you to help me, but if you are against me. I am walking now. I have had enough".

'Ross please be assured I am not against you! I want to work with you but I am frightened of the disasters which are happening within the company. She was trembling, I held out my arms she rushed towards me holding me tight.

'I might be strong in the office, but this situation is terrifying me'.

I suggested a coffee, she agreed, I found some coffee in the little kitchen. Boiling a kettle I made a jug, pouring two cups I gave one to Janine, she took a large mouthful, gulping it down she gasped for breath and started coughing, I thought she was going to choke, when she recovered, she cried what did you put in the coffee?'

The coffee from the packet, I showed her - she said this is French strong only two spoons per jug.

I thought a large jug, holding four cups, would need eight spoons; she quickly corrected the mistake by diluting the coffee with boiling water,

'I am very sorry'.

'You were not to know'.

'I bet that gave your taste buds a shock' Janine translating the sentence, replied 'English humour,'

'Yes'.

Janine regained her composure and suggested that with Max not in the office, it may be wise for us to have third party help, due to my   lack of knowledge of the French language. What I needed was a neutral translator to deal with all documents, meetings and discussions.

Who could I trust?

John might jump at the chance, but who would do his job?

'I will return to Laroche stay with John for the weekend then return on Monday. Can I use the telephone to call John'

'Mâis oui.'

John answered, it was good to hear a Yorkshire accent even if it was speaking French, I quickly explained the problems that had happened since my return to France. 'Sorry old chap; all my rooms are taken, why not call Madame Jacqueline, now she would have space for you.' John was laughing as he said it. 'What! are you implying?' I asked.

'Nowt, mate.' He was laughing again, but said to still call in when I arrived, he would be delighted to see me.

John said that he would not be able to take on the translator's job, but thanks for the thought.

'How is Elaine?', Elaine. I had not spoken to or even thought of her for nearly a week. Should I fly back to England to see her instead of going to see John? 'I will call her next, see you John, bye.' She was happy to hear from me, bringing me up to date on the English events, nothing really exciting was happening, my business was actually doing better with me not being there, she listened to what events were unfolding in France and mentioned that if it all went wrong, better not spend too much money.

One factor I had totally forgotten, I was am a director of this business and now responsible for the company debts. Elaine said, 'Why not stay with John, have a word with that policeman chap who saved me from the attack in the village.' Jules.

Of course, I had totally forgotten about Jules, he could be my eyes and ears.

I called Jacqueline regarding a room; she was happy to hear my voice. She said, "of course it would be no problem for me to stay", I would see her soon. Janine was privy to all telephone conversations and she referred only to one, 'Who is Jacqueline?'

'Jacqueline is the house keeper of Pierre's house in Laroche, I thought you knew that.'

'It was your pronunciation of her name, made me think that it was a different woman.'

I wondered if the Monteverdi would be finished, then I could drive it to Laroche for the weekend. I asked if Janine would like to accompany me for the weekend to Laroche. Monteverdi did you say you have a Monteverdi?

Yes. I bought Pierre's at auction, Janine was amazed. I thought I would not see it again. I told her of the damage and the repair shop, I should get it this weekend.

'I am flattered you have asked me to come with you this weekend, I must decline, but I will accept if you would ask me again at a later date.'

I made a telephone call to the hospital in Canada for a condition report on Max; he was still in a coma but breathing slightly better. When Max recovered, we needed to have a serious talk with him. Until such times we decided not to inform anyone of our suspicions. Janine telephoned the garage to see if the Monteverdi was ready. It was, and it could be picked up at any time. Janine asked for the car to be delivered to the office later that day, I read the paperwork in the folder from Max's office; alas the papers revealed little. 'I will take them and look at them over the weekend.' Janine asked, 'How did you get that?' Pointing one of her well-manicured fingers towards the earring inside the open valise. Picking up the earring I placed into Janine's hand, inspecting it closely, 'It is beautiful, it is missing its butterfly clamp.'
'You can have it if you wish, I also found this wristwatch I showed her the Cartier chronometer, taking the watch she looked, 'It has a broken strap,'
'No, it is only a broken bracelet pin, I intend to have it repaired but I have not had the chance,'
Janine said 'I will have it repaired for you,' and placed the watch on the table with the earring. I went to my room to select some clothes and pack a bag for the weekend, Janine called out my name from her bedroom. I looked in her room she was lying in her bed with the back of her hand resting on her forehead.
'Are you OK?'
She raised herself onto one elbow, the bedclothes slipped away revealing her naked breasts, offering me an outstretched hand I took hold as she pulled me towards her, 'I wanted you last night, but we both slept, I will have you now.' She smiled, my heart skipped a beat, situations like this did not happen to me.
Shocked but still excited I cautiously held her in my arms, we

made love with great passion relinquishing when exhaustion took effect, I could hear and feel my heart beat slowing to its regular rhythm.

My eyes wandered around the room coming to rest on the famous carved wooden headboard. The numbers that she had given me were written by the maker's name, similar to Jacqueline's headboard, but at the other side was a set of numbers: 14/5/99 35. I made a mental note of the number and this female returned my thoughts and actions to another encounter of our passion.

As Janine walked away from the bed, I finally saw the full beauty of her body; she was slim and walked gracefully on tip toe, her skin was slightly tanned, her breasts had not lost any of their firmness that age or gravity destroys. She stood awhile gazing far into the distance through the small paned bedroom window; the picture was carved in to my mind.

'A penny for them.' I asked.

'Pardon?'

'A penny for your thoughts, or are you are lost in your mind.'

'I said that to you the other day.' Janine replied smiling.

She slipped from the room then the sound of the shower working indicated playtime was over, she returned wrapped in a bath towel, I too slipped from the bed into the shower.

In the shower I could feel her presence, her excitement, I could smell her perfume.

I finished dressing in my bedroom, and returned to the lounge, picking up my briefcase I saw the earring I had given Janine, now lying with its partner on the table, now a pair.

Janine already noticed I had seen the pair 'Thank you, they are very special to me.'

Janine suggested a walk to the office some time it is quicker than driving.

I took delight in accompanying her on her promenade. Entering reception Janine and Claudette discussed matters bringing to her attention, two representatives of the commissariat de police.

Janine acknowledged the waiting officers; she would see them within 10 minutes requesting time to deal with urgent business matters.

The morning's post did not produce any further clues, all matters concerning the business were dispatched with her normal thoroughness.

She called Claudette and had the waiting officers shown into her room. She asked me to assist with the police interview.

The officers explained that the Canadian police had contacted them to make enquiries into the accidents in the Montreal factory.

We explained the best we could, the officers made their notes, and departed still confused but they were satisfied with the details so far. We were presented with their business cards so we could contact them if anything new or a similar event happened.

Closing my eyes momentarily I thought about the morning's events, a smile must have been showing, a voice asked, 'why I was smiling with my eyes closed?'

'I did enjoy making love to you this morning; we had no fear or embarrassment.'

'Did you not like it?'

'Yes, I did, spontaneous lovemaking is better than planned.'

Excusing myself I retrieve some toiletries from my case in the other office, requesting from Claudette 'Please make sure we are not disturbed for 15 minutes, no exceptions.'

Entering the office, Janine was sitting on the edge of her desk reading papers just arrived via the fax machine. Showing me the document.

'What is this?'
Taking hold of the document I viewed the Fax copy of the fax Whittle had received that morning 'It shows Pierre's secret formula.' Darrell sent it to me.
 Taking the original copy of the formula from my case, I laid them on the desk to compare, they were identical.
The only other copy was in Max's possession and this version when prepared will emit the green gas.
I had asked Darrell to send me a copy then I could try to identify the fax machine that it was sent from. Looking at the top of the paper the number and the fax ID were missing, however there were a couple of lines in the fax. These lines are caused by dirt on the sensor head in the fax machine, if you match the lines, you can sometimes identify the Fax machine it can be the same as a signature. 'Do you have any faxes from Canada?'
Janine reached across the desk to pick a document from the IN tray, not able to reach the tray this made her dress ride up her thighs, as she passed me the documents, 'are these any good?' she asked.
I took hold of her ankle sliding her towards me, 'what was I doing?' placing a finger to her lips. 'I will make love to you now' she did not protest, then I discovered why she was careful about her skirt sliding too far; she was not wearing underclothes, spontaneously she released enough of my clothing to satisfy the impending union. The impulsive act left us both flushed with excitement.
'I have never been taken like that,' Janine whispered, a slight tremble in her voice revealed her passionate side, as she stood her skirt fell into place a quick check of her hair, she resumed her unruffled poise, readjusting my clothes, we continued with matters in hand.
Picking up the fax document from the floor to compare, both

had transmission lines on them identical to the one from Darrell.

'Is this the only fax machine in the office?'

'No, there are two more, one in Pierre's office, and one in Max's office.'

'One more test to do.' I replied.

Just then Janine's telephone rang, she answered, 'Oui,' listening she replaced the receiver, she came to me sitting on my lap and looking me in the eye, she kissed me passionately and whispered 'Meester Ross's car has arrived, the driver is requesting a signature to approve the repairs.'

'Fantastic,' I attempted to stand with Janine in my lap.

'Un moment sil vous plait' she alighted then helped me up from the couch, blocking my exit from the office, she stood so close to me she had anticipated my enthusiasm to see the car.

She asked softly, 'Is this my competition?'

'Oui it might be' I held her hard against my hands gripping both of her buttocks.

'I will come to see my competition'

Just before Janine left the office, I spotted her blouse had slipped out of the skirt's waistband, I tucked her blouse back, I heard her gasp slightly 'Merci'.

Janine met the paint shop driver in the reception, beckoning him to follow: she led the way towards the garage using the private office entrance.

Through the door, a small balcony with a flight of stairs descended to the ground level, Janine's stiletto heels making a sharp click on the steel steps as she descended.

The Monteverdi gleamed in the subdued light of the garage, the driver fussing around the frontal area, made a great issue of the completed repairs, demonstrating the flowing lines and the perfection that they made the repair.

He explained that they had filled the car with the very best petrol, and he was fumbling with the remote which gave him a problem with the alarm. As he pressed the remote buttons, the alarm activated making the most annoying screeching sound, the poor chap looked lost, Janine spoke quickly to him she took the alarm sensor quickly pressed the correct buttons to deactivate the cars wailing siren.

The repairs were satisfactory, I signed his documents releasing finally the Monteverdi into my care, Janine by this time had gained entry into the car and was sitting in the driver's seat adjusting it, she inserted and turned the ignition key, the engine rumbled into life with a healthy growl, revving the motor a couple of times, listened, then drove the car forward, then skilfully turned the car 180° and reversed it into Pierre's parking place, with the car pointing in the direction of the open garage door.

Turning off the engine she closed the door firmly, and as she walked towards me, she lifted her hand above her head pressed the car remote control with a flash of the indicator lights the car locked and the alarm was set, she walked past me, handing me the keys, remarking 'Competition, None!'

The driver and I stood in amazement with the display of such confident driving; he opened his hands in a typical French gesture, bade me 'Au revoir' and sauntered out of the garage stuffing the delivery note into his pocket. Gazing in admiration at my new acquisition the repairs were perfect, I made a mental note to call Patrice to thank him, returning to Janine's office she was on the telephone, handing me the telephone she said, 'It is Darrell for you.'

'Darrell'.

'Mr Whittle has just dismissed me for sending you that copy of the fax. Whittle was ultra pissed when he discovered the

laboratory damage, he stormed about the office screaming 'Some bastard's going to pay for this!' Then found the formula copy in my Fax machine, I thought he was going to explode, I would not tell him why the copy was in the machine. He got one of the girls to make the machine produce a history report the minute he saw the Paris number he knew, that you were aware. 'Remember me old chum, if it all comes good, keep an eye open for Whittle, he is dangerous, he would stop at nothing to get his own way.'
'Thanks for the warning, Darrell I shall be on my guard
Janine was standing with a supercilious air her hands placed on her hips; standing on one leg, she rocked her foot on the heel of her shoe, she was waiting for me to say something, thinking for a minute, 'When did you drive the car before?
'Many times,' she replied still waiting for something; I was getting a feeling of being told off, for what? I told her about the fax from Darrell causing him being dismissed.
'Bad luck I am sorry for him' she retorted, 'I thought you're driving of the Monteverdi was very good you handled the vehicle better than I have.'
She thought over my comment saying 'thank you,' then fired back at me 'You have not driven the car yet'
I was deep in trouble and sinking fast, quickly recalling the actions of the last hour, prior to the car being delivered.
'Oh, if you are upset about me making love to you, I am sorry,'
'No, it was not that, it was where, the embarrassment if we had been caught, would have been too much.' Janine whispered, I had found the nerve, I took her hands touched my brow on hers, whispered I have a little secret to tell you, 'I told your secretary we needed fifteen minutes, for a private meeting without disturbance, no exceptions.'
Janine looked at me for a while, then said 'Please forgive me I

am learning more about you every minute', she kissed me quickly, then returned to her desk.

I returned to the testing of fax machines, as I left her office, I looked back saying 'I think you are wonderful.'

I closed the door, I went and spoke with Claudette, I explained Janine is a little upset, could she order some flowers for her, and get them delivered immediately.

'Who shall I say they are from?'

'A special friend.'

In Max's office I inserted a blank page pressing the copy button to use the machine as a photocopier, I copied the blank page and two distinct lines appeared on the copy. I tried to use Pierre's fax but the door was locked. Returning to Janine's office I repeated the test on her fax machine, two lines appeared. Marking each page with the respective fax machines and checking the copies, I had so far, none matched the fax from Darrell. Mentioning that Pierre's office was locked Janine slid open a small draw removed a small bunch of keys she curled her finger towards me intending me to follow, Pierre's office was in darkness, Janine turned on a small desk lamp which bathed the desk in light but keeping the ceiling in darkness repeating the same test; the resulting copy was clean with no lines.

'Finished' Janine requested.

'Oui' returning to her office, I talked to Claudette; can you get me Wayne in the Montreal factory on the telephone please?' A chirpy voice with a distinct Canadian accent came on the telephone. I have a special task, also if he did not know I had cracked all the passwords; things were looking good. 'That's cool, what is it you want me to do?' he replied. I explained the experiment with the fax machines in Paris: 'Send me a fax from every machine in the office and factory write on each page the fax machine it was sent from then send the faxes to this number, only this number.' I gave the fax number of Pierre's office.

'If anybody asks, what are you doing, say "Ross said to test the machines but keep it quiet.".'

'Skulduggery,' he replied.

'Skulduggery, do it now please.'

Claudette asked 'What is skulduggery?'

I looked at her gave her a wink, 'The most fun you can have with your clothes on, a special secret' Claudette looked puzzled then she wrote down what I had said, I bet that would keep her busy translating for ages.

I knocked on Janine's door.

'Entrez' as I entered, she was smiling again, I told her about the test facsimiles being sent from Canada to Pierre's Fax machine. While waiting for the papers to be sent I opened Janine's fax machine showing her the dirt marks on the sensor head, scraping them with the edge of my fingernail. I tested the machine again; it copied clean.

Janine enquired. 'What causes that problem?'

'Liquid correction fluid, People use it to blot out information they do not want others to see or read from a fax, but they do not give the fluid time to dry before faxing a copy.'

'As the fax is transmitted, damp correction fluid leaves a smudge on the sensor head, as the fluid dries a line is draw on the copy.'

Janine could hear the fax machine working in Pierre's office, she picked up her keys, and we went to inspect the evidence. Wayne was transmitting the faxes as requested, each fax displaying fax number and location. Six faxes arrived, but it was the one from laboratory 2 which attracted my attention: the lines matched the fax from Darrell, plus by adding the lines from Janine's fax machine, the copy was complete. I stapled all of the corresponding faxes together.

'We have our traitor.' Janine could not believe it but inspecting the documents showed that all the leads pointed to the Montreal factory.

The fax started to receive another fax, this one was a composition of hand writing, in a form of letter:

Although written in French I could read and understand most of the content

To the directors of Vista Plastics Paris.

I wish to tend my resignation, effective immediately from the post as General manager of the company, I feel that I am superfluous to the company's requirements now. I am wishing to follow a new course in career,

a line crossed out the next paragraph but it was still legible and the letter continued,

with the introduction of Mr Ross Todd, I feel that the company will fail, I have proof that he knows nothing about the business and I believe that this will lead to the company's downfall.

The next sentence was half written, I could not understand the words.

At the bottom of the fax was added, I found this paper on the floor by the fax machine in lab, #2 with the current situation I have kept it secret.

I am sure you will advise me what to do with the documents

Regards

Wayne.

Janine translated the document as she read, it took a second for the content to register, all this information was being collated in my brain.

I could see Max clinging on hoping that I would find or reveal the formula, and as I did not show him the latest version Max had nothing to act on. After he saw a copy of the latest formula retrieved from the laptop, once within his grasp he was prepared to sell it to the highest bidder, he would leave the company and watch from the side-lines leaving us the huge financial commitment and final failure.

The chance call to Darrell from Janine's flat only confirmed that the copy, only hours old, was sent from the factory in Canada, probably when I was 40,000 feet over the Atlantic.

The fax started to receive. It was a list of the numbers used by each machine in the Montreal factory. Only one number had the international dialling code for England, the fax machine in the laboratory. This was the positive proof Max had treacherous intent.

Janine made a very stern statement with harsh short words as she lifted the telephone, dialled urgently, then she spoke rapidly to someone, she continued being very forceful and precise in her conversation, and requested confirmation of her orders by return. A fax, would be acceptable.

'C'est la vie. Those who live by the sword die by the sword. I had just authorised payment of salaries and expenses to Max only this morning, as he has been discovered a traitor, I have cancelled all payments to him from us, and the bank manager is looking into retrieving other payments he had from us.

Boy, this lady certainly does not mess around when she starts.

She turned her attention to me 'Will you stay tonight? You could go to Laroche on Friday?' The glint in her eyes revealed an ulterior motive.

'I would love too but I made plans for Friday earlier.'

She locked Pierre's office as we left, she returned to her

office, Claudette gave me a little wave, 'The blooms have
arrived'
'Blooms?'
She translated 'flowers,' she passed me the receipt, pulling
some money from my wallet she took what she needed
giving back the change.
Entering Janine's office, she was stood by the huge display of
flowers, reading the card, are you 'the special friend'.
'Oui mademoiselle' she kissed my ear whispering 'I hope
Jacqueline does not make love to you.'
I shrugged at the last comment, 'I will see you when I get
back.'
The remote control for the Monteverdi had four identical
buttons set out in classic pattern. I approached the
Monteverdi pressing the first button the alarm activated with
an ear-piercing screech looking hurriedly at the remote I kept
pressing the buttons in order until the noise stopped, finally I
worked out the combination. Lifting the trunk lid, I placed my
case's inside.
Finally I sat inside, I took time adjusting the seat and rear
view mirrors, the engine rumbled into life, while the engine
idled I familiarised myself the controls, feeling confident and
all gauges were indicating correctly, I selected D on the
automatic transmission console, the revs dropped slightly
with the car momentarily moved forward, releasing the
parking brake I crept forward, applying pressure to the
accelerator spun the rear tyres, taking care on the
manoeuvre I inched cautiously out of the garage, I could see
Janine standing on the balcony watching me, she seemed if
she had a tear in her eye, for me or the car?
The side road was clear. waving her goodbye, I headed
towards the south west. the car's controls were simple to
use. It was the 7-litre engine you had to be wary of it was so

powerful that improper use of the accelerator firmly pushed you back into the well-padded contoured seats, knowledge of the car controls would take time, time I had plenty of. The southern toll road stretched out in front of me was free of traffic, an opportunity not to miss play or experimental time, switching the automatic transmission into manual mode. This option would leave tyre marks on the road, as it launched the car from a slow crawl to 130 mph in seconds, a projectile of serious proportions, this would get you in and out of trouble fast.

Playing with the cruise control this simple but effective piece of equipment enables the driver to set the speed of a vehicle then the electronics maintains the set speed all the time, a worthwhile addition in relaxed driving and fuel economy. Under the arm rest were a selection of musical cassette tapes, I played one and enjoyed classical music as I travelled. I missed the first turn for Laroche, and I took the short cut that Jules had shown me. I eased the car into the village, parking outside John's bar.

Entering the bar brought a cheer.

John exclaimed, 'I thought you were not coming.'

'I was playing with the new toy!' John poured me a brandy, 'that's on the house, mate, we also now have a room if you still need one.'

'I have already arranged to stay at Jacqueline's hotel, she has a room available.'

John winked, 'I know whose room.'

'I will go and see how things go, see you later.'

Simone, poking her head around the kitchen door, said, 'I thought I heard your voice, welcome back.'

Leaving the bar, a gendarme stood by the side of the car, it was Jules, 'Bonsoir Ross.'

'Bonsoir Jules comment ça va?,

'Très bien, Et vous'

'Bon, I am staying at Mme Jacqueline's hotel, please could we talk in the morning?'

'Avec Plaisir, I will look forward to it.'

Driving the short way through the village, I saw Jacqueline standing by the front door bathed in the evening sunshine, she came running down the path to meet the car 'Bonsoir Pir... correcting to Ross at the last second, she kissed me in the French custom. Settling into the room she had made available I took a quick shower then presented myself downstairs. Jacqueline had prepared a meal. She had prepared a magnificent table I was hungry taking great delight in sampling all the food presented, the wine was plentiful, many questions were asked during the evening. It was hard explaining complex problems, Jacqueline was not as easy to talk with as Janine, however she was a very different person, the change was pleasant. Two brandies were already poured and waiting on a table in front of a large fireplace. Sitting on a comfortable couchette, I sampled the brandy, it was excellent, A clock chimed 12 midnight. She suggested that we retire and enjoy a goodnights sleep.

Chapter 10

A song thrush was giving a superb performance, totally oblivious and regard for anyone sleeping, my eyes opened slightly and I surveyed my location. The sunlight streaming through the window made the room bright and warm, raising myself onto one elbow, I could see outside through the partial open curtains, all the early signs of a lovely day were present. A day without any pressure would be acceptable, glancing at my wristwatch it was six in the morning.

I could hear the sounds of someone moving around, sitting on the edge of the bed I surveyed my kingdom, two doors, one window, one chair, a bed, dressing table and wardrobe, and a polished wood floor, a light-coloured rug lay by the side of the bed.

My overnight case was on the floor in front of the window, the door to the bathroom was open displaying a shower unit bath and other utensils, I stood, on the floor the floorboards creaked under my weight, the wardrobe door made an eerie sound then slowly swung open the hinges creaking as it stopped.

Trying to move around quietly seemed to cause the house to make a new noise, turning the shower control the water pipes started to bang and shudder; as the air hissed from the pipes then the shower coughed then water spurted from the shower head.

I slipped off my shorts collected some toiletries and returned to shower; the hot water was bracing; it felt so good sometimes it is better than sex.

A gentle knock on the bathroom door puzzled me. Stopping the shower, I wrapped a towel around me before opening the door, it was Jacqueline, begging my forgiveness; there was a telephone call for me downstairs.

I pulled the towel tighter around my waist before sprinting downstairs to take the telephone call. It was John. Listen mate call home something dreadful has happened, see you.

I called Elaine; her voice gave away the fact she was upset, she had been trying to find me. She went on to say that someone had broken into the house last night while she was out, there was a terrible mess, Pongo, my little dog, had been killed, the Legend had been set on fire, the police told her that somebody was looking for something specific or had a grudge against you.

'Why?'

'No money or valuables had been taken, just the damage to the car and the dog.'

I told her to stay with someone until things settled down or I came back.

'Can somebody make the house secure; I will arrange a flight home today to help sort things out?'

'No point really, stay there and sort that problem first, you could not do anything here. Elaine protested.'

'Only if you are sure,'

'Yes, I will be ok I can stay with my pal Phyllis.'

'I will give you a call later, take care.'

My facial expression must have relayed the problems thrust upon me, Jacqueline quietly enquired, 'Un problem?'

Explaining the best, I could, I started to shiver, the house was cold. 'I am going to shower, get warm, then dress before other guests come down for breakfast.'

Show her? Get some warm? Then address? Jacqueline raised an eyebrow as she enquired.

'Le douche' I replied shivering violently. She seemed amused, opening a side cupboard removing a bathrobe thrust it towards me then removed my cold damp towel, giggling as she disappeared into the kitchen.

The news from Elaine was disturbing, my mind began to race, why, after such a short time, should these serious problems be affecting me, what I had done to deserve this misfortune. Running back upstairs to the bathroom, I threw the bathrobe onto a chair. Hastily I climbed into the bath turning the shower faucet simultaneously, the pipework coughed I looked up at the sprinkler it erupted blasting me with Coldwater. I cursed loudly with shock warmer water quickly followed. my eyes were stinging from the unexpected blast of cold water, unbalanced slightly I slipped and collapsed into the bath tub. I sat awhile recovering myself, then switched the faucet lever from shower to bath and stretched out in the rising warm water. Mulling over the news from home, someone was having a go at me, but why poor Pongo. Why would anyone want to hurt my little dog, I shall miss it, my thoughts browsing over the other damage, the many hours of hard work, that I had put into the Legend, for what, to end its days incinerated. 'If I find out who?' All forms of retribution with untold harm flashed through my mind's eye.

Jacqueline tapped discreetly on the open door; she was concerned after hearing me callout. 'You like, your wash back washed?' She asked. her translation was poor but it made me smile.

'Oui madam', better to accept then wait and see what she meant, 'No mademoiselle' she replied indignantly, 'Pardon mademoiselle.' She smiled and disappeared from the room, I became aware that I was laid naked in the bath, talking to another lady without shame or embarrassment. I think she had offered to rub my back then walked off.

Although she had done more for me in the last ten days without hesitation, Janine had also been the same. Was this demeanour normal or the way of women who want something? I draped a face flannel across my groin giving myself some modesty, then shutting my eyes, leaving the hot water renovate the cold parts. Something touched my leg, Jacqueline had returned and was standing with one foot in the bath, she was carrying a small basket. Sitting astride the bath edge she placed the basket on the floor, it brimmed over with brushes sponges, soaps and bottles of mysterious looking concoctions.

Selecting a small round brush and a bar of pink soap. 'Turn round,' she ordered. Whatever she said she was going to do it was about to happen.

Rubbing the soap with one hand on my back she used the brush in small circular movements. She started at the top of my spine continuing until all my back had been soaped and brushed. This was ecstasy, occasionally opening my eyes I watched the reflection of her working in the bathroom mirror, she took great care in what she was doing. Scooping a beaker full of cold water from the basin she poured the contents over my back. Wow! The hairs stood to attention. Using the brush in reverse motion she brushed the skin again. I was ready for the water the next time but it did not happen.

'Turn around,' she requested. The hot water made my skin feel as if it was on fire.

'Is this the way landladies in France treat their customers?'

'Non, la personne spécial. '

'Could I rub your back?'

'Bien sûr.'

It was the most enjoyable bath I had encountered, what pleasure soap and a soft brush can give. Towelling each other dry became so stimulating, it concluded in passion.

'Avez vous parlez Jules.' Was Jules coming here to meet with me I could not remember. looking out of the window there was no sign of him on the road. Jacqueline was holding the shirt to help me dress. I put my arms into the shirt the wrong way, I held of her in my arms. responding she lifted her legs to grip me around the waist, making a slight moan as we coupled, we fell onto the bed, without breaking our union, later we lay our passion spent. I removed the shirt. 'This will not do,'

'Pourquoi?'

'This one is wet.' Holding the shirt to the window the damp patches replicated Jacqueline's torso.

She joined me in the shower, towelling me dry again making sure I was presentable; I kissed her cheek lightly smacking her bottom. I made a comment that she should put some clothes on before she walked around the hotel; she had not bothered to dress after our little episode. Looking out of the front door there was no sign of Jules, deciding not to walk, the Monteverdi was given an early morning airing taking me to the bar.

Jules was waiting for me John, bringing some coffee, joined us. Over the coffee they both sat enthralled as I portrayed the events of the previous week. Jules eager to help, had seen the opportunity that I had offered but he must discuss the matter with his superiors first. 'Jules, can you tell me exactly how Pierre Saar died?'

'Sure, not a problem.' Jules speaking in sombre voice proceeded, 'The body of Pierre Saar was discovered at the base of the staircase in the garage at the Vista Plastics Paris. It would appear that he had slipped and fallen down the flight of steps. His injuries included, a broken neck, wrist, ribs and the right ankle.

He had lain in the garage for nearly six hours, but he died within the first. The Paris Sûreté investigation was complete. All properties of Pierre Saar found at the scene, his wallet, monies, files, although the leather attaché case was open, were scattered around the base of the stairs and on the garage floor, but nothing was missing.

A Madame Janine his secretary confirmed the documents were all intact. The coroner's court verdict: was accidental death. Pierre Saar had no apparent enemies or any health problems. The police have closed the files on this case; however, if information to the contrary became available, they would, of course, be prepared to investigate.'

Jules continued to say that Pierre Saar was wealthy. Mme Janine and Mme Jacqueline knew him best, there was a rumour about another woman but neither Janine nor Jacqueline had knowledge of her. We had discussed the matter for many hours, with my input and the case history we were wiser into Pierre Saar's past and present, Jules suggested that he depart to consult his superior with the proposal. Stretching as I stood the comfort of the wood bench left a lot to be desired, I had noticed a lack of comfortable seating in rural France. It seemed local folk did not think it important to have a comfortable chair, a smoke free table outside the bar, was an attractive idea, taking my coffee with me, I day dreamed as I soaked in the sunshine

Elaine sprang into my mind, using the bar telephone, I called her; she was feeling better but still was upset about Pongo, the police had been checking the area but they had found nothing. Elaine had scrutinised the house contents, nothing appeared to be missing, she said the intruder had gained access to the house from the front door, two large flat jemmy marks had appeared in the plastic surround.

What were they after?

Who were they after?

Elaine decided to stay with her pal Phyllis, she was having a good time, Phyllis was a good laugh, she also lived close by, Elaine could keep an eye on the house until I returned home.

The insurance company said they would get their builder to repair the property, but assessor had written off the car.

We discussed some of the problems I was encountering, I decided to stay on in France, and ride this one out. Never had so much excitement come my way, the scrapes, the situations, the compromising entanglements; I wanted to see what was going to happen next.

Jules returned to the bar with his superior officer, a man I had already met, Captain Louis thought it would be a good idea for Jules to work with me, they had contacted the Paris Sûreté detective who had controlled the Pierre Saar case. Being updated about the recent events, his interest was re kindled, considering that a bright up and coming officer working undercover, unknown to the Paris workforce, would be an opportunity not to be missed.

Simone appeared with some more coffee plus some tasty looking chocolate covered donuts. Cutting one open revealed a centre of custard. A nice change, but over indulgence with these pastries would easily give you the portly look. Captain Louis pausing from a sip of coffee and a piece of the donut asked how I would explain Jules's presence. 'Very simple,' I explained, 'Jules came to my aid during the assault on me in Laroche. Due to a change of my circumstances that everybody is aware of, I now require the services of a translator. Nobody outside the village knows of Jules, or that he is an officer of de law, I simply reply if anyone inquired, that I offered Jules a temporary position as personal translator and guide while I was in France.' 'With me knowing of your special circumstances that would be the normal actions of an intelligent business man, there would be no reason to doubt you, it even fools me,' Capt. Louis chuckled, looking at me and touching his nose with one eye closed. It seemed that the subterfuge had his approval.

Jules was officially on the case.

Simone asked, 'Would you and Jacqueline like to eat with us this evening?'

'Could you call her as I am busy at the moment.' Simone came back within a minute whispering in my ear that she would join us in 10 minutes.

Jules and Capt. Louis departed for their evening meals.

Sitting with John outside I overheard Capt. Louis say to Jules 'Ooh, la, la Mme Jacqueline' again touching his nose with his finger, then she drove into view, Jules and Louis turning to observe her, saluted as she passed, keeping a watchful eye on her as she walked from her little car to where we were sitting, Capt. Louis, shaking his head as he walked away, there is a story there but in what context I would hate to enquire.

Jacqueline greeted us in a profound display of cheek kissing, as I leant forward a muscle in my back seem to spasm, making me wince, Jacqueline noticing this made me sit on a high stool at the bar, while John served aperitifs, Jacqueline sipping her drink was rubbing my back with an occasional finger prod in different locations. As she found the painful spot, I reacted instantly; she teased the spot with her finger end, making small circles around the area, I could feel the muscle tension releasing as she manipulated the problem. After a couple of minutes of manipulation, she declared 'Voila, il est fin.'

'Merci Mademoiselle.' I thanked her.

Simone calling us for us to join them in the back parlour, John topped up our aperitifs, a local mushroom soup for starters the soup was black in appearance with an earthy and interesting taste, however I personally felt a little black pepper would suit my palette.

This was followed by fresh roasted pork with a cream pepper

sauce with huge quantities of various vegetables. After, followed a change of wine to complement the apple pie concealed a taste unlike any other apple pie I had experienced before, I could not place, the spice or additive to the apple which made this pie different. With every course served, John had a different wine which complemented the dish. A brandy was a welcome end to the meal.

The evening consisted of eating, drinking and discussion. This way of life is as important as food, it was good.

Driving back to Jacqueline's hotel, a brilliant full moon made it as bright as day, but bathed in an eerie grey light.

Jacqueline wanted to walk around Pierre's chateaux. the house was still and seem to be sleeping, probably ready to waken when the next owner took residence.

The evening air together with the exercising climb around the terrace, assisted the digestion, the view of the valley in the moonlight was magnificent.

The cigarette smoke from the bar started to make my eyes water, I excused myself to wash and freshen up, I felt rejuvenated, and returned to the lounge, Jacqueline had poured two brandies, taking hold of the goblet the delicate aroma complimented the taste.

'Qu'est ce brandy?'

'It was one that Pierre liked. Do you like it?'

'Mâis oui! ' I replied giving her a wink. She did not understand the satire, she just smiled back.

She noticed my glass was low 'vous desirez autre?

'Oui. '

Through the open cupboard door, I could see the shelves filled with many types of bottles, the top shelf was crammed with this particular brandy, retrieving the open bottle, she replenished my glass. A box of floppy computer disks tucked in the corner of the cupboard. I found this strange, as I had

seen no computer at Jacqueline's house. The evening had been splendid and a cooling breeze was now chilling me. The brandy was having an agreeable effect and sleep would take hold if I did not retire. 'I must go to bed'
Jacqueline replied, 'Would you like some company?'
Smiling back at her, I said, 'That would be nice.'

Chapter 11

There was a movement in the bedroom, through squinted eyelids, I saw Jacqueline was busying herself in the room; a breakfast tray had been laid on the bed. Watching her for a while she quietly slipped in and out of the bathroom, quickly but silently tidied the room. Sitting up quickly I greeted her, 'Bonjour. Mademoiselle,' my voice croaked, the suddenness made her jump.

Oh! She cried, holding her hands across her chest, smiling back at me she sat on the edge of the bed, 'Le brandy, made u slept as we bed to came.'

'We came to bed?' Pardon Jacqueline, 'je regret to, err sleep,' a beautiful companion, who wanted more than sleep.'

Pouring the coffee, she watched me eat my breakfast. 'Do I breakfast alone?' 'I said that to you the other day.' She replied.

'Have you eaten?

Are you sharing with me?

What do you want to do?' Looking thoughtful for an instant a glint in her eye hinted on other activities, she put the tray on the floor, sliding back into the bed she embraced me as she positioned herself astride me.

'I wanted you last night but you were incapable.'

'Was I?'

'Yes, I tried, oh how I tried.' She sighed.

I was not at my best to give satisfaction in that dept, but she had her mind set, a roaming hand found me sleeping, taking a firm hold she increased her grip, I felt pain where I did not want to feel pain.

My muscles reacting to the delicate movements of her hand, slowly, twisting, pulling and pushing movements. Her other hand encircled my chest scraping the skin slightly with a finger nail causing my skin to shiver, leaning forward she pressed herself the softness of the bathrobe teased my nipples until they were hard.

'Voila, yu av changed your mind, I can see.'

My body was responding to her caress, as she sensed the change, she was enthralled in the command of the situation, slowly removing her bathrobe, her gyrating hips were moving slowly down my stomach towards my groin. 'Be careful, I feel a little sore in that department today,' I remarked. She lent closer to me, moving her breasts she touched my nose softly with her hard nipples, slowly sliding them from side to side.

She started to kiss my brow, moving down to my eyelids, my mouth, progressing downwards to each nipple, slowly but surely sliding her kisses moved down my stomach until she had reached her target. Her mouth was soft, her stimulation was unbelievable. She progressed, to caressing my stomach then chest, moving higher until she had positioned herself to take full advantage. She slowly mounted me with intentional pushing of her hips until no further movement was possible, the flexing of her vagina muscles bringing pleasure then final satisfaction.

She managed, a nonstop session of pure sexual pleasure. A sudden breeze caused the net curtain to rise quickly momentarily, only to descend very slowly our entwined bodies; heavy with perspiration the freshening breeze was well timed.

The noise of someone walking on the gravel path, alerted us to a visitor. Whispering in my ear, 'I will see.'

'No, let us make love again.' She laughed quietly as she slipped from the bed and moved to the side of the window. 'Someone is looking in your car.' she whispered, as she backed away from the window just enough not to be seen, she kept watch on the visitor: the light from the window was emphasising her feminine curves, I was enjoying watching her, she was so engrossed in her vigil without thinking she instinctively, gathered her hair around her hand curling it into a bun then placing it on the top of her head, she looked around, saw a pencil on the dressing table, she used it to secure her hair in place, she turned and beckoned me to join her, standing in her shadow, I could see a man looking in my car, it was Whittle. 'Whittle!' I hissed, Jacqueline, slipping into her bathrobe, ran from the room, to appear at her bedroom window enquired what he wanted.

Whittle replied in perfect French, 'Bonjour madam, where is the owner of the car?'

'He has left for Paris but will be back later, can I take a message?'

'Is this car for sale?'

'No! It is not, is that the message?'

'Yes,' he replied.

Jules, in uniform riding on his bicycle pedalled up the lane during his early morning duties, recognised Whittle, stopped, sitting on his bicycle enquired, 'What is your business here in Laroche?' I could not hear exactly what the reply was. Jacqueline, with her super hearing, as all women have, heard every word, and joined in with the discussion. She informed Jules about what he had said. Jules assumed this chap was up to no good and instructed him that he was to move on, and not bother people in the village, even suggesting that he did not come back to the village. He had told him that they still had details of the last trouble he had caused; these details would be given to other police forces in the immediate area.

Whittle, not wanting to aggravate the situation, agreed to leave. Jules kept watching as he drove away, Jules recorded the registration number in his day book, turned to Jacqueline greeting her, 'bonjour,' Jacqueline asked Jules to breakfast with them he readily accepted. Jacqueline returned to my bedroom, closing the door behind her. 'Vous désirez?' She enquired, placing her hands on her hips blowing me a suggestive kiss.

'Non mademoiselle, je douche' Pouting, she murmured 'ok,' watching me go into the bathroom, I heard the outer door close as she left the bedroom.

The shower was good, my thoughts of the morning's activities were inconceivable, my memory had a field day recording this morning activities, recalling the event would give stimulation for years to come. I dressed then went downstairs to breakfast; Jules in discussion with Jacqueline were enjoying a coffee, their communication was so quick that it was difficult to grasp. 'Bonjour Jules,' 'Bonjour Ross,' Jules told me more about Whittle appearing outside the house, Confirming I had watched the incident from my room; not wanting to make myself known, I wanted to have a good look at him.

Jules also wanted to discuss with me details about what he was to do tomorrow in Paris. 'We will just take it as it comes.' Whittle was prominent in my mind: his was a name that one would not forget easily. I wanted more information on this man if he was proving to be an adversary, I wanted to level the playing field. I called Darrell explained recent events and Jules's secret involvement, I introduced Jules to Darrell over the telephone, Jules, asked many questions, Darrell gave what answers he could.

Now finished, Jules passed me the telephone, 'Strange,' as Darrell continued 'I saw Whittle in a Manchester restaurant last night with a woman; you know come to think of it, it looked remarkably like that lady I saw in your office.'

'What woman? Which office?' 'That secretary woman, I cannot remember her name, you know who I mean,' 'The

Paris office.' Darrell replied.

'What time did Whittle leave?'

'After me, I left about quarter to eleven, they had not finished eating.' Darrell confirmed.

'How could he be in England late on Saturday then mid France only hours later? No ferry is that fast.'

'Oh! Did I not tell you; Whittle has his own aeroplane; he is always flying around Europe to business meetings. He had assumed that with Pierre Saar dead, he would get the formula without a problem, he had plans to become the major world player in the plastics industry.' Darrell who seemed to be enjoying our discussion, let me into a confidence. The chemist, whose life he had saved was upset about Darrell's dismissal, was prepared to inform Darrell on all updates. 'We had a spy in the other camp.' Also, Whittle has had a meeting with the head of the chemistry dept at the university, they are prepared to give as much assistance as they can, the professor reckons to understand the formula; together they had analysed the formula to find that one of the symbols was incorrect. With this problem discovered he was trying different elements to achieve the correct results.

Doom and despair uncertain feelings confused my mind, the race was on again, another experienced industrial chemist was working on the problem with a copy of the exact formula. We were at a disadvantage with our main chemist's dead and Max out of the equation precarious times were looming. Making plans to call Darrell during the week he replied he would call with any new information, we rang off.

Passing the information on the aeroplane, to Jules, he replied 'Dacor, there was an airfield nearby. It would be worth a look to see if this man's aeroplane was there. 'Let us go'. It will also keep me away from this woman's clutches for a couple of hours.' Jules hinted heavily that he would enjoy a drive in the Monteverdi, cycled home to change into his civilian clothes.

Leaving Laroche via the short cut, we cleared a small amount of traffic, the clear road stretched out in front of us, 'Are you sitting comfortably?'

'Why?' Jules asked, quickly pressing hard on the accelerator, the Monteverdi rocketed forwards sending the speedometer needle scurrying around the dial to 130 in seconds, the Monteverdi was trembling as the powerful engine kept accelerating, the engine noise was perfect. Jules was elated, never had he been so fast. 'This car is fast, quicker than your old Legend, do not forget the speed limit.' Jules cried out, instinctively I lifted my foot from the accelerator pedal letting the speed reduced to a sedate 80mph. the engine was whisper quiet.

We turned into the airfield Jules suggested to park next to the control tower. He would be a couple of minutes I will talk with the air traffic controller, he returned with good news, Whittle had left twenty minutes earlier, he was heading for another airfield south west of Paris. 'He had one passenger, a dark-haired female' Jules had told the air traffic controller the police were now watching this man, if they had any information, they would be appreciative.

The silver car Whittle had been driving, was parked outside a car hire office. Jules checked the registration number it matched the one recorded in his pocketbook, Jules sauntered over and talked with the car hire receptionist again he informed them of the official interest, and request for any information. He spent some time in discussion with this girl; I assumed he must have been asking her for date.

A public telephone kiosk was nearby, I decided to seize the opportunity to call Janine, just to say hi. Her phone was busy waiting a couple of minutes, I called again. This time the answer phone replied her voice giving instructions also a number, she spoke too quickly for me to understand. Jules had just joined me; I passed the phone to Jules, he listened then translated 'She is out, call her on her mobile.' Telling me the number, I called. As she recognised my voice, the tone of her voice softened. 'Was I enjoying myself and taking it easy?'

'Oh yes, I was, it is very interesting.' I told her what Darrell had told me for us to advance we need expert help. She would make enquiries on Monday if we could get help in Paris with our problem.

Whittle appearing in the village did not seem to worry her, I asked her about Pierre's girlfriends, she knew of Jacqueline, remarking something in French which I could not understand, saying our bye byes, she would be waiting for me on Monday.

Joining Jules at the café du airport, as I sat down, a sudden stabbing pain in my lower abdomen made me gasp and cry out, collapsing into the seat, it buckled under me throwing me to the ground.

'Ross!' cried Jules, 'what has happened?' The pain was so severe I was unable to talk, slowly the discomfort subsided enabling me to sit up.

'Phew! That was sore.' Judging by the concerned look in Jules face I must look grim; 'I will be ready in a minute.' Gradually the pain eased letting me regain composure then Jules helped me to the car, passing him the ignition key, you drive I cannot, this pain is too severe.' Jules told me my face had changed colour to grey, then white, slowly the normal colour returned. He wanted to call a doctor immediately to attend to the problem.

'If this pain has not ceased when arrive at Laroche, we will go and see the doctor.' I agreed.

He drove the Monteverdi so carefully back to Laroche, as not to give me any more discomfort, I remarked 'Be careful of the speed limit we might get arrested for going too slow.' He hit the accelerator hard, the car took off like a frightened rabbit. The acceleration threw me into the back of the seat causing the pain to hit a new level.

'Could it be the food poisoning?' Jules asked, as he drove straight to the doctor.

The doctor laid me out on his table slowly prodding parts of my body, he checked all the vital signs, no problems found. He was frowning deep in thought, as he performed his diagnosis, the abdominal area caught his attention, applying pressure to a couple of points, my reaction was what he expected. Was I, a sportsman? he enquired.

'No, not really.'

'Had I been in a fight?'

'No.'

'Have you been exercising in the evening with your wife?'

'No, I am not married.'

Being very diplomatic he rephrased the question,

'Exercising with a lady friend.'

'Yes. I will agree with that,'

'Bon you have a simple strain, take it easy, it is important no more heavy lovemaking.'

'Love making?' Your English people call it Bonking I believe,

The Doc referred to another patient history, 'Another person, I knew of once had a similar problem.'

'Did he recover?'

'He is dead now.'

'Resulting from this problem?'

'No, from another accident.

I think you understand exactly what I mean.' The doctor gave me some pills that would give relief to the problem however the pills do have a side effect.

'What is the side effect?' I enquired,

'Le Peepee, he no standing up.'

Without naming him, the Doc indicated Pierre also had this problem, As Jules was driving me to Jacqueline's, he referred to the problem.

'Excessive exercise.' I replied

'For the exercise's' Jules explained, 'I ride my bicycle vigorously in the morning.' Silently I reflected, this damage was done during a riding related more enjoyable but just as tiring exercise, this condition was not going to become common knowledge.

Jules stopped outside John's, suggesting a small aperitif to toast our new venture on Monday.

John requested that I call Elaine, 'she called, can you call her back.' she did not answer so I left a message on the answer phone, concerning Whittle's aeroplane. I suggested telling the police, they could check to see if he had landed at our local airport. He may be the perpetrator who burgled the house, torched my car then killed the dog.

John was attending to customers in the bar while Jules discussed Monday with me. I suggested a 6.00am start the drive would take two hours to Paris, and an early night with a good sleep was required, by me anyway, wishing everyone a good night, I carefully drove back to see Jacqueline. She had prepared a small evening meal combining mussels in a fish sauce, a pleasant change, eating fish on a Sunday, followed by a banana cooked in fresh orange juice lightly dowsed in brown sugar, with a liberal splash of brandy finished the meal. 'Est ce que vous désirez un cognac?'

'Bien sûr.'

As she opened the cupboard door standing out like a sore thumb was that red box of computer disks.

'Do you have a computer?'

'Non.'

'Why do you have a box of computer disks?'

'What are they?'

'That red box on the shelf.' She stretched to retrieve the box, in doing so showed more thighs with a glimpse of pink panties. 'Voila Rose,' She turned smiling, realising what I had said, then threw the box of disks at me; the flying disc box opened spilling floppy disks over the floor.

'Pardon.' She was laughing.

'You will be,' I replied with a grin.

I found nine floppy disks; the box indicated ten. A spasm stopped me looking for an instance, as it abated; there was no sign of the lost disk. Jacqueline came to help,

'What is it you were looking for?' She asked, placing a brandy on the small table.

'One of these.' I showed her a diskette, after ten minutes of looking still no sign of the lost disk, maybe there never were ten, only nine. While we were on hands and knees Jacqueline decide it was a good enough chance to entice me with another idea, one that I was a little tender with. I told her of my predicament.

'I have a cure,' disappearing upstairs, she called me, 'Bring your brandy, hurry.' she was in her bedroom in front of an open cupboard, she was preparing something, inside the cupboard a good array of little pots, and different coloured glass jars, as I entered the room she pointed to bed 'assez vous'.

She pushed me backwards onto the bed, pulled off my socks, and then removed my trousers.

A tub of white cream with an enticing perfume was plonked on my chest.

'These smells nice, what is it?'

'Just a special cream.' Jacqueline gently removed my shorts, proceeding to view the painful area. She prodded away at a few areas, coming to the same conclusion as the doctor, 'He, is not used to everyday work', I was enthralled she was talking to my parts as if he was a person. She generously covered the cream into my upper thighs and base of the stomach, expertly she smoothed the cream into the surface of the skin, this manipulation stimulated me, I was aroused, but the pill the Doc gave me was fighting back, the pill eventually won. At this point in time, I had totally forgotten any pain with the effects of the cooling cream.

It would be nice to spend the evening with her in bed, the bed with the password on the headboard, the bed that had started the search, the bed which had given much pleasure. It was still giving pleasure, would I be able to enjoy more, would the bed hold any more secrets?

Dimming the lights Jacqueline slipped into bed cuddling up to me, giving me a feeling of contentment, quickly we slipped into a deep sleep. I woke around three o'clock, feeling extremely hot, our bodies were dripping with perspiration.

Easing my arm from under her I released myself from the entanglement, and slipped from the bed.

Peering through the open window all was still; the full moon illuminated the empty road. I stretched my arms above me touching the ceiling with ease, I collected my thoughts; in three hours I would be going to Paris. I felt shivery with the cool breeze from the window, I returned to the bed, I could see a reflection in her eyes, she was awake, watching me.

'What are your thoughts?' she asked quietly

'Many.' I replied.

She pulled me back into the bed I had no feeling of pain; with her assistance we made sensual passionate love over the next two hours.

Then the alarm fired its deadly buzz, it is always the worst sound one could hear at five o'clock. I did not want to get up and drive to Paris, I was content where I was, alas the morning was planned, no more distractions, I gathered my clothes and returned to my room, I took a refreshing shower. By the time I was finished Jacqueline had a freshly pressed shirt, with a business suit, laid on the bed.

She appeared as if by magic with coffee, and then assisted me with my dressing. She prepared me for the coming day; she had done this before, and I knew for whom Jacqueline went to let Jules into the house. I greeted Jules. He too was dressed in a suit ready for the office.

'Okay, let's go.'

Giving Jacqueline the customary cheek to cheek kisses my hand secretively caressed her breast as we departed.

'Jules, do you want to drive?'

'No, this car has affection for you, it responds better to your touch.' The Monteverdi snarled into life as we edged the car out of Laroche towards Paris. The traffic on the road from Laroche was light. As I flexed my right foot the car responded taking us safely into the high nineties, the miles disappearing beneath us as we headed for Paris. Jules keeping me up to date of the areas where police cars lay in wait for speeding drivers. He made me aware of the toll road speed trap; if you leave the motorway too early, the speeding ticket follows the payment of the toll fee. It is always worthwhile taking a break before leaving the motorway.

As we entered Paris we encountered heavy traffic, slowly we made our way to the office and drove around the rear of the building, in the car park a place was reserved for Pierre Saar, he would not be using it, so I decided that I would, parking the Monteverdi, I pressed the remote-control button, the car bleeped once, the car was alarmed.

The entrance to the office was on the first floor this was accessed by a balcony with staircase, I sprinted up the stairs catching Jules unawares he trotted along behind me, he said for man crippled with pain yesterday to running upstairs was a miracle.

Jokingly I said 'It must have been the meal Jacqueline prepared.' I looked back down at the stairs then remarked to Jules that these must have been actual stairs on which Pierre had fallen from to his death.

Pressing the outside bell push, we waited, then the little speaker on the wall requested who it was calling, I replied it was I and a friend; the electric door catch clicked releasing the door to let us in.

Walking through the corridors to the reception area, we met Claudette, I introduced Jules to her, and requested Janine's whereabouts, Claudette replied that she had slipped out for a couple of minutes.

'Is Pierre Saar's office open?' She removed a key from her draw and passed it to me, 'We will wait for Janine to arrive in the office.' Unlocking the door, the room was still in total darkness, searching for the light switch, clicked the lever, hidden lights illuminated around the ceiling, the room finally revealed itself.

The décor was unique, even the office was strangely shaped, one end opposite Pierre's desk the room was circular, fitted wall units bowed slightly in the middle and connected the floor to ceiling.

The office was situated at the corner of the building. Sliding open the closed window blinds gave one a commanding view of both streets. Outside both windows were wall mounted cameras I could make out the initials CCTv on each of them.

Claudette entered the office with some coffee on a tray, she stayed for a moment, her interested in Jules was obvious. I took my coffee Jules kept silent, replying the coffee was most appreciative.

Drinking the coffee as I walked around the office, I perused the room; sitting down in different locations, the room was so different; it was coloured dark blue, all seating and ancillaries matched. I was interested what lived in what cupboard. The one of the wall units professed a well-stocked bar, under the shelf of cut-glass tumblers and other glassware, lay a small preparation area, beneath that, sat a small fridge.

This fridge contained a variety of fruit juices, some bottles of wine and on the inside of the door, a plastic tub opening the lid, it was Jacqueline's special cream, I continued looking, the variety of drinks from around the world, there was one, with the light behind it was a beautiful emerald green its name was 'Absinthe.' Jules also spotted it, he remarked on the bottle, 'he had heard of Absinthe but never had seen it.' Jules explained. 'Absinthe is a high alcoholic drink banned from sale since the 1900s in France, it has some strange effect on the central nervous system if the drinker abused it.' I pointed out to him that there are three bottles of this drink on one shelf, a Green, Red, and Black, removing the Black Absinthe from the shelf, I read the label, 'BLACK ABSINTHE 80. 160 proof 80%Vol. No wonder it was banned. Curious the Red Absinthe had the same proof; however, the Green Absinthe was a mere 40% proof. Maybe that was the starter drink. Putting the bottle back I closed the door.

A concealed door in the wall unit led to a bathroom with shower, and smaller storage room, this room housed a large cupboard containing a filing cabinet, and a white metal cabinet with security padlock and latch.

'Look! There is a secret in the office.'

'What is it?' I replied.

He pressed the rocker switch; a section of wall slowly descended similar fashion to a drawbridge, settling firmly on the floor. It was a bed, with more blankets and bedding, stacked on the inner upper shelf. He pressed the rocker switch again the bed disappeared back into the wall recess as quietly as it appeared.

'I wonder what other secrets this room has.'

As we stood surveying the room, Janine entered, seeing that I was not alone she suppressed her greetings to me. I introduced Jules to her with the story that we had agreed.

Janine asked Jules many questions, and seemed happy with the replies, she requested a private moment with me, I asked Jules to replenish the coffee this would give Janine and I time to talk.

Each of us were happy to meet again kissing and holding each other.

I suspected something was wrong in her manner, I asked her what was wrong, she was upset that I had not consulted her before engaging Jules. I explained that this was just a temporary assignment for him. 'After all, Janine it was your suggestion,'

She had forgotten, then realised it was her idea, she perked up. she had convinced herself It is handy to have another capable of helping out, just in case.

She quizzed me about the weekend and I told her about the problem with a small strain, and the doctor telling me to rest; the weekend gave me the rest that I needed.

'Was this an old problem?' She enquired, cautiously looking at me with anticipation in her eyes. 'It comes and goes but it is getting better and I was feeling so well I sprinted up the stairs this morning'.

'Bon.' She smiled cautiously,

'What is the plan for today? And how is Max?'

Max was still in the coma, as for plans, I talked with a government minister on the formula problem, He would make enquiries into the possibilities of assistance, and he would be in touch.

Jules returned to the office, bringing a small tray of coffee and some biscuits. Janine wishing to know more about this stranger asked him to join us. Before Janine started her inquisition.

I asked Janine, 'What was Pierre Saar like? What did he do?' I want to know this man better, his habits, leisure activities, hobbies, likes and dislikes; to know one's adversary one must assemble all the facts.

Janine was still cautious about Jules being present. I said that if there was anything sensitive, we could discuss it privately. For the next two hours, Janine shared with us her entire knowledge of Pierre Saar, but I could sense she was keeping some details to herself. Pierre had a fascination for photographic gadgetry, and his other hobbies he enjoyed opera and ballet. The plastic industry was his life 'It was his release,' Janine sighed.

'What was Pierre carrying when he had the accident?'

'He carried an attaché case.'

'What happened to that?'

'It is here.' Janine went to the side of his desk, picking up a light tan attaché case with a zip closer and a magnetic over flap.

'This was found at the bottom of the stairs with Pierre, its contents strewn about on the garage floor. We picked up all the documents then put them back in the case. As far as we could see everything was intact.

'One thing was missing.'

'What was that?'

'His mobile telephone, it was never found.'

'I could do with a mobile telephone; it would be beneficial to me while here in France.'

The attaché case; had a zip closer and a magnetic over strap. I emptied the contents onto the large leather covered desk, checking every corner of the case. There was nothing left. I even felt the sides just in case Pierre had hidden something, as when I made the discovery in the Monteverdi.

Jules asked, 'Could I look at the papers?'

I was agreeable, looking at Janine for her approval, she gave her consent. Jules quietly scrutinised the papers, nothing new had surfaced. As Jules looked, I played with the zipper it glided so smoothly, and as you laid the case down the magnetic flap closed holding all items secure.

Leaving the zipper open the case closed and still the case was secure. Putting the same number of blank papers in from the office printer I left the zipper open and dropped the case the flap closed before it could reach the floor, and the contents stayed intact. Thinking for a while I flung the attaché case across the office, a bit harder than I expected, it crashed against the panelling but it stayed closed, Janine watched me bemused, 'You have found something?' she asked 'un minute s'il vous plait' going to the balcony in the garage I made sure the contents were secure, and the flap and zipper were open I stood at the head of the stairs and dropped the case, it bounced then cart wheeled down the stairs, slithering to a halt at the bottom. Retrieving it I tried again from halfway, and tried to land the case on the banister rail, it hit the rail and again cart wheeled to a stop halfway across the garage floor. 'That is where it was found,' Janine spoke from the top of the stairs; I collected the case and ran back upstairs. Meeting with her at the top of the stairs, I slipped my arm around her waist and kissed her. 'It did not open,'

'That is true, I watched you,' Janine confirmed, when Pierre had it, for the last time, it was open and papers were spread around.

I smoothed my hand over her bottom; 'Perfect', then I opened the door for her to enter the office.

Jules was nearly finished his perusal of the contents, he asked 'What was in this?' he held out a plastic document sleeve towards Janine.

Taking the sleeve, she looked at it 'I do not know what it contained or what Pierre had inside it, it is different to the style that we use. This is also dirty; someone has stood on it.' She was just about to throw it into the waste paper bin.

'No, please could I have it, I wish to take another look at it. also, could I see one that we use?'

'Bien Sûr.' Going to the wall unit and opening a draw, she picked a new plastic sleeve and gave it to me. Both items were identical apart from the ring binder section. The one used in the office had a silver sheen to the edging strip, whereas the one found in the valise was dark grey. 'Who makes the one we use in the office?'

'We do.' She pointed to the bottom of the sleeve a code, '"VP197gie." VP stands for the company, Vista Plastics. There are three numbers and three letters. The code is pressed into all the sleeves, which indicates the production date. If the item became defective, records could be checked as to the construction components, it is our normal business practice.'

The other plastic sleeve stamped in almost the identical place a code: 'βWPfhfc2'. 'Any idea as to the make of this one?' I asked,

'No.' Janine replied, she glanced at a wall cabinet briefly then returned her attention to me, we had discovered earlier in the same cabinet a video recorder, television plus a large quantity of video tapes.

'Did Pierre watch much television at the office?'

'No,' Janine replied, what is the television in this cabinet used for, swinging open the door revealing the equipment.

She looked on edge, 'Err, it is the CCTV system.'

'CCTV?' I held my hands out in a French manner, of not knowing what is CCTV?

Janine switched on the equipment to demonstrate. She pointed to the screen le monitor, then to the video, le recorder then to a small logo badge on the front displaying CCTV. the picture displayed on the monitor, was showing a split picture giving excellent views of both streets, the cars parked in the garage. The views changed presumably as the system switched from camera to camera, a view of reception area, with Claudette talking to a gentleman at the front desk.

'Oh!' Janine exclaimed. 'It is the government minister; I will go and greet him. She looked at me with a serious look, tapped on the door with her fingernail, close this cabinet before you leave the office, nobody knows about this CCTV system in the office.'

Jules and I chatted for a few minutes. Jules explained that, it was easier to speak French and translate later; he would of course make sure I was informed. He had so far concluded Janine was hiding something, and she was still very protective of the company.

'I think she was in love with Pierre, but as a confidante and not a wife.'

'That would explain matters,' Jules finalised his conclusion.

A discrete knock on the office door heralded the entrance of Janine followed by a gentleman, Janine introduced us to a Thomas Boisseneau, secretary of state for industry and commerce, and he had some very good news.

A retired but well-respected Austrian chemist was presently in Paris, and would be willing to assist. He once worked with Pierre many years ago, and would take it as a great honour to help. His name was Otto von Gertle; he would arrive at 15:00, to take a look at what we had.

Thomas, apologised for his hastily retreat, another matter of great importance required his presence. Janine thanked him graciously on our behalf for his assistance. Thomas's exit was a speedy as his entrance, we sat and discussed the coming Austrian chemist and how we could accommodate him, Janine added she remembered a von Gertle, he had worked with Pierre many years ago on a project.

Suddenly Jules asked for the number of Pierre's mobile telephone, as Janine rattled off the number, Jules picking up a telephone dialled it; Jules asked if he could speak with Albert; The line went dead. 'It appears that someone has Pierre's telephone.'

'Who is Albert?' I enquired.

'Nobody,' he replied, 'I just wanted to make a contact, but the location and area would now be recorded. It is now possible to triangulate the location of the telephone by which transmitting mast was used. It would be worthwhile letting the officer in charge of the Saar case check out this new information.' I asked Jules how he knew of the radio triangulation, 'Ah my Papa was a radio operator in the résistance during the war, and he was chased by Le Boche for years, the never caught him.' Janine agreed, and then departed to her office to make the call. Jules was still looking for other secrets the room might have.

I sat in Pierre's desk chair and surveyed the office from his everyday view, taking note of each location, and the layout of the office, we had looked in all but the desk. His desk was large and covered in black and blue suede leather, with a grey stitching and hand engraved in places, it was an expensive desk, in such expensive desk's secrets can be hidden. Systematically I started inspecting each drawer. Each drawer was emptied on the desk and contents inspected; a single coin glued onto the back panel in the top right-hand drawer.

I too did this custom in my office at home, as long as you have that coin, you will never be short of money. Strange how, countries apart, still adhere to the coin superstition. Many items of interest were discovered but nothing was of importance to the current problem.

Jules found another cupboard full of video tapes, all marked with dates and marked with a number 1 to 32, one tape for everyday of the month. Used in rotation the tapes would give a history of what had happened during the last month.

'Regarde vous' Jules cried

'What have you found?'

'I do not know what it is.'

'If you pull open this door it opens, to reveal a shallow cupboard this was different from the other cupboards. But, when you slide the door up, Regarde.'

The secret compartment included precision weighing scales, a microscope, an electronic spectrum analyser, selection of glass jars and a variety of laboratory equipment. On the top shelf were video and micro cassette tapes some marked with dates, others had little messages written on them. Some tapes were still boxed and kept apart from the others obviously these were the new stock.

Jules said, 'Let's investigate later when we are assured nobody can disturb us.' He closed the door, just as Janine reappeared.

'I have told the police about Jules's experiment; they will be looking into it. Ross, I have some work to do before Otto arrives. I also have something for you in my office, will you come now?'

I followed admiring her as she walked, she had an excellent poise and statue, I detected a slight limp in her gait but it was nothing detrimental, taking something from her desk drawer. She asked me to close my eyes, I felt her presence and smelt her perfume as she came close, the feeling of pleasure as her soft lips kissed me, and she pressed something into my hand. I tried to make out what it was without opening my eyes, I was torn between enjoying the embrace, and what was in my hand, Janine would not let me go to look, we started laughing as we broke the embrace, she was purposely making sure, I could not see but curiosity won, I held a mobile telephone.

'I have put my numbers in the telephone memory, it will work anywhere in Europe.' I kissed her she responded, I gave her a hug, I decided to tell her what we were doing.

'We are examining the contents of Pierre's office and intend to look through all the video tapes.' she looked back at me, 'Thank you for telling me, I felt rejected, with Jules being here, be careful what you find do not tell anyone.' I was just about to leave she called me back; taking a tissue from her handbag, she removed a trace of lipstick from my lips, 'merci madam.'

I showed Jules my new acquisition, Janine had written important telephone numbers onto a small label stuck in place onto the back of the phone.

We started to look through the video tapes. The tapes were stacked in a daily order but the video tape for the day of Pierre's accident was missing. There were a couple of extra tapes and also a tape which had a label with a bold red X. This tape had completely rewound itself, snapping the tape inside.

'I wonder what was on this tape,' I said, showing it to Jules.

'Run the video tape,' Jules said.

'The tape has snapped inside.' Sitting down at the desk, I took out my penknife selected the cross-head driver attachment, and removed the case screws and removed the cassette top. Using a strip of cellophane tape, both the damaged ends of the tape were reconnected. Re assembling the tape and placed it into the video machine.

The video machine had two slots; there was a tape in the slot marked (A). a bright red neon light above indicated that it was recording. The repaired tape went into slot (B). The machine accepted the tape and started to wind the tape into the machine; the screen flickered for a while then displayed pictures of both sides of the street. The date and time were also displayed on the bottom of the screen. This was the missing tape; this tape had hopefully recorded the happenings on that fateful day when Pierre died.

The video was displaying scenes in sequence from each of the four cameras, then for the first time I saw Pierre Saar.

He was sitting behind his desk with lots of paperwork. After watching for ten minutes, we watched as the recorder displayed the entire sequence of video shots, changing every fifteen seconds.

Janine was in her office, sitting at her desk talking with Claudette from reception. Claudette took some papers then in another shot Claudette was seen filing the papers in a cabinet. The sequence jumped to the garage.

'Hey, the car is missing.' Jules said, 'What car?'

'The Monteverdi.' Jules, viewing the screen intensely, said, 'Ah, you English, you are always joking. This is a video tape, look.'

Switching off the playing tape, we saw that the garage camera was in operation and revealed the car was still there. He took a second look. 'Look who is at the Monteverdi, that Englishman Whittle.' As we were watching him, he crouched down taking a long look under the car, then reached under the driver's side front wing, he was under the wing for some time, he then reached under the floor and then under the rear suspension; as he moved to the other side, he went out of camera view.

Jules made a quick telephone call to his contact in the Paris police, explained the situation, and continued watching as Whittle played around under the Monteverdi, two uniformed policemen walked into the garage looking around, they noticed Whittle crouching down behind the car, they must have requested his motives. Whittle, started gesticulating, waving his hands in the air and pointing to the car. We could see what was happening but could not hear what he was saying to the officers. We watched as one officer talked into his radio; the other officer beckoned to Whittle to come with them. He stood his ground, shaking his head. Taking hold of him by his upper arms they force marched him from the garage taking him into custody. Jules remarked, 'Whittle is still searching for something, I shall find out later what happened.'

I decided to telephone Darrell.

'Hello, are you working?'

'No.' Darrell replied,

'How do you fancy a bit of covert work?'

'That sounds exciting please explain?'

'Information on Whittle, I need as much as I can get, what he is up to now, and what he has been up to, even verbal chit chat from the secretaries could give me a lead',

'Why not, that bastard needs taking down a peg.' Darrell commented

'Try and find out from the university professor how far he has got with the formula.'

'Leave it up to me; I will call with any news. Are you still at the Paris office?'

'Yes. Have you got enough money to cover your expenses for a couple of days until I can send you some?'

'No problem.' I gave him my new mobile telephone number he could reach me on. I also told him that Whittle had been detained by the Paris police; again, he had been playing with my car. 'Watch him, he is slippery.' See you soon, bye for now.

The desk telephone started to ring. It was Claudette, she announced that Mr. Otto von Gertle, had arrived. 'Show him to the office and please bring some refreshments, and could you inform Janine that we have a visitor'

'Janine has slipped out on an errand.' Claudette replied,

'Does she normally slip out of the office on an errand?'

'No.' She replied.

I wondered, the lady with Whittle at the airport looked like Janine. Also, Darrell said, she was with Whittle in Manchester, also when I called her at home, she was not there, I called her on her mobile, but she could have been anywhere. The only time I had been close to her was at the auction, and I was not taking any notice, then today, Whittle is arrested and Janine disappears on an errand, could this be a pattern that I did not want to know about? Or did I.

My thoughts vanished as the office door opened, Claudette made the introductions, Otto von Gertle, to Jules, and myself.

Otto was what I would believe would be a typical Austrian chap tall white hair, moustache wearing half-moon type reading glasses and a sports jacket and light tan brogue shoes, there was something about him I could not place, then I saw it he had a look about him from the film Pinocchio, he looked like Giuseppe Pinocchio's Father. I explained to him that Mme Janine, who is in charge of the office, is out at the present time. If it would be acceptable, I could give you the account of the situation to date.

'Please, if you would prefer call me Otto, my name is a mouthful in general conversation,'

'Likewise, please use our first names,' Otto also had a good command of English. He listened to the recent events then requested a copy of the formula. Providing him with the latest copy that had been prepared in Canada, I continued to tell him of the green gas that it had produced.

Otto studied the details of the formula, thinking, then going through it all again. 'I have it! The formula in this format will kill everybody. But if you change three items it should work. Do you have a laboratory here?'

'I have not seen one, but I will ask Claudette, she replied that Pierre worked most of the time in his office, and late into the night, but nobody was allowed to enter when he worked.

Conveying the reply to Otto, I enquired as to what it was, he would need. 'All the ingredients in the formula; some weighing scales; standard scientific glassware.'

'Enough!' I cried,

'Show Otto the sliding cabinet.'

'Are you sure?' Jules asked. I nodded my approval, we displayed our discovery, Otto, rising to inspect the array of equipment, said, 'This is typical of Pierre, always had everything that you need and more. There will be a fridge somewhere.

Jules pointed at the small fridge. Otto, inspecting it, said, 'No, another fridge, one with bottles of powders and granules.' Otto taking stock of the drink, remarked I wonder what he was doing with the Absinthe, especially the black.

I consulted Claudette again. 'Yes, it is in the side room by the bathroom in Pierre's office, the key is hung on a small nail behind the door.'

'Thanks again.' that girl knows more than Janine, I wondered if Janine was aware. Otto, opening the fridge door, started to select what he wanted, giving the bottles to Jules to carry.

With the amount of ingredients brought we needed a table to place them on, there was none.

Otto requested more lighting, the office illumination was not as good as he would like, then Otto noticed a blue switch placed at the back of the cabinet, he reached out and pressed it. Things started to happen; a section of the office ceiling moved downwards then proceeded to slide to one side, a bank of fluorescent strip lights automatically switched on; then a sectioned stainless-steel top slid slowly from the wall, small holes were all around the edge of the table.

The distant sound of a large electric motor starting. Two sides of the office wall units, moved slowly towards each other stopping with enough space, for one man to walk in and out. The holes in the edge of the table were air jets, they produced a wall of moving air, little fibres strands attached to the sides of the holes stood to attention, indicating the air movement. We could feel the air around the work area drawn up out of the room. Otto, taking notice, said, 'All these safety features have been installed for a reason.' Rechecking the formula again, Otto asked, 'Is this the formula that was made in the Canadian laboratory?' I could not say, only Max had that knowledge. Otto scanned the room with the altered layout, the design of the room had changed then cried, 'this room is a Venturi.'

He explained that all the air in the room would be sucked out through the roof vents, and fresh air drawn into the room via the bottom, and sides vents of the table.

Pierre was so worried about this gas for him to have built such a complex secret into his own office,

'Were any other safety items found in the room?'

Jules mentioned the sliding bed, also these were found he opened a drawer and removed some respiratory face masks. Otto picked up a mask, 'These have special charcoal filters; they will be perfect protection against any gas produced but make sure that they are fitted correctly around the nose.'

Otto started, by laying out the items that he would need. 'What about the gas?' 'It will not bother us,' declared Otto. Looking at Jules, I gave a surprised look and hunched my shoulders, but we let Otto continue. He selected each ingredient, weighing them to the gram then laid everything in order, while Otto was preparing himself and adjusting the mask to his face he was chuckling, I asked him what the joke was.' He remarked, 'Pierre had not changed, safety first and a bed in his office, still the stallion.'

Donning the masks, we started. Otto said, 'We make my version first, then we try Pierre's.' Otto quickly looked at us inspecting our face masks and ensuring the seal around our noses was snug, anyone had laboratory training, we both shook our heads. OK. Keep your hands away, even if I drop something, I will pick it up. Unless: I ask you.

Otto's version of the formula, commenced, and within thirty minutes we were finished, and there was no sign of the infamous green gas. The first additive was finished, and was ready to test. Placing the formula in a sample jar, it was identified as: Batch 1: Otto 1: Aug: The second batch commenced. Otto measured the exact measurements, then asked, 'Are we ready, please recheck our masks?' Otto worked furiously, placing chemicals into the mixing beakers then placing beakers onto the electric heater, Luis and Whittle's Chemist had used a gas Bunsen burner, which had ignited the gas, Otto adding more of the chemicals. 'I think Pierre had problems at this point.'

Just as the words left Otto's lips the colour of the chemicals in the mixing beaker changed to a light yellow, the electric heater bringing the liquid to boil, bubbles formed in the liquid, clearly, we could see inside each of the bubbles, was the deadly green gas.

The escaping gas from the beaker, itself was sucked away immediately into the extraction system, a flashing amber light with a label Gas and a muffled klaxon buzzer gave an audible warning as the gas was detected.

'Pierre built all these safety features because he knew this would happen.' Otto stated, 'the room is working well, the gas is being extracted from the room into the roof.' Thinking I must take a look in the roof, 'There must be some serious filtration placed there.' 'We should be finished in twenty minutes.'

Suddenly the office door opened, Janine, walked into the circle. Otto yelled, without turning his head, 'GET OUT, NOW,' The gas was escaping the venturi, the airflow was compromised by the open door. A secondary alarm buzzer on the side of the table was screaming its warning with a flashing red light. That door had to be closed now.

Janine, stood her ground viewing the strangest sight ever to be seen in an office, replied, 'Do not, tell me what to do,'

She was not going to move, and she was totally unaware of the immediate danger. I could see the wisps of gas curling along the ceiling heading for the open door.

I launched myself towards her, grabbing her we stumbled out into the hallway pulling the door closed behind us. We collapsed onto the carpet. I was not sure whether I had knocked the wind from her, she was gasping for breath; if the gas had got to her fresh air might help. I grabbed her hand, pulling her towards the outer door into the garage and fresh air. She was still gasping for breath as I flung open the door to the garage. Realising I still had my face mask on, I removed it, she saw it was me, the hostility in her face relaxed, but was pale. She held firmly to the balcony railing while she recovered. She was furious, 'What was that all about?' She demanded. 'We were making the formula; you walked in at the wrong time.'

I explained, 'Otto had arrived at 15:00, you were not in your office; Otto is an impatient man so we continued without you.'

She was still shaken, grasping the facts quickly. 'You saved my life.' I offered her the safety of my arms and she eagerly accepted, holding me tight while she settled herself, she slowly relaxed and stood back leaning against the balcony railings.

'I will go down to the garage and take a walk around outside.'

'OK.' Just as she started to descend the staircase, she slipped recovered herself then stumbled and started to fall headlong down the stairs, I reacted by lunging after her, I managed to catch her ankle but the momentum of her falling she was pulling me down as well. Grabbing for anything secure my hand locked onto a metal balustrade long enough to impede the fall. She also managing to hold onto a banister rail, she held on.

Hanging on we had stopped, I reached out to help her, one of us was bleeding, we were both covered in blood, the steel stairs were brutal and unforgiving. Her dress was torn, and she was trembling violently, we helped each other to the top of the stairs and safety. Kicking on the closed back door, I shouted for someone to help us.

Jules first to arrive quickly took control; picking up Janine in his arms he took her to her office. I followed close by.

'Janine nearly fell down the stairs.' I cried, Claudette seeing the state of Janine she ran to her assistance. Jules ran back to the office carrying a damp towel, he wrapping it around my hand and wrist; only then did I realise that I was bleeding making a mess on the carpet.

Sitting down, my arm was aching with pain. Claudette realised the injuries were serious telephoned for expert help from the doctor in the medical centre on the next floor. They responded immediately, a nurse cleaned my damaged wrist and bound it, Janine was shaking, she was in shock, the doctor was giving her an injection, she had bandages to her shoulder and upper arm, one of her ankles was swathed in a bandage from her knee to her toes. She gave me a brave smile, but she was hurting, I suggested taking her home but she declined.

Otto, totally oblivious to the happening events, came out of Pierre's office shouting, 'Eureka, I have made it.' Then taking note flurry of doctors, nurses and bandages, said, 'Oh my, what did happen?' Jules suggesting to Claudette 'Please lock the office and garage doors.' She went to her desk, pressed a couple of buttons, the office was now secure.

Otto surveyed the situation, enquired how the lady was who had opened the door. 'Shaken but alive.' 'Lucky, that gas is highly toxic, you know, she probably would not have been in any danger standing in the open door. The rush of air passed her and let more air in from the outer office, but the extraction system was still evacuated the gas anyway,' Otto added his theory. 'Come, take a look.'

He showed me the two jars containing the two samples, the second one now marked 'Otto2' was placed on the leather topped desk. Now all we had to do was to extrude some plastic, add the formula and test the results, we could do it in the morning at the factory.

Otto with everybody so busy, he would write up the formula, at his hotel, including the method, 'Ross, this is important remember, it is the method, not the formula, without that you die.' It was certainly unique. He would return in the morning at 9:00 and come with us to the factory I will look forward to the visit.

Otto said his farewells and left, within the next hour we had settled the office back to normality, Jules said it was late and he should go, Claudette had booked him a small hotel nearby. Janine was the type of woman who was indestructible, but she and I could have gone the same way as Pierre Saar.

With the rest of the staff departed the office was quiet, I sat at Janine's desk, she was stretched out on her couch with a damp towel covering her brow, she was still pale, 'Can you make it to the front door? I will get a taxi to take us to your apartment.' She shook her head she would like to rest, giving her time; I returned to Pierre's office, turned the blue switch off, the ceiling panel and side panels returned to their original positions, the whine from the extraction system slowly reduced to a stop, I replaced the lab equipment back in the cupboard then sliding down the door the office regained its prior appearance: I deposited the two new sample flasks in the large fridge.

Janine had come to see what I was doing she was sitting on the small couch, she still looked ashen. I suggested that she should lie down, she laid back and I lifted her legs onto the couch, she winced, as I lifted the bandaged leg.

'Would you like a drink?'

'Yes, is there a brandy?' Janine enquired. Retrieving the bottle of special brandy, I poured two glasses, passing one to her. She sipped it slowly as she manoeuvred herself to ease her pain. 'We could stay here tonight if you wish, I am not hungry, just tired. I have feasted over the weekend and could do with a period of abstinence, in both activities.'

'There is enough room on the couch for two, but we have no

cover and will get cold.' 'I have something to show you,' standing by the sidewall, I pressed the switch. The secret bed, slid silently from the wall, her eyes opened in amazement, she had never seen that before, I could see in her mind, she was trying to work out when Pierre had it installed. She attempted to slide across to the bed, but was cried out. I lifted her, the pain in my wrist stabbed; as I placed her on the bed.

My wrist ached; I closed the shutters giving us privacy. I dimmed the lights leaving the glow from the desk light, then joined her on the bed.

She was still frightened and in pain, but feeling more secure, she snuggled in and we fell asleep. I awoke later, I was feeling cold, and I pulled one of the blankets from the shelf. Gently covering her with the blanket, I removed my clothes, Janine asked me to help her out of her dress; the reassuring warmth of our bodies and the extra comfort of the blanket, we cuddled as we fell asleep.

A crashing sound outside the window woke my slumber. Alighting from the bed I took a quick look out into the street; a municipal waste disposal wagon was working its way down the street removing garbage, emptying trash cans and bins as they went.

Returning to the bed, I found it was empty; a flushing toilet, then a shower starting in the bathroom gave Janine's location. As she returned to the office she was crying.

'What is the matter?'

'Look.'

She let the towel slip to her waist she was covered in bruises, they were starting to turn dark blue, and crimson, they looked very tender. As she slid back into the bed she lifted the bed sheets, 'Have you seen your body?' Janine answered, my chest was covered in bruises, with a blood-soaked bandage around my lower arm and hand. 'Go and shower, it will help.' Janine said. Entering the shower I had an uneasy feeling, what it was, I could not put my finger on, the warm shower soaked away the dried blood, turning the shower head to a close stream of water the extra power pummelled my skin helping to relieve the taut muscles, the wrist bandage, now completely sodden through I unwound it, I had a cut to the edge of my wrist, it had stopped bleeding, I washed it gently, then towelled myself dry sat on the edge of the bed Janine still wincing from her pains. I think Pierre has something that would help us, Picking Jacqueline's special cream from the shelf; I started to smooth the cream on her bruises. Janine shivered as the cold cream touched her body but she persevered.

Janine said quietly, 'How do you have such a soft touch' as I rubbed on the cream',

'Rubbing down car paintwork, also applying cream to the eczema that my little dog had,' I replied. She looked at me, smiling closed her eyes and fell asleep, she looked a bit happier I rubbed some of the cream on my bruises, and while I had chance, also on my strained area. Sliding back into the bed I then fell asleep for the third time.

Chapter 12

Noises made by the arriving office staff woke me from a deep slumber. Kissing Janine on her cheek I whispered it was time to get up. Janine asked could I get the brown valise from the side of her desk in her office.

I dressed quickly then retrieved the brown valise from her office, without I thought being noticed. She disappeared into the bathroom, and after a couple of minutes, a changed lady appeared dressed in a smart grey suit. Her attention to her makeup disguised the bruise marks on her face.

'I am impressed.'

'I always keep a change of clothes here in case I have to go somewhere at the last minute. Pierre also kept clean shirts here.'

Going to a cupboard in the bathroom she came back with a dark blue shirt. 'This will look better than the other one. It is dirty and it has blood on it.'

Changing the shirt made me feel better. Inspecting the closet, I found a sand-coloured linen jacket and a pair of charcoal grey trousers, they were a good fit. My black shoes had been torn in the accident, A box with a new pair of tan shoes, were also in the closet they were a slack fit, but so what.

I returned to the office. Janine gasped, 'You look like Pierre in his clothes.'

Just as she departed, she kissed me on the lips. 'Thank you for yesterday, I am indebted. Oh, I nearly forgot.' Going to the cupboard, she changed the video tape, replacing it with the one from the bottom of the pile.

'Have you thought, our lovemaking in your office the other day will have been recorded.'

Stopping for a moment, and looking at me she said, 'That

could be worthwhile keeping.' She opened the cupboard and removed the tape for that day. 'For us only,' she whispered and placed it in my hand.

The desk intercom requested the locality of Janine. Janine answered, 'I am here.'

'A telephone call for you.'

She listened for a couple of seconds and replied.

'Please wait while I transfer you to my office.' Transferring the call she looked and said, 'We are at work now.' Then as she departed, she said, 'Keep it safe please,' and kissed me gently on the lips then slowly caressed my shoulders her hand gliding down my back and firmly holding my bottom, the glint in her eye as she left was exhilarating, the affection made my heart flutter, a moment I would cherish for a lifetime.

Jules appeared carrying two coffees. 'Claudette said you were in, I presumed you could do with one.'

'So, what happened last night at the police headquarters?'

'Whittle has not broken any laws; he still claims that he is in love with the Monteverdi and wants to buy it.' He had not done anything but with him being in a private car park with an open public entrance, we could not hold him even on a trespass charge.

'He was discharged in the afternoon. The other officer told Jules that a woman came to meet him at the police bureau, and one of the officers thought it was Madame Janine.' I remember she had gone out during the afternoon, 'how do I ask her?' I could not believe it; I would not believe it. I was thrown in to a dilemma. Telling Jules of this I was now unsure, and I thought I was getting on very well with her. 'We will check later, all visitors to a police bureau are video recorded, we will go and view the tape later, but we have some work to do first, at the Paris factory.'

Collecting the two sample jars, I placed them into a black leather case I found on top of the refrigerator. The flasks fitted perfectly; there were other compartments capable of carrying up to ten flasks. Ten flasks would make the equivalent of a huge stock of plastic, I thought.

1 gram per 1 ton of plastic.

1-kilogram equals 1000 tons.

1 case of 10 flasks equals 10,000 tons. Now I was realising that this additive did not have to be made in vast quantities. Sliding open the cupboard I placed one of the full beakers on the scales. There was approximately one kilogram content in each beaker. Pierre could easily make six months' supply in one evening in his office. Nobody would be any the wiser and with the shipment controlled by Janine, even she would not know where Loyplas was made. It was the perfect cottage industry; no wonder sinister greedy eyes were watching.

We prepared to go to the factory, calling in on Janine to let her know where we were going. 'Are you going by car?' She asked. 'Prenez le metro.'

It was after 9:00, there was no sign of Otto so we left instructions to stick him in a taxi and send him to the factory when he arrived. 'Stick him in a Taxi?' 'Pardon, Mme please send him to the Factory when he arrives by Taxi.' 'I will do as you wish,' she replied.

'You will do as I wish, that is a statement worth reviewing later' I replied with a touch of my nose, Janine just smiled and proceeded with her work.

Claudette was giving Jules's directions to the factory. also, the name of the manager, who would be waiting for us. We left by the front door and as we walked past the entrance to the side street, I took a quick look at the garage door, it was closed.

Down the street was the Metro station, we were just about

to enter, the station when I changed my mind.

'No, we will go by taxi.' I said, a gut reaction. Jules flagged a taxi and I explained the gut reaction to him as we sped off towards the factory.

Mr Albert Jacks, was glad to see me again. He had remembered me from the head office meeting.

'I have heard of your problems, are we going to make plastic today?'

'Oui Monsuire,' Jules did most of the talking, as Mr Jacks' English was poor. We explained the two sample batches. As we proceeded to the factory floor, the rows of plastic extrusion machinery were impressive. The factory was making precision parts for electric drills, the automotive industry and the French aerospace industry. The allocated plastic extruder machine was waiting, our machine operator, Jean Pierre started the machine, the massive heated pressure screw started to turn, the molten plastic was then forced through a die ring, exiting as a tube, which made a large bubble about three meters tall. Then after the plastic was cooled, overhead rollers nipped the tube of plastic which was then fed through a series of rollers, until the plastic tube finally would be fed through a series of flat heated bag sealers and a guillotine. The plastic tube was then guillotined, while simultaneously a seam heater sealed the bottom edge. The end product a simple bag was ejected onto a waiting pallet; bag after bag followed as the machine kept running. The chosen machine was to produce basic bags and the master mix 'Otto1' was being added to aid identification, a different colour was allocated to identify the plastic later, it also assisted the operator, to the special mix was coming through the machine.

The bags we made were of a good quality, they had an oily feel to them. Albert and Jean Pierre inspected the sample bags. They were interesting and different, and could have a special use. Taking enough samples, then adding mix 'Otto2' we waited for the extruding polymer to change colour. As Loyplas was self-colouring it started to change to its silvery transparent colour.

'Très bien.' Sample bags were taken again, then Jean Pierre cleared the machine.

'Now the final test we make plastic with the original master formula,' Adding the original, we let the process repeat itself and then samples were made and duly marked accordingly to identify them. All bags were taken to the laboratory for the final test.

Mr Jacks, jotting down his report, started with,

Le method Otto 1.

On the stretch then puncture tests results were good but to a different specification, not what we were looking for. However, there were unknown properties we did not understand. Further test on this sample will certainly commence.

Le method Otto 2.

The second batch tested, superior results, passing all the tests. A huge success.'

Mr Jacks exclaimed, 'Un instant! Let us test the final samples.'

Le method original.

The third batch tests repeated. The second and third tests proved to be identical, the tests matched perfectly.

Mr Jacks enquired, 'When did we make this sample?'

'Yesterday afternoon.'

'Then it is the same, does this mean we have duplicated the secret?'

'It would appear so.'

'Thank God,' Mr Jacks cheered.

'Keep this secret please, until I can discuss this with the other members of the management.' Monsieur Jacks agreed, he was happy knowing that the factory's future was secure. Monsieur Jacks invited us to his office and we had refreshments. A lady who was serving coffees had her back to me. A slender body and shapely bottom attracted my attention,

'I have seen that bottom before.' I nearly said, 'Janine, what are you doing here?' but something stopped me. She was the same height, as she turned round, she was of a similar build, but with flatter chest and her hair colour and style were the same as Janine's. Passing the coffee, I asked her in my splendid French,

'Comment vous appelez vous?'

'Je suis Mademoiselle Maxine, le secrétariat a Monsieur Jacks' she replied.

'Merci Maxine.'

She gazed around everyone had a coffee and the cakes were on the table. She left the office, but her perfume lingered. A niggling feeling about that woman taunted me.

She came back into the office taking a seat behind me, she prepared to take notes; we discussed the work on the agenda. Jules translated for me as Mr Jacks spoke.

'With the batch 'Otto 1', we want to try other tests. New formulas are always worth looking at, we might not have the correct application for this yet.'

He confirmed that the second batch was identical to the original. Mr jacks was pleased and happy with the rediscovery, holding his finger to his lips telling everybody in the office it is still a secret, my niggling fear made me uneasy during the meeting, I stood and walked around the room taking a better position to observe Maxine carefully, she did look similar to Janine but even I could see where the similarities stopped, looking at Jules I caught his eye, I expressed through my eyes for him to look at Maxine. We had finished our work at the factory, delighted with the outcome, we returned to the head office by taxi.

Jules asked about Maxine, he had taken a good look at her, and wondered why I had brought his attention to her, it was the similarity to Janine, I expressed,

'No.' he replied, totally different,

'Ok.' I replied.

A small commotion at the Metro station attracted a crowd of onlookers; an ambulance in attendance was parked together with a police car, with their blue lights flashing. As we drove passed two medics operating a wheeled stretcher cart, a body was covered by a sheet. The taxi driver uttered, 'IL est mort'

'Look, the garage door is open, Jules; Let us enter by the garage, I want to have a look at something.'

My knee creaked as I stooped down to look at the area of the car Whittle had been interested in, but it was dark and I could not see clearly. Pulling from my pocket my bunch of keys, I had a small flashlight on the keyring. Shining the pencil thin beam into the darkness of the Monteverdi's wheel arch, I saw a shiny black thread standing out against the grey wheel arch. Slipping my hand into the wheel arch, touching the thread, I found it was slack and was laid across the top suspension link, then it disappeared behind the road wheel. 'Take a look at this,' I said, pointing to the thread. Jules said, 'Do not touch it.' Shining the flashlight through the spoked wheel I could just see the end of the thread tied round the rubber flexible brake pipe. 'If one end is connected to a brake pipe, what is the other end connected to?'

I was about to place my knee on the ground to get a better look. Jules remarked, 'Your trousers, with the dirty floor, use this.' He picked up what looked like a piece of paper, from the ground, passed it to me. It was a plastic document holder, similar to the one found in Pierre's valise. 'Where did you get this?' I asked, looking at Jules.

'It was laid on the floor.'

'Are there any more lying around?'

'I will have a look.' Jules started looking around the garage for any more plastic folders.

Pulling a tissue from my pocket I knelt on it, I managed to get a better view. I followed the thread with the light beam from the front of the car to the rear axle, the end of the cord had been wrapped around the open drive shaft in the rear suspension, 'if I drove this car in any direction, this cord would cut through the rubber brake pipe.' As we talked, I untied the end of the thread and removed it from the drive shaft then unhooked it from the front brake pipe. I checked the other brake pipes; they were clean.

'But it is only a thread,' Jules said, looking at it.

I took the thread outside to inspect it further in the sunlight. 'This is carbon fibre cord. It is like flexible steel wire; you cannot snap it; they use this product it to make racing car bodies light but incredibly strong' we decided to have a mechanic check the car as a precaution. Jules passed me another plastic sleeve.

'Where did you find it?'

'It was on the staircase, folded against a step. You would not see it if you walked down the stairs.' Folding it over, I placed it into my pocket. We now had two of these today.

We climbed the stairs to the office, looking around for anything out of the ordinary. There were scuff marks in the dust, possibly caused by Janine and myself as we had fallen.

Entering the office, we were spotted by the eagle-eyed Claudette. 'You have returned, Janine is in her office.' I asked

Claudette to have the chauffeur check out the Monteverdi
for any possible braking and safety problems. I gave her the
car keys and she replied that he would report to me when he
had finished.

I knocked lightly on Janine's door. 'Entrez' She stood up as
we entered, walking awkwardly towards us. 'Is it the
bruising?' I asked. She nodded her head.

'We have some good news. A completely new batch of
Loyplas with new properties has been made. The second
news is that Otto's batch of the formula was perfect. A
perfect match with the original; by the way, has Otto
arrived? We have not seen him at all this morning.'

Janine held her hand out, she was still in a quiet mood; taking
her hand, I asked, 'What is the matter?'

'Otto died during the night,'

'No,' stunned, I sat on the couch she sat beside me, then
explained, 'He had returned to the hotel and had dinner with
his wife; he was saying to her that he was pleased that he
had found the secret of the decade. Replicating the secret of
Pierre, he had also managed to replicate the method; the
method also had a secret.' It was too complicated for his wife
to understand or even repeat and she took little notice. Otto
was intending to put in a written report in the morning and
present it to us today.

Otto had died in his sleep. He did not complete his report.
'Did anybody observe the formula procedure in its entirety?'
Janine asked 'I did not, you entered the room just as the gas
was appearing, I did not see the final minutes.' Jules also said
that he too was distracted with the mêlée.' 'What does it
mean?' 'We might not have the complete method. I
remembered Otto saying that the method is the secret not
the formula,' Something else happened someone at the
metro station fell under the train this morning, he was

dressed in light brown jacket and dark trousers, he was killed instantly, the police think that the man was pushed, thinking it was you I called the factory and I enquired if you had arrived safely, they told me you had. Janine spoke with a renewed frailty in her voice, 'did you not see it happen,'

'No, we took a Taxi at the last minute.'

Why the concern, Janine glared at me annoyed 'what are you wearing' light brown jacket and dark trousers, so what, the same as the man who died at the metro, Shit! It could have been me.

'That is correct.' she cried, 'I was concerned.' I stood and gave her a hug, she gripped me holding on tight, 'please, don't leave me, I am frightened.'

A ringing telephone broke the silence Janine answered, listened, 'for you'.

Taking the telephone and still holding Janine close, it was Darrell, he was full of excitement, I called in the university to see the professor, our chemist was with him, he thought that I still worked for Whittle Plastics; the old Prof was getting excited that he had nearly finished, and would have the solution in a day or so.' Then I told him,

'Whittle had omitted to say that this formula kills anybody who makes it incorrectly, also there was a world patent on it.' Boy, was he upset.

'Why was I not told this before I started?' he claimed.

He immediately aborted all testing, instructing Darrell to remove the samples and paperwork from his laboratory; He was muttering, 'Your company will be invoiced for the work done.'

He then stormed out of the laboratory, leaving Darrell to remove all the samples, chemicals and polymers together with his working notes.

'I have the lot. Whittle has nothing.' Darrell claimed, 'I am travelling today to Paris bringing the items with me.'

'Have you got access to a fax?'

'Yes.' he said.

'Great, fax me all the paperwork you have now.' I gave him the personal fax number of Pierre's office.

Sitting back down, I said, 'We are so close to cracking this problem, let us make another batch.'

Janine gripped my hand. 'No, not without a chemist. There is a certain way to put it together and I do not want any more people to get hurt.'

'We were not the ones hurting people.' There was a knock on the door. Claudette entered then closed the door behind her.

'There is a Mr Harold Whittle from England to see the managers.'

'Isn't this remarkable all these events are occurring and that bastard walks into the office as if nothing has happened, what will he want this time?'

'Let us see.' Janine explained something to Claudette, giving us twenty minutes. A brief plan flashed through my mind. Hurriedly I typed away on Janine's computer a plan formulating as I typed.

Claudette returned and gave Whittle our reply, 'The managers will see you in twenty minutes, please have a seat. Would you like a coffee? Have you your business card? Please sign the visitors' book.' She opened the book and presented it to him. Whittle signed.

Claudette left to prepare the boardroom as instructed. She called into Janine's office, giving me Whittle's business card; looking at the card, staring back at me, were the letters after his name. He was a chemist; how good a chemist was the deciding factor.

I was typing quickly and another idea had come into my head. Line by line the document took shape. Janine, looking over my shoulder at it, was amazed. 'He will not do it.'

'We can but try.' I placed the finished document in my brief case. Spinning around on the swivel chair I said 'Jules cannot be seen in the office. He has met Jules before.'

'Oui, Jules after we go into the boardroom go to Pierre's office and watch us on the CCTV.' Jules agreed.

'Janine and I will meet this man, then we will play the game he knows. Let us see what he wants, but we give nothing away.' Agreeing, we prepared for the meeting in the boardroom. If we were settled and confident, we would hopefully have the upper hand.

Claudette returned to reception to find Whittle thumbing through the visitors' book, making notes from the names in it. Claudette said, 'That is private, that is not allowed,' quickly taking the book from him, she snatched the piece of paper on which Whittle had been writing the names from the book. 'Give me back the paper.' Whittle snarled. 'No,' She replied, dropping the paper into a shredding machine, destroying the information. 'Please come with me.' She ushered Mr Harold Whittle into the boardroom, showing her dislike of the man, closed the door behind him sharply. Whittle took a prominent seat at the opposing end of the boardroom table. He taking his time he surveyed the room as he settled himself; then he turned his attention to Janine and me. He erupted into his proposed evaluation of the problems Vista Plastic was experiencing. He perceived that now he and only he was in the position to assist us in surviving within the industry.

'That is very generous of you, what is your intention?' Janine asked.

He was prepared to underwrite all the company debts and supply the expertise to get us through our current problem. However, for this consideration and expertise, this was under the strictest condition that all European and Asian distribution fell under his control, final details etc, etc, could be thrashed out later.

Not much, I thought. The European and Asian markets were the primary profit-making markets. Janine requested his business plans for our perusal. He retrieved a folder from his briefcase and presented his business plan, laying it on the table. Janine thanked him graciously for his concern and interest. 'We shall consider your proposal, and shall get back to you within the coming week.' Whittle looked at Janine with a leery eye, 'Madame, please do not waste any time. The offer is for 24 hours only.' Whittle sneered

'Thank you again, we will get back to you within the specified time.' Janine replied. Whittle rose from his chair, replacing documents into his briefcase, turned, then left the room. 'That man is arrogant, discourteous, and he is a pig!' Janine retorted. The internal phone buzzed and Janine took the call. 'Max has died, without regaining consciousness.' Well, that is one crook out of the equation.

Jules joined us bringing a tray of coffee, I included him in my thoughts, if we took Whittle on board then we found out he had killed all these people what would happen under French law. 'Arrest, prosecution, and imprisonment, the company would get bad reviews in the press.' Jules replied. The company might fail with the bad publicity; it could eventually close in either of the directions we chose.'

'What would happen if we were to sell him the formula, realise the assets, then place any monies outside France, keeping information about the method secret, another secret he would have to pay for again?'

'Ross, you have a devious complex mind, but he has the formula and I bet he is chasing now for the method' Jules exclaimed. 'Whittle is preparing to steal the most valuable asset from this company. It is becoming apparent that he could well be responsible for the death of.'

'There is no hard evidence as of yet.' Jules interrupted. 'OK. We must play him along for the time being, this will give us time to see if we can duplicate the formula again, but this time we will record the events.'

Record!

Record the!

Record the bloody events!

'We have already recorded them!'

Leaping to my feet, I opened the panel concealing the video recorders, pulling the previous day's tape from the stack. I inserted the tape into slot (B) and rewound the tape, searching for the time setting of 15:00, the time Otto arrived. I pressed the button we all sat down to watch. The tape displayed Otto in reception, Claudette was asking questions. The video camera scene changed, following Otto's progress. The video machine sequence would scan around the other cameras, then return to the scene we wanted. Although missing some of the process, the view we wanted came back. As the liquid was changing colour, the image was clear enough to see details we required. The scene lasted long enough to observe the arrival of Janine and my spontaneous actions to get her away from the gas. The camera shots changed every 15 seconds, following us to the staircase, Janine was attentive; watching her recovery. She watched intently as the image of her showed the reality of how close she came to disaster, even my quick action of catching Janine was by my fingertips, I had nearly missed. Then the scene changed back to Otto. He had clearly finished the gassing part of the method and was continuing with the next part and the addition of the 12th compound. The switching scenes gave everybody an update on the situations around the office, finally arriving back in the main office to show Otto holding up the beaker, shouting, 'Eureka! I have made it.'

There was still part of the method missing. With the scenes changing, the final parts were in no doubt. The odds of trying every sequence until we produced the perfect product would take time, but this could be achieved, as we were now down to the last 9 additives. So, the equation was 81 tries to get the formula correct, we were in a far better situation than Whittle. Janine brought my attention to a slight error in the calculation it was not 81, it was $9 \times 8 \times 7 \times 6 \times 5 \times 4 \times 3 \times 2 = 362,880.00$, even if you did 10 formula variations a day, it would take over 1500 days to complete, we do not have that time. I was so sure that I had this in my grasp, I felt deflated, feeling as if the wind had been knocked from me, I sat watching the tape, it was still displaying scenes around the office; the distressing scenes of the doctor, nurse and Claudette attending to Janine and myself; I switched the tape off, not wishing to see the grim scenes again.

Although something in that recording was very obvious, but we could not see it. We persevered making notes of the assembly always it stopped at the critical time. It is a shame the sequences were not that little bit longer as it would possibly have shown the entire mixing from start to finish.

'Remember we have serious business today,' Janine remarked. I had not forgotten, but my mind was disturbed from the normal train of thoughts; Pierre's family required payment, although Max was history, he was still a problem, and the odd bank or two, my U.K. businesses, and Elaine, I must call her, and Whittle what a pain in the backside plus the long-suffering wholesalers, all waiting for a decision, pressure, loads of pressure, and I came for a holiday. Now because of Max and Whittle tampering there were many copies of the formula in existence, an urgent factor was, others were now trying the first with the product would recover the market again.

I seem to be sitting on a drifting ship with no forward motion, we were paying people and they were waiting for us to make decisions, Otto had already made the formula once, it will happen again soon I was sure, our office staff were watching us, all worried about their security, bad news and rumours travel fast in the office environment. I suggested to Janine a delaying tactic it would remove undue pressure and restore confidence, the sales team would launch a promotion for Loyplas, call the wholesalers, accept any advance order for Loyplas, this would ensure confidence that we were in production again. The word would quickly discourage the opposition and deter opportunists. She was delighted with the out of character marketing ploy and called the sales manager to issue new sales targets for the coming days.

An unexpected visit from one of our bank managers threw us into a spin, we graciously received them in an impromptu meeting letting the news of the sales promotion slip out, one minded person is always suckered, they took the bait, and congratulated us on our discovery. Janine made a strange suggestion, we could forget to contact Pierre's family for a week or two, they were not poor, and do not need the money, they could wait. After an hour we had removed the immediate problems, finally one more thing to do.

I called Elaine. Some kind person had telephoned her telling her of my lurid affairs in France, and exactly who with, when and where. She did not want to believe him, but she knew it might be true, and it had upset her. She was disappointed with me, and was leaving me while she reconsidered.

'I could do without this extra pressure at the moment,' I replied, but she was adamant; she droned on and on, while I listened, I was absentminded searching around in my pockets; I found the fibre cord I had removed from the car earlier, it was black, soft and silky knowing of its great strength. I tried to prove it wrong, bad idea; the cord cut into the skin on the edge of my palm. 'You have done it again, you are not listening, and you are too easily distracted.'

'I told you I cannot deal with this problem at the moment.' She slammed the telephone down, holding the receiver in my hand for a moment the silence was pleasing, in reflection I suppose that's the end of that episode.

I wrapped the cord around my fingers making a small ball, I put it back into my pocket. I went to see Claudette for a plaster to stop me bleeding on the carpet again, she made such a commotion for such a little cut, first she had to tell Janine, then disinfect the cut, then dry and carefully place the plaster in the correct direction, so it would give maximum protection. If I had a hanky, I would have wrapped my hanky around my hand until it stopped bleeding. Janine fussed and made me a coffee to steady my nerves; it is only a small cut, I cried, Janine replied it was only a cut from madam guillotine but look what happened.

The plastic folders that Jules had found I compared with the one in my briefcase, they were identical three of these had been at the same place where serious accidents had happened, I noticed a speck of dark red on one, it was dried blood, could it be mine or Janine's.

'Jules, I wonder which airport Whittle used, I would like to see this aeroplane that gets him around so quickly; I have an idea.'

Jules made some enquiries, 'Voila, it is at Beynes Thiveral a small airfield nearby, only fifteen minutes on the Metro.'

'Let us go, I would like to see it in daylight.'

We told Claudette our plans. She would inform Janine of our

itinerary; she passed me a small envelope containing two rusty steel nails about 4 cm long. I looked at Claudette mystified, the chauffeur had found them under the front tyre, one at the front and one at the back, a puncture in any direction. Had I driven down the road with punctured tyre, and a cut brake pipe, the resulting accident could have been nasty. Was this another little present from Whittle?

I certainly knew of a place on his anatomy, I would love to stick these.

The short train journey was uneventful, but I was treated to seeing Paris from another view when we emerged from the tunnels, Beynes Thiveral airfield was across the road from the metro station, Jules made some enquiries and found Whittle's aeroplane.

It was a twin engine, Navajo Chieftain, a magnificent piece of machinery; I would love to own something like this.' Looking inside it could seat eight people it was compact inside I could see a laptop computer together with a small printer laid on a dividing side table. Other items required to print documents were laid around, plastic sleeves, lots of them, Whittle had enough office equipment on board to make any paperwork he desired upon demand, I was getting a feeling this man acted upon instinct, and he was flying by the seat of his pants. Jules had seen enough evidence in the aeroplane Whittle must remain in France; he would go to the officer in air traffic control and get take off permission for this aircraft revoked. With Jules gone, I tried to gain entry by the rear door but it was locked. However, the emergency exit door was not, keeping low I opened the door, giving me enough space to grab hold of some plastic sleeves.

I couldn't reach the laptop on the table but I saw another laptop computer by the side of the exit seat, I recognised it as Pierre's broken one, the laptop he paid a fortune for at the auction. I decided to borrow the laptop, after all, if we're going to become business colleagues, he could help me collate the pieces of this fantastic jigsaw.

Holding the laptop inside my jacket, I walked back to the main building, handing the plastic sleeves to Jules. 'Our man has the same plastic sleeves as the ones found on the stairs.'

'Portraying a scenario for Jules to contemplate: Whittle placed these sleeves on the stairs, both Pierre and Janine have slipped on them, they were on the stairs again this morning we could have slipped on them going into the office this morning.'

'Slipped on the plastic sheets?' Jules scoffed with disbelief. 'Try standing on one.' Jules stood on the plastic sleeve, 'I am here nothing happened.'

Rethinking, I was so sure it would work. The as Jules stepped off the plastic, he collapsed to the floor, as I helped Jules to his feet,

he said, 'They are dangerous, somebody could get hurt.' The statement had just cleared his lips, when he realised, 'This could be the proof that we need, certainly enough to bring him in for questioning,

An idea was forming in my mind, I ran back to the aeroplane; fishing the carbon fibre cord from my pocket, I eased myself into the undercarriage cavity behind the landing wheels. I attached one end to an undercarriage bracket, bringing the cord through the undercarriage strut then securing the other end to the main ignition lead on the port engine.

If Whittle made any attempt to take off the carbon cord would tighten then simply pull out the main ignition lead from the magneto, then causing the engine to stop.

Walking around the front of the aeroplane, the sleeves kept sliding out from my pocket; keeping one, I stuffed the remaining ones into an air vent on the starboard engine.

I met up with Jules as I walked back. 'Air traffic has been told. They gave me this list, all the dates that Whittle has visited France in the last six months are listed here.' Cross checking the dates confirmed that Whittle was the pilot when his aeroplane landed in France, He was also here on the fateful day Pierre Saar died. He had logged a flight plan from my local airport to Paris on the same day that my house had been burgled; all the pieces were falling into place, we took the next train back to Paris. During a scheduled stop the inbound train was taking on passengers when an outbound train stopped next to us. Jules told me to look into the other carriage without making it obvious, Whittle is sitting with Janine in that carriage Cautiously looking in disbelief, I saw Whittle but not Janine. She looked very like Janine; it was Maxine, Mr Jacks' secretary.

Jules looked again, I can see the similarity now, you were very observant at the Factory.

I muttered, 'The plot thickens.' Jules requested an explanation of Plot and why it thickened. 'The connection is complete, let us get him now.' Jules whispered. 'I would prefer if we leave him alone for now; we shall call him tonight to tell him that we are ready to negotiate in the morning. That should keep him in Paris and give you time to check that video in the Police office.'

'How did this woman get hold of the secrets from Pierre?' Jules asked.

'How does any woman get secrets from a man?' Jules did not understand. After another brief explanation Jules fully understood, I wondered what these people did for excitement in the village at night, although I knew of what one woman liked doing, 'You are a man of experience,' Jules said.

'No, a man who has experienced,' I replied, 'and do not ask

me to explain.' The trains departed towards their respective destinations.

'I have a good feeling about tonight; I think we will succeed at the first attempt of remaking the formula.' 'Confidence, I like that,' Jules said.

Janine was still working as we arrived back. 'What have you two been up to?' 'We have positive evidence of the leak in the office; before I can tell you of its Jules is going to the police bureau to check out a video with a friendly gendarme.' 'Bonne chance!' Janine replied. 'We could do with some,' Jules responded. 'I am going to check the fax machine; I am expecting some details from England.'

I put the borrowed laptop onto Pierre's desk, there were a pile of documents waiting in the fax machine. Sitting down, I started to read through them, Darrell had included a written list of the documents he had sent. The professor's report was detailed and interesting, the report gave me an insight into the formula and how it worked; reading through the test report showed the tests that had been carried out.

This professor was very cautious, I think he as well as the late Otto, had an inclination, of a gas problem. By following the professor's detailed report, together with the snippets of the videotape, I reckoned to have a good chance in producing a finished product. After reading and digesting the contents of the documents, the thought of calling this professor to ask for his help were not dismissed, what other problems lay waiting, in the final closing minutes of method and formula.

Glancing at the wall I saw the video camera, a wild thought sprang to mind, manufacturers are intelligent and clever, they employ intelligent engineers. With over ninety percent of people not reading instruction books, they often miss the extra facilities that machines are capable of. Pierre was fascinated with photography and gadgets, if each camera

records all the time the timing sequence is only for a single multi-screen monitor. Each individual camera might record events in their entirety; the trickery is controlled by the recorder electronics. What if there was a facility on the video recorder to watch one camera, regardless of what was recorded on the tape. Searching the video recorder cupboard, I found the instruction book for the:
Compact covert Tele vision & multi track video recorder.

Operating instructions.
Menu.
English version page 12,
Turning to page 12, I eagerly read the instructions. The options I thought of, were available. This meant that as there were four cameras, there would be four tracks. Consulting the instructions I checked the settings on the recorder, referring to the manual, to replay the single track. I adjusted the video to play any track from any tape.
I didn't want to damage any of the tapes so I set the video to 'observe'.
A numerical pad was set into the front panel of the recorder it seemed complex, but following the hand book there was a mention of a remote control, it was laid by the side of the recorder, step by step using the remote control it was so simple, pressing the # & 0 button, the four images were displayed.
Pressing the # & 1 button, the No. 1 camera image displayed a full screen.
Pressing the # & 2 button, the No. 2 camera image displayed a full screen. I browsed through the camera's images.
Pressing the zoom button, I found that you could zoom in on the picture, Wow! What fun could be had.
A volume knob located on the front panel indicated that the

video had recorded the sound track as well. By increasing the volume, I could hear what was going on in each room.

Taking the tape from last Thursday from Pierre's desk, I loaded the tape and advanced to the time when Janine and I were talking in her office. I pressed the correct camera button and the full screen appeared. By increasing the volume, I could hear myself and Janine discussing matters. My voice sounded terrible, the coming events I knew would become passionate, I watched the scene; it was stimulating using the zoom, you could get a close up if you wished. It was getting me excited. A knock on the door brought me back to reality. I reduced the volume control, closed the door. 'Come in.' I called out, No reply, 'Entrez!' Claudette came in. 'I thought I heard two voices.'

'No, telephone I waved my mobile.'

'Ah, oui, coffee?'

'Oui Claudette.'

Opening the cupboard door after she had left; I removed the tape cassette and returned it to my hiding place in Pierre's office.

I inserted the tape marked for Monday, selecting the time and the correct camera scene. I watched Otto prepare the formula in its entirety then rewound the tape and watched it again. I now had two formula and methods, on video. Removing the tape from the machine I put it with the other private one.

As a gut reaction I removed the video tapes from the desk and hid them with the other tape. The secret was discovered and finally safe. Only I had the location, I quickly wrote down what I had done and where the videotapes could be found, I faxed the letter to the secretary in my office in England, saying I would see her soon and to keep this paper safe. I shredded the paper before going into the reception for coffee and cake. I telephoned Janine's office. She answered.

'I want to make love to you now on Pierre's desk.' I said, I could hear her gasp slightly. 'Oh, err, you have a visitor.' Darrell was in reception.

'Hello, have you been waiting long?'

'Just arrived, Claudette is getting me a coffee.' She returned, and had already anticipated my thoughts, thrusting the cup in my hand. Janine came from her office.

'Have you met Darrell?'

'Just briefly,' Janine replied. 'I have it,' I whispered to Janine.

'What do you have?'

'The formula and methods.'

'How?'

'I will tell you later, but it is safe and secure.' Unseen by anybody Janine stroked my back, sticking her nails into my flesh just enough to distract my thoughts.

'Later.'

'A lot is going to happen later,' she said.

'Follow me,' I said to Darrell, 'come into the Lion's Den.' I sat him down in Pierre's office and Janine still taking her walking carefully joined us for the impromptu discussion.

'Darrell, what is this game about with Whittle and his world domination theory?' Darrell virtually spilt the beans he told me more about this man and some of the shady deals he had done in the past.

'Does he have a wife in England?'

'Yes, and four children, she is an American.'

'Are they happy?'

'No. She is suing him for a divorce.'

'Ouch, settlement costs in America are huge, serves the bugger right.' Darrell continued to say, 'Do you know he has a French girlfriend who works for our company in Paris? I think I have seen her at EXPO in Germany. He has known her since the last EXPO, with her working for the main opposition, the attraction was even greater.' Darrell added I thought it was this lady when I talked with you the other day but now that I see her close to, she looks similar.

Janine had listened to our discussion, she raised an eyebrow when Darrell referred to the other day, and including her as friendly with Whittle, 'The only female person who went to the EXPO was Maxine, and she has dark hair,' 'It would appear you have dark hair too.' I said quietly. 'Did Maxine have a relationship with Pierre?'

'Maxine did try to get close to Pierre three months ago, she was very attentive,' Janine replied. 'Pierre once remarked that if a woman was suddenly heavily attracted to him, he would play her along to see what it was, the woman wanted, and enjoy any favours offered.'

Janine flashed her eyes at me, and changing the subject, said, 'The business plan that Whittle has put to us is all in his favour, he will give us nothing and take everything.'

Darrell commented, 'That's Whittle: take all, give nought back.' Inspecting the areas Janine had ringed with pencil, I checked the figures. Janine was correct; the plastic folder still held some other paperwork from Whittle, and one sheet of paper was inside a plastic sleeve, immediately I looked for the manufacturer's mark. It was the same, as the three I had in my brief case in the office. I passed the plastic sleeve to Darrell I asked, 'Do you recognise this?'

'Yes, I made these personally as a costing exercise, it proved too expensive to produce in England, so we got prices from Taiwan. Certainly, no more than 500 made, most were used in the head office, I think Mr Whittle may have a packet of them, we also had to recall them out of the office, they were dangerous.'

'Oh, In what way?'

'One of the office girls slipped on one. As she fell, she cracked a vertebra in her spine, she has been off work for months and has lodged a huge insurance claim against Whittle Plastics. She stands a good chance of an out of court settlement.'

Another piece of the jigsaw clicked into place, 'Got him, bloody got him', not wishing to alert Darrell to my elation, I kept quiet, Janine sensed I had made an important find; spoke directly to Darrell 'We will of course put you in a hotel for the duration of your stay, are you on your own or did you bring your wife?', 'No Darrell replied I came on my own, my wife does not like travelling,'

'Janine and I will be busy tonight, we have lots to do but I want to see you about 08:00,'

Janine conferred with Whittle over the telephone, He accepted our invitation to the meeting at 10:30, and to finalise the details.

The trap was nearly set. Jules arrived back, confirming that the woman in the video who met Whittle at the police bureau was Maxine, she was also niece to Max, he filled in the latest details, and Jules intended to arrest Whittle immediately.

'Who is Jules?' demanded Janine.

'May I introduce to you Jules Cabot; he is a friend and a gendarme I met in Laroche. He was the only man I could trust, because he had no connection with anybody. He was also very handy if I needed a man for translation or a bodyguard, Jules is the man. 'I made another plea to halt the arrest warrant destined for Whittle; we want something from this man, if you arrest him, we will not get it.' Jules listened intently to my plan. 'Jules unsure about my intentions, but I have never been wrong, said he would go back to the police bureau and would return early in the morning with some plain clothes officers.

Claudette had arranged a hotel for Darrell to stay, 'Keep a low-profile old chum while old Whittle is around.' Janine asked Claudette to show Darrell the hotel and make sure he was settled; as they left Darrell said, 'Bye for now, toodle pip.'

Janine asked Claudette to lock the office as she left, we would let ourselves out later.

'Janine, can I make Pierre's office, Ross's office? Of course, it is yours.'

'Thank you.' I stood went out of the room then re-entered, I took my seat on the edge of the desk in my new office.

Janine also left the room, then a discreet knock on the door. 'Entrez.' I called, 'Mr Ross do I have to knock on your door to come in?' Janine enquired, standing halfway through the door, 'No of course not, you are welcome anytime, please come in.'

Entering the office, she said with a mischievous look, 'You will not need a bodyguard from me. What is the meaning 'toodle pip'?' 'It is only a local English saying,'

Janine was carrying a paper bag containing some sandwiches. 'We have not eaten today, so I got you something,' 'how are your bruises?'

'They are better, easing slightly, but still painful.' She put the sandwiches on the desk and saw the laptop computer on the desk.

'Where did you get that laptop?'

'It was in Whittles plane.'

'That was Pierre's last laptop computer; he only had it for a couple of weeks, before it stopped working. He was disappointed that he had lost so much work. The engineer said it was not repairable.

He took it home to have a look at it himself the weekend he,'

Janine sighed, 'Died.'
I said quietly. 'You loved him very much.'
'Yes, I did, but now he has gone, life will go on.'
'What was it you said you had found earlier?'
'Oh yes! I want to show you something.' As I retrieved one of the videotapes, Janine questioned why I had hidden it.
'For security reasons one of the tapes has the formula and method on it,' Placing the tape in the machine I played the tape of our little episode. The entire love making session was displayed. She asked, 'How did you do that?'
'I took hold of this lady, lifted her dress,
'No, I do not mean what we did, the tape complete viewing scenes.'
'Simple, I read the instruction book and pressed a couple of buttons.'
Turning the volume up, we watched in amazement as the recording showed Otto as he progressed through the formula then the method as if he was demonstrating to an audience. He picked up the chemicals one by one, giving their name and exact weight, systematically, he continued until the method was finished, whilst Janine was watching I listened to the tape. Taking the laptop, I tried switching it on, nothing, maybe the battery was flat. Turning it over, I found and removed the battery, inside the battery compartment was a small flap, prising it down the computer hard disk slipped out from its tray.
I removed the tray and replaced the hard disk into its correct position, in the previous search we had found some tools and a voltmeter, using it I checked the battery, there was voltage but it was very low. A battery charger found in the same drawer proved to be the correct one to charge the laptop. I replaced the battery and connecting the power supply, a flashing green neon showed that the battery was on charge; I

pushed the switch to start, the laptop emitted a strange series of bleeps the screen flashed on then off, but as I listened to the it, it continued to start up, If the screen is broken, I could simply plug it into a monitor. Quickly I removed the monitor lead of the desktop computer, and connected it to the laptop. And as they say in France "Voila," the monitor displayed the information.

Janine, who had finished watching, the CCTV, came over to see what I was doing; she was astonished that the little computer was working. 'But how?'

I explained that the computer hard drive had jumped out of its socket and the screen was possibly broken. I think it had been dropped, the computer repairman was correct; it would be cheaper to replace the entire laptop rather than try to repair the old one, but that was no excuse for not offering to try and copy the information from this broken one to a new one.

Pierre had only lost a couple of weeks' work and his old laptop was still working. He could remember what work he had done in his own memory would have been easy for him to continue on his old machine.

Janine, opening the paper bag, passed me one of the sandwiches; we ate while reading the letters stored on the laptop. A few documents were not on the other machine, one called jan5.doc was for Janine, it asked for the password, which I entered then the second password.

The document flashed on the screen. Written in French; Janine read and translated the document. She decided to sit on my lap while she read the letter; it was a private letter from Pierre to Janine but did give a clue to the whereabouts of a video that she should find and watch. The video had 'Janine 1996 08 29,' printed on the label. We looked at other letters but nothing sinister. Another letter confirmed our now suspicions of Max, Pierre had also the same conclusions and also the connection of Maxine and Max.

The Max Whittle connection, plus more info and dirty tricks were listed. There was a letter to his father giving details of a last Will and testimony, That Will and testimony had so far not been found and the name of the solicitor who held the Will.

'How are your bruises?'

'You tell me.' Janine stood up, going to the window. She closed the blinds; then slipped her blouse from her shoulders. 'They look sore.'

'They look worse than they are.' She slipped off her trousers lifted her bandaged leg onto the desk, I slowly unwrapped the bandage the bruising still prominent and swelling around her ankle made the skin shine, taking some of the special cream I smoothed into her ankle and lower leg slowly massaging the rear of her calf muscle she seem to melt, 'are you alright' I asked, 'that massage is so nice I am feeling helpless, she helped me remove my shirt and she applied the cream around my shoulder and wrist smoothing and the cooling cream into my skin, we inspected each other's body and applied cream to any bruise showing or starting to show, standing up she made her way slowly and in some discomfort to were the hidden switch was, she pressed the switch making the bed slide quietly from the wall, and she then went to the drinks cabinet and poured some of the Absinthe green liquid into two glasses, pouring in some ice cold water and dropping in a sugar cube giving the drinks a quick whisk she offered me a glass. I remarked 'This looks interesting.' taking the glass from Janine and tasting a small sip. It tasted of medicine,

'Is this special?'

'Yes,' Janine replied. 'Like you.'

'If you say so.' I dimmed the lights, came and sat on the bed. 'Show me that video again.'

'The video or real thing?'

'Ladies' prerogative,' I replied. She pushed a button on the remote control switching the video recorder off.

Chapter 13

Sitting up in bed, I reviewed over the pending activities, a cough from behind me brought my attention to beautiful naked lady reclining on a comfortable bed, in my office in Paris.

'Would you get me a drink of water please?' I returned with the glass full for her; she had a couple of pills in her hand.

'What are those?'

'Pain killers for my aches,'

'I could do with two pills; my wrist and shoulder are still painful from the accident.'

'We should be getting dressed, we have a busy day and I could really eat something.' I only had a sandwich to eat yesterday evening, Janine, pulling me onto the bed, whispered, 'You can breakfast in twenty minutes, after a correct morning stretch.' Janine and I exercised what she wanted to stretch before a refreshing shower, I helped myself to another clean shirt from the stock I had in my office.

I had a good feeling about today. It was a good feeling yesterday, but today's feeling felt better. Janine had disappeared to obtain some items for breakfast. I discovered the coffee machine and made a fresh jug, her shopping trip produced fresh croissants and a 'pain au chocolate,' We ate breakfast,

'You know,'

'We do not need Whittle now; I hope that Jules and his men are close, so they can arrest him, I do not wish to meet him again.' Said Janine, in a cold voice.

Jules arrived with two colleagues from the serious crime bureau. It has been decided to give Mr Whittle a loose rein until after your meeting; we shall then arrest him so he could assist us with our enquiries.

'I wondered if I could get Whittle to admit anything or make him mad enough to start his little tricks.'

'A moment, I forgot something.' Janine went back into my office then returned, as she passed, whispered, 'CCTV.' I winked at her. She opened her eyes wide for a moment. 'Later.' she whispered.

Darrell appeared in reception I waved him to come to the boardroom offering him a seat I asked him 'Whittle, what does he really like?

What item would he really go out on a limb to get?' and what does he hate?

'Power, secrets, and something new,' Darrell replied, 'He hates, being caught out, if he missed something, in fact he acts like a spoilt child sometimes if he cannot get his way.'

'What are you going to do?' Darrell enquired.

'I do not know, I have an idea, but it will come in the final seconds, but the most important thing is, I want you out of the way before Whittle arrives, for the meeting at 10:30'

'I am out of here.' Darrell said, calling Claudette into the office, I asked will you take Darrell for a tour of Paris and show him some interesting places, my expense, please go now, and I do not want to see either of you before tonight at 20:30 at Gee Patron's for dinner.' Taking some money from my wallet, I passed to Darrell, I said, 'Go down the back stairs and look out for any plastic sleeves on the stairs. Do not, under any circumstances come back here regardless of what you hear or see, if you get bored, give her one.' I mentioned, jokingly.

Claudette overheard the last instruction, and as they left, I could hear her ask 'What is the meaning of 'give her one? One what? Darrell could explain that phrase.

Explaining the intention of this meeting to Jules, I suggested

that one of your colleagues replaces Claudette on the reception desk during the time Whittle is here.'
'Of course, he would be able to cover the front door, and stop him escaping,'
'Whittle, Janine, and I shall be the only ones in the meeting. With an officer in reception, you and the other can stay in my office watching on the monitor. Then if things get out of hand you can assist quickly.'
I sat at the computer typing amendments to the original proposal; it included a counter offer, a backup strategy I intended to throw at Whittle.
Janine watched as I typed. 'It is in English.'
'I don't care, Whittle and I are English, you can read and understand the document.'
'I think he will not go for those terms; I certainly would not sign it.' Janine departed to answer another enquiry, I finished the documents, printing two copies of each of the two versions, I placed them into my brief case.
Whittle arrived early, he swaggered his way into reception, informing the new receptionist that he was here for a meeting at 10:15. 'Oui Monsieur, please have a seat and I will inform Madame Janine of your arrival.' Leaving Whittle for a minute, the receptionist officer entered my office and announced that Mr Whittle was here for his appointment; Jules said look at the CCTV monitor Whittle had left reception and was looking into Janine's office, Janine rattled off a rapid reply and the officer returned to reception.
Janine picked up her bag refreshed her make up, stood smoothing down her blouse and skirt, picked her valise, took a deep breath letting it slowly exhale, 'I am ready,' I kissed her lightly on her cheek, sliding my hand over her bottom, 'Trust me, let's do it,' we both proceeded to the boardroom.
My heart was thumping with uncertainty for the coming

meeting. Janine sat, while I preferred to stand. Mr Harold Whittle made his entrance into the boardroom. He decided not to be seated, but to stand at the other end of the room pacing up and down, looking at us and waiting for our input. I approached him, gesturing to shake his hand. He accepted, I wish he hadn't his handshake was limp cold and sweaty, not wishing to dry my hand on my trousers, I found my hanky making a display of wiping my nose from an impending sneeze I managed to dry my hand.

'Please be seated and we can continue.'

'No, have you decided to accept the offer?' Whittle replied bypassing what I considered standard methods of negotiation, he stepped into my territory.

'To begin with, how do you intending paying us for the transfer of this trade secret to you officially?

This shall be a consideration, and will be a private matter between the three of us.' Whittle was shaken, he did not, expect to pay a consideration, he thought he had won.

'I know you do not want the Monteverdi, just the hidden secret. That item has been removed. I believe this is what you were searching for.' I said, removing the bearer bond share certificate from my case, flicking it with my finger I purposely made the light reflect from it into Whittle's eyes. The look of greed in his eyes was evident he wanted this item at all costs

'100,000.' Whittle opened.

'Bugger off.' I replied. 'Do not insult me with that kind of offer. If you want control of this secret, you will have to increase the offer.'

'How about a Million?'

'Dollars.' Whittle Snorted,

'Sterling.'

'No chance.' Whittle replied,

'£250,000.'

'£800,000.' I replied.

'£500,000.' Whittle said. 'Final offer.'

'£500,000 plus' I replied,

'Plus, what?' he replied

'I will accept the sum of £500,000 and to clinch the deal include the keys and title for your aeroplane,

Now, how would Sir like to pay that?'

'You cannot have the aeroplane it belongs to the company.

Worth a try I thought

'I will pay Now,' he replied. 'I have £200,000 in cash and $350,000 in traveller's cheques.'

'Are they American Express?'

'Suppose that will do fucking nicely.' Whittle sneered,

'As the advert says.'

'Upon full payment we have a deal.' I replied quietly, turning my head in Janine's direction I winked at her. We will accept the consideration.' Janine confirmed.

Whittle, throwing his briefcase on the table, opened it, then he removed two large envelopes, I moved closer to him as he placed the envelopes onto the table, passing them to me.

I opened one. Looking in it, I saw and counted 25 sealed packets of £10,000 in £50 notes to the total value of £250,000. In the other there were seven books of Express traveller's checks with a value of $350.000, giving a total approx. value of £500,000. Sealing the envelopes, I placed them in the centre of the table, walking back to where Janine was sitting. Her facial expression was intent on observing the transaction.

I opened my case taking out the pre prepared document upon which I had typed the full formula. I had also the added the merger plan giving us the same interest in his company. I had added the usual small print on the bottom and following paper.

The Vista Plastic Company.
Paris, France.
We, the undersigned Managers and Directors, accept the proposed merger with:
The Whittle Plastic Ltd England.
And,
The Vista Plastic Company France.

For Vista Plastic.
Managing Director: Ross Todd.
Director & Secretary: Janine Bouillon.

For Whittle Plastic Ltd.
Proprietor & Managing Director: Harold Whittle.

In signing of this document, all pre agreed terms are binding. Vista Plastic directors will be entitled and gain equal managerial positions within Whittle Plastic ltd.
In the event any company failure or directors demise the surviving company and directors will assume control.
Any misrepresentation of any act or facts will be deemed a criminal action against the company and this agreement will be null and void.
General rules of merger apply plus I included lots of minor regulations, which if we wanted, we could make Whittle run around for ages.

Whittle spluttered, 'I am not signing that.'
'Mr Whittle, sir, if you do not sign, you do not get the formula.

Also, your university professor in England cannot crack it, so you are stuck with us.'

Whittle scanned through the document repeatedly then he must have seen a way out of his dilemma, relented, and reluctantly signed. Inspecting his signature, I signed, giving the document to Janine. 'Sign there please.'

She read the document. 'No, I will not sign.'

'Please, sign.' I said sternly, winking at her again.

'Under protest, I sign.' Janine replied solemnly

I had made two copies of the agreement, each party to retain a copy for their records.

I checked the documents. Both were signed and dated correctly. Nothing could stop any official body not recognising these as a legal document.

I walked to the end of the table where Whittle was now sitting, on what would have been the chairman's position. Graciously I presented him with a copy of the agreement; Whittle checked the details again. He bent down and retrieved a document from his briefcase. Can I now have sight of the formula; I laid the formula in front of him, He slowly checked the listing of values and calculations, with one he had in his care, raising an eyebrow. 'They are the same.'

'My copy is slightly different,' Whittle rescanned the figures then he saw the change.

Picking up the two envelopes containing the consideration, I placed them in to a drawer at the end of the boardroom table. Locking the drawer, I gave the key to Janine.

Whittle, producing a packet of cigarettes, proceeded to light one, blowing the smoke in my direction.

He followed this act of defiance by placing one of his feet on the boardroom table, displaying a totally cavalier attitude. Now it would seem that he was in control, he sat looking at us with a smug look on his face. Whittle asked, 'With reference to the formula, has anybody else seen it?' 'Only Madam Janine and I, my assistant and the manager at the Paris factory saw the finished product.'

Gloating he replied 'I know all about it, you also made batches of the main formula and it was perfect.'

I replied 'That is very remarkable, how did you know?'

'I have my contacts and informants everywhere, but now I have access to both the formulas as well. You think you are both very clever,' boasted Whittle.

'I beg your pardon what do you mean?'

'I bet this lady does not know about your relationship with that tart Jacqueline in the hotel at Laroche.'

'I even bet your wife does not know about you and these women.'

'My wife? Mr Whittle, I am not married.' I remarked quietly and a muffled gasp came from behind. I did not turn. Whittle had now threatened blackmail. 'What if photographs appeared at a certain address at the wrong time, you would be finished.'

Whittle had played his hand, and was waiting for a reply.

He was playing me at an old sales technique; make your sales statement or play, then do nothing, be quiet and the first to speak has lost. I coldly looked at him, not wanting to give him the pleasure of my unease. He was correct, I did have a problem, but so did he: an American wife and four children with separation settlement costs would cripple him. He had more to lose than anybody around this table.

We glared at each other, although it was seconds, it seemed as if an hour had passed. I could hear Janine moving in her chair, if she spoke, we would have lost. I casually slid my hand as if to scratch my scalp, crossing my fingers behind my head. Janine saw the signal and stopped moving.

Finally, Whittle blurted, 'Show me the laboratory in this building?'

'Sorry I cannot,'

'Why not?'

'There is no laboratory here,'

'I don't believe you.' Whittle snorted.

'What would you like to do now, Lunch on me?' I enquired.

'I would dismiss the both of you,' he sneered, 'but you have both made sure that you have jobs as directors, though I can rectify that later.'

'I intend to ship the entire contents of this office and the Paris factory to my factory in England; I will tear it apart, making sure that you have nothing left.'

Changing the subject, I said, 'Remember the auction we were both at?'

'Yes,' He replied.

'I am curious why you paid a huge amount for a broken laptop?'

'I knew it was Pierre's and he had all the latest information and data on it. The bloody thing was broken and it did not work! You had the other, I knew that you had the same information and were still stuck.'

'This information, did it come from Max?'

'Yes, the unlucky sod died before he had finished and you had taken the computer back to France and,'

Whittle stopped mid-sentence, 'What's your game?' I ignored his question.

'Ever seen these?' I asked, removing a plastic sleeve from my inside pocket I placed it on the desk in front of him.

'It's just a plastic sleeve, what's that got to do with anything?'

'Quite a lot actually. That specific folder is one of your personal document sleeves, made in your factory in Manchester. It was one of those that caused Pierre Saar to slip and fall to his death;'

'You can get those bloody things anywhere, there are millions of them, you can't blame me for Sarr's death!' Whittle cried out,

'Wrong! I have indisputable evidence on these particular items.' Whittle was showing a concerned expression. 'The first one was found at the foot of the stairs in the garage, just after Pierre Saar died. The second one was found in a similar place again at the foot of the stairs; after Madame Janine and I nearly fell down the same stairs. Luckily, she survived and is here today. The third we found placed on the stairs after we had checked them clean. The fourth we have been given to us by you personally, with your Business Plan inserted. This one the fifth I took from your aeroplane which is now standing at Beynes Thiveral airfield in the south west of Paris. The sleeves all bear identical manufacturer's production marks, the date stamps are from the same batch; and finally, these marks are the property of the Whittle Plastic Ltd, in England.

Only 500 samples were made, they were hand made by your Ex-technician manager Darrell, who until recently was in your employment.

I am also informed that a spinal injury claim against Whittle Plastic is in progress. The full facts are long winded but I surmise that the poor office girl slipped on one of these sleeves. I surmise this and your twisted mind gave you the idea of how to hurt people.' Whittle was now white with rage, squirming in his seat.

'Do you have a problem?' I asked.

'No,' 'Then I will continue.'

'Harold Whittle. I put it to you that you dropped or placed one of these document folders on the stairs, knowingly that anybody, stepping on this plastic sleeve would cause them to slip and possibly cause them serious damage. As a result, Pierre Saar died.

I also put it to you that you placed another document folder on the stairs the other day, hoping to achieve similar results.

I also put it to you are personally responsible for setting fire to my Legend motor vehicle, burglarising my house and killing my little dog.'

'I did not!' Whittle leaping to his feet.

'Sit down, Whittle or I will give you another one of what I gave you at Laroche, no policeman will stop me this time.' Whittle slumped back into the seat looking dejected. Now I had the little shit where I wanted.

'The other day you interfered with the Monteverdi, wrapping carbon fibre cord around a brake pipe and drive shaft, placing these rusty nails in front of the tyres hoping to do anyone driving in the car actual bodily harm. I consider that you are crook, a murderer and saboteur.'

'You have no proof,' Whittle spluttered.

'When you leave here you will be detained by the Paris Police who are waiting in reception to interview you in connection with the death of Pierre Saar.'

Whittle snapped back at me, 'How did you work that out? Nobody saw me, there was nobody around.' I pointed to a small video camera in the corner of the room behind him. He spun round to see.

'As you are obviously unaware, your presence in the acts was recorded on the office CCTV system.' At that precise moment, a mobile telephone began ringing. Whittle pulled a telephone from his pocket, placing it to his ear. He listened for a second then slammed the mobile down on the table.

Janine sprang to her feet, and cried out 'That is Pierre's mobile telephone, how did you get it?'

'I will get you for this. You're dead.' Whittle cried.

'Try it now, if you can, my dog did nothing to you but wag its tail.'

'That stupid looking soppy eyed, black and white thing.' Whittle launched himself at me, pushing me aside, grabbing at his briefcase as he made his escape. making for the rear exit, Janine kicked my briefcase into Whittle's path, causing him to stumble, and fall into the closed door.

He was spouting verbal abuse towards Janine. She responded by throwing a large heavy glass ashtray at him, which struck him on the back of his head and he slumped to his knees.

Janine screamed at him, 'Tell Maxine, she is suspended!' Stunned Whittle slowly regained his composure, taking stock of his surroundings he ripped open the boardroom door and sprinted towards the rear fire exit, bursting out and making his escape down the stairs, and out of the garage. I chased after him. He was out of the main garage door by the time I reached the door. Whittle jumped into a waiting parked car then sped off down the street, searching for my car keys, I pressed the cars remote control it had unlocked the Monteverdi, stuffing the key in the ignition, the engine fired immediately, Jules close on my heels jumped into the passenger seat. Flooring the accelerator, the car launched itself backwards into the back street, before the car had stopped reversing. I slammed the transmission into forward drive, and buried the accelerator pedal into the carpet. The rear tyres screeching with plumes of blue smoke as they tried to find grip on the shiny cobbled roads, slithering to a halt at the junction, to my right I saw two cars had been accidentally damaged, both drivers were out of their cars surveying the damage and gesticulating obscenities in the direction of the disappearing car.

I followed a line of damaged vehicles Whittle had left in his wake were slowing our progress. As the road opened into a dual carriageway and the traffic cleared. The Monteverdi engine growled as we sped after our quarry.

'He is heading for his aeroplane.' Jules was talking into a police radio, informing his colleagues in the office, he was talking so fast I could only grasp the odd word.

A Police siren wailed from behind, I moved over to give the police car room to pass and as he pulled alongside of us the policemen in the passenger seat pointed at us to pull over.

'He is after us for speeding, not assisting;' Jules exclaimed. He pulled out his police I D. trying to identify himself to the police officer in the traffic car that he was also a police officer. The young traffic police office insisted that we pull over by pointing his gun at me. I cursed him, slamming my brakes hard on, the traffic cop stopped further down the road, the police officer slowly started to walk towards us.

Jules was out of the car, running towards the police officer who now pulled his gun on Jules. Jules was shouting something like 'Idiot' and showing him his Police I D.

Another car with a flashing blue light pulled up. The policeman shouted lots of instruction to the traffic policeman who was stopping us. He saluted as he stood to attention immediately, taking the constant verbal from the other police car.

Jules, jumping back into the car, shouted, 'Go for the airport!' Leaving the quivering officer in a cloud of blue smoke, we caught the unmarked police car quickly. Jules suggested, to follow him, he will clear the way.' Beynes Thiveral airport was only 2 kilometres and at the speed we were travelling, it would take seconds; we arrived screeching into the access road at the airfield.

Whittle and Maxine were already in the Chieftain, one of the engines was accelerating the other cranking to start, the plane was moving forward,

'Do not worry; air traffic will not let him take off,' Jules said, 'We have him now.'

'I do not think he is going to ask air traffic,' with the both engines now screaming, the Chieftain rapidly gained airspeed, he had seen a gap in the parked aeroplanes which gave him a clear line to take off. He was airborne in seconds and climbing rapidly into the sky.

'Shit, we have lost him!' Jules cried, Whittle was climbing, heading for freedom, cursing him, I hoped beyond hope that the worst things in the world would happen to him right now. The Monteverdi slithered to a halt on the grass. We watched as he flew low banking the aeroplane around to flyover us, he had a supercilious expression, waving a two-finger gesture; Maxine was also looking and was laughing at us. To chase him through the courts would take ages.

We only had circumstantial evidence; Whittle's money would buy him time, and out of any situation, we watched as he climbed higher. Whittle busied himself preparing the aircraft for flight, sliding the undercarriage lever up, the undercarriage motors started to retract the wheels the carbon fibre cord which had failed to stop the engine as I intended it, when the aeroplane was on the ground, started to tighten as the undercarriage assumed its closed position. The other end of the carbon cord I had tied to the main ignition wire to the engine. The steel strength of the cord ripped the lead from the ignition, the port engine immediately ceased function and stopped, with one engine dead, the chieftain started to bank to one side. Whittle, reacting increased revs to the other engine, to compensate for the lost power; the starboard engine now working hard was overheating, the plastic sleeves I had stuffed into a hole in the fuselage was unbeknown to me, the main air intake, for one side of the flat six-cylinder engine, it quickly overheated and started to seize.

The chieftain lost speed and height, Whittle fought in vain to regain control; the aircraft nose dropped, then it started its final downward plunge. Whittle, together with his female companion in crime, paid the ultimate penalty in an empty cornfield on the outskirts of the airfield. The chieftain was engulfed in a huge fireball as the fuel tanks exploded. A once fine piece of precision machinery was reduced to pile of twisted scrap metal. Jules and I together with a few officials were in attendance, there were no survivors. The paramedics recovered two bodies from the wreckage. I stood in silence with no feeling of remorse or grief for my adversary, my mind screaming, got him at last, bloody got him, farewell Pongo, also Monsuire Jacks, would require a new secretary.

Returning to the car, Jules said he would stay and co-operate with the officials and would call later. While driving back to the office, I was glad Whittle was dead. Of course, Jules would be informed of what I had done, maybe sometime in the next eighty years.

The mobile telephone in my pocket started to ring. I answered it. Janine asked, 'Are you OK? I have wanted to call, what happened?' I explained what had happened, she went quiet.

'I am nearly back at the office; I will see you in a minute, bye.'

We met in the garage car park, holding each other tight,

'I was thinking the worst.' While we walked back to her office she quizzed me, 'Why did you give him half the company?'

'It was the carrot to catch the man, but in return he gave us half of his company; we merged the two companies. Whittle is now deceased. Vista Plastics now own his company.

We will need a manager; I think we will just find one at 'Gee Patron's.'

'What about that money upstairs? We have a company to

pay for and we will be requiring some expenses for the travelling.'

'We are also in possession of a signed legal merger document. As far as I am concerned, we show this to his directors to complete the merger and unfortunately Whittles copy would have been destroyed in the crash.'

'I do not think so.' Janine replied,

'Why?'

'He did not pick it up, it is still here.' She slid the document from her desk draw.

'We will take advice from our lawyer; we can always forward the signed document to Whittle Plastic directors, informing them of the merger by security messenger.'

'I would take it as a great honour if you would accompany me on the trip.'

'I should like that very much.' Janine replied.

'While you were away, I was reading the rest of the letters on Pierre's laptop. There was a letter concerning a last Will and testimony. I contacted the lawyer concerned and I asked him why he did not come forward when it was advertised that Pierre had died.

He replied giving a suspicious story about how he was unaware that Pierre had died. I mentioned this to the other officer in Pierre's, office and he decided to take a walk round to the lawyer's office. He is bringing him back round here with the details and a package.'

'What could it be? Remember when we opened the second letter on the laptop; there was a number and a code? What was it, can you remember?'

'One moment.' Janine started the laptop and quickly entering some details pressed the button and a laser printer produced the document.

She read the document details of 'Janine Privée 1996 08 29'

label. As she translated the clues, I started to look for the video, following the clues, we looked for the hiding place. The secret laboratory room emerged, this time the blinds closed and the door to the office opened. Jules and co. walked in together with our company lawyer, Jon.

'What is going on?'

Janine explained to them and everybody was interested. Jules had seen the table open before, and then he explained that all papers in the plane were destroyed when it crashed, nothing had been recovered.

Jon asked about the papers in the letter Janine was reading. The other solicitor handed them over; while we were searching, Jon started to digest the documents received. The room had completely adapted itself into the laboratory, generating the venturi effect. Janine gave a few more clues, many people were looking, the tape was found by the side of a fan duct sealed in a waterproof bag.

The tape was given to Janine.

'What do I do?'

'It has your name and is labelled 'private', it is intended for you. You watch it in on your own then if, anything is important, you can tell us but, only if you want to.' Jon was reading the Will. 'There is connected with this Will a video tape. Do we, have it?'

'Yes, it is here.'

'The Will is not complicated. There are lists of items to go to certain members and a list of beneficiaries from the family and the company. I can see no further need for the Police.'

Upon hearing what Jon had said, the officers agreed to retire and let us have a discussion. Jon said directly to me that there was no provision for me to be present, unless listed parties had no objection.

'Let the Will be conducted as Pierre had intended.'

Janine requested me to stay,
'No, you will tell me if there is anything of importance for me to know.'
We retired and joined the others in reception. They had found the coffee. Procuring a cup, I joined the little group. Jules updated me on the events. Janine had explained only so much about what had happened in the boardroom but the boardroom video was a bit of a problem.
Evidently, as I was walking around, I had been blocking out the camera views most of the time. They were having problems understanding the English Whittle and I were speaking; we had been talking quickly and using words they could not understand or translate. They had a list and one officer read me the list of words. I explained them, much to the amusement of the officers, and as the translation was understood, they wrote the meanings next to their questions.
This man had died and there would be an inquest into the cause, but as the man was suspected of many murders, he had taken the life of Maxine in the aeroplane crash; there was nobody to make a charge against. 'This will generate a lot of paper work.' Jules said with a sigh. 'I will require you to stay in France for a couple more weeks.'
'I think I will be staying in France quite a lot from now, travelling to and from England as the need requires.'

Chapter 14

Janine joined us. She had watched the video tape from Pierre and also the tape from the lawyer. It had given precise instructions on the making and the methods of how to make the Loyplas, and how to use the laboratory room correctly. Pierre had gone on to say that both the Ontario and Paris factories were to have similar laboratory rooms built. The plans were also shown and other details were supplied.

She walked into her office, beckoning me to follow.

'What did he say to you in the video?'

'Pierre talked to me in the video as if I was across the desk. He told me exactly what his suspicions were and who not to trust. He included the lawyer that he had left the last Will and testimony with, also Max, and Maxine, he also mentioned that under no circumstances should Harold Whittle ever have any interest in the business. "He will steal it from you.".' 'Did Pierre say the last sentence exactly as you said it?'

'Yes.'

'Do you know what it means?'

'Yes, he has given me Vista Plastic, with provision for pensions to members of his family.

However, there is a problem.'

'What is it?'

'The car was sold to you before the Will was read, because of the fault of the stupid lawyer. You found the bond and you are the legal owner of fifty one percent of the business, and I am the other forty nine percent shareholder.'

I said 'Is that a problem?'

'No.'

'OK, come with me,' I said, leading her by her hand into Pierre's office. I consulted Jon. 'Will you please carry a transaction out for me?'

'Certainly, what is it you want me to do?'

'I would like you to draw up paperwork for Madam Janine to have equal shares with me in this company.'

'Are you sure? You will be giving up the controlling share.'

'I met this woman only three weeks ago but I have always found her to be honest and true. And I would consider that equality within this business should be fair. In addition, we have another acquisition for you to check over.' I slid the signed merger document from my pocket.

'I think we also own a factory in England as well.'

Jon replied, 'I will go through the documents and see you first thing in the morning.'

'Remember, we have a dinner appointment with the new factory manager at Gee Patron's at 8:00 or was it 8:30,' 'We need to change first, of course.' She replied. We closed the office, returning to Janine's apartment. Janine showered first, then I followed. Janine asked, 'What about your English lady friend?' Before I replied, many years of companionship flashed through my mind.

'She has decided to leave me.'

'Why?'

'She did not say.'

'Are you upset?'

'A little, are you upset about Pierre?'

'Yes, a little.'

Janine let her bathrobe slide from her shoulders to the ground, revealing her slender body. I viewed a splendid sight, only blemished by the yellow bruising that was slowly disappearing.

'What did you do in your early years to keep your body slender and trim?'

Replying, she said, 'I trained in the Paris ballet school, but an accident stopped my career.'

'That is a shame.'

'I still keep up the exercises; they are still good for the body.'
I heartily agreed. 'Your bruises are clearing nicely.' Glancing
back at me, she said, 'Your bruises are getting better, too.'
Walking over to me she started to rub the bath towel over
my back. I turned and held her in my arms, she responded
with a suggestive kiss, then standing on her toes, gracefully
she lifted her leg and placed it on to my shoulder. No more
words were spoken. We took our time over consummating
our new business partnership.

We arrived late at 'Gee Patron's' and Darrell and Claudette
were already there. Over dinner we talked, then informed
Darrell of an immediate general managerial position that
would be coming available in the near future in England. He
was delighted to hear of the job.

I said to Darrell, 'Did you get bored today?'

'Only twice.' he replied.

Jokingly I said, 'But what about her indoors?'

'Probably giving the window cleaner one.'

'Never would I have thought of her that way.'

It was time to go to our beds, we had enjoyed ourselves.
While saying to Darrell and Claudette, 'See you in the
morning,' I was considering driving back to England to sort
what problems would require my attention.' Walking to the
Monteverdi, I opened the door for Janine to slide into the
seat. Taking my position in the driver's seat, I caressed her
long legs. She enjoyed showing a bit more than the last time
we were together in a car. She looked content and at ease.
'What were you doing to lose an earring in the back seat of
this car?' 'Ross! I cannot say, but would you like an
adventure?'

'What did you have in mind?'

Janine giving directions, we motored out of Paris, heading through the villages. 'Park the car over there.' She pointed. 'Come.' I followed her down a small pathway towards a small cottage situated on the edge of a wood. She opened the front door. 'Close your eyes.' She took my hand. 'Let the adventure begin.' I was led somewhere in the house. Janine said, 'Sit here and keep your eyes closed.'

I listened to her moving around the room into other rooms and returning. There were mechanical noises and a distant sound of an electric motor whined into life. I resisted the temptation to peep through my eyelids, but I was content to wait for the surprise. She had refreshed her perfume. The intoxicating allure appealed to my senses. There was a click behind me. I responded by turning my head towards the noise. 'No, please wait.' There was a distant sound of an orchestra playing a classical piece of music, with the volume increasing as the music reached a crescendo.

'Now open your eyes.' Music flowed into the room. In front of me a picture of a theatre was being projected onto the wall. I looked at Janine; she had changed into a knee length, small, black cocktail dress, revealing all of her shoulders, she had rearranged her hair into a classic French style on top of her head.

'Madame, I am impressed.'

'I do hope so.'

The image being projected on the wall changed and the curtains opened.

The music changed to a quiet introduction. Dancers began to dance onto the screen from all directions, proceeding to play the ballet. I watched, trying to grasp the ballet and the story. I saw a recognisable shape of a much younger ballerina. The ballet scenes progressed and the music continued and the dancers danced energetically. 'The dancers must be very

tired after this story has been played.'
Janine said, 'the discipline is strict, always the exercises and
constant rehearsals for the future ballets.' 'I thought that you
danced very well in the last scene.' 'You saw me?' 'Yes, the
third one to enter the stage. And how many years is it since
you danced like that?' 'Many, years ago.' Janine replied.
'After the accident I had to have physiotherapy to stop my
ankle causing future problems.'
'What happened?'
'I was in an accident on the stage. It happened so fast; two
leading dancers collided during a high spring, collapsing on
me and breaking my ankle. I still do the physiotherapy during
the day. I had to take time off for a few hours the other week
to have a check-up.'
'That was the day Jules and I went to the factory.'
'That is true, how did you know?'
'I was told that you had been missing for a couple of hours.'
'Were you checking up on me?' Janine said, looking at me.
'I was checking up on anybody who might have caused me
problems.'
'After the accident, when I caught you, was that the leg you
broke, the one that I had caught?'
'Yes. I had to go to a physiotherapist to have a check. The leg
was painful, that cream that you used was very good, it
worked well. Where did you get it?'
'Madame Jacqueline makes it; she gave some to me when I
stayed at her hotel.'
'But that jar of cream came from Pierre's office fridge.'
'He too must have got some from Jacqueline.'
The ballet finished. 'Where are we?' I asked. 'In my little
house.' Janine proudly waved her hand around. She switched
the projector off, turning a small table light on. Janine was
standing, offering me her hand. 'Come, time to sleep.'

The dawn chorus woke me. I was so comfortable that I did not want to wake. It was one of those mornings when time was going to stand still until the next day. Janine's eyes flicked open, looking at me. 'Bonjour.' 'Would you like to come to England with me today? We can take Darrell back then go to Whittle's factory and present our credentials to their management.'

Janine sat up and leant across to look at me, 'You do like living dangerously.' Janine slipped out of the bed disappearing into the bathroom and taking a shower. I followed and after cleansing the sweat of the night from my body, returned to the room, refreshed.

Janine was standing by the window. The sun, streaming through the window, silhouetted her slender shape. An alarm radio crackled into life and a news station started to give out the breaking news of the day.

Janine moved close behind, gripping my neck and shoulders and kneading then rubbing my back, rolling my neck and head in a half circle then reversing the direction. I could feel the neck muscles grinding and creaking. Starting to massage my shoulders then neck, she finished by rubbing in some cream. She finished by kissing me in the corner of the neck and shoulder, causing me to lean my head into the direction of the kiss. She pulled me onto my back, climbing on top of me. She needed no encouragement from me to make love. This time love making had no heavy physical movement. Slight muscular movements and relaxing and tensioning certain muscles together with small thrusts helped us enjoy pure stimulation.

We showered again. Janine was talking to me in French now. I was starting to understand her language and was replying to her in French. If I made mistakes, she would explain the mistake with the correct pronunciation. She was doing what she said, teaching me French and making it her pleasure. I was a willing student as she was tutor.

Janine said she would be delighted to accompany me to England. She had been once before on a business trip with Max, he had tried to make love to her and she had refused to go anywhere with him after that, unless Pierre was with them. She did not trust him; a distrust that proved to be correct. We breakfasted on coffee. Janine was packing a few items she would require. She would get the remaining items from her apartment before she left. I wished to make sure all things are correct. She would give her secretary instructions and also take a mobile telephone with her so she could be contacted by the office.

Leaving her secret hideaway in the depths of the French countryside, we travelled back into Paris. Janine, using my mobile telephone, called the office, giving Claudette instructions on what she wanted to take with her to England. Arriving first at Janine's apartment we retrieved some clothes; I followed her inside as she packed a case of clothes for the trip. 'Put something warm in, it can get very cold in the north of England even in the summer time.' Placing the cases into the boot of the car we made our way into the office. Claudette and Darrell were enjoying a coffee. 'Janine is to accompany us today back to England.'

I spoke. 'That's fine.' Darrell agreed.

Inside the boardroom we surveyed the scene. It was untouched. Things had been left as they had fallen. Picking up a mobile telephone from the under the table, I switched it on. It displayed 'Tel Com' and a small picture of an envelope in one corner was flashing, indicating that a text message was waiting to be read. I displayed the waiting message.

Janine translated it as an old message from Mr Jacks

concerning the latest mix. Checking the date of the message we saw it was the same day as Pierre had died. Inspecting the telephone received calls; we found there were calls from the Paris office and the ones from Jules when we tried to see if the telephone was still operational. Monsieur Jacks had already confirmed with Janine that he had sent a message to Pierre. No other secrets were gleaned from the telephone. The telephone directory was holding nearly 100 names and telephone numbers in its memory. While searching through the telephone menu we found that this telephone had an IR Infra-Red port.

Looking around the offices we found that one of the laser printers had an IR port on the front. Walking to the printer I adjusted the telephone to print the directory. The details were sent to the printer. Two pages of names and numbers were printed, which I placed in my brief case, as I opened the lid one of the hinges broke, remembering, Pierre's valise in my office I emptied its contents into an empty drawer and transferred my paperwork to the valise.

I opened the draw where all Pierre's electrical gadgets and battery chargers were kept. I found the charger for the telephone. A car charging lead for the same telephone would charge the battery from the lighter socket in the car. Placing them into my valise, I looked round the room that had changed my life, I wondered what the future would bring. One thing was certain: my business in England was going to get a rude shock when I got back.

I thought how although the business was making money, there is making money and making money. I thought of the English term 'flogging a dead horse'. Lame duck enterprises were going to have their neck rung, or be sold to the highest bidder. A sudden idea came to me. I had bought and sold goods and the contents of businesses by public auction. Why not offer my business the same way, or even advertise the business then see if anyone would like to buy me out. It would be an interesting exercise.

Making a telephone call to the company of auctioneers I used in England; I informed them of my intentions. They suggested an appointment, making it in three days at my office. In Janine's office I found her in full flow, her secretary taking notes and Janine checking items we required in England. 'Make sure we have a copy and original of the signed merger with us.' I mentioned. Janine looked quickly and pointed to her valise.

Darrell was still talking to Claudette. 'Put it down, you don't know where it has been.' 'For the last three days I definitely know where it has been.' He replied.

'If you gentlemen are ready, we can go.' Janine said, 'I was impressive with her eagerness to travel.' Guiding the Monteverdi north away from Paris we cruised effortlessly towards the hovercraft terminal at Boulogne. Driving a left-hand drive car in England was interesting; my reactions as I negotiated the first couple of roundabouts were mind boggling. But quickly the brain adjusted and driving became a lot easier. Taking the car through the centre of London I showed Janine places of interest, the infamous M25 motorway was reduced to car parking status. As we negotiated our way towards Manchester Darrell became a guru, telling snippets of information on areas we passed through.

Approaching Whittle Plastic factory, we parked the car in the Managing Director's parking place. We entered the reception and approached the desk, it was unattended. We had to press a bell push for attention. The lady, who came to tend to our enquiry, saw Darrell with us and greeted him with glee. She told him about Whittle's demise and the major problems that administrators were causing. Evidently the bank had panicked and placed the company into administration. I mentioned quietly to Darrell, 'I will keep in the background for the moment, let Janine do all the talking.' Darrell introduced us to the receptionist and requested a meeting with the acting manager.

At that meeting Janine introduced and made her greetings on behalf of The Vista Plastic Company, Paris, bringing to the attention of the administrator the meeting, with Mr Whittle and the management of Vista Plastic Company a merger which had been proposed, accepted and completed.

With the demise of Mr Whittle, the Vista Plastic Company had a controlling interest in the company Whittle Plastic. The administrators listened to what was declared and wished time to consult their immediate management. Janine allowed them a period of 4 hours to complete their investigations. Janine, fully aware of her business law, together with the signed documentation, gave them no option but to hand over the business immediately.

The administrator making the call to the main bank resulted in the bank manager requesting an immediate meeting with the new management, at the bank. Janine simplified the request. We would be glad of a meeting but it would be appropriate to meet at the company office. The bank manager, accompanied by his area manager, arrived for a review of the current bank account.

Janine had found irregularities in the account statement. She shredded the manager's integrity with references to the atrocious charging that had been added since the date of Whittle's death. Janine insisted on an explanation. The bank manager gave what he thought would have got him off the hook but he was not dealing with an ordinary woman. She confronted him in the company of his superiors and spluttering, he tried to pass the blame to another. Janine referred to the bank account prior to the sad event. The account had been extremely healthy. On the following date, a huge amount of money had been removed from the account. She wanted an explanation. Reference was made to outstanding loans made to Whittle Plastic which had to be repaid. Janine asked, 'Were these loans listed and terms agreed?'

'Yes, they were.'

'Were these loans to Whittle Plastic or Mr Whittle personally?' The cautious reply confirmed that it was the Whittle Plastic Company who had taken the loans out.

Janine was keeping quiet while going through the statement. Her calculator was in full activity and she pencilled a couple of figures to the bottom of the statement and also indicated the areas where the statement had been adjusted. 'What is the charge in this country for theft of funds from bank accounts, appropriated by the controlling bank?'

There was a look of horror on the managers' faces but the area manager had a smile. He turned to the manager. 'I think this lady is correct, I too will be interested in your reply.' She had them; the banking professionals had been caught. She would allow them ten minutes in private to find a solution before she would take the matter further to rectify the situation.

The managers came up with the solution that monies taken from the account would be returned immediately, plus interest for the period at 1 percent above the base rate. This would of course have no further implications or comeback to the bank, and Janine contemplated, replied, 'I will agree subject to two weeks interest paid to us at the rate you have just charged us.' The manager bleated that that would cost the banks hundreds of thousands. 'It could be construed as a good basic fundamental lesson.'

The area manager agreed the rectification of the account and said that it would happen today. Agreeing, Janine closed the meeting and dismissed the two managers, and requested a replacement coffee, after someone had got real coffee and learnt how to make it properly.

Glancing at Janine I whispered, 'You had them by the balls.'

With a puzzled look she enquired, 'Balls?'

'Yes, the Balls.'

'Janine, I think Darrell is well placed to become acting manager, reporting to you directly.' 'That would be good, he has the respect of the business staff. It should work.'

Darrell was installed as manager that afternoon; he asked Anne to make reservations for us at one of the better hotels in the Manchester area. Anne had already anticipated and had made provisional bookings with a hotel not far from the factory.

'We would be pleased to meet with Darrell there for a meal tonight. Please advise the company accountant, including that if any members of the board of directors wish, they would be welcome to join us.' Feeling tired, we headed for the Royal Claret Hotel near the M60. During the registration process, Janine requested a private room large enough to accommodate a business meeting for six to eight persons and also the possibility of meals provided afterwards for, say, four to six persons. She gave a partial list of names to attend and said that if anybody enquired about Whittle Plastic to show them to the room, please. The reception staff, eager to help, would be pleased to carry out the request and would inform us when the guests arrived.

Going to our room, I stretched out on the bed and closed my eyes for a second. I fell asleep and wakened to find Janine had curled up beside me, she also had succumbed to sleep.

As I moved, she also woke, I am taking a shower looking into the bathroom a huge bath dominated the room. I remarked to Janine, 'Have you seen the size of this bath?'

'Yes, but you were asleep.'

'Sorry.'

'But I fell asleep as well.'

'Janine, we have an hour, what would you like to do?'

'I would like to f...' the moment was interrupted by the bedside telephone tinkling into life.

Listening, I asked, 'I thought people were coming at 7:30 for 8:00'

'Yes sir, that is correct.'

'Quell heure it il, Pardon, what time is it?'

'7:30, Sir.'

'Thank you, we shall be arriving shortly.'

'Bollocks! We have lost an hour, of course, the infamous British summertime.'

'We have guests, are you ready Madame?'

'Oui.' Janine was checking her makeup. 'Cinq minutes.'

Five minutes, more like five seconds. With a splash and dash shower, ready or not, we made our appearance.

Entering the room, we were directly approached by a gentleman dressed in a classic, dark blue, striped business suit. He requested our names and Janine presented him her business card. She introduced herself and then me, she was playing the game and keeping me in the background. The man replied, introducing himself as the company accountant. He presented his card: 'Thaddeus, Thaddeus & Grimshaw, respected chartered accounts since 1876.' He was the son of the grandson of the original Grimshaw, James Grimshaw. Also present in the room were the two directors, a Mr Smith and a Mr Joiner.

These two were hurriedly voicing their worries on the

condition of the company. Would their investments be safe? Janine decided she could not reply until she had further information. During the meeting, James Grimshaw the accountant was kept under pressure by Janine, requesting an explanation of why he had not challenged the bank over the spurious charges displayed in the statement and many other irregularities.

Could Janine prove the accountant, inferior in the position he held in the company? Janine was asking Grimshaw to his face if he had prepared the accounts personally, or did he subcontract the account to another accountant? His reply shocked the directors; he had been subcontracting the accounts. 'For what period have you been doing this?' Janine replied faster than a snake striking.

'A couple of years,' Grimshaw replied, 'but I still finalise the accounts.'

'Couple?' Janine enquired.

'What is Couple, I do not know this word.'

'Sorry, five years.' Grimshaw replied sheepishly. I decided to stay silent and listen and whispered my intentions to Janine. She realised. 'Bon.' She replied.

Rising, I went to the bar. Darrell joined me. 'You are playing a game with the accountant and directors.'

'Why not? Grimshaw seems incompetent and they are worried about their little investments, never question nodding donkeys.'

'The office staff were asking about you, who are you.'

'I hope you have not given the game away.'

'No, you are a business colleague of Janine, but I did add you were responsible for Whittle's black eye. Simply don't mess with this guy. It is working great; you have the shirkers worried.'

'Good, let us keep it that way.'

Darrell was amazed that Janine was so meticulous. 'She has a wonderful discipline.'

'Yes, in more ways than one.' Janine had blasted her way through the establishment and the bank manager, the accountants, and the directors were now unsure.

One question the accountant came back at us with was why the company, was not informed of the merger. Grimshaw claimed he had not had sight of the merger document. Janine replied, 'Is its normal practice for a managing director to consult his accountant if he thinks he has chance of an excellent business opportunity?'

In the exact words of Mr Whittle in my office in Paris, 'There were only twenty-four hours to accept.'

'Ah, that opportunity.' Grimshaw had now confirmed the merger, Whittle did contact him referring to a twenty-four-hour offer.

Janine continued, 'You were advised. Are there any other matters you wish to discuss or may wish to forget?' Pausing for a moment, giving everybody time to make their replies, she said, 'Please be aware that I have been recording this meeting.' She pointed to a mini cassette recorder laid in front of her in the middle of the table.

'There will be a business meeting tomorrow at the Whittle Plastic office. Any details not discussed this evening can be reviewed at that time.' She declared the meeting closed.

The waiter announced our meal was ready. A table was prepared in an adjacent room.

Grimshaw, deciding not to join us, departed. We had the pleasure of Darrell with the two directors during our meal. During dinner questions abounded from the directors. One of the directors asked me, 'Did I understand English?'

I replied in a croaky voice, 'A leetle bit.' That seemed to satisfy their curiosity.

The meal was excellent and the wine acceptable. The guests were agreeable and settled; after plying them with wine, a slip of the tongue can reveal many things.

One director let it be known that he was the father of Whittle's wife. He enquired about any money that his daughter would be receiving or entitled to after Whittle's death.

Janine suggested that it would be advisable that they consult a lawyer if a Will and testimony was in existence. They assured us that there had been a Will.

'We would be pleased to have a copy of this document then we can consider the options. Please remember that this merger was completed before Mr Whittle was killed.'

Deciding to retire for the evening, we wished the guests a pleasant evening.

Darrell's wife arrived. I had not seen her for such a long time, I was not sure if she would remember me, she did remember but it was a long time ago, she wished us luck in the venture, promised to make sure Darrell would work hard, yet she was a little plain lady, obviously the significant force in the home, she extracted him from the wine and took him home.

Returning to our room, Janine was in good spirits. 'You have enjoyed yourself tonight.'

'So have you.'

'I watched a man say nothing all evening and people told him everything.'

'It happens.'

Janine disappeared into the bathroom, returning a minute later. I required the services of the toilet. The huge bath was slowly filling, a hand towel was draped around the faucet and the bath was filling without making a noise. Returning into the bedroom and taking a couple of brandy glasses from the mini bar and collecting a bottle of brandy from my valise, I poured two drinks from Pierre's special stock.

Janine, letting her dress slide to the floor, she stepped out of the dress laying it neatly over the edge of a dressing mannequin, dressed in her underwear she helped me removed my jacket, and shirt. I watched with amusement as she fought with my trouser belt.

I asked, 'Would Madame like a hand?'

'No, I start a job and finish it.' She pushed me onto the bed and proceeded to unbuckle the belt, sliding it from my trousers. She threw the belt over her shoulder, removing my shoes and trousers, they went in the same direction.

She pulled me to my feet, placed a glass of brandy in both of my hands, then slid her hand into the front of my shorts, taking hold of my testicles.

She looked into my eyes saying, 'by the balls, come with me.'

'Madam, I, have no option.' She guided me to the bathroom. The bath was nearly full, turning off the tap: she stepped into the water and urged me to follow.

'What about our underwear?'

'What about them?'

I was laughing to myself, what is the joke she asked being lead around the bedroom, then made to climb into the bath.

'Do you have a problem with that?'

'No,' I replied, 'you only had to ask.'

'Oui, but it was more exciting this way,' we lay relaxing, amusing ourselves and discussing the day's events. With the warmth of the water and the expanse of the bath it was easy to assume a state of total relaxation.

'What birth sign are you?' Janine asked.

'Pisces.

What birth sign are you?'

'Sagittarius.'

'What does a water baby do?'

'Many things, in water.'

The morning silence was shattered by doors opening and closing. The house maids were cleaning and vacuuming with a total disregard for any residents. We breakfasted in the room. I was planning our movements for the next two days.
'Janine, I, have an appointment in my home town with an auctioneer in two days.'
A muffled ring from a mobile telephone could be heard. Janine said, 'It is not mine.' I immediately started digging into my cases I recovered my old mobile telephone.
A company which sold businesses had heard that I was intending to sell my business. They happened to have a client who required business premises similar to mine immediately. I had a preference to sell the business as a going concern. They would confer and looked forward to meeting with me shortly after my 10:00 appointment. That was two days from now at 11:00.
'Why sell your business' she asked.
Explaining my notion of selling, I told her how vista plastic would demand a large amount of my time and the possibility of me residing in France was very high. She, agreed that was a wonderful idea.
Arriving at the factory, someone had parked in the MD parking place. I left the Monteverdi parked in the next available parking bay and entered the front doors into reception. We were had assumed control and were ready to take over the establishment. Now for the daunting task of what lay ahead of us the challenge was exciting.

Chapter 15

Anne, Whittle's personal secretary, came to meet us in reception, welcoming us to the offices. She assured us unquestionable assistance in any matter connected with Whittle Plastic.

Madame Janine, assuming her official self, asked Anne, 'Parlez vous français?'

'Oui madam un petit per,' she had learned it at school but was willing to take a refresher course if it would prove necessary.

'Please, if in doubt, have any questions or statements clarified.' A short tour of the office brought us to Whittle's personal office.

'Eees that Monsieur Whittle's computer?' I pointed at the computer on the desk. Anne said, 'Yes, he also had two laptops. One he had in the aeroplane, the other is here.' Then she pointed to an empty space.

'Well, it was there a minute ago.' Embarrassed Anne, quickly looked around trying to find it. Whittle's office was not pleasing to the eye.

None of the desks or furniture matched. It would appear that he had bought the cheapest regardless of shade or colour. After all, it was only a desk or a seat for somebody to sit at and work.

Anne returned, smiling nervously, having found the laptop, it had been placed by the side of a filing cabinet, in my office. It had never been put there before.' An irritating thought came to mind, was someone starting, to play games.

Was Whittle the man, or was he just a pawn, was there another character hiding in the wings.

Janine quickly contented herself browsing the current accounts, purchase and sales ledgers, recognising some of our customers' names in the sales ledger.

Anne switched on Whittle's personal desktop computer, she entered Whittles password: 'MAXINE'. there you are Mr? Janine interrupted her, Monsieur Ross Todd.

The way she pronounced my name even made it sound French, I started to investigate what Whittle had stored. I removed the disk with the super spy program courtesy of Wayne.

I loaded it onto the computer quickly checked his most recent documents then using a search engine I searched for any document giving keywords 'Loyplas', 'Pierre Saar', or 'Maxine,' setting the computer to do the hard work I waited twenty minutes before the task was finally finished.

I gruffly murmured, 'Zis computer iz slow.' Anne replied, 'They are all old systems. Mr Whittle did say that he was going to acquire a company with state-of-the-art computer system, and we were to get that.'

The crafty sod had already convinced himself he was taking us over, and had earmarked our computer system, tough luck. Starting up the laptop computer which was faster I checked his files for recent documents; to my amazement I discovered collaboration with the Schyne Plastix in Darmstadt.

They were intending a joint venture to take over our business and as usual it looked as if Whittle was going to screw them as well. Showing this to Janine,

'That was the company that placed that large order.'

'We will make sure it is delivered on time. After they have paid, I will reduce cost of the product; that should bring tears to their eyes.'

'Why tears to their eyes?' Janine asked, 'it will hit them where it hurts: in their pocket.' I found a comprehensive list of properties owned by Pierre Saar, Janine and Jacqueline.

There were lists of other items and addresses and a full spec sheet on all the properties held in the name of Vista Plastic France. All the patents held together with telephone numbers and personal details were also documented. This was one copy I must have.

Preparing to copy to a floppy, I took a disk from the box I had found in Jacqueline's cupboard. The computer reported that the floppy disk was full. This message appeared on all the disks from that box.

Aborting the copy process and checking all the disks, they all reported a file with a number corresponding to numbers 1 to 9. If these disks held a computer backup, what were they a backup of.

Looking around Whittles desk, I found a full box of blank disks. I copied many files, letters and spreadsheets that I considered important.

If we had a closet thief, the disappearing, reappearing laptop might just disappear for good.

When Anne left Whittle's office, I told Janine about the letter listing all the properties, locations and details on telephone numbers of Pierre, Jacqueline and her.

'I would like to see a copy of that later.'

'Sure.' I said, and copied it onto a floppy disk.

The search list on the master computer had finished. Preparing to copy the files onto floppy, the computer was beeping every time it beeped a file on the list disappeared quickly, I realised somebody using the network were deleting files on my computer. I looked at the back of the computer saw the network cable and unplugged it from the base unit.

The file deletion ceased looking to see what had gone to the file deletion bin; I found it had not been cleared. Quickly I restored the deleted files to a hidden directory, and then I copied all the documents left into the same hidden directory.

If somebody was playing, they would not see this directory and having seen the document directory was empty, they might stop interfering.

Just as I was trying to re connect the network cable, a wiry looking chap came into the office.

'Hello, my name is Sydney. The network is down; I am here to fix it.' He reconnected the network cable. 'Everything here is OK; it must be somewhere else. I might have to switch off to reset the computer server.'

I beckoned him towards me, 'Oo sed it wuz down?' He understood, leaned towards me 'Eet wuz de accountant Meester Greemshaaw, hee iz wurking inn de ennd uffice.' Sydney replied. I quickly realised he was pulling my leg, about my accent. Dropping the accent, 'OK dipstick take me to him fast,' I said. Sydney showed the way. I followed, walking quickly, making him hurry to the point of nearly running down the corridor into the end office. Grimshaw spotted me coming and slid from his seat onto the floor. He was trying hide from me. 'Good morning Grimshaw, are we playing games this morning?'

Grimshaw, sliding backwards from under the desk, sat down on his seat, looking straight at me his eyes occasionally glanced towards the computer screen.

Sydney cried out, 'Grimshaw what are you doing?'

Grimshaw lunged for the keyboard, alerted by Sydney's cry, I grabbed Grimshaw's wrist, wrenching it away from the keyboard I spun him round forcing him to his knees, I pushed him hard, he crashed into the wastepaper bin spilling its contents over the floor. The bin was full of floppy disks, with a few crumpled papers on top to hide them.

Turning my attention to the computer screen, it displayed.

'Do you wish to format drive C and erase all data? Y/N,'

'Y' was selected.

'Enter volume name to erase?'
'Master Server' had been selected.
'Press Y/N to complete task.'
'Y' had been selected.
A flashing a message displaying 'Press any key to continue'
The computer was waiting, for the final key press to destroy the all programs, documents and data files.
Not taking my eyes from Grimshaw I asked Sydney, to confirm that command on that screen would effectively destroy all data on the Master computer.'
Sydney checked the screen. Grimshaw cowering in the corner; looked shaken with my; command of English.
Sydney with total disbelief looked at Grimshaw said, 'You stinker, your absolute rotter, it would have taken me days to rebuild this network if you had done that.'
'Sydney! How do we get out of it, we touch a key, it's all gone.'
Grimshaw leapt from the corner his arms outstretched he wanted to reach that keyboard at all costs, and send the command to destroy the important data. Clenching my fist, I punched him as hard as I could, sending him sprawling onto the edge of the desk.
The keyboard vaulted into the air. Just catching it would be fatal. Sydney grabbed the power lead, then ripped it from the computer. The terminal ceased operation a millisecond before the keyboard came crashing onto the desk.
Sydney managed to catch the base unit before it hit the floor. He gently replaced it on the desk then went to check the server from another computer. He returned, and claimed that it was all is safe.
'Grimshaw you are a berk!', Sydney exclaimed.
He lunged at me this time; without hesitation I smashed my fist into his face. He moaned slumping to the ground out

cold. I quickly established he had something, something very important to hide.

My fist was hurting, it was the same hand that I damaged saving Janine, rubbing my knuckles I asked Sydney, to help me empty his pockets onto the desk, everything, leave nothing in his pockets, his inside pocket held a folded envelope. Opening the letter, I found a copy of a last Will and testimony for Harold Whittle. I folded it back and placed it in my pocket. I dragged Grimshaw's body out of the little office, 'Is there any rope?' I asked 'Use one of these.' Sniggered one of the office girls, she passed a couple of large nylon tie wrap straps. 'We make them for the Police; they tie up criminals with them.'

It was a good product Grimshaw was securely restrained to an old cast iron heating radiator. He slowly recovered his senses, seeing the results of his idiotic action he appealed to my better side, claiming it was Whittle's fault, he made him do it. He confessed to helping Whittle steal as much money from the company as they could. He bleated that the pending court action with the insurance claim and the looming divorce settlement would financially cripple him.

Whittle knew that Vista plastic had in their possession another polymer additive, which made plastic bags decompose. This one product would really place Vista Plastic as the main player in the industry, they had to be stopped.

A telephone conversation with the Manchester fraud squad; quickly despatched a couple of detectives to the office, the resulting interview produced enough details to have Grimshaw arrested, and presumably they would have enough reason to investigate Grimshaw and his Accountancy Company for months.

During the following days Sydney became indispensable

assisting me in the search for lost and deleted files and documents.

I noticed from Sydney's office a couple of people being shown into Janine's office, I joined her to receive Mrs Whittle and her solicitor they brought a copy of his Will for our inspection.

The Will made provision for his wife to receive a modest pension and the sum of £25,000 for each child; this was to be placed in trust until they reached the age of 18. Mrs Whittle did not want anything for herself, but if the children were taken care of, she would be satisfied with that.

Harold had always paid the domestic bills; bravely she admitted that she was foolish with money squandering it on trivial items. I enquired if she had sufficient funds; to which she replied the housekeeping were low.

I decided to make payments to cover modest expenses including her domestic bills for a period of six months while this affair sorted itself out. This satisfied her solicitor and she was more than happy with the outcome. I took a photocopy of the Will giving my assurance that I would look into it. After they had left Janine declared that I was human and had a heart.

Taking the paper from my inside pocket I passed it to her, as she read the document, her face changed to a frown, 'Where did this come from?'

'Grimshaw had it in his pocket,'

'The Pig! What a nasty pig.

Sydney burst into the room carrying a sheet of paper. 'Have you a moment Boss?'

He came to the side of me he bent forward the make sure nobody would hear, dropping his voice to a whisper, 'I think, this is important, it was not listed on other computers and was under a hidden file, I think it is a list of overseas bank accounts and account numbers.

I fitted a new keyboard to Grimshaw's computer, and started it up; it is working fine. I had a quick look at it, although he had deleted a lot of stuff, he has not cleaned the waste bin of deleted documents, all the files are back in place.

Unfortunately, he managed to delete all the files on Whittle's old computer and I cannot get them back.'

'Try looking under a directory called 'D,' I made a secret hidden directory and transferred the files to it, if anybody checked, it had all gone.'

'Sneaky,' he replied and disappeared into the office complex.

Janine had been busy, not distracted by my actions she had finally estimated the value of Whittle Plastic, to around twelve million, but there was little money in the bank, even with the money returned a large amount of money had disappeared.

'Any idea how? Where? Or even to its location?'

Janine shrugged her shoulders. 'Although the money is represented in the books, the company will have to cease trading within two weeks, it has no money.' I mentioned to her this weekend was a bank holiday. 'Why do Banks av a Holiday?' returned the question, I explained the English quirks and days of holidays.

It would give us time, we shall drive over to the North East and tidy my business affairs, I could show her my humble dwelling.

Sydney returned back, triumphant. 'Boss, not only did you save the deleted files, you also saved the backup file for the main server. While I cross checked the data, I found two more documents, I printed them, here they are.

Document 1.

The Ajax air company Bridgeport Mass.

Purchase order.
1. Lear J23, serial Number LJ2 #000123045.
Call / Sign F.W.T.T.A. Transferred.
The agreed payment has been transferred to your account.

Document 2
A rental agreement.
Aircraft parking and office space.
Location: Hanger B3a Tel 0161 3899 343456.
Manchester International Airport Authority.

I wondered if that is where Whittle parked his Chieftain aeroplane. 'Sydney please, keep, quiet about these documents until I can make some more enquiries.'
'OK Boss.'
'Have a look at these and tell me what they are.' I passed him the nine disks found in Jacqueline's cupboard. Sydney reappeared fifteen minutes later.
'Boss, those disks were a backup for a spreadsheet, one of the largest I have seen. It is on the network, have a look on your computer.' Opening the file, I scanned through, Janine stood behind me looking at the screen over my shoulder, she moved closer pressing her firm breasts into my back, she had found a new way took distract me and took pleasure enticing me in this way.
She whispered, 'It is the last formula for the latest additive Pierre was working on when he died. I thought it was lost after the computer crash, where did you find it?'
'It was on some computer disks I found in Jacqueline's house,' Janine, now resting her chin on my shoulder as she read the spreadsheet. She placed one hand on my shoulder digging in her finger nails, the other hand hidden from view slid around my waist and down the front of my trousers

intentionally scratching the skin. She was definitely distracting me.

Sydney gave me back my disks. 'I have put a copy of the file on this CD Rom and a backup copy of all the documents from all the computers.'

'With all the crazy things going on, I thought you should have a copy.'

'Great work, Ace. We have a chap like you at the Montreal factory, you and he should meet, thanks Syd.' I placed the CD on the top of the desk.

I called to Anne, 'Can I take the laptop with me so I can check it out?'

'Of course, it is yours now.' Janine was successfully distracting me, to the point of arousal, and I was being restricted by my clothing, things were pointing in the wrong direction. I stood, discretely repositioned myself and sat down again. Janine was taking delight in this torment. she pressing her hips into my shoulder. As I was easily observed by, Anne I had to be sure any return intimidation was hidden.

I placed my hand on the back of her calf and caressed the area then continuing the caress up between her legs, she moved one leg slightly apart to give my caressing hand an opportunity. 'Ross there is a telephone call for you.' Anne called from her office. Phew, saved by the bell. The call an eager telephone sales girl from a call centre trying to sell me insurance. I did not say one word just quietly replaced the receiver. What a waste of a moment like that, moments like that do not happen every day.

I called out to Anne, I instructed her to shield, calls like that from me, then enquired, 'Where was the Chieftain aeroplane kept prior to the accident?

She replied 'He used to park it at Manchester airport in one of the smaller hangers.' I thought about a refund on hanger fees then I had a gut feeling, that document Sydney found 'Purchase order Lear J23 C/S FWTTA.' A Lear is not a Piper. What, is parked in the hanger at the airport.

Hesitantly, I called the telephone number on the receipt. A company called Tiny Trees Air Services answered. They confirmed that an aeroplane of that description belonging to Whittle Plastic was parked with them, I explained the situation to them and requested 'Would it be possible to make arrangements for two, destination a north east airport for 10:00 the next morning?'

They replied that it could be ready for any destination with 2 hours' notice, subject to pilot hourly schedule, they would check flight time and slot availabilities; taking my telephone number they would return my call within ten minutes.

In less than a minute, they were on the telephone to Anne requesting confirmation of who I had claimed to be.

Anne, corroborated my authority; any instructions from me could be acted upon without question, I requested the phone call to be transferred to me. I complimented them on their security, also gave them further instructions. That the aeroplane was not to be used by anyone without mine, or Madame Janine's, specific authority. This change in orders as they were a charter company they requested in writing, otherwise it was fine. They would be pleased to accept any future arrangements without having to confer with Anne. By the time I had finished talking with them, Anne had slid the amended order of instruction on my desk for signing.

They would collect us from the hotel in the morning at 8:30 Janine sat at her desk browsing through a sheaf of papers, looking up, 'Oui Ross.'

'Instead of driving to the north east we will be trying an alternate method,'

'Alternate method?'

'I have just discovered that Whittle had two aircraft not one,' 'but there is only one listed in the paperwork, the one that crashed in France.'

'He has a Lear jet parked at Manchester International airport.'

Looking bemused Janine replied, 'Lear jets are expensive, I wonder where the money came from for that acquisition.'

I think when we go this evening, we take all the paperwork we are working with, away from this office.' Anne acquired a stout cardboard carton, we started to pack the papers into it.

We gave Darrell and Anne instructions on what we wanted to be done, then departed for the hotel. Janine enquired, 'Was there a problem about leaving anything in the office?'

'I was not sure, just a feeling, these feelings have never failed me yet.' Janine stroked my thigh as we motored back to the hotel, 'Will I be safe, and make it to the hotel,' I asked cautiously,

'Only until the bedroom door closes, then you are mine,' she leant across the car kissing me on the ear, and rubbing the front of my trousers. 'Please, I am excited, but this traffic is also excited, and distractions could lead to accidents,'

'Humph, she slid away reclining herself into the passenger seat. The hotel car park seemed rather empty, at least I could pick a space to park the Monteverdi. In reception, I requested a safety deposit box; placing the carton of papers and Sydney's backup cd into the deposit box I felt an easier. Janine informed reception that we will dine in our room this evening, and made arrangements to have a table prepared. Taking a menu with us she confirmed that the meal would be ordered within the hour, Janine held open the bedroom door as I was struggling in with two laptop computers and valise.

She kicked the door closed behind her and told me; I was going to be her partner in sex. I had no option, skilfully she made me respond to her demands, leaving me recovering, on the floor. she called reception and gave the order for our meal, then she disappeared into the shower.

While the meal was being prepared, I made the room presentable, I found another item, that should be in the safety box. I took a walk to reception, to deposit item, then I returned.

The door to my room was slightly open, cautiously before entering the room I looked through the door jam, I saw a waiter setting up the table for the evening meal, as I entered the room the waiter had his back spoke to me 'Good evening, sir, your meal will be arriving shortly.'

The bathroom door was open enough to give an admirable view of Janine taking her shower then I wondered about the waiter letting himself in. Janine surely would have closed the door if she knew the waiter was here, walking into the bathroom I enquired if she knew the waiter was preparing the table, 'No, she did not,' I spun round to challenge him, but he had gone.

A knock on the door revealed another waiter bringing the meal. I mentioned to him 'The other waiter has laid the table.'

'What other waiter?' he enquired, looking at the table, it was not laid. Then I noticed the broken laptop together with Whittle's own laptop had gone. I called the reception desk and told them of the theft. The hotel manager appeared within seconds. I explained the fact that we had had two laptop computers stolen from the room by the waiter who was serving us.

The second waiter, who had just arrived, claimed that he was the only waiter on room service tonight; he enquired 'Shall he continue with the table?'

'No please wait.'

The manager and waiter discussed the matter about a second waiter; the manager would check this problem out immediately and get back to us. Before he left, I insisted that the room is left untouched and we were transferred to another room immediately. Also, it was my intention to have the Police take a look at this room before anything was touched.

I called one of the fraud squad's officers I had met earlier, explaining what had just happened. He quickly suggested not to eat the meal; it might have been tampered with, someone, would be arriving soon he would ring through the report. The manager, allocated a new suite for us further down the hallway.

I joined Janine in the bathroom quickly informing her of the problem, my concern was to ensure she did not walk from the bathroom in her normal state of undress. Janine, dressed in bathrobe and a towel draped around her hair, emerged from the bathroom to see our luggage being taken out of the room.

'Where are we going?'

'An emergency relocation,' the manager informed her, collecting our personal items from the bathroom we transferred to the new rooms. Our new room were superior; and the replacement meal was delivered in record time overseen by the duty manager.

The mysterious waiter could not be found, evidently, he was a casual worker supplied by an agency during staff shortages.

A firm knock on the apartment door announced the arrival of a uniformed policeman, with him were two plain clothes detectives, I pointing to the room, and gave him my key, 'We have moved our personal effects into this room, leaving all and sundry for you chaps to investigate.'

'OK, we will check and call on you later.'

A French Experience.

'Try and give us an hour to finish our meal.' I requested
'OK.' he said and went to investigate the room.
Sitting down to eat, Janine with concern in her face asked,
'What happened?' I gave a brief explanation, an item for the
security box, a bogus waiter stealing the two laptops, I called
the police, and the manager decided to put us in here.
The police officer was as good as his word; he did give us an
hour, virtually to the second.
They had found some items and needed confirmation
whether they were our property.
One item I certainly recognised was a large nylon tie strap,
commenting 'I used a couple of them today to restrain an
unsettled person at the office, I was sure I had not brought
any from the office.
My company, makes them, and evidently the British and
other Police forces are some of our customers.' The plain
clothes officer agreed, he had used them himself, then he
put this one in a sterile bag to take away. 'We will call you
when we have something,' He gave me his card and left.
Janine settling herself into the new room opened the
bathroom door, a large circular bath with holes in it was
prominent in the centre of the room.
'There is bath with holes, the water will run out of the little
holes,' she quickly understood my explanation, 'Dacor! C'est
un-Jacuzzi.' I poured two glasses of brandy.
'We will have to make a trip to France tomorrow, we have no
brandy left.' With a nice smile Janine, produced a bottle of
Brandy on the table.
I commented. 'You are full of surprises.'
'I could not believe it when you hit Grimshaw today; are you
a violent man?'
'No'
'Something strange happened after you hit Grimshaw, the

office girls clapped.'

'Oh, I did not notice, maybe Mr Grimshaw was not a popular character in the office.'

'What are we doing tomorrow?'

'We are being picked up at 8:0 flying to the North East, I have a meeting with and property agent to arrange the sale of my company and its assets, then we will be returning here maybe for a day or two, then if we are finished return to Paris.'

Taking an envelope from my jacket pocket. 'What are your comments on this, Sydney found it on Grimshaw's computer', Janine perused the paper, 'If these are Banks and bank accounts, it would be interesting to see what is in them.'

It is a long way and all that driving we would be away for at least three or four days.

'If we use our aeroplane, we can be there and back in hours.'

Janine went into the bathroom and started filling the bath with water, she returned to top up the brandy glasses. 'Come, join me in the bath.'

A prominent button located by the side of the bath had no identification, so I pressed it; the sound of an electric motor starting and a surge of warm water came from the little holes in the bath followed by millions of bubbles, dancing and probing their way around us. The evening passed quickly in this unbelievable relaxed atmosphere and wonderful company.

The telephone buzzed discreetly, it was the early morning alarm call, the room was distinctly cooler, the sound of raindrops hitting the windows, it was a cold, wet Manchester day.

Exactly at 08:30 we were in the courtesy car and on route to the airport. The Lear jet was magnificent its white coachwork gleamed brightly against the grey morning. it was smaller than I imagined. It would seat four plus pilot and co-pilot. Captain Frank; introduced himself and welcomed us onboard. 'Take any seat you want.' The customary pre-flight checks were already completed; we taxied to the main runway, taking off almost immediately.

The climb and acceleration of this aircraft was indescribable, the jet seemed to quiver as it climbed into the sky, within minutes we appeared into brilliant sunshine leaving the grey Manchester clouds behind.

The journey was short, we cruised for twenty minutes then started our decent into the patchy cloud covered north east of England. Frank on final decent settled onto the runway at 9:35 Captain Frank gave us his card; his mobile number is on the back. 'Call me when you are ready to go, I only need a half an hour to prepare.'

'If we decided to go to Switzerland from here would that be a problem?'

'I would need city of destination and extra time for refuelling etc.'.

'Can you make a provisional flight plan to go to Zurich and one to Manchester as the option, and also refuel the aircraft?' that's good Frank said 'If we buy fuel for an overseas trip, we do not pay the Vat,'

'That sound good to me,' I replied.

'Sure, no problem.'

Strolling out of the airport we hired a taxi to take us to my office. I suggested to Janine, 'Go inside the office and ask for me at reception, see what happens.'

Janine walked gracefully into reception, telling Gladys my receptionist that she had arrived from Paris for a pre-arranged meeting with me. Gladys, tried to explain that I was not here, Janine, just stood there waiting.

Gladys looked stressed as I walked in, 'Hello Gladys, how are you,'.

I greeted Janine, giving her a gentle kiss on the cheek. 'Bonjour Madam common allez vous, you look as lovely as ever, will come this way, we will be more comfortable in my office' holding the door open we entered before closing the door, I said, 'Will you remove your clothes,' then I closed the door.

Janine, stifling a laugh, asked 'What are you playing at'

'A moment.' I started to count one and two and three and so on, before I got to 15 there was a discreet knock on the door. 'Please come in Karen,' I called out.

Karen entered I introduced Janine to her, 'This is Janine, this is Karen, my business secretary, she likes to know what I am getting up to, and in Karen's case into,' Remarkable, it took about fifteen seconds for the grapevine to inform everyone I was in the building. Peeping through blinds on the hall window, I watched Gladys coming out of the workshop, I imagined the workforce sliding off the work benches and now trying to look busy and still producing nothing.

Karen was wondering what was happening, she had heard rumours and jumped to the conclusion I would close down the business.

'I think you should not presume what I am going to do,' I replied. I updated Karen, of the pending meeting in ten minutes with some people. 'Show them into the office when they arrive and please, could we have some coffee, Karen asked how Janine took her coffee. Janine replied, 'Like my men; Très chaud, et fort.' Karen, trying to translate the sentence, looked at me, I whispered Black and strong, a strange look came on Karen's face as she left the office.

Janine started to undo her blouse.

'What are you doing?' I asked.

'You told me to take my clothes off as I came in.'

'That was a joke for the benefit of Gladys, but now that you have brought the matter up it will take five minutes for the coffee to be made.'

I slipped the lock on my office door, so many just tended to walk into my office without waiting, I was not going to have this opportunity embarrassed, at least I achieved an ambition on my executive desk. Shiny surfaced wood desks are not as good as the leather covered ones.

I heard a partial crash from outside the door, Karen had tried to walk in and found the door locked, had dropped some of the cups on the floor, a cold stare from her was enough; she suspected something had happened, but was not going to commit herself until she could talk with me in private.

Philip who ran the auction house and Harry from business sales, arrived together, we sat and discussed the possibilities; Harry currently had a client who could be well interested in the business, he had just received a large pay out from an industrial accident, and he was eager to invest.

This chap knew of my business and was aware that it was profitable; I was trying to calculate a price for the business when Janine suggested the French formula for pricing, this was slightly different from the English, I let Janine calculate the price it increased by £30,000. Nothing ventured, nothing gained, I offer the business at Janine's price,

'You can get me on any of the following numbers if you have need.'

I turned to Philip, 'Let us take a walk around the property and try and give a value, he was keen to establish, if we intend to clear everything at auction, or leave the premises to be sold or rented separately.' Janine joined us as we walked around the premises, I surveyed twenty-five years of business in a different light.

'We might have a problem with a specialised business but we can try.' Philip concluded.

Returning to the main office; I asked Karen, 'To order me a taxi for two to the airport in 15 minutes'

She asked, 'What is going to happen? Who was the French lady in your office?'

'That is Janine; she is my partner in the Vista plastic company, a little something, I picked up while I was on vacation in France.'

Kareen wanted to know more, than I wanted to tell her at this point. 'Karen, what I would like you to do for me, is run this place for me, you can do it. Keep on top of the boys, work fashion, not in the physical sense. You can sign cheques; you have helped me greatly in the past. You can be a great help while I am busy, on other matters.' Karen decided that she would do it, until I get back, which should be in a couple of weeks.

'Where are you going now?' Karen enquired. 'Switzerland.'

Taking Frank's card from my pocket, I called him. 'Hi Frank, can you make the trip to Zurich?'

'If we leave within the hour, we will be there for about 15:30.'

'See you shortly.'

'Affirmative.'

Janine waved to Karen as she climbed into the waiting taxi.

'How are you getting to Zurich?'

'Oh, In the company jet.'

She laughed nervously, 'Now I know you are joking.'

'I will take you for a flight in it later, after these problems are sorted out.'

She looked at me with sad eyes. 'I heard; she left you.'

'That is correct.'

'I will be here when you get back.'

'While I am travelling, see if you can get my mobile telephone switched to International Service.'

'I Miss you,' she said as I kissed her on her cheek, she kissed me back, still with a hesitance in her response.

The taxi arrived at the airport and we were in the air and heading for Switzerland within minutes, rapidly climbing to 10,000 feet Frank trimmed the Lear jet for straight and level flight, re checked his figures then set the automatic pilot.

Then he turned around to address us. 'Coffee?'

'That would be nice.'

Janine offered to make it. 'Where is it?' '

Just here.' Frank demonstrated as he pulled open a cupboard door. 'The door hinges down and duplicates as a small table.'

Janine busied herself with making coffee.

Frank enquired, 'Have you ever flown a plane before?'

'A long time ago, a friend of mine had a small air taxi service, I used to help him out, he taught me to fly, but it was at a time I urgently required relaxation to remove stress and flying gave me that release.'

'Let us see how much you learned?' I sat in the co-pilot's seat and Frank explained the controls and operations, distinguishing the differences between jet and propeller engine power. I could immediately see the difference between the aeroplane that we flew in the early years and this one was a superb high-speed cruiser. 'If you intend to fly in this plane on a regular basis, how to land the craft in one piece is a worthwhile acquisition.' Frank switched off the auto pilot, telling me 'Take control.' After ten minutes of flying, climbing and descending, trying to keep flying in a straight line was not easy, Frank chirped, 'But you are not in straight flight, you are in a shallow dive, keep your artificial horizon dial level. We are well off track, switch on the autopilot.' I switched on the autopilot. Frank gripped hold of his seat arm. I wondered why; then I found out. The aeroplane reacted so quickly as it made its course correction, I was thrown to one side.

A cry came from the rear compartment; Janine wanted to know if there was a problem. The Lear jet quickly achieved straight and level flight. I agreed with Frank; it would be good to take lessons.

A radio message from French air traffic control said that they had been monitoring our progress and that they noticed our deviation from the flight plan. They were inquiring if everything was OK. Frank said, 'French air traffic control are concerned, I will be busy for the next 15 minutes telling them something.'

Returning to the passenger compartment, Janine asked, 'Did you like that?'

'I always wanted to fly but could not afford it. When I can afford it, I shall learn.'

'Sensible.' Janine replied. 'Would you like to join the mile high club?'

'What is that?' I told her, she was interested but would only consider when we were on our own.

'I would have to learn to fly to fulfil that ambition.'

'That would be something, for you to look forward too.' Janine whispered.

Frank's voice came over the intercom. 'Landing in ten minutes, please be seated and put on your seat belts and make sure all items are safe and secure.' Landing at Zurich, our first port of call, Frank informed us, 'I will be out of hours so I cannot fly until tomorrow.'

'That's fine, do you know of a good hotel in Zurich?'

'I believe that The Romanoff in the central square is good.'

'OK, we shall see you there later.' We found a taxi and

headed for the nearest bank on our list.

We enquired at the customer service department. with the list of accounts, we had with us. They sympathised but they could not help us unless we gave them exactly the correct codes and account numbers together.

We left the Bank feeling dejected, with the second bank, we tried a different tack. We requested a balance on the account. Giving the bank account details then the account key, we had a balance sheet printed off and given to us. It was over $800,000.00 'Would it be possible to transfer that amount by a bank-to-bank transaction?'

'That would not be a problem.'

Deliberating for a moment whether I should take a cashier's cheque for that amount, I replied to the clerk, 'We will conclude the transaction in the morning, thank you. Could you direct us to the Romanoff hotel please?'

'Oui Monsieur, out of the front door and take the first left. It is on the right side of the square.' Leaving the bank, we met Frank sitting in the foyer.

'They are full,' he said as we entered.

'Just a moment.' Janine strode to the reception desk and requested two rooms, for one, maybe two, evenings.

'That is no problem, Madame. How will you be paying for the room?' I gave Janine my credit card. 'Use this please.' The receptionist glared at Frank as he passed the keys to Janine.

'Capitaine.'

'Oui Madame' Frank jumped slightly to attention.

'Here is your key, we will see you in the morning. If you want anything, put it on the bill. However, please limit your woman guests to three.'

'Three, Pardon Madame, I will make sure it will not happen again.' Frank doffed his cap towards Janine. This play acting was noticed by the conceited reception clerk. Climbing the stairs to our rooms, Frank was chuckling. 'Great, three by command, things could be worse.'

Entering our bedroom I asked, 'Are you enjoying yourself?' Janine did not reply. She turned and held me close, kissing me and pushing me backwards onto the bed. Then standing, she slowly stripped her clothes from her body and stretched herself in ways I had seen her exercise before. She disappeared into the bathroom to shower. I lay on the bed contemplating whether to join her in the shower.

Her mobile telephone started to ring. Janine walked from the shower, answering her phone, listening to the caller then talking quickly and sternly. She laid across the bed on her front talking and making notes on her notepad. I teased her to see if she would push me away, she made no attempt to refuse. I made love to her slowly, she kept her composure and her voice never wavered; she continued with the telephone conversation without any emotion. Calmly switching off her mobile phone, she raised her hips higher, making me kneel on the bed. Her head was laid on the pillow. This was a sensual position and a deep experience. Finally climaxing, we laid together and slowly unwinding we slept for a while, and then showered.

'I think you are enjoying this.' She commented.

I replied 'Every centimetre of it. the translation took a little time; she collapsed into my arms shaking with laughter.

Later we left the hotel for something to eat taking an evening promenade.

We noticing most of the banks were in the immediate area. 'We can deal with each bank one at a time, first thing in the morning. Look, there is Frank.' He was in a bar having something to eat. 'We could eat there with him.'

'No! it is not possible for two pilots on the same flight to eat the same food or food prepared in the same kitchen.'

'But you are not a pilot,'
'I wanted to have dinner this evening with you, not Frank' I replied, she liked that and gave my arm a squeeze.
 Frank spotted us walking past and gave us a large grin and gestured with three fingers.
'I returned the gesture omitting one finger.'
Our hotel overlooked the lake and it had a good restaurant. Over the evening meal we discussed past and present problems including the disgusting way Mrs Whittle and her children; might be excluded from the Will, if the Will I had taken from Grimshaw had been registered she could well have a serious problem. We concluded, if, the money is found, it would be possible to do something for her
Placing my jacket over the back of the chair I spied a paper standing proud of the inside pocket, quickly glancing at it.
'Remember this,' I passed it to Janine. It listed details and telephone numbers of key staff within Vista Plastic and their properties and locations.
'Who could have made a list as comprehensive as this,'
'Max.' Janine proclaimed.
'A census officer came round about six months ago. He and Max had a long meeting. I wonder if this was the result of that meeting, a copied or pilfered document. It is not complete; it does not show my house in the village.'
 'I see Pierre had a flat in Paris.'
'He never used it; he rents it to students.'
Within the listings there was the main house at Laroche, the office, a house north of Paris,
'His parents live there.' Janine replied, 'there is nothing sinister about this list.'
Satisfied with both the meal and the excellent bottle of wine we decided to retire. Going through my paperwork in the bedroom I found within my valise another list of telephone

numbers printed out from Pierre's mobile telephone. Some had names by the numbers and some just had the letter or a number. 'Janine, I cannot recognise some of these names and numbers.' 'Pierre was a private person and had many friends more than I knew of.' I concluded another possible dead list.

As we reclined on the bed as we talked, she caressed my chest. She whispered, 'We have made love more in the past weeks than I have in ten years.'

'Are you complaining?'

'No, I am not.'

'What about Karen?'

'She was a very old friend, more of a sister than lover. She might tease, but never play.'

'I think not. She watched you all the time when I was in the office, we ladies know these things.'

Thinking to myself, it might have been nice once, but now any thoughts in that area had diminished.

Chapter 16

We were both awake we dressed and made our way to the restaurant for the breakfast. It consisted of boiled eggs, sliced hams, various cheeses, and black coffee.

A new task now lay ahead the best tactics on how to approach the banks. If we intended to investigate these accounts today, if they were fruitful, how we would move the money with the minimum of risk. Janine suggested that we open an account and initially transfer the money from the other accounts to it.

We would have the assurance that the money was safely under our control; then decide its fate later.

Deciding to open the account at the bank that gave us a frosty reception.

We learnt a lot from the accounts manager as we opened the new account, as it became operational our confidence increased. We discovered the account numbers were coded, each bank used different figures, it was either a numerical or alphabetical code set the approach method; we decided to apply to the teller for a statement, before we commenced any further actions. Visiting each bank on the list we successfully transferred all the monies from the accounts. There were three banks remaining, one here in Zurich and two in Bern. I wondered why he had chosen Bern.

Returning to the second bank we visited last, we asked for a balance and statement of the account. The statement showed that that morning, a transaction of $400,000, half the funds, had been transferred. Shocked and taken aback I requested details of where the money had been transferred. It had been transferred, to the Linen Bank in the Isle of Man, to an account of a Mr J Shawgrim.

Janine requested the immediate transfer of the remainder of

the account, to our account in the Frosty bank.

Returning to Frosty Bank we requested the transfer of the funds in both the Bern accounts. I passed the account details to the clerk taking them he disappeared into a rear office. We observed him as discussed, the transaction with another man, he rose from his seat and looked at us over the diffused glass screen.

The clerk returned. 'For one of the banks it is not a problem. It can be done immediately. However, the other bank is independent, they will only deal with people on face-to-face transactions.' Authorising the instructions to transfer the Bern account contents we also requested $50,000 to cover our expenses.

I passed an envelope to the clerk. I told him 'It contains a password and pass code. Both these are to be asked for in any future transaction.'

'This is a most unusual request sir, but your instructions will be adhered too.'

Janine was perplexed as to why Grimshaw had all these accounts hidden in many different banks, as we left the bank, she confirmed that I had all the necessary paperwork.

'Yes, I have.'

Janine telephoned Frank. 'Hi.'

'Can we go to Bern,'

'Whenever you are ready madam; I am at the aircraft and it is ready to go when you arrive.' Collecting our luggage from the hotel, we departed to the airport, destination Bern.

Capt. Frank suggested to me, to join him on the flight deck, it is a better view as we negotiated our flight through the mountains. Waiting on the approach road to the main runway a commercial cargo jet was in front of us to the rear our little aeroplane, was overshadowed by a huge Jumbo aircraft, waiting his turn to depart. It was our turn we had the green light.

'We go.' Frank's voice was clear in my headphones. He anticipated the signal and had the twin jet engines screaming. Rolling down the runway and gathering speed, Frank eased back the control column the nose of the Lear jet rising as the wheels left the runway the rumbling stopped, the undercarriage retracted into the body of the plane causing the aircraft to leap forward with the air drag now diminished.

Silence apart from the distant whine of the twin jet engines as we climbed into the blue cloudless sky. Frank pointed a finger at three green neon glowing, 'they indicate the undercarriage is up and locked, very important.' He systematically checked the instruments, checked the settings and rechecking everything again, keeping a wary eye for anything that could go wrong. Frank thumbed towards the mountains. 'You do not get a second chance in this part of the world with those large lumps of solid rock with snow covering the top.'

Levelling off at 8,000 feet Frank asked me to select a heading southwest, and climb to 10,000 feet. We were at that time heading in a northwest direction. Taking hold of the control column to perform the desired turning manoeuvre, the aircraft responded quicker than I anticipated, this caused the aircraft to bank steeply as it turned, my stomach had a feeling similar to when you are riding a roller coaster and you reached the bottom of a big dip. Frank quietly remarked, 'It is good practice to keep the coffee in the cups and not down the front of a client.'

'I am sorry.'

'You will be, if she has spilt some on her dress.' Glancing back, Janine was oblivious to our antics, and she looked charming as she gazed out of the window.

Frank was busying himself with never ending paperwork. He glanced at the instruments giving me little prompts now and again to correct my actions. I flew through the wide valleys on our route from Zurich to Bern after fifteen minutes I started our descent into Bern. 'According to the flight let-down chart, we simply follow the motorway towards Bern; the flughafen is just south east of the town, gradually I was reducing height until I saw the motorway clearly on the left side of the valley, I levelled off at 1,500 feet above the motorway, Frank voice in the head phones commanded, 'I am taking control.'

'Over to you Captain,' I replied, his hands instinctively darting to operate switches on the front, side and overhead panels, as he moved the undercarriage lever downwards, I could hear the muffled whine of the electric motors operating as the undercarriage locking out into the landing position, simultaneously three red neon indicators had turned to green, also gave visual conformation. Landing a plane on a runway without a severe bump is termed 'greasing it.' Frank took great delight in greasing every landing, he remarked that it saved tyres, air traffic control stopped our chatter and gave us directions to our parking bay.

'If everything goes well, we will be ready to go within a couple of hours.'

'Will the return trip, be to Paris or Manchester?' Frank enquired

'I am not too sure yet. If everything goes ok, we can be finished quickly', He would work out two flight plans and submit both. Janine quickly getting used to this executive level of travel chastised a security official for delaying to check our paperwork, I hailed a taxi, then proceeded to the bank. One of my gut reactions was twisting my stomach. I commented 'I think we may have a problem ahead.'

A French Experience.

page 252

Chapter 17

The taxi stopped outside the bank, I surveyed the building it had a daunting atmosphere, as if it was telling me to go away, do not enter the feeling sent a shiver down my spine. Janine not receiving the same signals, walked briskly up the stairs and entered the bank.

Once inside, she paused surveyed the layout then walked over to the enquiry desk, we made application to the clerk as we had done at all the other banks for a balance on the account. The clerk invited us into a private office, there we were met by a small, impeccably dressed man; he introduced himself as the account manager.

He enquired, 'Who it was requesting details about this account? We have specific instructions concerning this account. As I the account manager do not recognise either of you, we must have the verbal password agreed with the client to continue.' 'Would that be the name password or the number password?' I enquired. The manager did not reply, he just sat and looked in my direction. I asked him again whether it was the name password, or the number password. 'Le nom ou le numéro, s'il vous plait?' Janine retorted.

Possibly shocked by Janine's intervention, he quickly replied, 'Nom.'

'Maxine.' I replied as quickly

Checking his document a few times unsure, he asked me again for the password. 'Maxine.' He seemed still unconvinced I spoke to him I am afraid my accent maybe pronouncing the password name incorrectly, as the client and I both lived on opposing sides of England and accents and dialects differ greatly, he perused my explanation, but finally concluded, 'What is your wish of the account Monsieur?'

'A statement please.' He pressed buttons on his keyboard and a small printer by the side of the computer produced a slip of paper. Tearing the slip from the printer, he checked the figures against the screen details then handed the slip over to Janine. He waited for further instructions. Viewing the figures, I saw the digits on the slip read.

$12,800,000 Janine looked at him. 'And the statement?' Expressionless, he tapped another key, another printer below the desk rattled into action. Tearing off the statement, he passed this to Janine. He asked would we be long.

I replied 'Why?'.

'If this is all you require, I will bid you good day.'

'I think we will be transferring money from this account in a couple of minutes.'

'That is very good, can I offer refreshment a coffee perhaps?' This was the first indication he gave that he belonged to the human race.

'Deux café sil vous plait.' 'My pleasure.' Tapping a key on his computer, he retired to bring the coffee.

Janine was checking the deposits and balances, making notes as she went on the statement. The gentleman returned, carrying two coffees and placed them onto the desk. He resumed his position in front of us.

'Je crois qu'il y a une erreur dans ce compte.' She had found a mistake and was already on the attack.

'A problem,' I asked.

'Oui Ross, these figures are incorrect.'

The clerk inquired the nature of the problem, quickly looking at his computer screen browsing, and then checking again with his computer screen. 'I assure you Madame they are correct.'

'Mademoiselle' she replied, 'Pardon mademoiselle' he begged her forgiveness' 'I assure you, Sir, they are incorrect.'

She indicated the error to the account manager. He checked again, tapping more keys. The account problem was rectified. He profusely offered apologies. We waited while he recalculated the balance and printed out the correct statement. The new balance had increased by $1.5 million to $14.3 million. Janine replied 'This costly mistake would have lost us $1.5 million. Regarding the severity of this one circumstance, this account should be transferred to another bank immediately. Please transfer this account in its entirety to this account in Zurich.' She passed him details of the recipient bank. We had our coffees replenished while they were organising the transfer. Confirmation that the transfer was complete was handed to us reading the statement, Janine remarked to the executive that they were laissez faire with their charges.

The manager replied, 'That is simply our standard charge for such a transfer.' And he enquired would there be anything else we required of the bank?

'Yes. Have you any outstanding paperwork to go to this client, we are flying back today to conclude matters with him tomorrow.' He checked with the office, there was a document, destined for posting, but as we had offered to take the document, the bank would be pleased if we could take the document for him.

Sitting in the taxi, elated with our success and a substantial sum of money recovered, Janine opened the letter addressed for:

Mr Shawgrim.
Manchester
England.

Dear Sirs

We received your transfer request today for the contents of your account to be transferred, we were concerned as you are aware of the person-to-person transactions rules which govern our banking practice. We were most relieved when your representatives arrived and we have adhered to their instructions on your behalf.

We remain yours truly
T.W. Wizter, Accounts Manager. Bern Credit CH.

Janine could not believe it. 'We had transferred the account and only just in time, minutes later someone had attempted to move the funds elsewhere: who was this Mr Shawgrim?'
'Grimshaw, who else.'
Leaving Bern on a heading for Manchester, Captain Frank in charge rapidly let the Lear jet rocket to 10,000 feet. I had joined Frank with the take-off, this enabled me to take a break from banks and so-called officialdom all done in the word of making money, and I gained more flight experience, once the flight plan was safely logged in the autopilot's memory, it was engaged, and we headed for Manchester.
Janine came through onto the flight deck. 'Would anyone desire a coffee?'
Frank thought that was an excellent idea. He had paperwork to attend to, two hours would see it finished and he would cope better on his own.
'Why not tell me to push off,'
'OK.' Frank chuckled 'Push off,'
'The coffee will be ready in two minutes.'
Serving Frank with a coffee, Janine asked Frank 'One or two?'
Frank grinned. 'I thought I was allowed three.'
'Is it possible to make a mobile phone call from an aircraft?'
'Try it if you wish, we are passing into French air traffic

control.' Using my telephone, I called the Manchester factory. There was no reply. I gave the telephone to Janine. Before she could put it in her handbag the phone rang. She answered, then listened and gave me a wide-eyed expression. 'Please, if you have any other information call immediately.' Relaying the content of the telephone conversation Janine reported that the factory in Manchester was destroyed in a fire last night.

'We will see it from the air, when we get closer.' My mind engaged a higher gear and was racing through the calculations and probabilities of accident or sabotage.

I was feeling drowsy so I reclined my seat full length. Noticing this Janine went forward to talk to Frank, returning she closed the curtains to the flight deck. She disappeared into the toilet at the rear of the plane, as she came back, she closed the window blinds darkening the cabin interior. She reclined the adjoining seat, slipped her hand under my shirt then joined me in sleep.

The seatbelt warning light chime, woke us from a lovely sleep. Janine kissed me whispering, 'je vous en sais gré.' Over the intercom Frank was declared landing in 20 minutes.

'Please prepare for landing.' Frank had been notified by air traffic of the closure of the main runway at Manchester. Evidently a cheap charter flight had blown a tyre, and this was obstructing the main runway.

We would have to come in from the South. A factory fire was producing a large plume of dense black smoke, which was drifting across the flight path. Frank confirmed directly with air traffic reported the current state of the smoke column. Indicating the density of the smoke would not affect the landing. Sitting with Frank gave me an unrestricted view of the factory fire, the devastation was impressive. 'I think we have just lost our factory and everything in it.'

Frank replied, 'What an insurance claim that will be.' And passed me a small camera, 'take some pictures it will look good from up here.'

I clicked away with the camera using up all his film.

Conversing with one of the customs officers attending our arrival, I asked about the factory fire, she told me the television news claimed a small fire in a central heating boiler had been the cause, together with a leaking gas main to the factory and the rest you have seen.

Saying goodbye to Frank, I thanked him for the safe flight. He thanked us for such a good time, he had not laughed like that for ages. He would look forward to flying us anywhere anytime. Frank organised a courtesy car to return us to the hotel. As we were at reception retrieving our door keys, the receptionist gave us a large envelope stuffed full of messages and notes. Sitting down in the room, we methodically ploughed through them. There was a note from the police saying please contact them urgently on the number given. Another note from Sydney, call urgently.

Switching my mobile, it quickly indicated that the answering machine had received lots of messages.

I called Sydney first, he was glad to hear from me. He told me about the fire It was terrible; everything was lost. He had heard the police had been reliably informed that I had started the fire and then skipped the country. He filled me in on a couple of other items of interest. He had taken another copy of the CD home and had been going through the documents letter by letter.

'I have made a list of urgent letters that I think you should see.'

'Come to the hotel now if you wish.'

'See you soon Boss.'

I made the phone call to the police officer as requested. 'Yes,

Sir we are glad that you have contacted us, would you be going on or planning an overseas trip within the next day or so?'

'No.'

'Do you have a problem?'

'No.'

'Would you be so kind and put me through to D. S. Harris?'

'Why would you be requiring him?'

Giving sergeant Plod an update he gradually realised I was already dealing with a supposed higher level of intelligence within the Force.

The desk sergeant put me through to D. S. Harris.

'Hello, it's Ross Todd.'

'Have we got news for you?'

'I saw the factory fire from the air as we flew back to Manchester.'

'As well as that, the samples we took from your room showed the meal had been interfered with. A substance had been wiped onto the plates and cutlery it would have incapacitated both of you for days. The lab boys are finalising the tests on the substance.'

'How are you getting on with Grimshaw?'

'We had no option, but to let him go.'

'What, you are joking!' I declared 'Why?'

'He claimed that he had not been officially discharged or suspended from his appointed position within the company and he was only fulfilling his obligations to the management of the office until the new managers took over.

We had to charge or release him; he had a high flyer of a lawyer.'

'And you believed him, I bet you daft buggers, even believe in the Easter Bunny and Fairies' I replied angrily, I was fuming, with anticipation I asked 'When did you release him?'

'We released him two hours after his arrest'

'What! two hours after you arrested him? I do not believe you guys, I had lots of things happen to me in the last couple of days, now that I know Grimshaw is free and on the streets, I have a good idea now, who is responsible, bloody thanks a lot.'

'I take it you are not happy with us.' Harris replied.

'Now here is a case for you to ponder. With Grimshaw on the loose, could there be a connection.

He attempted to destroy all the computer records for Whittle Plastic.

A mysterious waiter at the hotel tried to poison us, and then only steal two company laptop computers.

The transfer of $400,000 from Whittles secret Swiss bank account, to an account in the Isle of Man under the name of a Mr J Shawgrim.'

I kept details of the other accounts secret for the moment; we still had a crazed idiotic accountant on the loose and what seemed to be a bigger idiot in charge of the case.

'We have details of the transfer if you if you would like a copy.'

'I will come and see you straight away.' Harris replied.

Sydney was the first to arrive; he brought with him his own laptop computer. Showing us the business letters, he had discovered, we took note of the content.

D.S. Harris finally arrived, tempting him with a coffee, I declared that we have a connection in which both Grimshaw and Whittle had been skimming funds from the same bank account without each other's knowledge, so much for the age old saying 'Honour amongst thieves.' D.S. Harris remarked that the account must be pretty thin by now.

Janine confirmed the discrepancy, she had checked over the accounts, and a substantial sum of money was missing.

'Have you got copies of these documents?'

'No, they were all on the master computer, at the factory.'

Sydney butted in, 'No they were not; we have a copy remember, I gave you that CD before you left.'

Of course, the computer backup, I had forgotten about that, excusing myself I quickly retrieved the CD from the safety deposit box and returned to the bedroom.

'I will make you a copy of the files from the master CD.' Sydney replied.

Harris insisted, 'I will take the master as evidence; our technical boys will get what we want from the disc.'

Sydney instantly replied, 'Not a chance Mush! He was not letting the police's great boots stamp on the only copy.'

'You will get what you require, there are secret formulas are on that disc and we will not take the chance with it, you might just release it to somebody with a smart lawyer.'

'OK, point taken.' Harris replied.

Harris and Sydney sat in the corner of the bedroom making lists of files Sydney thought he should have, and between them polished off the last dregs of the coffee, Sydney produced from his laptop computer a cd copy of the information that would require. Harris happy with his new details returned to the Police station.

'Did he get everything?'

'No.' Sydney replied.

'How do you fancy a job in our Montreal or Paris factory, we could do with a bright lad like yourself.'

'That sounds good.'

'We will talk with you later.'

Janine had ordered more coffee to be sent to the room, while waiting I read and listened to the long list of messages on my mobile telephone. Harry from Business sales requested that I call him fast, Harry, had a client, a Mr T Davis

was interested, and he was prepared to pay the asking price.
'Accept it quick.'
'He is with me now as a matter of fact, would you like a word?'
'Hello Mr Todd, will the staff be staying?' Terry asked.
'I saw no reason why they should leave.'
'What about the Lady in charge of the office?'
'Which one?'
'Karen.'
'I think so, I have not heard from her as yet, so I cannot say.'
'I think she is really smashing; she would be able to teach me the business.'
'Provisionally I cannot answer for her until I ask, but if you are intent on having the business as a going concern, I will consider the offer but I must discuss this Karen first. I will do that now then get back to you in a couple of minutes.'
I called the office an unrecognisable bright voice answered the telephone. 'Good morning Todd's how may I help you?'
'Could I speak to Karen please?'
'Yes, it's me Ross.' Karen always answered in dulcet tones.
'How do?' she answered.
'I am fine, what's going on in jolly old England?' we chatted about general things but I detected a shine in her voice, I had not heard for years.
'Yes, we have been busy business is good.'
'And' I replied
'That chap Terry who was interested in the business wants to buy it.'
'And'
'We have nearly sold all stocks.'
'And'
'Why are you asking me "And" all the time?'
'Did Terry take you out?'

'Why?'

'I thought as much.'

'If Terry was to take over the business, would you be prepared to stay on with him?'

'Yes, I would, I am sure, positive, yes I am positive I would stay.'

She quickly updated me on the simple events at the office and we quickly scoured through a list of questions she had made.

She asked when I coming back, in a week or so, would I go and see her when I did. '

Of course, I would, OK I must go I will see you when I come back. Bye for now.'

Calling Harry back I told him to please inform Terry that Karen was prepared to stay with the company, and I would be pleased to accept his offer.

'Prepare the paperwork, use my solicitor for any legal stuff.' I said, giving him details of the solicitor's address.

'Call me with any problems, thanks again.'

Chapter 18

I must have looked pleased with myself as I put the telephone down. Janine enquired, 'I think you have good news'

'I, have sold, my old business.'

We discussed details of our trip; nobody knew what we had discovered in the secret accounts in Switzerland. And we both agreed to keep these matters confidential. Our money problems now a figment of the past, but unexpected thrust upon us, was a disastrous fire and an out of work, workforce. Anne, called us at the hotel, she was requesting an update on the future of the business.

Thinking quickly, I gave her a list of orders to contend with, 'Can you make some arrangements for some portable cabins to be used as offices and have them placed in the factory car park, then ask the telephone company to reconnect the telephone lines to the cabins. We can cover the production of goods from the Paris factory for the time being. We need a presence at the factory site; also inform the insurance company, and find an independent insurance assessor to work on our behalf.

Make sure the cabins are fully equipped with desks and chairs. Give Sydney the power to obtain a full computer network system, whatever he needs to get going; also, the need of 24-hour security. I will arrange for a room here at the hotel for minimal staff while we get back on our feet.'

I explained the problem with the factory also the urgent need for emergency office space to the hotel manager. Offered an arranged a working environment from this suite. The manager let me see the rooms and we agreed a favourable rate and took them for seven days.'

Ann called back within the hour.

She had worked wonders; the telephone company had made available ten mobile telephones with our telephone lines diverted to them. Sydney's pal had a computer business and can do us a deal, we will have the systems ready for tomorrow, I called an insurance assessor he was dealing with a similar factory fire, and had everything at hand, he suggested that the work force be laid off immediately, we can claim lost cost from the insurance company.' Anne declared it would save the company, thousands in payroll costs, and we can employ the good staff when we are rebuilt, she did suggest this would be a good plan, as there was some problem staff that could be dispensed with.

Janine suggested that she could go back to Paris. 'I think that Anne will be capable to control matters here she can discuss any problems over the telephone.'

I called Frank. 'Any chance of a trip to Paris tonight?'

'Yes, but I shall be out of hours; I shall have to stay overnight. I have been trying to get hold of Anne, we have had an enquiry from a Mr J Grimshaw, he claims that he is the financial advisor for Whittle Plastic, and wants to use the Lear jet,' Frank continued 'I have flown this chap around before,'

'Where does he want to go to?'

'The Isles of Man, then onto a small French Riviera airstrip. He has given me the location and I checked, it is a tiny private airstrip, possibly it is too small for this beast to land safely. I told him I could not do it today but he insisted he would get another pilot to do it.'

'If you log the flight plan for Paris now, we shall take Janine to Paris then return in the Morning.'

'OK.'

'Frank, do you think you could land the plane at this French airfield?'

'Yes, I could, problem is taking off would be risky, we would have to break a few noise regulations but it would be possible.'

'Call Grimshaw, tell him a story, there is a problem with the aeroplane a CAA rule or something broke, but that you would be prepared to take him tomorrow. Give me a call back if he goes for it, also enquire if he will be on his own.

'You will be requiring another pilot as well.'

Frank enquired. 'Anyone in mind,'

'Have you got a uniform jacket that will fit me?'

'I think so.'

'That will do nicely.'

'Janine?'

'Oui Ross'

'I will take you to Paris tonight then I will join Frank on a charter flight tomorrow.'

'With all this going on you want to go on a charter flight' Janine replied, looking sad.

'It is possible this flight will be important and you will be impressed with the outcome.'

I enquired from D S Harris if there was a problem with Janine returning to Paris and myself leaving the country. 'No problem, why are you asking me this?' 'Just to keep you informed, of our movements, also the main office of Whittle Plastic will be operating from this hotel for the next seven days and then the operation will resume from portable office cabins in the factory car park.' 'That is good.' Harris replied, 'thanks for letting me know.'

Janine had packed her valise; she was ready to return to Paris. Leaving the Monteverdi sleeping in the secure underground car park, we arrived at Manchester airport, quickly cleared passport and the security check; we clambered into the Lear jet. Frank had finished his pre-flight checks. Janine took her seat, I proceeded to close and secure the outer hatch, checking everything was secure I joined Frank on the flight deck. Leaving Manchester we headed for Paris, Frank had logged a flight plan, 'Last minute change of destination, we are bound for Beynes Thiveral.'

'Beynes Thiveral, South West of Paris. I have been there with Mr Whittle, and a couple of his chums it was the time when Whittle was learning to fly. It might be tight but I will call air traffic to inform them of a change in plan.'

Frank called air traffic on the radio, they accepted the change of plan and transferred us to Beynes Thiveral, they would be prepared to receive us. Previous larger aircraft than ours had used this airfield, so there was no problem in us landing. The Wind was from the south and the local conditions were dry and clear skies.'

'Affirmative' Frank replied 'we should be landing within the hour.'

'I am going to sit with Janine, I am feeling tired, the air seems stuffy.'

'I will increase the fresh air flow to the cabin; you will feel better in a couple of minutes.'

'Why is it that,' I asked, 'if you travel above 15000 feet you have to pressurise the cabin area or the passengers could die with lack of oxygen? Light aircraft usually have a maximum ceiling height of 12,000 feet.

If your aeroplane cannot be pressurised and you have the necessity to climb higher, then the pilot will use his personal air supply. He then pointed to an air bottle and face mask by the side of his seat. Also, in emergencies we are compelled to use it. Co-pilots have the same equipment on their side of the flight deck. Passengers have their face masks drop from the overhead panel. Occasionally if we have noisy or drunken clients, we can reduce the oxygen level. It puts the clients to sleep then we raise the level again and we have a quiet flight.'

'That is a sneaky trick to play.'

'Yes, but it works. It can subdue violent passengers as well.'

Frank said, 'I have the usual international paperwork to fill out, see you before we land.' I closed the curtain and joined Janine. She looked charming as she reclined in the leather armchair, taking the adjacent seat, I blew gently into her ear, she jumped. 'I did not hear you arrive.' She rubbed my chin, 'You have not had a shave.'

'I have not had time. Do you have any hair dye?'

'Why?'

'I wish to do a bit of undercover work. If I colour my hair a darker colour, I think I could get away with it.'

'Tell me more, this sounds incredible.' Janine sat on the edge of her seat as I explained the plan and what I intended to do. She agreed it was worthwhile.

'I have some dark hair colour in my apartment.'

I touched her hair, 'Is it this colour?'

'NO, this is natural. I looked closely at her hair, she admitted 'Well possibly the occasional grey hair, I had to colour it black when I was dancing.'

'Will I suit black hair?'

'It would be interesting but you will have to do your eyebrows and forearm hair and either shave or colour the beard, as well.'

'Will you help me? I need to be as invisible as I can for tomorrow's flight.'

Janine moved over and sat on my lap. She snuggled into my arms and stroked my hair.

Sliding my hand up her leg, I said, 'You have shaved.'

'Oui Monsieur.' I teased her while caressing her legs. She

suddenly stood, sliding her hand to my belt buckle, undid it, continued to unzip my trousers.

'What about Frank?'

'He is busy with his paperwork.'

Sitting astride me, we both slipped into the membership ranks of the so called exclusive 'Mile high club'.

With all this sexual activity and change of diet, I was feeling fit. My trouser belt required tightening further, when I get chance, I would weigh myself, I must have a good twenty pounds in weight. My new fitness level increased my endurance, unfortunately all the activity had to cease as Frank switched on the seatbelt sign, then informed us we were about to land in ten minutes. Adjusting my clothing, Janine smiled, 'That was the best inflight entertainment I have ever had.'

'Thank you, Madame, we at Tiny Trees Air Services wish to please.'

Janine thought for a second replying' I thought we were flying united,' I saw the mischievous side of her, I gave her a longing embrace then went forward to experience another landing this time at a small airfield.

With the light fading we used our own landing lights. They illuminated a path into the darkening night sky ahead of us. Landing safely, we were directed to our waiting space by the ground crew.

'Did you get the jacket?'

'Yes, I did.'

'I tried it on it is a bit tight across the shoulders.'

'Just leave it open; you won't be wearing it inside the plane. Frank passed me a plastic bag containing a shirt with four bars epaulets a black tie with the company logo, you will need black trousers, socks and shoes.'

'I have those clothes in Paris, I won't let you down.'

Frank pointing toward a small hotel across the road 'I shall stay there, the lady owner was very friendly last time I was here,' I gave Frank Janine's telephone numbers for the apartment and her mobile. You can call me on my mobile, it works in France.'

'See you 7:00 departure.'

'Au revoir.' Janine, giving Frank a kiss, said, 'Will you look after him please?'

'I want him to look after me,' Frank replied smiling.

Taking a taxi to the apartment the journey took ages, all the streets were backed up with cars and slow-moving traffic; Janine asked the driver what was causing the problem, he answered there was an illegal demonstration by groups of immigrants complaining about something or other, adding a curt comment about foreigners he continued to negotiate his route.

At last, we closed the door to the apartment, she started her efficiency check of the area, first on the list was her messages on her answer phone, then she made her home habitable, she retrieved the hair colour. There should be enough, it is not permanent, and it will wash out after a couple of washes.'

She had quickly prepared a light meal, as the meal was cooking, said, 'Remove your shirt, I will prepare your hair.' Putting an old towel over my shoulders, she applied the colouring thoroughly into my scalp, eyebrows, then my stubble beard. She was careful as she applied the substance and made sure none dripped onto anything. She started to giggle as she applied the preparation to my forearm hair and the hair on the fingers and back of the hands, Janine was only just containing herself blurted out; 'Only one small part left, would Monsuire require that doing as well?'

'No, no a shave would do nicely.'

she laughed, 'Oh, I have something much better than a shaver.' she chuckled
'Later, Wow later.' I smiled
The meal was nearly ready; she looked at her wristwatch it was time for me to shower and remove the surplus colouring. As I emerged from the shower, I observed a strange reflection in the mirror. The colour change had worked well, Janine, giving me a good look over, as she helped me into a bathrobe.
'You are dark on the top and blonde from the waist down.'
'This is a direct result of a mixed marriage.' I declared, we both collapsed with laughter.
'I am not likely to have to take my trousers down so what people can't see they will not be worried about.'
We enjoyed our meal followed by some brandy. I was having an early start. Just then, Frank called, 'I could hear a female chuckle in the background.' And, 'I hear you have found your friend.'
He was confirming the time of departure. 'See you at 6:30, immediate take off.'
Frank relayed back. 'Affirmative.'
As I dozed on the couch, Janine lay by my side. She was caressing my chest and stomach; it was so soothing I kept drifting in and out of sleep. I suggested bed; Janine agreed and suggested making love. I was a bit tender in that area and she hinted, 'Where is the special cream from Jacqueline?'
'It is in the bathroom,' she went and returned with the tub in her hand rubbing the cream carefully into the painful area, it was so soothing. I fell into a deep sleep only to be shocked back to life by Janine's alarm at 5:30 in the morning.
Janine helped me dress. 'You will be sitting all day, here is a little help.' She came towards me carrying a tin of talcum

powder. Shaking some powder into the back of my shorts, she gave me a lingering kiss as she shook more talc into the front of my shorts. It felt good, and comfortable.

'Merci Madame.' Dressed in the white shirt Frank had supplied sported the four barred epaulettes, the company black tie, trousers, socks and shoes, I looked a different man. If you put on sunglasses like the ones pilots use, the transformation was complete.

Janine was inspired. 'This mile high club, do you have to renew membership, or, is it a lifetime appointment.'

'Madame, I think in your case a special rule might apply the renewal of your membership every flight.' Returning a sultry look, she sidled over sliding her arms around my neck and gave me a big hug and another lingering kiss. 'Do be careful, very, very careful.'

She came to the door to see me off. I slid my hand through the fold opening her bath robe, holding her close I caressed the cheeks of her bottom,' perfect,' I whispered in her ear. I could feel her nipples stiffening though my shirt, it was not the time to leave, but plans had been made, picking up my briefcase and a change of clothing in my suit holder I left.

The taxi arrived on time; the driver took a second look as I approached 'This taxi is not for you Monsieur, for another person, an English man with the blond hairs.'

'It is me; I am incognito.'

'Oh! Crazy Englishman.' He said, and he opened the rear door.

'Beynes Thiveral Airfield, s'il vous plaît.' We arrived on time at the security gate. I thanked him with a generous tip and he sprang out of the car, helping me remove my luggage. He saluted me and then drove off.

As I entered the gate and approached Frank, he asked me, 'Are you he?'

'Yes, that is correct I am he.'

'Who are you waiting for?' He said in a lower tone of voice.

'I am to meet the infamous, Captain Chaos, from TyT.A.S.' Frank appreciated the joke and went into fits of laughter.

'I did not recognise you,' he said, as we walked to the Lear jet.

'We have to be perfect today; a lot depends on it.' We discussed the plan on the way. Frank was intrigued, landing at Manchester, I complimented him on his good landing, as we were picking up passengers, air traffic directed us to park adjacent to the main terminal, to board our passengers. I want Grimshaw to go through security; we did not want him carrying anything nasty.

Frank said, 'I shall go and bring our clients. You walk around the aeroplane, looking busy as if you are doing the external pre-flight check.'

Grimshaw and a very large companion accompanied Frank as he returned. Greeting them and offering to take their luggage and briefcases, I asked, 'Is there anything you need from the cases before they are stowed in the hold?'

'No.' followed by a grunt from man mountain.

'Excellent. Please take the two centre seats and make yourself comfortable.' I placed all non-essential baggage in the hold. I locked and secured the hatch door. Frank watched as I shut the hatch, 'Impressive.'

'What, closing a hatch door?'

'No, remembering to secure the safety latch.' It was there and very obvious; it must be there for a reason, nothing special.

Mr Grimshaw and companion Mr Twist were introduced by Frank, continued to introduce me as the co-pilot, engineer, Troy, taking my position in the right-hand seat in the cockpit, I made myself look busy.

Frank sat with the clients, briefly reconfirming instructions and making sure that Grimshaw reconfirmed the destination of the Isle of Man, then onto Cannes in the south of France as their final destination.

We were cleared for immediate take off. All items secured, we taxied to the main runway. Mr Grimshaw slid open the dividing curtain between us and the passenger compartment. Frank, immediately challenged his action, speaking sternly, 'Please take your seat, we cannot take off unless you are sitting down and your seat belt is secure.'

'I want to watch you operate the Jet; it fascinates me.' Frank was increasing the power to both engines. The scream of the twin engines drowned out any further conversations between flight crew and clients.

Grimshaw returned to his seat, buckling his seatbelt then relaxed and observed our actions. Mr Twist, oblivious to the surroundings, was just looking out of the window. Frank's voice spoke from my headset, 'If he wants a show, we will give him one, we will "stick it" all day. The autopilot has a problem, it is malfunctioning.'

I confirmed his instructions.

'Follow and shadow my hands on the throttle levers only, change the radios as I ask you to, make notes on your clipboard, write down anything you want, just look busy.'

The green light on the runway flickered 'On' giving us the visual instruction. We cleared for flight, air traffic confirming simultaneously in both our headsets. Going for the record take off speed we departed Manchester. The Lear jet eagerly quivering in the fast climb, we rocketed into the grey morning clouds. The undercarriage clunked safely into place, full power, and I.O.M, here we come.

As requested, I shadowed his hands on the controls as we climbed. The Lear again was eager to be airborne. Just as we were levelling off at 3,000 feet a voice in our headsets said, 'Tango, Alpha, do you have a problem?'

'Negative.' Frank replied. 'Is there a problem as we took off, that we should be aware that', We evidently had exceeded air traffic noise reading as we left.

'Sorry about that frank replied immediately, we will have the engines checked at Ronaldsway, to see if there is a problem. Thank you for the information and concern.' This seemed to satisfy them; they wished us a safe flight. Finally trimming the aircraft for straight and level flight, Frank started the normal paperwork. Frank, speaking to me via the intercom, instructed, 'Take control, straight and level heading North West.'

'I have control.' concentrating hard I was not going to make a mistake. I kept the aircraft straight and level. The artificial horizon instrument has the outline of a small aeroplane on the front glass. Keeping the image matching the rear of the instrument will keep the craft in level.

Frank gave another instruction in the headset. 'Radio 1, channel 2.' Changing the radio channel to the number 2 tuned our radios for the next leg of the trip. Frank hailed the Prestwick air traffic control.

'Foxtrot, Whiskey, Tango, Tango, Alpha, good morning, Prestwick.'

'Good morning, Tango Alpha, destination?'

'Ronaldsway I.O.M.'

'Affirmative.'

'Climb to 10,000, weather reports heavy air turbulence. Please report back to us any undue weather conditions upon arrival at Ronaldsway.'

'Affirmative.'

'Have a safe flight.'

'Thank you, Prestwick.'

As we eased the control column back to climb to new level of 10,000 feet, the ever-nosy Grimshaw asked why we were climbing again.

I replied, 'Air turbulence.' and switched on the seatbelt sign Levelling off at 10,000 feet, Grimshaw was leaning into the cockpit area. Frank, intent on filling in paper work, did not notice him. I turned to him, 'Please return to your seat, we are informed of serious turbulence. It would be safer if you sat down and refrained from moving around.'

Grimshaw was about to say something when the aircraft entered an air pocket. The aircraft dropped about one hundred feet, everything not secured in the cabin bounced off the roof.

Grimshaw hit the roof of the bulkhead, and collapsed onto the floor, cursing as he crawled back to his seat.

I enquired. 'Are you OK,'

Mr Twist, looking at Grimshaw, grunting disapproving 'Just sit down, he told you to sit down.' Before Grimshaw managed to get his seat belt secured, the plane dropped another hundred feet. He must have hurt himself as one side of the seatbelt dug into him as he was propelled into the ceiling again. Twist just looked at the cursing lump beside him, and grunted something obscene in his direction.

Frank said firmly, 'I have control,' making the aircraft climb back to 10,000 feet. Again, the aircraft dropped. Frank called Prestwick,

'Request to climb to 15,000 feet, encountering severe turbulence.'

The reply came back, 'No traffic in your vicinity, you are safe to alter height.'

At 15,000 the flight was smoother; Frank reported the condition to Prestwick air traffic. soon it was time to descend to Ronaldsway for final landing instruction. Starting our

descent into Ronaldsway, steeper than I thought we should have, my ears were hurting with the pressure change, Frank passed me a boiled sweet chew on that I will help, my mother told me about accepting sweets from strangers.
'But, I protested, we have been introduced,' Frank replied, 'Well, that's alright, Mum would have approved.'

'Take a quick look round the passengers for me, make sure all the cupboard doors are closed, all loose item stowed before we land.' Moving back into the passenger area I secured the drinks tray.
Grimshaw said, 'Give me a whiskey.'
'I am sorry, we are about to land, I am securing for landing.' Grimshaw had poked his nose into every cupboard, every door was unlocked. Frank's voice came over the intercom, 'Landing in five minutes.' Returning to the flight deck I talked with Frank over the intercom. 'Grimshaw is upset, his head hurts.'
'He should have sat down.'
We broke through the cloud bank covering the Isle of Man perfectly lined up for immediate landing on the main runway. It was raining slightly with a 5-mph crosswind.
We parked directly in front of the main terminal. After shutting everything down Frank went to talk with the clients, 'To be absolutely sure we have enough flight time for southern France, we must be airborne by 2:30 pm. That should give you about three hours to complete your business, is that OK?'
Grimshaw replied. 'That should be enough.'
'If you follow that Air stewardess coming towards us from the terminal, she will guide you through, there is a taxi rank just outside the main entrance. We shall get your luggage from the hold for you.' Grimshaw requested his briefcase.

The rest stays on board Mr Twist vacated his seat and lumbered off following Grimshaw.

Frank turned and asked, 'Want a job?'

'Why?'

'You did most things correct.'

'Thanks, just basic courtesy, and common sense.'

'What was the idea of manual flying?'

'We do not want some people to see how easy it is to fly.'

'Grimshaw is one of those clients who are a pain, always want to sit in the co-pilot's seat and play pilots. He probably flies one of those flight simulators on his home computer, after a couple of hours, people like that think they can fly, they can be dangerous.'

'What did you think of Mr Twist?'

'Big.'

'He is, it was possible him that I needed extra power to take off, and exceeded the noise level' chuckled Frank.

While we were waiting at Ronaldsway we took the chance and refuelled the Lear then checked over the so-called noisy engines only for the benefit of the air traffic tower. They would have been informed by Manchester about the noise problem. We looked busy then sauntered over to the café in the terminal and savour the delights of a light lunch.

'Drink small amounts.' Frank said.

'Why?'

'What goes in has to come out.'

I chose a light sandwich and an espresso coffee. During lunch, I updated Frank about the suspicions we had with Grimshaw stealing money from the company bank account in Switzerland.

'I have a feeling he is clearing his bank accounts in Douglas then when we get to France, he will be, as they say, doing a runner with the cash.'

Frank replied rubbing his chin. 'Mmm, that's why you were running around in Switzerland that is very interesting, we could do something to stop his little tricks.'

I made a call to Anne, 'Hello Ross, everything is going like clockwork, also D.S. Harris was trying to get hold of you.'

I made a call to Harris. 'Hi Ross, I am glad you have called,' he confided with me, 'They now have a positive proof of a conspiracy to defraud not only Whittle Plastic, but large number of his other clients, the fraud investigators found discrepancies within hours of starting to investigate. We are looking for him to help with our enquiries, but he has disappeared, his girlfriend said she thought he had left the country on a business trip.'

'Would he have a large gentleman with him called Mr Twist?'

'Yes, he would, Twist is known to us as a thug and one of his employees.'

'Is there a reward for finding him?'

Harris replied. 'No!'

'We have them both with us.'

'Where are you?' D.S. Harris replied with urgent tones.

'He chartered an aeroplane from a pal of mine to go to Ronaldsway then onto Cannes in the south of France. This pal of mine wanted a second pilot with him, so I am here.'

'But he will recognise you.'

'No, he hasn't. Grimshaw and Twist are both in Douglas at this present moment.' Frank touched my arm and pointed to the main entrance.

'Oh no they are here now; I will keep you informed of what happens.'

'I will inform Douglas Police,' said Harris. 'You won't have time.'

I gave our flight number to Harris,

'Bye now.' Grimshaw had spotted us and was walking

towards us.

'We have extra luggage; it is in the taxies with Mr Twist.'
Calling a porter to assist them with their Luggage, Grimshaw was intently looking at me. Noticing this interest I enquired, 'Anything wrong?'

'I know you.' Grimshaw replied.

'Not unless you live in Outer Hebrides, and lived in South Africa, I have never met Mr Twist or your good self before.'

I was thinking, I have met your bad self and that was a pain. Mr Twist, assisted with a team of porters, was pushing trolleys each one was stacked high with parcels and packages.

Frank said, 'Time to go.'

We passed separately through the security check, leaving Grimshaw and Twist to follow with the packages.

I took a position by the side of the X-Ray monitors as Grimshaw's parcels came through, most of the packages displayed the same thing: thin metal strips, apart from the last one which was full of flat metal strips and bags of round discs. I noted the latter package and would make sure it was packed in the rear hold. Frank was past the total weight of the excess baggage and the dimensions; quickly calculating the safe carrying capacity of the Lear, I realised we would be over loaded by 800 kilos.

Frank brought this matter to Grimshaw's attention. 'We can put the excess baggage into storage and have them shipped to France by air freight today or tomorrow if you wish?'

Grimshaw replied, 'Leave the Co-pilot and Twist behind.'

'Impossible, absolutely impossible! International flight rules say we must have two pilots on the flight deck.' Frank quickly replied.

'I can fly so I could do it.'

'You are not trained on Lear jets.'

Mr Twist snarled at Grimshaw, 'You are not leaving me here.' Frank made a suggestion, 'If we leave the excess packages here in Ronaldsway storage area, we return in the morning from France, pick the up the packages then fly them back to France. It will only take about 7 hours.' Grimshaw was not happy, but with airport security watching our every move, he had no option but to agree.

Loading the packages, the best we could, we filled all the outer lockers and most of the seating area.

We deposited the leftover packages, including the heavy parcel in the cargo shed. We arranged pickup for tomorrow, but because of the weight only one passenger would be allowed as the craft would be bordering maximum weight.

We waited for clearance on the main runway. It took nearly all the runway to become airborne, finally lifting clear just before the runway ceased and the Irish Sea started. Frank was calling Prestwick, he informed them of the destination. They immediate replied, 'Tango Alpha destination of Cannes, confirmed. We have a severe weather warning: storm clouds with a ceiling of 18,000 ft dead ahead, you are cleared to climb to 20,000 ft.'

Frank replied quietly, 'Can we continue at 10,000 ft with the option to reroute?' Frank was still in discussion with air traffic control as Grimshaw stuck his head into the flight deck. 'Is there any food available?'

'Yes, a moment, I will come through.' Frank finished with Air traffic, explained to me There are two chicken dinners for them. If you remove them from the fridge located under the drink's cabinet, then use the microwave next to the fridge, give the meals 5 minutes at full power, they will be ready.'

'Also, there are some complimentary drinks.'

'I think they have found them.' Both Grimshaw and Twist had large glassfuls of spirit and looked in a jovial mood.

I went into the cabin and informed them of the available food, 'Yes please.' Grimshaw said, 'Well, if that is all you have, I suppose I will have one.'

I prepared their meals; there were two cakes in the fridge for afters. Before I could serve them the dinners, the aircraft shuddered violently. Frank reacted with a fast correction to the power and prepared to climb. Glancing portside a huge bank of dark grey cloud. The same cloud stretched as far as I could see. 'What's up mate?' Mr Twist asked.

'A storm clouds dead ahead and it looks a nasty one. Captain will climb over it.'

'Is it dangerous?'

'Only if you attempt to fly through, we would be tossed around like a cork in a tumble dryer. Please put you seat belts on and stay seated.

I will serve your dinners.' I said, giving Twist his meal. Suddenly the aircraft lurched to one side, the boxes sitting on the seats moved and crashed onto Mr Twist. a quick movement of his arm pushed the boxes back into place, thanks for that help we could have been in bother with a shifting load, I dropped onto one knee holding the boxes and pushing them backwards. Grimshaw blurted out, 'What is a man with dark black hair doing with blond hairs on your legs,' Looking back at my leg I saw my trouser leg had slid above my socks revealing my natural light blond hair. I was going to tell, the mixed marriage joke again, but Grimshaw was not happy.

'I know you; I know who you are, you are that bastard who thumped me in Manchester.' He swung at me knocking me sideways, sending me crashing into the bulkhead. I felt the sickening crunch as I collided with the door mechanism and everything went black.

Grimshaw ran through to the flight deck and said in a

menacing voice to Frank, 'Your mate's knocked out in the back, I am taking over command.'

Frank asked, 'Sorry? I did not hear what you said could you repeat?'

Grimshaw repeated, 'I am taking over command.'

Frank looked at him and repeated, 'you, are taking command, and intend to take control of this aeroplane. I must ask, can you fly this Lear jet aeroplane?' As he repeated Grimshaw's order to take over the aeroplane he was secretly pressing the radio transmitter button on the control column. With this single action the entire air traffic control network became informed that the plane had been placed into a hijack situation. We had become a marked aeroplane: every radar screen tracking our progress would have the radar blip isolated.

Frank replied, 'We must climb to clear that thundercloud, I must ask permission to climb.'

'Don't you touch that radio?' menaced Grimshaw. Too late Frank had double clicked the send button, as from now whatever was said in the cockpit was also transmitted to the listening authorities and the Police.

'Just fly through that cloud.' Grimshaw gesticulated at the black cloud in front of the nose of the aircraft.

Frank sternly replied, 'That is not advisable; we could have our wings ripped off.'

'I have flown through a storm cloud before.'

'What in?' Frank replied. Grimshaw swung at Frank and connected. Frank feared the worst and felt blood running down from his ear. 'What is it you want me to do?' 'Fly through, that is your order.' Frank levelled off. At 17,000 ft he slid a hand down by his seat turning off the oxygen in the cabin.

'What are you doing?' Grimshaw observed Frank's

movement.

'I am turning the oxygen off in case of a lightning strike, then we do not become a fireball.'

'Why are you not using the autopilot?'

'It is defective, we had trouble yesterday, and we had no time to repair it.'

Regaining consciousness, I quickly became aware of the surroundings; I was still laid on the floor, without moving I tried to determine the situation. Mr Twist, oblivious to the events developing in the cockpit, was tucking into the last cream cake. He then reclined his chair, closed his eyes and went to sleep.

I could hear Grimshaw and Frank talking loudly to each other. The outside buffeting was constant, indicating that we were in the cloud. Hopefully we would be through the cloud fast as we were travelling at 350 knots.

'Why can't we see where we are going?'

'We can, we are using the radar.' Frank claimed.

Grimshaw was getting agitated, 'It is only a cloud and we are in it.' The buffeting was getting worse, we were being thrown around like a feather in a whirlwind. Frank was working hard to keep the Lear straight and level.

Grimshaw was getting jittery, 'We are going round in a circle.'

'No, we are not.' Frank replied, 'read the instruments.'

'They are faulty, I know, I can fly.' Grimshaw cried. With a loud bang, the plane dropped at least fifty feet. Twist woke up, looking out of the windows. It was very black on both sides. He grabbed hold of me and pulled me onto a seat, then he started to fasten my seat belt. I opened my eyes. Twist asked why it was black outside.

'Because that daft bugger mate of yours will kill us if we do not get out of this cloud.'

Twist replied, 'He is nuts, can you stop him, I am frightened of flying.' The racket of the rain pounding on the outer skin of the plane was deafening, then we were struck by a brilliant flash of lightning, and the plane bucked to one side then dropped another 50 feet. Frank hit his head again on the side window as the plane bucked and twisted, he slumped into his chair.

Grimshaw shook him, shouting, 'Wake up!' Shaking him, he was starting to panic.

I looked around, the plane bucked then rolled over. Grimshaw, not wearing his seatbelt, crashed into the ceiling. The plane, rolling over, started its downward plunge.

The plane bucked again then stopped rolling momentary. Grimshaw landed onto the floor between the two pilots' seats. Jumping from my seat I made my way into the cockpit getting back into my seat. Pulling back on the control column I managed to compensate the roll, stopping the plane from rolling by pulling back on the column. The nose of the Lear jet responded to lift, pulling us out of the dive.

I gave Frank a shake, he was being thrown around in his seat blood trickling down the side of his head, the plane still was bucking violently in all directions.

There was an almighty bang the plane jumped sideways I felt the sickening crunch as I hit my head again against the side window. Dazed I could feel myself slipping into the darkness of unconsciousness. Fighting against the outcome, I glimpsed the amber glow of the autopilot switch. I made a stab for the glowing amber switch, I was now unconscious unaware of the following the effort I made towards the switch had worked, the indicator light turned green, I managed to open an eye and what I saw was in slow motion, I tried to hang on to the seat as the Lear jet banked quickly to port. The autopilot began to corrected the flight problems and revert to the last stored flight plan the Leah jet levelled automatically and compensated for any problem the storm threw at us.

The craft climbed back to 15,000 feet, and flew out of the storm clouds with four souls on board, one scared stiff and two unconscious, and one desperately trying to regain control of the situation.

Withing 10 minutes we had control again I recovered a bottle of water and a serviette Placing the wet serviette on Frank's brow. He moaned, but he was made of stern stuff, he recovered slowly checked over the situation then checked the aircraft, made some adjustments then called Prestwick and conveyed the recover status.

I asked Twist to help me get this idiot out of the cockpit and back into his seat. Twist placed a massive hand on Grimshaw and dragged him to his seat.

Looking in bags for something to restrain him we found a roll of wide brown tape. Removing Grimshaw's jacket, we wrapped the tape around him and the seat and then taped his wrists and feet together. I also requested to bind Twist. Last thing we wanted was this man mountain jumping around within the plane. Twist promised me that he would not cause any trouble to us, without us he would now be dead. Still, he said, if we were worried, please tie him up.

Grimshaw woke, realising his situation he struggled and shouted for Twist to get us. Twist, half awake, looked at the situation then his bindings and remarked to Grimshaw, 'He told you to sit down.' Then closed his eyes and went back to sleep.

Grimshaw was screaming obscenities at us in desperation and we required peace of mind and silence, I taped over his mouth, peace prevailed.

I said to Mr Twist, 'Sorry about tying you up, are you OK?'

'Let me sleep, I am tired.' We landed at Manchester, and were escorted to a secure location inside a hanger; armed security guards surrounded the plane. Frank had requested in advance that we should have security handy when we landed.

D.S. Harris was leading the team of local special police. They arrested Grimshaw. He was cursing that he would get me, he would not forget, he was placed into the back of a police car. The police then turned their attention to Mr Twist, giving him a bad time. I intervened in to their endeavours, 'What's the problem with Mr Twist?'

Plod answered. 'He is under arrest.'

'What for' I asked.

'He is a crook.'

'Maybe so, but not today, he has done nothing wrong and has not threatened us in any way. He has been courteous and pleasant at all times during the flight, and even helped us secure Grimshaw.'

Plod remarked, 'We will take him anyway and release him if there is no cause.' D.S. Harris came to see us, asking Frank, 'Where is Ross?'

'Over there.' Pointing at me. Taking a second look, he said, 'Bloody Hell! 'What is this all about?'

I told him of the situation, how there was a connection with my company and this aeroplane, then about when I went from the north east to Switzerland, then about the discovery of who owned the plane.

'Well, who does own this aeroplane?' D.S. Harris enquired.

'I do.'

'Captain Frank called me and told me of this person claiming to be from the company who wanted to fly the plane to IOM, then to France. Until that time only four people had knowledge of this plane, this enquiry made five. Grimshaw knew he was on the run; he wanted to move the money he stole from the company, then move the deposited money from the I.O.M. to where? We did not find out.

The quickest way to move anything and secretly is by private plane. Grimshaw wanted to get the money; I thought I would tag along, incognito.

Frank and I took two clients to the Isle of Man to pick up their goods, then I called you, you told me Grimshaw was wanted for other conspiracies. Can you wait please I need to go to the toilet very urgently.'

Frank pointed, 'There is a toilet over there.' Dashing in and sitting down, I looked down. All my pubic hair had gone; it was as if I had been shaved but softer. Then it dawned on me, I remember Janine saying, 'only one thing to do.' I said a shave, but later, yes later, when I was asleep, Janine must have used hair removing cream instead of the soothing cream. I thought, surely, she would know the difference. Of course, she knew the talcum powder would not make me feel the loss. Walking back, I was chuckling to myself.

D.S. Harris enquired. 'Something funny'

'No, just a private message from someone in France.'

Frank was explaining the rest of the story to Harris. 'During the onboard fight and actions, the autopilot had not been reset since we returned from Paris. Once the autopilot was re-engaged the plane automatically reverted to the last flight plan stored in its memory. The last flight plan entered into the autopilot was Paris to Manchester, the plane simply turned around and flew back to Manchester away from the storm cloud. Air traffic, aware we were in a hijack situation, would be watching, making sure we had priority clearance in any direction.'

D.S. Harris asked about the items which were in the aeroplane. We unloaded the aeroplane of everything that we had loaded, nothing was left. Customs even put a drug sniffer dog on board. They thought they had found something when the dog slithered under Frank's seat, only to emerge eating his sandwich.

We had to tidy the mess which officials leave when they are searching. The efficient investigators forgot to take Grimshaw's jacket. The entire consignment of boxes Grimshaw had placed onboard was impounded as evidence until investigations were completed.

Frank enquired, 'We were charted today, and Grimshaw has not paid his account. Could we be paid from the money on board?'

D.S. Harris replied, 'No, you will have to wait and see if there is any left.'

'That's nice, that's bloody nice, you bring the wanted crooks home then ask to get your bills paid, then they tell you to stuff off.' Frank appeared to be livid, 'We cannot run this company on fresh air, landing charges and fuel have to be paid the same day.'

'I wish to make a protest.' Frank started to wave his hand in the air, at which Harris and the other officials just walked away, leaving us alone.

'Swine's. Ve vill vin in the end.' Frank was grinning from ear to ear.

'Frank.'

'Yes.'

'Ronaldsway, tomorrow then Paris?'

'Why,'

'We have not finished our charter. Our client requested the remainder of his consignment air freighted overseas tomorrow, if you remember, we are paid when we deliver.'

I was holding the cargo receipt from Ronaldsway storage in the palm of my hand. I slowly turned my hand towards Frank,

who looked over the rim of his spectacles,
'Is that Grimshaw's Jacket?'
'I do not know, I found it on the floor in the back of the cabin; we will have to place it in lost property in our office, until someone claims it. By the weight it feels like there might be a wallet in the inside pocket, he may have already left payment for the charter in this pocket.'
Taking out the bulge in the pocket was a long brown leather wallet, it was stuffed full of £50.00 notes, and some traveller's cheques.
'Maybe we were too quick to judge this client,' Frank claimed,
'I think that we should complete the trip and the charter and place the remaining goods in a safe place.'
'Have you any suggestions?'
'One of the establishments in Switzerland, they appeared very secure.'
I called Janine, 'Hello.'
'Bonsoir, how are you?'
'Smooth as a baby's bottom.'
Janine laughed then whispered, 'I am the same, when will you be back?'
'Tomorrow. Frank and I will be landing at Beynes Thiveral on route to Zurich; we are taking a shipment to Switzerland. I will be requiring the help of a delightful lady; would you like to come?'
'Oui Monsieur.'
'Would Madame like to renew the club membership you enquired about?'
'Would that be renewed on the outbound or inbound flight?'
Janine replied in a sultry whisper, 'Both.'
The removal of the remaining shipment from Ronaldsway went without a hitch. Frank handed me the controls as we

cleared Ronaldsway. He gave me the heading. Proceeding on, I climbed to 15.000 feet, levelling off, then checking the set procedure with a little prompt from Frank. I set the destination into the auto pilot and double checking the details, I switched on the auto pilot. Captain Frank grinned.

'Anything wrong?' I asked.

'We will find out when we get there, coffee?'

'Good idea.'

It seemed to take minutes then we were on final descent to Beynes Thiveral airfield. 'Why not bring your lady friend along for the flight?

Frank stammered, 'Are you sure?'

'Why not? We are at work! Whatever we work at is our business.' Frank, picking up his mobile telephone, made a call. I overheard him discussing the matter, and he turned and replied that we would have two passengers to pick up at Beynes Thiveral airfield. My landing was not good; I bounced the Lear on my first attempt the Lear, recovering immediately then settled on the second touchdown. Frank passed comment that those pesky French rabbits had been digging up the runway. Frank alighted from the aircraft and disappeared into the terminal building returning with Janine.

'I shall go and collect another passenger; I should be ten minutes.' Janine was delighted to see me, enjoyed a lingering embrace.

'We have ten minutes before Frank comes back with his lady friend; I asked if he would like to bring her on the trip.' Janine pouted, 'We will not be alone.'

'What did Madame have in mind?' She gazed around the cabin.

'There is no room; every corner and spare seats are lost under boxes and cartons, is this??? Yes, it is the remainder.' She slowly made her way past the cartons disappearing into the aft toilet.

I noticed Frank returning with his companion. I opened the outer cabin door for them; Frank introduced his companion as Hermione. She was very attractive and spoke a little English. She was amazed as Janine joined us; it turned out that they were old friends from school days. Frank gave me another look, one of those looks when you just know ladies will be exercising their jaws for the next two hours or so.

Chapter 19

We took off, heading for Zurich, ensured of an evening's entertainment. We requested a security hanger to park the aeroplane; I did not want any problem on that front now. We had made arrangements to stay at the Romanoff Hotel, before Frank and Hermione disappeared, I told Frank we would see him in the morning about 10:00.

'Affirmative.' He called back then they hurried away for their own evening's activities. Janine was delighted to have met an old friend. She was able to talk and get up to date on times gone by. She found out that Whittle had stayed at Hermione's guesthouse a few times. He was not the nicest of people but she was still sad that he had been killed with his lady friend.

Janine informed her about the nature of the business and deception those two had been up to, Hermione was astonished and disgusted.

Taking hold of Janine's hand, I held it tight and pulled her close to me, our noses were within two millimetres, 'I have something to say.' Her eyes looked deeply into mine as she anxiously waited for me to speak. I could feel her heart beating and I held her the cheek of her bottom with my hand.

'I am extremely hungry, and must have food before sex.'

'Why not the other way round?'

'No problem we shall eat first' we showered, together she made sure the hair dye was thoroughly rinsed from my hair I shaved enjoying the removal of the beard growth, donning casual attire we took a walk to find a quiet restaurant. During the meal I relayed the flight adventure with Mr Grimshaw and Twist. She showed great concern that Grimshaw could have easily caused an accident and all would have been killed.

I agreed, and she made me promise not to do it again. She was curious about the contents of the boxes.

'I am not sure as to their exact content but I know it is money, lots of it. We should investigate before we make the deposit to avoid embarrassment.' I felt something touching my leg, it made me jump. Putting my hand under the table it was Janine rubbing her foot on my leg under the table.

'You have eaten.'

she whispered 'Shall we'

'Yes, On or Under the table.' I suggested

'No! In the bedroom.'

Our stimulating foreplay was greatly increased with the lack of lower body hair; making love, we settled into each other's arms, slipping into deep sleep.

A resounding crash woke me from my slumber, I totally forgot about the bloody dustcarts in the morning.

Looking out of the window, there was movement in one of the windows on the floor below. I observed the person, looking out of the window. It was Hermione, she was naked and she had a plump body; her breasts were larger than I thought, still they had a pleasing shape with dark nipples. The pallor of her body was stunning against the darkened background of the room. A hand slid around my shoulders. I felt the contact of a warm naked body pressed against mine, which brought my attention back.

'Do you see anything of interest outside?'

'Only Hermione on the floor below.'

Janine took a look and was noticed by Hermione. She waved back and smiled, disappearing back into the room.

We met at the breakfast bar. I discussed a full inspection of the goods with Frank, before we made the deposit. Frank suggested we use the inside of the Lear for a quick inspection. We would reseal the boxes and place them outside the aeroplane ready for a security company to take to the bank. Driving back to the airport we passed the frosty bank, where we intended depositing the shipment. Hermione said something to Janine. Janine translated informing us that Hermione's son worked at the frosty Bank. Entering the secure hanger, Hermione, not realising what we were going to do, offered to go and get some food and other necessary items. Janine gave her some money to get some other items she required. We examined the cartons; of all the boxes were crammed full of money. Janine tried to count but there was too much. Judging by counting one box then comparing it we estimated an excess of fourteen million pounds in bundles of Fifty and Twenty-pound notes.

There was one box that contained silverware and lots of jewellery and trinkets, plus other interesting objects. Frank deposited that carton in the rear hold on the Lear jet, we would take a detailed look at the box and contents later. One box contained gold bars and gold coins of different countries and size plus bullion in large amounts. Hermione, returned with a plentiful supply of food and bottles of wine and a small package which she secretly gave to Janine. Taking the food inside the Lear she busied herself preparing a small meal for us.

Hermione said she had telephoned her son in the bank; he would be delighted to meet with us sometime during the day or evening. I suggested that we should take the plunge and deposit this consignment, picking my words carefully so as not to make Hermione aware of the amount of money on hand.

We requested a security van to attend us to remove the boxes to the bank. At the bank I made the deposit into the account, while Janine and I dealt with the clerk. Hermione located her son and a mother and son talk commenced.

Her son was more interested in us and how she was connected with us; she explained the little that she knew and he seemed happy with the information. A well-dressed man in a light grey suit called him to the desk for a couple of minutes. They were in deep discussion with the occasional secretive look in my direction. As we were about to leave the same man approached Janine and I requesting that we meet with him in his office; he was the bank manager.

Janine and I sat listening to what he had to say; he was most apologetic referring to earlier in the month when the bank had not co-operated correctly. He now found himself in an embarrassed situation that they had not informed us of the all the bank accounts held for Whittle. He produced a sheet of paper, which Janine quickly read then discussed quickly in French about the new matter on hand. She sat quietly going over the details on the document. With no reference to me she requested that the entire contents of these accounts be transferred to our present account. The manager made the order and offered us coffee while we waited, he then discussed the possibility of investing the money for us in a plastics company in France. He had heard they had a remarkable product and he was hearing extremely good reports of this company.

Janine gave some orders to the movement of money to the two accounts, one in France and one in the other Credit Swiss bank that we had also opened during the earlier visit. When Janine gave the name of the company account in Paris, the manager exclaimed, 'But that is the plastic company I was telling you about.' We thanked him, then informed him, we are that plastic company concerned.'

He asked us a barrage of questions about the company; he was interested in acquiring shares in the company if they were available. We said that upon return to Paris, we would send him details by return.

The clerk appeared with the new statement and balance of the amount of money contained in the cartons, what we wanted to do with the bullion, and coin. Please record the registration and deposit in a security box for us, the registration was completed and receipts and balance sheet were passed to us to check, and sign.

Janine, leaning close to me, said quietly, 'It is time to go.' Bidding the manager farewell Janine held my arm as we left. I could feel her shaking through the grip on my arm. Sitting in the car she looked at me and in a shaky voice said, 'I think the bank made a mistake with the accounts and they have transferred over fifty-four million dollars into our account. This I transferred the bulk of the money to our account in Paris and the remainder to our account in the Credit Swiss.' 'But whose money, was it?' I replied. 'Remember the connection with Whittle and the German company Schyne Plastix who were going to take us over?' 'Yes, I do.' 'They intended to steal from us,' I replied. 'It was their money but it was deposited under the name of Whittle. The German company, with their money gone, will have trouble surviving; there might be a possibility they will cease trading.' Janine went on to say it was Hermione's son who brought this account to the notice of the manager; they had no option and with us being present at the bank, were forced to make a decision. Evidently, under new Swiss banking laws, if they had not advised us and we discovered the deception, the bank would be liable to huge fines and compensation costs. 'I think we are in a position to fly over to Darmstadt in Germany and have an impromptu visit with this company.' Janine replied, 'we shall wait a week then go.' 'Why a week?' Janine looked at me, 'I have something planned.' 'Frank is flying us to Cannes on the French Riviera when we are finished here; I want to show you something.'

The Lear jet climbed briskly, unhindered by the excess weight, into the afternoon sky heading for south west. The weather was clear with little wind, perfect flying weather. Hermione appeared with two coffees and a biscuit. Frank said, 'Do you fancy flying this for a while?' He had a glint in his eye. 'Why not, Mon Capitaine?'

He passed control to me then disappeared into the rear cabin. The Lear jet was on autopilot and would not deviate from the route unless switched off. Janine came forward and joined me on the flightdeck, closing the curtains giving Frank and guest a moderation of privacy. She sat in Frank's seat, pulling a folded paper from her blouse and passed it to me. I read the paper, it contained a comprehensive list of deposits and the banks it had been transferred to. That was a good list. 'Do you think there is any more money hidden anywhere?'

'It is hard to say, knowing Whittle Plastic's prior state of accounts. Now that he has destroyed the German plastic company, I am glad we are rid of him and his accountant Grimshaw.'

Hermione had been given a slip of paper from her son as we left the bank.

Janine passed me the paper, it read,

17 Rue de l'océan

Cannes

Codex 4573 France.

'Whose address, is it?'

'Whittle's Secret residence.'

'Madame I am amazed; you are starting to be as devious as I am.'

'I have had a good teacher.' She smiled, sighed and stretched her arms. A hand hit a switch on the overhead panel. I quickly returned the switch to its original position. This was not a good place for activity.

Sounds of sensual passion could be overheard from the rear cabin. Janine placed her hand over her mouth, 'Do you not think Frank heard us?' 'No, you were very quiet, it was the smile on your face that gave you away.'

Air traffic control hailed us, I returned their call asking could I change heading for approach into Cannes. They gave me the heading and I dialled in the new heading. The auto pilot did the rest, turning us towards the new heading and dropping the engine power. We started reducing altitude. Frank's head popped through the curtains, 'Hello Captain, Janine could I have my seat back please?' Climbing from his seat she gripped my shoulder with her hand giving me a secret nip then she disappeared through into the rear cabin. Frank, taking control, took us along the coast on a long let-down so we could see the properties and villas and estates on the coastline. They were magnificent, and expensive; nearly all had parking places for boats and some had landing pads for helicopters. We landed at Cannes International Airport at 5:15. We arrived at the hotel at 5:45 and had to be ready to go to by 6:30.

Frank and Hermione had other plans and did not wish to come. We dressed the best we could with the limited clothes that we had brought. Janine and I were taken by taxi to this secret place. As the taxi turned into the square, the auditorium was well displayed. It was the ballet. I read the title of the evening's ballet; it was the same ballet Janine had her accident. Taking our seats she said, 'some of my friends are still associated with this ballet it would be nice if we met them.' The lights dimmed and the music quietly commenced.

The curtains opened; my eye caught a flash of light from Janine's earrings. She was wearing the earrings I found in the Monteverdi. I leant towards her saying your perfume and earrings are exquisite, whispering 'merci', she slid her hand into mine, looked at me and smiled. Her grip noticeably tightened as two of the dancers leapt across the stage, both landing gently and graciously then bowing to the audience. The curtain closed; it was the interval.

She had tears in her eyes, 'Is that where the accident happened?' 'Oui let us get a drink.' The foyer was filling; I collected two white wines, returning to find Janine talking to a group of people. I stood back, she looked, happy as she talked.

She saw me waiting and reached out her arm for me to join her; she proceeded to introduce me to the people present. They were part of the original cast that she had danced with in the early days. Many questions were directed towards me, I could not understand them all. Janine told them that I was English and spoke limited French.

The sound of a gong indicated the end of the interval and the Ballet was about to resume. The foyer emptied quickly leaving us and two others were gesturing to return to our seats. Janine suggested if I did not mind that we go and have a drink with this couple. Janine introduced me to Edith and her husband Jack; it was he who had crashed into Janine, ending her career so swiftly. They were still good friends and they lived just outside Cannes. We went to a nearby theatre café, it was quiet now and but when the ballet finished this café was packed, history unfurled itself with the discussions these three were having.

My understanding of the French language was becoming clearer; as the evening progressed, I found myself contributing to the conversation. Edith invited us back to their house for a nightcap; we agreed and eased ourselves into Jack's small car, which chugged along the sea front. Jack turned and started up the hillside. We were near the area where the expensive properties were situated. I asked Jack did he know of 'Rue De L'Océan?

'Dacor, il est deux cent meters

'Can we go and have a look at number 17'

Jack turned and drove into Rue de L'Océan. At the end of the road was number 16, a small turning circle and the edge of the cliff then the sea. The cliff towering above us was silhouetted against the bright moonlit night sky; there was no number 17 to be seen. Just as we turned, a car entered the road and stopped outside number 15. Janine went to speak with the man driving the car; he shook his head then pointed in the direction of the other side of the hill. He was indicating to go back around and come in from the other direction; his hand signals took no translation. We retraced out route back to the main road.

We travelled another kilometre and entered the road from the other direction. The houses on this side were not as grand as the others but still impressive. We drove slowly along looking at the driveways and house numbering. They were very sparse, then we saw a small sign, number 17 was carved into the weathered wood, an unmade track led into the darkness. Jack said, 'We are here.' Getting out of the car we tried to see what was at the end of the drive. A small glow from a light came from a corner window of the distant house, other detail could not be made out. 'We shall return in the morning and have another look.'

We proceeded with Jack and Edith to their little house it took about 20 minutes to reach the house. Edith asked who lived there. Janine told them a business colleague, who once said when in the area call in to visit. As it was late, we could go back in the morning. Edith said, 'You will both stay with us tonight, I will not hear any objection.' I was not objecting; I was in the back of a little car with a delightful woman, why should I complain? Jack's house had been constructed into a hillside overlooking the city; it was an unusual but distinct location. It was a cosy house, which was burrowed into the hill side., it would be cool during the summer and warm during the winter. Edith showed us to our bedroom it overlooked the bay, which was clearly visible in the moonlight. Quickly taking a comfort break we returned to the lounge area, Jack had poured brandy for everyone. Sitting in this casual environment was to my liking, it was warmer than Paris and definitely warmer than England, I could very easily be acquainted with this way of life, we chatted and drank until the early hours then retired to bed and sleep.

Chapter 20

A shaft of sunshine piercing through the gap in the curtains bathed me in a brilliant light. Turning my head, I could escape the intense light; no further sleep would be achieved in this bed unless I closed the outside shutters. A female figure walked across the shaft of light, making a silhouette that I had seen many times before. 'They have a swimming pool!' Janine exclaimed, 'I am going for a swim.' Rising from the bed I followed her down to the pool, 'What about swimwear? I have nothing with me.' 'Do without!' Janine cried, as she jumped naked into the pool. It is a wonderful feeling swimming nude. Shortly we were joined by Jack and Edith, judging by their immaculate all over tan, they too did not bother with swimwear; no need of anything in the privacy of your own home. I swam for an hour and played in the pool; I could feel the sunshine becoming unbearable on my skin. 'I getting out of the sun.' I climbed out of the pool taking a seat under a parasol.

Edith also had left the pool, she returned with some towels, disappearing again to return with coffee and croissants, and pain au chocolate. They were a distinct favourite. Janine came and lay on a sun lounge bed she draped a towel across her to hide her modesty. As she lay drying in the sunshine, I remarked that her earrings looked pretty. She turned her head smiling and blew me a kiss. Edith was smirking what is the joke, it is the colour of your hairs,

'Pardon, could you elaborate' Edith seemed slightly embarrassed and explained the dark hair on my head changed colour as it went down my body. I looked and it was true it did.

Janine explained to Edith it fits of laughter why I had dyed my hair, and of course mentioned the hair removing cream,

Edith asked for a view of the clean area, as if she had not already observed it, now I was feeling embarrassed Janine came and sat on my lap and consoled me.

Nature took its course, she realised she could not leave my lap as she had excited me and this would be a problem, she could not move, I could not make the erection go away, we had a problem, Jack and Edith seemed to be settled for the next hour or so, there was only one thing to do and let nature take its course. Jack had dropped off to sleep, Edith sensed something was happening kept us under observation, as we tried to give the appearance of one sitting on another's lap. Finally, the sex urge waned and Janine stood throwing her towel onto me she jumped into the pool.

Edith smiled at me giving me a longing look, I was getting a feeling if she would love to take Janine's place, this inclination caused me to become erect again, I turned over and tried to hide the problem.

After ten minutes I managed to control my ardour, stood put on my shorts and took a walk around the pool.

I walked around and gazing down the gradually sloping hillside down to the sea, I could make out the hill and rue de L'Océan.

The road went to both sides and I could just make out the house tucked into the hillside with what looked like a long straight road coming from the front of the house for about two hundred and fifty meters along the cliff edge.

There was a single post with what I thought was an orange flag hanging limp, but a slight gust of wind caught it and as it lifted, I saw it was a windsock.

That strip of road was a landing strip. I pointed this to Janine, she asked Jack if he had noticed any aeroplanes landing there.

'Only in the early part of the year, quite a lot of activity, but not now, most of the rich people have helicopters. Also, I think there is a problem with that property.' Jack suddenly became aware that that was the property we went to last night.

Jack had remembered something recently in the local paper about that place, he left to go and search for the newspaper. He returned holding the paper open at the page and he read the article. The local government had placed a compulsory purchase order on the property; the owner had only so many days to appeal.

Janine enquired. 'When is the last day'

'It's today at 15:00.' Glancing at my watch it was 11:45,

'Janine, I think it is time to pay a visit to the property at Rue de L'Océan, Edith was sad to see us leave so soon, but we promised to return soon, I thanked Edith for our stay. She wished us bon voyage, and gave me a big hug as well as the normal kisses on the cheek; Jack drove to the property and then on up to the house.

A security guard met us at the gate requesting our intentions. We told him we wanted to look at the property, as we were sure it belonged to us.

He was not willing to let us enter. Janine influenced him with a promise of a permanent job and a pay increase, this certainly swayed his judgement and he opened the gate then beckoned us to view the property. He gave us a comprehensive conducted tour of the estate. There was definitely an airstrip with a hanger big enough to house a Piper Chieftain, it might even take the Lear jet, but the Lear created so much noise that as it took off this would be horrendous for the surrounding neighbourhood.

The house was well furnished throughout, rooms downstairs and all bedrooms contained their ensuite facilities an indoor and outdoor pool complemented the property. A small stairway cut into the cliff led down to the sea and our own private beach. A jetty jutting out to sea, at the end of it was a fair-sized boathouse; looking through the window, I could see a yacht with its mast laid flat, and a speed boat, moored alongside all seemed to be silently waiting.

I asked the security guard; 'Is this part of the property?'

He replied. 'I believe so.' next stop the government office. Arriving, we were glad of Jack driving us, as parking would have been a nightmare. He said he must get back, departing he wished us good luck and to come and see them anytime. Janine comes into her own in the office environment. She carved a way through all the officials and clerks quicker than I could have. We made claim to the said property at Rue de L'Océan due to the last-minute discovery of this acquisition by the Vista Plastic Company.

After an hour of discussion, the compulsory order was waived. We were thrust into negotiations with the local government. They were intending to expand residential dwellings in that area, and the runway on our property was causing untold problems. During the discussions we were informed that many persons had made enquiries about the acquisition of the property. Janine had already replied that we would make a decision at a later date, as we had just discovered this undeclared asset of the company.

Leaving the office, we decided to take a leisurely walk back to the hotel by the route of the promenade. Janine seemed to give the impression of contentment.

I asked, 'is everything fine or do we have a problem?'

'No, everything is good.' Today at the last minute we had avoided losing a lovely property to the government. We reminisced about the recent events and discoveries. The situation now was better than I could ever have expected; we had overcome some dangerous situations and survived.

As we arrived back at the hotel, Frank and Hermione came running to meet us looking worried. 'Where have you been? Your beds had not been slept in, nobody knew where you were, and we could contact either of you on your mobile phones.'

I asked. 'Is there a problem?'

'Only where you were; we were worried!' A brief update put all minds at rest. Janine's telephone bleeped into life and simultaneously my mobile telephone rang. I received a call from Darrell; he was happy as ever and in Paris with the factory destroyed. He decided to drive the Monteverdi back to Paris then see if he could help out in the office. 'The Monteverdi was in the office garage safe and secure. I suppose Claudette is helping you?'

'Yes, in more ways than one.'

The new formula Otto had discovered with the degradation factor was better than the one Pierre had on file. With the political situation going green due to pressure from environmentalist parties, plastic carton and reeled film manufacturing companies were showing interest, with orders already materialising. I informed him about the possible acquisition of the German plastic factory. He thought it would be an excellent move. Then let us in on a secret, when Whittle started to have an interest in the factory, he talked them into the installation of new equipment; this would be a prime factory to expand to manufacture the new products, and it was only about three-hour drive from Paris.

A coffee with Frank and Hermione proved interesting. They had discovered a mutual interest; Frank quite liked the idea of living in France and subject to the location of where the Lear jet could be parked would be prepared to relocate as well.

Later Janine and I took a walk along the promenade. As we

turned a corner a sign inclined against the wall advertised an auction of fine items was taking place. We casually entered. Watching the auction take place Janine stood in front of me and leant on me. I was holding her around her waist then casually she suggestively rubbed her bottom into my lap. I winced slightly, gripping her waist, 'What is wrong?' She enquired with a concerned expression.

'Stubble.'

She deliberated for a while, 'I have some cream that will help. We must attend to that immediately.' Playfully pulling each other by the hand along the promenade, our arms interlocked, we walked back to the hotel.

I whispered to her, 'Will that be the package Hermione got for you in Zurich?'

'You don't miss anything' Janine stopped, sitting on a promenade bench. She opened her handbag and placed a small soft blue pouch in my hand. I opened it, it was the gents' watch I found in the Monteverdi; the chronometer was gleaming, it looked new.

'Yes, they repaired it for me in Zurich.' I once gave it to a man that I loved; now I give to another whom I love dearly.

Janine's suggestion to wait for a week or two was perfect, I made a courtesy telephone call to the sales dept of Schyne Plastix, the receptionist, explained that they were closed, and passed the call to the factory administrator, I talked with him giving him the story that we happened to be passing and it was possible that we could visit them and discuss future supplies of the Loyplas compound.

He was sorry to say that the company had ceased trading, and our journey would be wasted, when I offered to have an interest in acquiring the business, he was absolutely delighted, and he would be pleased to meet with me.

Frank flew us to Darmstadt for the meeting with Schyne Plastix, they picked us up from the airport, in the company limousine, then wined and dined us even assisted us to conclude sale.

We stayed at a hotel in the centre of Darmstadt, we made sure that we had a quiet room with no early morning noises from frenzied refuse collectors. As we were concluding the final paper work Janine was in her element, she enjoyed the final capitulation of the last enemy, the administrator passed me a bunch of keys, I looked at them asking 'what they were for',

'Your Mercedes' he replied,

'I do not have a Mercedes,'

'The car belongs to the company you now own the company, and that is the transport of the previous managing director.' this set my mind thinking what happened to Whittles car, I looked out of the window into the parking lot and pressed the remote button immediately a black Mercedes Benz saloon lights flashed a couple of times, pressing the remote button again the lights flashed only once, I repeated the action again, I did not know of the Mercedes range of cars, and this saloon was a mystery.

Janine came and stood behind me she secretly stabbed her finger nail into my side, 'I suppose it will do for now, you could keep the Monteverdi safe in the garage.'

'We shall drive to Paris in this new vehicle; and see exactly how long it took to make the journey by road.' I had flown so much I was missing the excitement of driving on the road.

With all the business transactions completed we sat a while in the vehicle. The car was unusually sparse in documentation, a paper in the glove box, stated that this was a loan car from the Mercedes distributorship.

Janine called them on her mobile, 'Yes, they were waiting for the car to be returned, the car was now repaired and ready for collection. Janine asked directions and we drove to the garage.

Taking the paperwork to the receptionist she gave me a paper to sign and passed me a set of keys, I asked her to show me the car in question, she pointed outside in the car park the fourth car down in the first line, it is the green one.

Walking to the line of cars there was a gap in the roof line of the parked vehicles, in between two saloons was a two-seat coupe, painted in a metallic dark green, Janine was delighted, she took the keys inserted the key in the driver's door and unlocked it, the car erupted with an incredible noise, it shrieked loudly I seem to be stood in the perfect position to receive the full blast as the siren.

I stepped back in shock of the noise, a mechanic walking by, came over, and spoke to me, I raised my hands in a gesture of not understanding and hearing, he took the key from her, pressed the Mercedes symbol on the key, immediately the alarm ceased. I replied to him, 'I do not speak any German,' he was taken aback with the reply, he thought for a moment then turned to Janine. He demonstrated the alarm and the ways to arm and disarm the security system, Janine spoke to him in French, he had little French and even less English, but we managed to understand what was required.

The interior space was limited; lifting the boot lid I discovered an empty black valise, the spare wheel, a toolkit and a first aid kit. Packing our luggage into the boot I tossed the black valise into the front seat.

Janine had already inserted herself into the driver's seat, and was ready to start the car. The mechanic helped her adjust the seat and showing her the controls, she was displaying a generous length of leg as she pressed the pedals up and down, she was playing for the mechanics benefit, when I took my seat in the passenger seat, the mechanic stopped being so attentive, the engine roared into life, it had the sound of eight cylinders, as Janine revved the engine again, definitely a rumble of eight cylinders.

She selected D on the automatic transmission, and released the parking brake, slowly inching forward out of the car park, a quick scan of the road signs, we headed for the airport.

Once on the dual carriageway she gave the accelerator a quick jab, the kick we received in the back as the car shot forward into an incredible speed, surely this was not the way these cars performed.

Frank was amazed when we arrived in our new acquisition, after he walked around the car, he noticed a small badge on the rear panel, and it read Mille Miglia,

'Is it the V8 version?'

'Yes, I believe so,' Lifting the bonnet to reveal the V8 engine rested snugly in the engine compartment, emblazoned across the cast aluminium air filter casting was the name Mille Miglia.

'Wow!' Frank exclaimed and immediately offered his services to drive it back.

'What about Tango Alpha?'

'If you wish you could fly the plane home,'

'I would love too,' I replied, 'but I would need more than a couple of days flying experience to pilot that beast.'

Frank was drooling over the new car.

'I am vague on this model what is special about it?' I asked Frank, 'The power output, and many little tricks also they were limited to a certain number,'

'Janine is enjoying this car, even I have not driven it yet,'

'Can, I, erm, polish, possibly have a drive, can I have a drive when we get back, Frank begged,'

'Get off your knees, and put your tongue back in your mouth, you are making a mess of a clean car,' I replied 'Of course you can.'

Frank delighted with a chance to drive his dream car, flew back to Paris after we dumped onboard our surplus luggage, keeping an overnight bag with a change of clothes. I browsed the route map working out a route via Mannheim, and Saabrücken then either use the A4 into Paris stopping around Metz for the evening.

Letting Janine drive, I read the cars instruction book, according to the book the car had more accessories than the standard car, increased brake horse power, this was definitely being put to good use, she just overtook anything that unfortunately happened to be in front of her.

I continued to test the accessories as I found them, browsing through the hand book, and around the car interior, the cream leather seats were very supportive and comfortable, this made the hard suspension bearable, the car was sophisticated and easy to drive. I rediscovered the black valise, opening the case it had a couple of papers in it, taking a quick look they were the registration documents made out in the name of Schyne Plastix, the cars emblem, was embossed in the front of the valise, it was a nice addition.

The evening was drawing in and Paris was still a good drive, the sign for Metz to the right, and a town called Nancy to the left, we decided to stop to eat and stay in a small hotel, travelling south on the road to Nancy, we came across a small hotel just north of the town, and secured bed and breakfast and including an evening meal.

I finally managed to extract Janine from the driver's seat, later we sat in the little café and enjoyed our meal, during the evening many couples came to dine, it was a very popular place, I sensed Janine was pleased with herself, I requested

an insight into her thoughts, she explained her exhilaration,
'It was the surprise,'
I enquired, 'What was the surprise?'
'The car,'
'Ah, yes, the car, I have had thoughts about this car, this green sports car with the cream leather interior, and superb powerful engine.'
'Oui mon cherie,' she was leaning towards me, anticipating my reply, I wondered how long I could keep this attention.
You did say that it would do for me to run around in and park the Monteverdi in the garage.
The look of disappointment was creeping over her face, and 'I wonder if you will let me, let, me,'
she whispered, 'Let you do what?'
'Let me drive, your car, tomorrow.'
She realised that I did not mind her having this car, slipping around the table she sat on my lap, she kissed me much to the surprise and delight of the other people in the restaurant.
'I take that, as a yes then'
'Come,' she pulled on my hand, 'it's time for bed.'

I was glad she liked the car I was not fussy on the colour; we made Paris the next day before noon, and almost immediately returned to the general toil of the office life.
The days turned into weeks the weeks into months and then years, time passed so quickly it was frightening, the exciting times waned as we settled into a period of progressive business and prosperity, Whittles car turned out to be a medico British saloon, together with a lease agreement.

The English Factory now fully rebuilt with many thanks to the Gas supplier' insurance, although the fire started in the boiler room the sprinkler system would have easily dealt with it, the flames were fed from a nearby fracture in the main gas main. My foresight in hiring the insurance assessor to work on our behalf saved us a serious amount of money; he certainly earned his fee minimising our loss.

Schyne Plastix under the direct supervision of Janine was producing our new polymer products. The international press had a field day once the story broke, resulting in the best free advertising we had ever encountered, our products, had become worldwide market leaders overnight.

Vista Plastic expanded at a tremendous rate, we included only loyal employees within the new company management, Janine's input in structuring of the management tree gave us security and time to oversee the monthly reports.

Patents for all the formula's we had under our control; were applied for and granted, this gave us the final security against any future industrial espionage.

'Le grand vacation' was upon us, France closes and goes South, all the overseas factories were in full production, this gave us an opportunity for a break, eagerly we seized the chance, Janine packed the cases, and within hours we taxied out towards the main runway at Beynes Thiveral. Franks excellent tuition helped as I acquired a pilot's license, now Janine was also learning to fly. We decided to keep the villa in Cannes, although it was in need of urgent maintenance, we left Jack supervising the workforce as they laboured for months. The repairs were completed; now we were going to take advantage and spend our week there.

As I eased back on the control column, the Lear climbed swiftly to ten thousand feet, within the hour we were on final approach, preparing to land at Cannes International airport. The Lear jet was due a service and there was a good service company at Cannes, we pre-arranged for the aircraft to have a full service, they organised transport to the villa in their helicopter.

We were given a lift by a female pilot, she was dressed in a fetching cream and dark blue flight suit, the word 'Bruyère' embroidered above the left-hand breast pocket. I thought of the old joke, if one is called Bruyère, what the other is called.

She handled the helicopter with expert ease, we flew for only ten minutes but she impressed me, I had thoughts about offering her the position as personal pilot to me, but with foresight, she might not want to change her lifestyle, delayed my question being asked.

Preparing to land at the villa she hovered for a while as she surveyed the landing area, the helicopter rotors were clearing the pathways of dust and loose branches, finally satisfied with the landing area she settled the craft onto the ground.

Thanking her for the lift, she returned an attractive smile and replied 'Anytime it was a pleasure.'

Janine had left us and was opening the front door, I unloaded the cases from the back of the aircraft, I referred to the possibility of a pilot's position within the company, she would consider the offer, I gave her one of my business cards, I asked her to call me, she replied she would, then warned me of the rotor blades. I watched her prepare to take off.

Her smile broadened as she prepared to take off, she gave a little wave then making her aircraft climb into the evening sky she flew onto her next appointment.

Although we travelled at great speed and luxury, we were still weary and tired, deciding to retire early, we slept in the new villa and were dead to the world until, the whine emitted by a searching mosquito, alerted me from my sleep, my hand reached out snatching the pest from the air.

a quiet voice beside me spoke, 'Did you get it?'

'Oui,' I turned my head to see a lovely smile. Now I was awake, I stretched out my hand, towards a switch panel on the bedside table, pressing one of the buttons, the large window blinds silently drew apart to disappear into their recess, a magnificent panoramic view of the Mediterranean was revealed, although the scene was normally bright and clear, today the dark grey clouds had turned the beautiful blue sea, grey.

It was hard to distinguish the horizon between sea and sky; there was a moaning sound from the wind as it oozed through a part open bathroom window; that gave me the clue, to how the mosquito had gained access to the bedroom.

'I fancied a swim,' she agreed throwing back the bed sheets we raced each other to the pool, stopping briefly to look outside, and then settling into the inside pool; within seconds we were swimming in warm water, I rolled over on my back and drifted in the water. Frances our maid entered the conservatory carrying fresh brewed coffee, and croissants; she placed the tray onto a small table bade us both a pleasant morning and then hurried back from the room.

Janine suggested, 'We could have an open house party this weekend for friends,'

'That would be excellent'. I approved. The coffee enticed me from the pool, the cooler air made me shiver, picking a coffee and croissant from the tray, I retired to a warmer room to eat my breakfast.

A telephone rang and ceased as Frances answered, realising that she would come and announce the caller to us, neither of us had dressed; I sprinted upstairs to gather bathrobes, throwing one to Janine from the balcony, she slipped the robe as the door opened. Frances carrying a portable telephone announced, 'It was the Paris office,' Janine took the call, listened intently occasional uttering several comments, and rectified the problem. I was still feeling cold so I showered, letting the hot water run over my back, Janine came to the bathroom calling out 'would I like some company?'

'Darling' I 'replied you can join me anytime,' we always enjoyed a shower together, as we washed our bodies, she mentioned, Darrell had been on the telephone, I thought it not important so he would call me Monday. 'Once upon a time we would not talk in the shower, we would not be able to keep our hands off each other,' she did not reply the instant passionate embrace led to the inevitable.

I replenished our coffees, Janine finished with her breakfast was making telephone calls to the group of friends we had in the area, giving out the invitations and marking the names onto a sheet of paper. We have five couples coming tonight, Edith and Jack I enquired he has done so much for us we must include them; she had not forgotten they would be expected without an invitation.

My mobile telephone rang,

'Hi' it was Frank,

'Good morning, and what do I owe the pleasure of your call?' Frank excitedly replied, 'It's, Its Grimshaw they have let him out!' I was on a stopover in Manchester last night I went to a Night Club, I met Mr Twist, he told me, 'Mr Grimshaw was out of jail, and he is gunning for you.'

'Oh,' Grimshaw and Twist, names from the recent past, names, I wished had they had been forgotten and left in the past. Frank had quizzed Twist, about what had annoyed Grimshaw.

He wants the money that was left in the storage on the I.O.M., he had called and they told him that you had collected it the following day. He knew the police did not have it, and put two and two together. I told Twist that the money was all returned to the companies it was taken from, and here was nothing left.

Twist thought it a huge joke, and laughed heartily, he said he would tell him and have a good laugh at his expense, 'Where are you now?' I asked,

'I have the clients to return to Paris, then I am free.

Something interesting, in the offering?'

'No, not at moment, how is the new aircraft?'

'It is like having wings, it reacts in the way you think, it is better with the extra 4 seats, we can accept larger parties, I will have to go, clients are arriving, bye.'

The grey day must have been an Omen, the most dangerous bastard of all time was released from jail, and is looking for me; Janine saw the concern in my face. 'What has happened?'

'Grimshaw, is out of prison, Frank has heard he is coming to get me,

'But why?' possibly because I put him in jail and recovered all his hidden loot, I placed a call to D.S. Harris at Manchester Police, to try and get the full story.

D.S. Harris was surprised and bemused to hear from me, he was even more surprised when I told him about Grimshaw being released from jail.

'But he got eight years for the embezzlement and other charges, a moment' Harris asked, the line became muffled, I could hear him mention to a colleague to check it out, Harris resumed talking with me, as we chatted about the last two years, Harris suddenly changed track, 'I have the details.' He could not believe what he was reading, as he was a perfect prisoner was eligible to apply for a special rehabilitation course, he satisfied the examining board, fully that he had amended his ways.

I replied, 'We all know that is a load of Bollocks'

Harris went on the say 'He has travel limitations, and no overseas travel his passport is being withheld.' I will look him up and see what he is doing now, make sure he does do anything untoward, if he is, then we will have to put him back,' Harris chuckled,

'I hope you do before he causes any serious problems,' I replied.

'I will let you know, what is your number now? He asked, I gave Harris my new number, and rang off.'

A strange feeling settled over me, I had never experienced such a sensation, my mind was racing, with the what ifs, and what to do's. As I laid back on the couch and stretched full length. Suddenly the one of the windows collapsed into a million pieces, something whistled past my ear and with a resounding thwack shattered a mirror on the wall just behind me, the mirror disintegrated covering me with large and small splinters of glass, I looked around quickly realising my predicament, I dare not move.

Trying to work out what had happened, I looked around I was barefoot and wearing only a bathrobe, if I attempted to move I would be severely cut and wounded by the many sections of glass, Janine was on her feet instantly, I called out, 'Stay there! get me some shoes,' she turned to go, then another noise similar to ice cube cracking in a warm drink, a small hole was punched out of the window, then another crunch, then another, the glass table broke into sections, propelling large dagger shaped splinters in all directions.

Janine was thrown against the wall, she groaned as she

slowly slipped to the floor, a crimson mark was left on the wall gave clear indication she had been hurt.

I was not sure what was breaking the windows or what was exactly happening until, Frances came running into the room another thwack, she stopped in her in her tracks, looked down to see a dark red spot had appeared on the front of her cream housecoat, the spot was growing and blood, dark red blood started escaping down her front. Holding her hand to the wound, she looked out of the window, swaying backwards she, recovered, faltered then slumped gracefully down onto her knees resting on her haunches; her head slowly falling forward came to rest on her chest. I called to Frances, she did not hear me, nor would ever hear me again.

Janine cried out, terror was in her voice, I assured her I was OK, her arm was bleeding, stay where you are, do not move. Whoever is doing this has a good view in this room, and is shooting at anything that moves, very gradually I turned my head to look at Janine, giving her a reassuring smile, the distant wail of a siren heralded an approaching police car, within minutes a gendarme was looking into the room through the shattered windows.

I called out for assistance: their presence attracted no more gunshots; I felt safe enough to move, entering into the room through the smashed windows the gendarme assessed the situation, holding both his hands outstretched indicating for me to stay, stay very still. I was still in a dangerous position, the millions of glass splinters were everywhere, another gendarme was talking on his radio for assistance, requesting an ambulance and a helicopter, the first gendarme reappeared carrying a pair of slippers, he lifted from me sections of glass, allowing me to put on the slippers.

Carefully extracting myself from the chair, pieces of glass were falling from the bathrobe; the gendarme helped extract the pieces of glass from my robe and hair. I leant forward and shaking my hair onto the floor; removing the robe I shook it free of glass, Janine quickly told one of the Gendarmes' what had happened and where clean robes could be found. He returned shortly with a robe, towel and a comb, I did my best to remove the glass from my body and hair, the gendarme quickly checked and could see no more glass, I put on the clean bathrobe and regained some modesty. Glancing back at the chair where I lay, if I had rolled off in either direction, I would have been impaled with jagged sections of glass.

At last, I was at Janine's side, she was hurt, I could see a small hole in the flesh under the collarbone with a blood coming from the wound, leaning her forward another hole on her back was bleeding, following the scarlet mark up the wall there was a hole in the wall could it be a bullet hole. Luckily, she was not covered with glass, but still hurt and bleeding I held the towel to her wounds Janine gripped my hand with a look of uncertainty and despair, who, could have done such a thing!

A second siren then a third announcing the arrival of help, two paramedics rushed into the room quickly one attending to Janine the other medic was examining Frances, glancing at one of the gendarmes, slowly shaking his head.

We were moved to a room deeper inside the house, the sound of helicopter rotor blades was above the villa, I could see many figures all in dressed in black, carrying rifles fitted with telescopic sights. One figure talking into a radio, and pointing in the direction he believed the gunman had been shooting from.

The medic turned his attention to me checking me quickly, I said to him, 'I was not hurt,'

'No' he touched the top of my ear and showed me a blood trace left on his finger tip, a bullet had missed me by millimetres he cleaned the graze then he placed carefully a strip bandage, covering the wound.

Poor Frances was carefully placed onto a stretcher then covered with a sheet, Janine was crying and shaking violently, the medic explained, she was going into shock; they put her into the ambulance then set off for the hospital.

Two new figures strolled into the room, one dressed in a dark suit aged about forty, and smoking a cigarette, slowly he surveyed the room, his companion a younger man wearing a dark coloured polo shirt and jeans walked over to the gendarme taking notes and displayed his I D, then turned his attention to me, 'Comment allez vous Monsuire?'

replying 'I have been better',

'Ah Monsieur is English,'

'Oui' he introduced himself as Sergeant Pascal, he asked me in perfect English 'Did I have any idea why anybody wished to shoot at me or either of the ladies here in this room.'

I explained the situation over the last couple of years and up to the present, including the telephone calls we received just this morning, the information about Grimshaw.

Pascal asked, 'Did I have details of this Grimshaw',

'I know a man who does,' picking up the telephone I placed a call to D.S. Harris, quickly explaining the current situation, could you liaise with the French Police, and passed the telephone to the young detective, he introduced himself to D.S. Harris, Another detective introduced himself as lieutenant René he wished to ask me some questions,

'Un moment lieutenant René, please could I get dressed,'

'Pardon Monsieur please, gesticulating his approval for me to leave the room.

I quickly changed into more sensible clothing, a warm shirt, blue jeans, and training shoes, due to the circumstances these were clothes I felt at ease in. I caught a glimpse of myself in a mirror, the dried blood mark ran from my ear and down my neck, slight red mark horizontal to the ear crossed my temple, that was so close, my spine shivered as the reality of what might have been.

I sponged my face and ear around the bandage, then a quick shave.

I felt better and returned to the room, glancing into the room, white clad figures were now working, taking measurements and recording positions of the bullet holes coloured tapes were being attached to bullet holes then stretched out to the corresponding hole in the window, the angle of the tapes gave a close enough proximity where the assailant had been laying,

Frances still lay under a sheet, more people dressed in white gowns were arriving and starting to examine the room, returning to the company of the two detectives I opened a small fridge offering them a glass of something Rene took a cold beer, Pascal, a mineral water, I served their drinks in cold glasses we kept in the fridge they seemed to enjoy the novelty, a radio chattered a quick message, officer Pascal immediately went outside looking in the direction of the hillside I looked from the safety of the house behind a window, the dark clad figure about three quarters of the way up the hill was waving, Officer Rene recommended that I kept back from the window, just in case the assassin was still around.

Pascal conversed into the radio waved back to acknowledge the distant figure, then returned to the room, they have found the place where the assailant was hiding.

'Did you swim this morning? Which pool?'

'Oui, in the inside pool,'

'Interesting, Rene remarked in a rough English, 'The assassin did not have a good view of that pool, but a perfect view of the outside one.

The room you were sitting in, the glass windows and blinds obscured the view; figures inside could be seen but not identified, that would explain anything that moved was a target.

I enquired 'I must call the hospital and find out the condition of Janine?' Pascal called on his radio, a reply to his enquiry arrived back within seconds, she was in the hospital and was being attended to; the helicopter pilot reported back there were no suspicious character's walking, but motorcycle tyre marks were found close by the assailants hiding place.

A gendarme answered the ringing telephone, he asked me if I knew of a Madam Edith, I took her call. She was watching the helicopters and the police cars, and was worried she had to call to find out.

I tried to explain what had happened but I was feeling upset. I passed the telephone and let one of the police explain matters, confirming that she was a close friend.

My mobile rang it was D.S. Harris, 'We cannot find Grimshaw anywhere, presumably that the chap who shot at you, was him.'

'That is the second time you bloody lot have cocked up I retorted back, pass my regards to the prison board, and bunch of do-gooders'

Harris quickly realised I was upset, requested to speak with the French detective if they were still there, passing the telephone to Pascal, arrangements and details were being sent to them now by Fax concerning Grimshaw.

Grimshaw had now annoyed me to the extent, if I ever managed to get to him, he was not going to survive in one piece, keeping my thoughts to myself, knowing if I mentioned my intentions to the police, they would ship me as far from the here as they could.

The Police recommended that I did not stay in the villa
tonight, then enquired where would I stay, I gave Edith and
Jack's address and telephone number, if Janine was released
from hospital she would be there as well.

With this maniac on the loose I wished to keep a low profile, I
requested both Janine's and my name kept from the
newspapers, and reporters.

The police requested I left everything in the house as it was,
a police guard would be posted.

Officer René and Pascal gave me a lift to the hospital, Janine
was ashen and still shaking, she forced a brave smile as I
arrived, the doctors said she could go home but to keep her
quiet and she must have rest, the doctor gave me some
tablets for her, they will relive the shock and pain of the
wound, but no alcohol must be taken with the tablets.
Thanking him we walked to the car Janine hanging onto me
tightly.

Pascal kindly drove us up to Edith's villa, Edith fussed over us
tremendously, Janine was worried about the guests we were
expecting this evening, Edith made a list of the people and
together they called everyone to inform them of the
unfortunate cancellation.

Jack came with a tray of coffee, and sat with me, and talked
about the event, he was sympathetic and said we were
welcome to stay in their house and use it as if it was our own,
everything here is yours. I thought what a lovely gesture.

I looked in on Janine she was resting on the bed, I sat and
quietly talked with her, telling her about the suspicions of
D.S. Harris and it was probably Grimshaw, who was
responsible.

'He must really hate you,'

'Us' I replied, her eyes were rolling she finally closed her eyes
and fell asleep.

Looking from the balcony, the lights from 17 Rue du L'Océan and many police cars were clearly seen.

Jack passed me some binoculars to get a closer view; we could not have been better placed to observe the villa. Then thinking all the high points around here would have a good view of our villa and it might be worthwhile to analyse the observed areas and protect them with privacy screens or walls.

Edith called us to see the television, it was headline news that people had been killed at our address, the police request any witness to the event were required to pass information to the them.

You are famous Edith claimed,

'What, for being dead,' I jokingly replied, just then Janine came from the bedroom, her transformation was incredible, looking her normal self, she came and sat beside me, Edith bringing her a small coffee and large brandy.

Jack remarked to me 'Did you get one, I didn't get one', Edith gave a look to Jack, stamped her foot on the floor, went out of the room muttering I only have one pair of hands, returned with a coffee and brandies from the kitchen for me, my pleasure Ross, she scowled back at Jack and spoke something very sharp and quick at him, I could not translate I got the idea of what she said though, finally came from the kitchen with Jacks refreshment.

Edith requested who would like to eat, we gave a simple choice and within minutes we were dining like kings, Edith I believed had prepared the meal beforehand, Jack retrieved a bottle of wine and the meal was complete. We enjoyed each other's company and the good simple food.

It was a disaster of a day with a welcome end we were alive, slipping into bed Janine's shoulder was aching, Inspecting the bandage it was tidy and secure, she took two of the painkillers the doctor had given her, and cried as she tried to find a comfortable position to sleep, she finally fell asleep, she woke me as she cried, she was dreaming and shaking her head on the pillow, I stroked her arm she seemed to settle, and resumed her sleep.

I dozed for about an hour, and then a strange noise sounding like a bottle being placed heavily on the ground outside the bedroom window made me wide awake.

Slipping from the bed, I looked out of the window, all seemed quiet, picking up the binoculars I scanned the surrounding area, like a fly is attracted to light, each time I scanned past a lamp or a light came into view I stopped and looked, a shadow slowly moving across a window attracted my attention, dropping the binoculars slightly to see the direction of the house that I was looking at. Looking again it was definitely a figure looking into a window then moving away into the shadows, a lady came to the window looking out, then she closed the outer shutters, was it a peeping tom or burglar, who could tell I could not see him anymore, a small light from a flashlight swaying back and forth lighting their way on the rough road, was two people walking up the road.

The same noise that woke me I heard again this time very close it came from the patio; someone was on the patio.

The house was in darkness, silently, opening the door to gain a better view. I could see a figure sitting by the pool, straining my eyes to see, the figure turned her head looking sideways, it was Edith she was sitting by the pool, glancing at my watch it was after 02:00.

I walked quietly towards her, Edith was already aware that I was there, invited me to come and have a brandy. I took my place next to her on the suspended swinging lounger chair.

She only had one glass and a bottle of brandy; we shared her

glass, as we consumed the brandy,
'Where is jack?' I enquired,
'Sleeping,'
'Janine?' Edith asked
'Sleeping,'
'Bon',
'I had not expected anyone out this late?'
'I have problems sleeping and spend the evenings out here by the pool, some of the nights are warm and comfortable tonight is cooler, she moved closer to me I could feel the cold of her body, she remarked how warm I was, then proceeded to lift up my arm and snuggled into me.

A warming wind materialised from over the sea, she said 'it is nice when the wind changes.' Slowly patting my tee-shirt with the palm of her hand, smoothing the wrinkles from the material, her hand paused momentarily then slipped into my shorts, her hand was cold.

'Are you sure?'

'Who will know,' she replied, 'only us, and the wind.' Hidden in the darkness she continued with her intimate caress and sexual domination, positioning herself carefully making only a brief murmur as she achieved maximum penetration, very slowly she moved her hips increasing the stimulation, methodically she teased and pressed her lips gently touching my lips with her erect nipples, we remained together enjoying the union until the final outcome as she gripped me so tight I could not breath, then collapsing onto me.

She did not move her breathing so shallow made her collapse onto me, she seemed lifeless, minutes seemed like hours as they passed by, then slowly she recovered from her petit mort; she stood turning into the wind outstretched her arms and embraced the warm breeze.

I watched as she slipped silently into the warm water, 'Come' beckoning me towards her, I slipped from my shorts and tee shirt and joined her in the pool, she pulled me towards her, she wanted me again, this time in the pool. The play was physical, it was lust for a body contact that drove us, I was unable, to complete the final act, the brandy was having detrimental effects on my bodily functions.

Edith was intent on more, to escape I climbed out of the pool and stood facing into the warm breeze. Edith stood close to me also taking advantage of the warm air, was more interested in caressing my bottom and inner thigh, trying to get me aroused again.

When suddenly from the direction of the villa at rue du L'Océan a brilliant flash of white light, preceded a fireball rising into the night sky, seconds later the deafening roar of the explosion reached us, My God! Edith cried holding her mouth, dumfounded I stood and looked in the direction of the explosion, Jack came running from the house shortly followed by Janine, the four of us stood and watched as the fire ball lit up the area, the villa was engulfed in a cloud of dust, the orange flames flickering through the dust came from different parts of the house, far in the distance electric blue flashing lights of the emergency vehicles could be seen leaving Cannes and making their way along the coast road. But what had happened to the Villa,

Janine standing at my shoulder remarked, 'If we had stayed in the house, we would be.'

I replied quickly, 'Having a sleepless night by now.'

Janine placed a hand around my waist and rested her head on my shoulder, slowly she caressed my back and finding no shorts,

'Ooh! What have you been doing?

'Swimming,'

'That's nice' she said and nipped the cheek of my bottom, I

became aware that another hand stroked me on the other cheek.

Edith stated 'This is all too much for me, I am tired, Bonsoir' and disappeared into the house. Janine recovering my shorts and tee-shirt while I observed the disaster scene, the fire service had arrived, figures could be seen attacking the flames; Jack also seemed unimpressed by the fire also returned to his bed.

The smaller fires were extinguished, the dust cloud was replaced by a vertical plume of black smoke, this rose until the breeze from the sea reformed it into a pancake shaped cloud, which slowly was drifting in our direction.

Janine cuddling into me pulled at me, she was wanting to go back to bed, just as I closed the door, for a brief moment I heard the sound, of a motorcycle engine slowly making its way up the road by the side of the house. I reopened the door slightly and looked out, while I listened intently, there were no moving lights to be seen, also the engine noise had gone. I dismissed the noise as a possible trick of the wind,

A slight cough from the bedroom indicated another, required my attention, Janine lay on top of the bed a picture of loveliness marred only by the bandage around her shoulder, the earlier brandy together with the unexpected attention from Edith had exhausted me, Janine however was feeling so inclined, with one willing partner bandaged and the other exhausted, love making was very slow and relaxed, we fell asleep in our snug embrace.

My morning started around 10:30, but I felt that another couple of hours would have been beneficial, I was alone in bed, low voices droned from the patio, looking from the window Janine, Jack and Edith were entertaining officer René and Pascal. I took a 30 second shower, the icy water shocked my system awake dressing in shorts and a tee-shirt; I joined my friends and visitors on the patio. Officer Pascal, greeted me with a good morning, he explained, they were making enquiries, if we were aware that the house at 17 du L'Océan was destroyed last night.

'Ah that was our house, I thought it might be'

'You were aware of the explosion? Pascal asked

'Oui Pascal, we watched as it happened' I replied, all of a sudden, the two officers were greatly interested in me, and asked to explain what I knew about this matter. I had nothing to hide, and proceeded to explain that, earlier this morning I heard a noise, and investigated, it was Edith on the patio having a brandy, I was awake by then and joined her, then we swam, as I was drying myself, I was looking in that particular direction just as the explosion happened.

A brilliant flash, followed by a huge fireball rolling high into the sky, similar to the fireball's you see in the movies. Pascal was very interested 'did you see anything else?'

Thinking only a receptive naked female, but I was not going down that road at the moment, 'Sorry, ask Edith she was with me.

'Wait, there was something,' I remembered, 'A prowler' pointing towards the house where I had saw him looking into the room through the window, Officer Rene making a note and position of the house, 'they would check,' I even told him about the sound of a motorcycle I heard early this morning by the side of the house. Edith appeared with a coffee, croissant,

'Good morning, Ross, how are you today?' she spoke to me, in well-rehearsed English,

'Bon jour madam, je vous remercie de vottre hospitalité,' Edith was delighted with my reply.

I walked over to the balcony and viewed the disaster area, picking up the binoculars I gazed at the devastation, it looked chaotic, figures dressed in white and black were steadily checking the area. Janine enquired do you think we have lost our clothes, and personal papers; if we had, we might have problems getting them replaced. Pascal said they were going there now if you would like a lift, 'Yes, I would, could I recover any clothing and personal effects I find, the officers conferred and agreed, under the circumstances they had no objections to me removing items from the villa.

Jack passed me a faded baseball cap, you should be incognito and hide if someone is searching for you, briefly glancing at Janine 'Remember the last time, if it is Grimshaw he would recognise me.' We drove to the area where once stood my magnificent villa, the devastation was incredible, the area was alive with men examining every detail.

I had difficulty visualising the house layout, making my way to where the bedrooms were, our room was totally destroyed the roof had collapsed compressing everything under it, by some miracle the adjacent bedroom was partially standing, the roof had not collapsed fully but hung in a precarious angle, pointing to the room,

'That is where we had put the suitcases,' a gendarme pointed to a dark blue van uttered 'Regarde Monsuire,' looking inside the back of the van were the remnants of our clothes and suitcases, my jacket had suffered a huge gaping tear in the sleeve, had rendered it to a rag, I felt my pockets and recovered the house keys and the duplicate keys for the aeroplane, my pocket book and passport. Did you find a brown valise with a zip top, 'No there was no sign of it, where was it?

'It was on the left side of the bed in the main bedroom, it has business papers and other important documents, nothing that could not be replaced,'

'There was this a well battered handbag, it was Janine's, it was intact but scorched,

'My god' I cried 'the cost of a new handbag for the lady, will this expense never end.'

'You are worried about the cost of a handbag,' Pascal remarked quietly

'No, I made a joke,' he started to laugh but still did not get the joke, he in turn tried to explain the subtle comment to the gendarme who in turn started to laugh, I passed the house key to the gendarme and asked him to lockup the house when they were finished, he went into fits of laughter, a laughing jovial Gendarme with a huge moustache and with large gaps in his teeth is not a pretty sight.

A detective dressed in a white coat came towards us, he requested why we had a huge container containing hundreds of litres of benzene.

'Benzene? thinking for a moment, it must have been Avgas, aviation fuel benzene,

I replied. 'It was fuel, for the light aircraft we used to have, I did not know there was any stored here.

Pascal asked the gendarme, 'What happened to the gendarme on guard?'

'He is missing sir,' Simultaneously a cry came from a somewhere under the pile of rubble, 'I think they have found him,' we stood back to give the medics space to move, very carefully they extracted the lifeless body of their comrade from the rubble, a paramedic checked for vital signs.

The medic looked in our direction called the attention of Officer Rene; he was pointing at something on the body.

I enquired. 'A problem'

'The gendarme has been shot it must have happened before the explosion.

With this new problem I think they were uneasy with my presence, Pascal offered to take me back to Edith's with the suitcases, I agreed, as I turned to go, the reflection from something shiny glinted from the rubble in the sunlight.

Pointing towards the object 'What is that?' Pascal asked one of the officers to investigate, he scrambled over the rubble moving a few planks and a broken door.

'It is a wall safe he called back to Pascal, he tried but could not move it, another officer joined him and they both pulled it loose, and slid the object down the pile of rubble.

Pascal asked 'What was in it?'

'I am not sure now' I replied, I was lying through my teeth; I didn't know what was in it, and I was damn sure that I was not going to let anyone but me open it.

'Can I take it with me and deposit somewhere safe?' Pascal saw no problem with that, but remarked it was too heavy for his car, the gendarme will take it in the van, I took hold of the safe and tried to move it was awkward and heavy, Pascal helped me lift the safe into the back of the van.

The vehicle rear springs compressed dramatically as the weight landed on the van floor. Pascal gave directions to the police driver, gesticulating towards the direction of the house, I glanced in the direction that Pascal had pointed, A flash of light higher up the hill flashed for an instant, it was similar to the sun being reflected from a binocular lens.

I felt that we were being observed. Pascal passed me one of his official cards please call me if anything happens or if you see anything suspicious.

I replied 'I already have.'

'What is it?'

'I saw a flash of sunlight reflected from something high up on the hill above Jack and Edith's house, do not turn and look' I said 'If we are being observed, it could be Grimshaw,' I manoeuvred around with my back to the reflection giving Pascal chance to see the reflection.

'I see it, it is moving too,' Pascal pulled his radio from his belt and spoke into it, 'they will be here soon,'

Who?

'The tactical team, with the murder of the policeman we too are looking for Grimshaw.'

'Let me know if you recover that brown valise, it is of importance to me.' After a few minutes a helicopter flew fast and low up above us climbing rapidly up the hill then turning in a tight arc it hovered over the area where the flash of light came from.

Men could be seen abseiling down ropes to the ground, Pascal now looked up, if he is there, they will find him.

We drove slowly up the hill to Edith's house the driver was trying to engage polite conversation, but my mind was perusing the contents of the safe, and how Janine was feeling after a good day's rest.

Parking the van in the drive, Janine was standing on the patio; she was dressed in a cut off tee-shirt and a pair of my boxer shorts.

'I have something for you,' sliding open the side door to reveal our suitcases, 'and not forgetting this,' I lifted the battered dusty handbag, instantly her face brightened, she took hold of her handbag, checked the contents, and held it close to her.

Jack and Edith came to meet us, the driver recognising Jack, Jack studying the face for a while, 'Il est Yves?

'Oui Monsuire,' the driver had been student to Jack when he was a metalwork tutor at the technical college in Cannes many years ago. They chattered for ages; he told Jack more about the explosion than I had found out.

We carried the suitcases into the house, Janine in hot pursuit where after a couple of minutes remerged transformed in fresh clothes, she looked enchanting.

Edith called us to the table which she had laid with coffee and small cakes, which were quickly devoured.

Yves asked about the heavy box, showing Jack the safe, he helped moved the heavy safe onto the driveway. Yves bade us farewell and drove back into town.

Sitting on the low sidewall by the drive, Janine came and placed one foot on top of the box asked 'what is this?'

'I found it amongst the rubble at the house, it is a wall safe,' Janine replied, 'but we do not have a wall safe,'

'We do, and that is it' I replied.

Jack commented 'And it is broken, the combination dial was smashed with half the numbers missing, and the door handle was locked.

'What is the combination,'

Thinking for a minute, 'It could be two turns to the left,' I replied, 'or two turns to the right,

'Which is it, right or left' Janine enquired, does not matter, Jack was in fits of laughter, he had already worked out what I had meant.

'Why were we laughing,' Janine asked.

'I explained, the dial is broken, the handle is jammed, so turn the safe round and cut off the back, Jack nodding his head in agreement.

'But how will you cut the safe open they are designed not to be opened,'

'Oui, but they are designed to be strong from the front, not the back.'

Jack asked 'What is in it?'

'I do not know,'

'Well let's find out,' he disappeared into the garage and returned with a small four-wheel trolley, we loaded the safe onto the trolley and removed it into the workshop.

'Secrecy is always best, if we are being observed.' Then it

dawned on me, if I was being watched, we could we be attacked again tonight, telling Jack of my thoughts Jack asked, 'Can you use one of these,' he opened a steel cabinet and lifted out two handguns, a revolver, and an automatic pistol.

'I have fired one many times but only at a shooting range, I have not used one in anger,'

'OK' he said 'Take this one' giving me the pistol, Jack proceeded with a demonstration how to load and make the gun ready to fire, all you have to do is point at the target and pull the trigger, the gun will load the next bullet.

Jack took both guns and loaded them with ammunition; we take them into the house later.

Now let us crack open this safe, he produced a petrol driven cutting machine, he selected a cutting disc from the array of discs on the back wall then fitted it to the machine, throwing me a face mask he started the cutter, the two-stroke engine spluttered momentarily, then screamed into life, standing over the safe, Jack placed the cutter blade midway on the side and proceeded to make a cut across one side turning the box to its next side repeated the cut, Jack cut four times. Then taking a heavy steel hammer I gave the back a hefty smack, the outer box literally fell off, and deposited a load of powder onto the workshop floor.

Inspecting the inner box Jack showed me the weakest spot, we continued our dismantling within ten minutes we gazed in amazement at the contents of the safe.

Lots of papers, bank statements and details, three sealed letters, many bags of gold coins and numerous bars of silver.

Jack took one of the bars and looked at it, 'It is not silver it is platinum.'

I lifted out a black soft leather bag, I carefully opened to reveal a quantity of jewels, if these are what I think they are. Jack uttered 'Oui diamonds,'

'We need a safe to keep these in, have you such a place' I enquired. Jack went to stand by the back door; he pulled back the doormat then lifting a steel plate, to reveal a hole in the ground, at the bottom of the hole was a floor safe.

Jack taking a key from his pocket opened the safe door; he removed a little package and locked it in a wall cabinet. I passed the items to him and he packed the safe with the contents of the old safe. He locked the door and gave me the key; it is the only one he said, take care not to lose it.

Taking a good look into the old safe there was nothing left it was empty; we cleaned up the workshop and made haste back to the house carrying our weapons. Edith was ready with the evening meal; she sat me down with Jack sitting opposite asking what we did in the workshop.

Jack replied trying to open the safe, Edith laughing I knew you would not do it, it probably is full of nothing, Jack winked at me 'how do you know these things.'

Edith replied, 'I am a woman.' Janine served wine she was still taking the tablets and was abstaining from drinking wine, she had spent her day relaxing by the pool, and managed to sleep, feeling much better today, she confessed, that yesterday was just a bad dream, what do you have planned for tomorrow.

'I intended to rent a car so I could move some items around,'
'Good idea I will help if you wish,' Jack replied,

I accepted his offer of help, relaxing after dinner on the patio, Jack had to light some anti mosquito smoke rings, Jack cursed, 'They were feeding tonight,'

'I am glad they were not feeding last night,'

'It was too cold last night,' Edith commented. Janine opened her handbag and passed me some cream, 'rub this on your skin it will drive away the mosquito,' almost immediately, after applying the cream the little pests turned their attention elsewhere.

We watched the late ferries as they arrived and departed, then the sound of a motorcycle engine, stopped me cold, Jack also heard the sound, turning his head to obtain the direction of the sound.

Janine was feeling tired, she leant over and kissed me, she was going to take some painkillers then she was going to bed. Edith flashed her eyes at me, she was lusting after more attention around the pool, the noise of the motorcycle was closer now and it had greater interest for me at the present.

'Jack, do you have a neighbour with a motorcycle?'

'No, we do not'. He stood up, then disappeared into the darkness

'Do you want a hand?' silence there was no reply from the darkness.

'He will be back after he has found what is making the noise,' Edith commented, the motorcycle engine stopped, then suddenly a single gunshot rang out, the motorcycle engine started this time it became very noisy as it was being accelerated fast up and over the hill.

Shortly Jack came back smiling, he had with him a rifle with a large silencer and telescopic sight, which he leant against the table.

'Who was he'

'Not sure, he was a dark-haired man, dressed in black and on a black motorcycle, I walked out in front of him on the road, he pointed his rifle at me, I did not argue, I shot at him with my revolver he dropped his rifle and drove his motorcycle away over the hill.

'Will he know which house you came from?'

'Maybe, I crossed the road coming on him from the back; he

was looking in the house over there, remember the house you showed the detective.

'Jack, I have this card from Officer Pascal, I had to call him if anything happens, I think this event is worth that call,' Jack took the card inside the house and telephoned Pascal.

Pascal quickly arrived; he inspected the rifle it was the same calibre of bullet that was used earlier in the attack on us. Jack pointed in the direction he was last seen travelling, Pascal knew that there was dense woodland at the end of the road.

'It might be worthwhile having the helicopter fly over and investigate'. Shortly after he relayed the information by radio, we could hear the beat of rotor blades but could not see the aircraft, Jack and Pascal decided to walk up the hill to see if anything interesting appeared. I looked in on Janine she was sound asleep, I picked up the automatic pistol from the bedside table and returned back to the patio.

Edith appeared carrying two glasses and a bottle of brandy; I studied the patio layout and moved the seats into the darkest area but still keeping a commanding view of the house.

Edith remarked, 'You like the darkness,'

'It is not a joke Edith, someone is trying to kill me and Janine, I am taking precautions,' she moved her chair closer then prepared a small table placing the brandy and glasses on it. Edith took delight in having company in the evening and nothing was going to stop her enjoying herself.

'Does Jack not sit with you in the evening?'

'No, he sleeps early now and I am never tired,' she replied

'Why not adjust your body clock with his and see if it makes a difference,'

'We tried but since his accident he has been incapable,'

'Incapable of what,'

'Having sex,' she replied quietly 'he has a problem.'

No wonder she was so amicable to me last night, she started rubbing my stomach again, Edith whispered, 'You do not have that problem,' caressing her hand down over my stomach, she certainly knew how to attract my attention.
'What if Jack returns,'
'I will hear him,' she replied,
'What if our assailant appears?'
'I will hear him,'
'How can you hear so well?'
'I have perfect hearing and can hear many things, I heard you making love to Janine after you went to bed, I could hear Jack talking to officer Pascal as they walked up the hill, I hear people walking up the road over two hundred meters.'
Just then she stopped speaking and listened, 'Janine is sleeping and we are alone.'
She was intent to have sex with me, and nothing I could say would persuade her, I suppose while we were waiting it would pass time for a couple of minutes.
She pushed me backward onto the sun lounger, then taking her chosen position sat astride me, and made love to me, she stopped the lovemaking momentarily, raised her head and listened, then resumed her tantalizing actions, I responded to her actions finally climaxing together.
Edit whispering, 'We are not alone, someone is here,'
I replied, 'Jack?'
'No,' she slipped from my lap, to the floor. Adjusting my clothing, I sat quietly listening, she held onto my leg gripping it slightly as a shadow moved into view passing the white painted wall.
The figure looked through the window into the room where Janine lay sleeping. Gripping the gun Jack had given me, I pulled back the slider the magazine sprung the cartridge into the chamber with a muffled click, the hammer locked back

the gun was ready for action.
Edith was fully aware that I had, and prepared to use it. Edith called out 'Jack,' the figure froze.
I placed my hand on Edith's shoulder to stop her saying anything else, I observed the figure intently.
'Well now, if it is not Jack, it must be Mr Grimshaw and without his companion in crime Mr Twist,' the figure slowly turned toward the darkness.
Grimshaw replied. 'And I thought you were dead.'
'I am terribly sorry to disappoint you, and I am perplexed, what it is you want from me,' Grimshaw moving his head trying to determine my exact location, replied, 'That wall safe will do for starters,'
'It was you, watching me from the hillside' I answered,
He replied. 'You notice a lot of things,
'If that is all you desire, you are welcome to it; by the way, it is outside the garage.'
Grimshaw limping slightly walked towards the remnants of the safe, he stood looking at the residue.
'Nothing left in it, just dust,' I commented from the darkness,
I watched as he knelt down, he flashed on a small torch and looked inside the box, then he moved the box with the door facing him, he removed something from his pocket, an audible click was heard as he unlocked and opened the door.
He removes an envelope from the inside, this secret place must be only accessible when the door is open.
I asked, 'Are they important?
He retorted 'None of your business,'
Thinking for a while whatever it was must be of immense value to him, a greater value than the other items found inside the safe.
Replying to his curt remark, 'Mr Grimshaw, I am afraid anything hidden in or on my property, belongs to me, it is my

business, and I intend to make it my business,'
I requested, 'Will you like to leave the envelope on the floor in front of the safe and go away now,'
'No Chance, this is mine,'
'What about the other items in the safe, who did they belong to?'
'Whittle, they belonged to' hesitating 'you, you told me the safe was empty,'
'It is now; but you have told me what I wanted.'
 'Clever bastard, I don't like clever bastards,' in a flash he pulled a short stumpy looking pipe from his coat, then pointed it in my direction, an orange flame leapt from the end.
I dropped to the ground landing on Edith. Simultaneously the shotgun pellets ricocheting off the patio wall hitting me on my back, and making my skin smart.
I cried out 'Oh you bastard,' he clicked the gun again took aim and pulled the trigger, the splattering of pellets pelted me, Edith protected by me lay flat on the ground. I stood up, standing sideways to minimise his target, raised the pistol and took careful aim and fired.
Grimshaw staggered back slightly as the shot struck home, he was trying to reload and dropped the cartridges falling to his knees, he recovered one cartridge and ramming it into his gun, took aim I could see he was pointing directly at me, just as Jack walked onto the patio.
Grimshaw spotting a new target fired wildly towards Jack, a large earthenware urn took the full force of the blast and erupted soil, plant, and pot debris covered Jack as he dropped to the ground.
I fired again, Grimshaw spun around dropping the shotgun, he quickly pulled a pistol from his pocket and fired twice in my direction, a bullet whistled past my head sounding like an

angry hornet. Another thudded into the wall by the side of me.

Edith groaned loudly, without looking at her, I returned fire again, Grimshaw faltered and fell backwards onto the wall, his legs buckled underneath him as he slid down the wall to the ground.

Pascal arrived breathless after hearing the shots, he had run down the hill. I could see Janine trying to open the bedroom curtains and looking out, not being able to see anything she switched on a patio light.

The patio light revealed Grimshaw slumped by the workshop door, he was leaning against the wall, keeping my gun levelled at him, I slowly advanced, his hand still holding the pistol, lay by his side.

'Have you finished? He looked at me cursing under his breath,

'You, you have shot me,' he croaked, I could see blood discolouring the front of his shirt from a shoulder wound, His eyes stared at me, he thought he had won.

Pascal had quietly manoeuvred behind Grimshaw swiftly kicked the gun from his hand making it slither away across the path, Pascal searched him for any more hidden weapons, then secured him with a pair of handcuffs.

Grimshaw was incapacitated I turned to look at Edith, she was rubbing her head, I had knocked her unconscious dodging Grimshaw's bullets, she could have easily become another target.

Her dress was still above her waist revealing far more than she should. I knelt down to help her to her feet.

She realised what could have happened, that her lust had clouded her judgment, her super hearing missed the appearance of the assassin, still hidden in the shadows she made herself respectable.

'It could have been your dignity or your life,' I whispered, then Jack cried out for assistance, Edith ran to him, he had been cut by the flying parts of terracotta from the huge pot.

Pascal reported the incident to his headquarters on his radio within minutes the entire area was brightly lit from the spotlight on the incoming air ambulance.

The medics helped Jack and Edith into the helicopter, then turned their attention to Grimshaw, he was still alive, carefully strapping a bandage and neck collar to him they securely tied him onto a stretcher, as he passed me Grimshaw glanced towards me.

'You will have fun bullshitting your way out of this one.' I walked towards him stopping by the stretcher; I slipped my hand into his coat and removed the papers he had taken from the safe, 'I do not think that you will need these where you are going'.

Officer René arrived, Pascal quickly updated him on the evening's activity, Pascal suggested that he go to the hospital with Grimshaw and René agreed, the helicopter departed with the hopeful and hopeless to receive medical attention.

René asking questions, another couple of gendarmes appeared, parking the now customary blue van in the pathway. I offered refreshments, a unanimous acceptance for coffee, making coffee I looked in on Janine, she was awake and looked shaken, I assured her it is all over now and gave her a kiss.

She wiped some blood from my cheek, then noticed the blood marks on the back of my shirt. she lifted my shirt and cried, your back is bleeding, it must have been the shotgun pellets when Grimshaw fired at me, 'What shotgun! when did he shoot at you?'

'He shot me earlier, when you were sleeping; I thought the pellets had just bounced off,'

'Some have lodged in the skin,' Janine replied she helped me remove my shirt then with a damp towel wiped my back clean, picking out the lead pellets, she had in her first aid kit some antiseptic cream.

Carefully she applied some cream to each wound, making them sting again. René came into the kitchen as Janine was finishing up, he saw the wounds and came to inspect, he asked Janine what she had put on the skin, she showed him the tube of ointment, it should be ok but it would be worth a visit to the hospital to check that all the pellets have been removed.

Feeling easier I put on a clean shirt then carried the coffee out on the patio, René stood by the remnants of the safe, 'What happened with that?'

'Grimshaw opened it and removed some papers,'

'Have you got them,'

'Yes, they are here, taking the envelope from my back pocket I gave it to René, he looked at the papers, 'This list of numbers, what are they?'

'Taking a look, yes I agreed, lists of numbers,'

He asked, 'What do they mean?

'I am not too sure, combinations for a lottery?' I replied.

I studied the papers in silence, in one corner a letter Z on one page, on another B, and another G and one Cay, judging by the way he had identified his other accounts, B for Bern, Z for Zurich, G for Gibraltar, and Cay for possibly the Cayman isles. All places one could bank large amounts of money without trace.

Officer Rene's radio bleeped, 'Oui,' he listened without interruption 'Merci' he replied, passing the papers to me, 'Mr Grimshaw has escaped from the hospital.

We will leave an officer on guard tonight and we will get him in the morning.

'I will come back in the morning,' confirmed Rene.
'Not too early please, I am on holiday, and so far, the holiday has not been good for us,'
 'Ok, sleep; if you can I will contact you in the morning.' With Jack and Edith at the hospital, I secured the house leaving a drink and washroom access for the officer. I joined Janine, falling instantly into a light sleep; my dreams were tormented with pairs of piercing eyes, and reliving the evening's events over and over again.
Oblivious to me the morning had commenced.
Janine was preparing breakfast, quietly she entered the bedroom with a breakfast tray, the aroma of full Arabic coffee gently persuaded me to join the world, I felt a pair of lips softly kissing me, my eyes flickered open.
Janine was close to tears, she kissed me, 'Let us get away from this place, too many terrible memories'
Where would you like to go, Switzerland, Gibraltar, or the Cayman isles, Janine perusing for a moment replied the Cayman isles, I have never been there.
I telephoned Frank we fancy a trip to the Cayman Isles, in the big jet, bring Hermione, we might have another couple coming, any problem with that.
'No, just keep the luggage to the minimum, it is a long way across the pond,' Frank stated, then enquired 'Do we have a reason for the trip?'
'Similar trip to the Isle of Man and Zurich,'
'Very, interesting see you later,'
'Did I know where Jack and Edith have gone?' Janine asked.
'Yes, when they come back, do you think they would like a trip with us to the Cayman isles?
I replied. 'I think they would be delighted,'
Janine picked a perfume bottle from the bedside table, very carefully she placed a small amount of the liquid onto her

finger tip, she lightly touched her finger to her skin, between her breasts, the alluring fragrance had the desired effect, making me succumbed to her charms.

A heavy banging of a fist on the front door, brought me back to the present, I glanced from the window before opening the door, it was Edith and Jack, swinging open the door I greeted them with large hugs and embraces, we chatted over the excitement and they told me of the incredible escape, Grimshaw had made from the hospital.

His wounds were light, this was being attended to by the nurse, and after she had finished, Grimshaw had feigned slipping into a traumatic shock, then as she left to get help, he tackled the gendarme wounding him. As the nurse returned stabbed her as well, he removed the keys from the gendarme releasing himself from the shackle, then he leapt from the 1st floor window onto a passing ambulance roof, and disappeared into the night.

We have a police guard on the premises until Grimshaw has been recaptured.

The telephone started to ring, Janine taking the call, chatted quickly a smile broke out on her face, she held out the telephone, it is Frank; he has landed at Cannes airport, and was awaiting our pleasure.

I asked Edith and Jack if they would like to come with us on the trip, they were both delighted and excited by a surprise trip and to get away present troubles.

Janine, going through the documents that we required on the trip, made a full set of photocopies, which I placed in the floor safe in Jacks garage.

We loaded Jacks car, and headed off to the airport to meet Frank. Hermione had accompanied Frank; she was so glad to see us after hearing all the problems that had beset us.

Frank and I planned the flight, first stop Madeira, to refuel, and a stopover. Then on to the Cayman Isles in the morning, I could take care of the banks at my leisure, take in some sunshine and swimming, we would then backtrack via Madeira for a stopover then onto Gibraltar, back to Cannes to drop off Edith and Jack.

Then Frank could resume our charter business; I could fly back to Paris via Switzerland and tidy the rest of the listed bank accounts.

Logging our flight plan we made ready for the trip, all final calculations were made, we fuelled for the trip and prepared to leave.

It is custom for the flight engineer, to walk around the aeroplane making final checks, as Frank started to warm up the engines, it was my turn to inspect the outside. Taking exceptional care to keep clear of the jet exhaust, I noticed a hatch panel had not seated correctly, reclosing the panel I secured the safety catches then turned to walk under the wing.

I was confronted by a man dressed in air service overalls, he waved a hand at me, he held onto his cap with the other hand, as I walked past him, he brought the waving hand, now a clenched fist crashing into me, hitting my shoulder I was sent sprawling.

He rushed over to me, offering what I thought was a hand to help me up, in his hand he held a small gun, looking into his face, it was Grimshaw, he was speaking to me, but I could not hear his voice, the scream of the twin jet engines drowned out any verbal communication.

He waved the pistol in the direction of the cabin, the last thing I wanted was him loose in aircraft holding any passenger's hostage, he prodding the pistol barrel in my back pushed me forward.

I purposely stumbled as he pushed me again, putting my hands down to stop me falling over, I lashed out kicking backwards my heel, it connected into his groin, I spun around kicking him again on his kneecap which made him collapse onto one knee.

He tried to point the gun at me, I kicked out again, this time my foot caught his wrist and spun the gun away out of his grasp.

His mouth was wide open yelling at me, both the engines were screaming and they drowned out any other noise. We fought in a most undignified manner under the wing, also the wing shielded what was happening from the passengers, kicking and thumping each other we emerged from the wing towards the back of the plane. Momentarily we separated, I smashed my fist into the shoulder where I knew I had shot him. He slumped down the look of pain in his face, then jumped to his feet taking a run at me; I caught hold of him by his wrists and I fell backwards placing my foot into his gut, I let the rolling momentum of him continue and launched him over the top of me.

I watched him pass over me, he seemed to fly, I leapt onto my feet expecting him to come back at me, then I saw him rolling, over and over like a wheel rolling down the tarmac behind the aircraft.

I had vaulted him into the jet exhaust and the powerful thrust had done the rest. I watched as this body was thrown about in the jet exhaust, slowly coming to a halt some distance from me.

The jet engines were slowing, glancing backwards I saw anxious looks from the open-door hatch, a distant fire tender was heading towards Grimshaw, flanked by two small vans and cars their blue lights flashing were converging on him.

Grimshaw stood and looked around saw the vehicles coming,

and limped across a runway, he walked into the path of a landing passenger aeroplane.

I watched, as he raised his hand in a defiant gesture towards the oncoming aircraft, one of the rear wheels, knocking him down onto the runway, then the powerful jet exhaust picking up the body hurled it down the runway like a rag doll.

An ambulance quickly took position and the two attendants quickly removed the body onto a stretcher and departed towards the medical centre.

I fell to my knees as I watched in total disbelief, in the instant demise of the opponent.

Frank now fully aware of my battle with Grimshaw had cut the power, Janine came running towards me, I grabbed her and kept her away from the jet exhaust, although the engines were spinning down the heat was still dangerous.

They only realised what was happening when air traffic had called Frank about two people fighting behind the aircraft.

Frank had observed in the last seconds the fight had cut power to the engines before coming to assist me.

In the back of my mind, I surmised we would not be travelling anywhere today, again that bastard, Grimshaw had caused me serious problems, the pending paperwork would be immense, I was glad he was dead.

Pascal arrived with the first group of security officers as they came out to the plane; he listened intently to my explanation of the affray, and then conferring with air traffic, 'Is the aircraft damaged?'

Frank replied 'No,'

Pascal saw no reason that we should not continue on our journey after all, Grimshaw was a fugitive and a murderer, he had at last died, Pascal declared you will be back and if I need any further information, he would call me. He bade me a good and safe trip and he returned to the terminal.

The sound of a helicopter about to land caught my attention, I recognised the pilot as Bruyère, the lady pilot who gave us the lift to the villa, she was about to land on a nearby landing pad, she saw me talking to Pascal and the Gendarmerie and walked over to see me.

I greeted her, 'Hello again, it is nice to see you,' she realised that I was in heavy discussion and said she would call me. 'Ok,' I replied.

I watched her climb into her helicopter and don her earphones, I was trying to remember her name but with all the current events I put it to the back of my mind.

I made another check around the aircraft while Frank called air traffic and by some incredible luck we were cleared for immediate take-off.

Janine inspected my face, a swelling just below one of my eyes was darkening, she touched the area lightly, I winched with pain, I should attend to your bruises now.

She whispered 'Come with me I will attend to you for other bruising, and clean them.' she led the way to the small private room at the back of the aircraft, Frank called out 'Be careful with him he has to pilot this on the return journey.'

I lay back into the seat, Janine wiped my face with a damp towel then laid a cold damp towel over my face to ease the bruising.

Finally, we were off, Frank calling over the intercom he was about to take off. I closed my eyes and listened to the aeroplane as she rumbled out then down the runway.

Clearing the runway we climbed into the afternoon sky, we would chase the sun across the Atlantic and land in Madeira then a welcome stop and continue to the Cayman Isles later.

I had a feeling of pity for the felled opponent, but leaving behind finally the Whittle Grimshaw period.

Janine sat beside me holding my hand as we climbed into the

sky, I felt the clunk as the wheels retracted into the aircraft, and settled back, while she would attend to my bruises.

I did not see the flash nor felt the searing blast of flame, I smelt the smell of singed hair and plastic, and I remember hearing a muffled crack, the plane shuddered violently, it changed direction, then immediately started its downward plunge.

Ripping the towel from my face, I saw the gaping hole in the side of the fuselage and floor, it was where Janine had been sitting, Janine was not there, I cried out her name, but the scream of the wind made it impossible.

I tried to open the door back into the main cabin, but the door was jammed, peeking through the doors secret peep hole, I could only see one person. Glancing from the gaping hole in the fuselage, I could see the coastline and the sea very close; too bloody close, I could imagine Frank battling with the controls before the final impact.

We crashed into the sea with a tremendous whooshing sound and I felt myself crunching into the door; my weight broke the latch forcing the door open. Quickly taking account of what I saw another gaping hole on the port side had taken out the wing and the row of seats, Jack and Edith had been sitting they had gone. Hermione still lay motionless still strapped in her seat, a piece of jagged metal protruded through the back of her seat, her gaze was transfixed forward, I could not see Frank, the curtain had fallen across the flight deck, water flooding in through the flight deck into cabin, gave me no option but to escape from the aircraft my means of escape was now the hole torn in the rear part of the fuselage.

The aeroplane was sinking as I dove through the hole into the sea, my trouser leg snagged on the rear tail fin It was now taking me down with it as an unsuspecting passenger to its final watery grave.

We plunged deeper I finally managed to loosen my trousers and shoes kicking them off I felt free of the doomed craft, I swam towards the light from the green depth back to the surface, I felt dizzy, my lungs ached, the sickening taste of seawater mixed with aviation fuel was in my mouth making me puke unable to spit it out until I finally broke the surface, choking and gasping for breath. Eventually I settled myself and began looking for any survivors, I was alone, there was little debris floating, nothing substantial to cling onto, I was getting tired, and although I could make out the coast, I had little or no chance in swimming there.

Leaking aviation fuel floated on the surface surrounded me, I swam slowly to find clean water, when in safe water I was tired and I tried floating on my back while waiting to be rescued.

I was using so much of my energy I could feel myself slipping beneath the waves; I felt that the ocean was trying to claim me as the final victim of the accident.

My memory cells came to the rescue as it retrieved some of the survival teachings from long ago, what I thought was silly at the time was to remove your trousers and tie the legs into a knot and use them as an inflation collar. However, they were still caught on the tail plane of the aircraft many fathoms below, trying to stay afloat a little longer. I searched the sea around me for any flotsam that would keep me buoyant, then as if by chance a bright yellow bag leapt out of the sea Infront of me and within arm's length then settling and bobbing around on the swell.

I made a lung and grabbed the bag it was one of the life jackets from under the seat, somehow must have freed itself, not caring the ins or outs the jacket was there, it was going to work for me it became my life saver,

I seemed to drift for hours my mind flashing through the events calculating the meaning of what, why, and who, the only thing I could remember was the hatch at the back of the aeroplane that was not shut correctly.

Grimshaw, bloody Grimshaw, it must have been, he must have planted an explosive device onboard.

The wonderful sound of helicopter rotor blades was coming closer, I looked up to see a small helicopter hovering only inches above me, I could make out a figure with his hand outstretched.

It was Pascal, he was leaning from the open door, his foot braced on the landing bars with his hand outstretched towards me, our hands locked, and he pulled me from the water into the helicopter.

Finally on board I was safe from the clutches of the sea, I heard a concerned familiar voice asked, 'Is he, alive?' I recognised the voice, it was Bruyère.

Pascal replied, 'Yes, he is', Pascal gave me some water to drink, it choked me causing me to vomit, taking another drink it cleared my mouth, spitting out the residue of the fuel contaminated saliva, I felt brighter, Bruyère had climbed to a safer altitude, looking down I could see debris floating in the sea, I looked intensely for any survivors. Wait! There was something I could see, asking Bruyère if she could go closer, for me to get a better look. There was a figure holding onto an orange life preserver floating in the sea, we hovered above the lifeless figure, feeling a little stronger I helped Pascal pull the figure from the sea, it was Janine.

Tenderly we laid her on the rear cabin seat, she coughed out sea water as we moved her which gave a good sign there was still life, although her eyes remained closed her breathing was shallow. Bruyère made her way quickly towards the Hospital.

Later as I emerged from the treatment room nursing my injuries Bruyère was waiting for me in the waiting room, her face brightened as she saw me. We talked about the last hours. The Doctor came looking for me, Janine had survived but only just, she was conscious and wanted me, taking her hand I looked into her eyes, they relayed the horror she had lived in the past hours, she spoke softly and slowly enquiring about the accident, then asked about Edith, Jack, Hermione and Frank, shaking my head I told her they had not survived.

She was frightened, I assured her that nothing like that would happen again, she held my hand tightly and closed her eyes, I continued talking to her as she dozed, the doctor came and checked her vital signs, he suggested a small emergency operation but he required her to sign a document, before he could operate. Would it be possible if I signed the document, I had been her companion for the last two years, Monsuire it would be possible the problem is the baby, she is carrying, it might survive, a baby, I was dumbfounded, Janine pregnant, and I was the father, why did she not tell me, I asked the doctor, how far on was she, only twelve weeks pregnant, it was possible, the doctor claimed that she does not know that she is with child.

I confirmed that I would be prepared to accept the responsibility for the operation, if he was sure and took great care, but of course, I would be extra careful.

She was rushed to theatre and the operation took place, I waited for her coming back, and she looked peaceful as she returned.

I returned to the waiting room, there was no one there, I was alone, my house had been demolished the love of my life lay in the intensive care ward fighting for her life, walking outside into the evening, I felt cold and tormented but exhilarated about the baby.

Pascal drove his car into the car park, 'Can I take you anywhere' he asked.

'I am not too sure on where I could go, unless I stayed in a hotel for the evening' he was just about to say something when a voice from behind spoke.

'Hello, you can always stay at my apartment, I turned to see Bruyère standing there, she had been having a cigarette and missed me coming out of the Hospital.

Pascal said 'Where will you be tomorrow?'

I replied, 'I do not know at this present time,'

Bruyère told Pascal that I would stay at her apartment nearby, then gave him her telephone number, we walked to her helicopter; then flew back to the airport, to park the aircraft in a secure area park.

In total silence without any words spoken she drove us to her apartment, showed me to a second bedroom, where I could sleep. I showered then climbed into the bed, the intended rest was a relive of the last hours I had endured, and the uncertain future.

I missed the sunrise that morning, and was spurred back into life by the smell of toast and coffee being prepared. Joining my host, I enjoyed breakfast with her.

'What did I intend doing today?' she asked.

'I will meet with Pascal and try to sort out some of the paperwork that this accident has incurred,' then thinking what I will do, my thoughts were interrupted the telephone ringing, Bruyère answered, it was the hospital, if I could attend the hospital that day, Janine had recovered from her operation and was wanting to see me.

Bruyère brought the coffee pot to me and refilled my cup,

standing close said 'will Janine be, ok?'
'Yes, but I have to go to the hospital sometime today,'
Bruyère replied. 'When you are ready, we go'
I had some matters to attend to, and most of them were waiting in Bank accounts in distant lands. Thrusting my hands into my pocket I felt something metallic by my hand, trying to take it out of my pocket, it was lodged in a small pocket in my under shorts, it was the key for Jacks safe, remembering one of Janine's tasks was to make copies of all the vital documents, the lists and other data was safe and sound.
I made a couple of telephone calls, and found that I would be required for a few hours at the airport enquiry, the crash investigators wished to interview me also Pascal would like to see me as well.
Three hours later, I walked away from that investigation room, I was mentally drained; I called to see Pascal, spending another hour with him finally concluding his enquiries.
I mentioned to him that I would like to retrieve some of my personal effects from Jack and Edith's Villa; he saw no problem and suggested that I should stay there if I needed an address.

We drove up to the villa, the place was ghostly quiet, glancing around I remembered the times, the good and bad, finding the hidden key I opened the villa and entered.
I walked into the kitchen and started to make coffee, there was no food around, of course I remembered we had started travelling, a flashback of the last seconds and the final scene as I burst through the jammed door, I leant against the counter holding on tight until the memory waned, Bruyère came and stood close holding onto me she had sensed that something was wrong, telling her that I was making coffee, my mind was still recollecting the accident, it was terrible,

the passengers had been killed and blown out of the cabin. Bruyère suggested that I go and shower then tidy myself, glancing into a mirror I saw the unshaven face of a survivor, Bruyère stroked the stubble on my chin, keep that it suits you.

It was good to shower using some of Janine's shampoo her perfume lingered, a tear swelled in my eye for her, then a feeling of happiness brought a smile came to my face, the baby, I had not fathered a child before, and the feeling I was experiencing was joy and foreboding. Discarding my dishevelled clothes, it was good to enjoy fresh clothes, something one easily forgets only remembering when you dress.

A found my second wallet, I carried two at all times, it contained a credit card some other items and duplicated papers, it was a custom I got used to after a pal told me always carry spares just in case your wallet gets lifted.

I tidied my clothes, and returned to the kitchen.

Bruyère had discovered some food in the freezer and prepared a small meal, as we sat and ate the meal, I poured a cup of coffee then taking my coffee I walked down by the pool, and surveyed the area, marks in the wall reflected the gunshots where the carnage had taken place earlier, a shiny reflection from the bay brought my attention to a distant group of vessels moored.

Taking Jacks binoculars from the side cupboard I zoomed in on the boats, recognising one of the men on board it was the crash engineer, from the investigation meeting, I gathered that I was observing the crash site, I watched intently as they were pulling a body on board, I could make out the four gold bars on his shirt epaulets. I knew it had to be Frank, pondering for a while over the scene I thought long and hard, I whispered to myself. 'Fare thee well old chum'.

A splash my attention turned to the pool, Bruyère was swimming underwater, rising at the end then turning she swam slowly back towards me. She climbed from the pool, her body glistened in the sunlight, her skin was paler but it was still impressive. Mulling over whether I should tell her that underwear had gone transparent with the water, revealing more than one should.

'How will you dry, your swimwear?'

'Oh my,' as she realised her garments had become transparent. 'The sun will dry them quickly in a couple of minutes,'

I threw her a towel from the pile in the side cupboard, stripping off her underwear she laid them on the top of a nearby bush to dry, and draped the towel around her body hiding her modesty.

She raised her eyes skyward as the distant beat of rotors blades was heard. 'You have to go and see Janine at the hospital first,' running her hands through her hair, she detangled and dried her hair in the warm wind.

Dressing herself, she was ready to drive me to the hospital, Janine was delighted to see me as we walked into the room, my heart jumped as I saw her sitting up in bed looking weak but alive. She chattered about her day, and the treatment she had been receiving, but nothing about the child.

Janine glancing over my shoulder towards Bruyère, 'Oh sorry I introduced her to Janine and explaining the important role she played in the saving of both our lives I spoke of her kindness and hospitality, and Janine thanked her yet again.

Bruere's, mobile rang, she listened, I have to go, she replied. She gave a little wave and walked from the room; I followed her and thanked her again and giving her a kiss on each cheek for the care she had shown toward Janine and me, she walked briskly out of the reception area, I watched her climb into her car and disappear into the traffic.

On the way back to the hospital ward, I encountered the doctor, he confirmed the operation was a success, and the baby was not harmed.

I sat with Janine; a tear was forming in the corner of her eye, 'What will we do now.'

'Well, I believe the jet is fully serviced and ready to go, we could fly onto Switzerland deposit the contents of the floor safe in the old Frosty Bank.'

Or, we would continue west, and discover what is lying in those offshore bank accounts belonging to. Mr Grimshaw.

We can take our time, go and then holiday as we like just the three of us.

Trois?

Pointing my finger towards Janine then at me, I placed my hand gently onto her tummy, and baby makes three.

Two weeks later, both of us were given a clean bill of health from the medical experts and the air crash investigation was now ongoing and would be for months even years to come.

I taxied out onto the runway and prepared to take off from Caan International Airport, although we were supposed to keep throttles closed and not make too much noise taking off, it was a courtesy not to disturb the rich and famous, ninety percent of them were deaf anyway, a mischievous thought crossed my mind throttling up to gain take of speed I held the throttles until I cleared the runway and once I had the displayed on the dashboard three green lights indicating wheels were safely up and stowed I pushed the throttle

levers hard back onto their stops as we climbed into the sky, the Lear jet was shaking with the demand for full power we climbed like a rocket into the blue sky.
We were still alive, now ready to take on the world and then give one in the eye of anyone trying to stop us.

THE END

Printed in Great Britain
by Amazon

13972858R00206